Aphrodisiac

◇◇◇◇◇◇◇◇◇◇◇◇◇◇◇◇◇◇◇◇◇◇◇◇◇◇◇◇◇◇◇◇◇◇

FICTION FROM
Christopher Street

Also from *Christopher Street*

"And God Bless Uncle Harry and His Roommate Jack, Who We're Not Supposed to Talk About"

Relax!
This Book Is Only a Phase You're Going Through

Le Gay Ghetto

The Christopher Street Reader

APHRO

DISIAC

Fiction from Christopher Street

A PERIGEE BOOK

Perigee Books
are published by
G. P. Putnam's Sons
200 Madison Avenue
New York, New York 10016

The Publisher gratefully acknowledges the following for permission to include these selections: Farrar, Straus & Giroux, Inc., for the selection from *Sita*, copyright © 1976, 1977, 1980 by Kate Millett; St. Martin's Press, Inc., for "Love Lifted Me," from *Who Was That Masked Woman?*, copyright © 1978, 1980 by Noretta Koertge. These pieces appeared in somewhat different form in *Christopher Street*.

Library of Congress Cataloging in Publication Data

Main entry under title:

Aphrodisiac, fiction from Christopher Street.
    "A Perigee book."
    Originally published: New York: Coward, McCann & Geoghegan, c1980.
    1. Short stories, American. 2. Homosexuality—Fiction. I. Christopher Street.
PS648.H57A6   1982   813'.01'08353   81-15406
ISBN 0-399-50603-9   AACR2

First Perigee printing, 1982
Printed in the United States of America

Aphrodisiac

FICTION FROM

Christopher Street

Contents

EDMUND WHITE

◇◇◇◇◇◇◇◇◇◇◇◇◇◇◇◇◇◇◇◇◇◇◇◇◇◇◇◇◇◇◇◇◇

First Love

*W*e're going for a midnight
boat ride. It's a cold, clear summer night and four of us—the
two boys, my dad and I—are descending the stairs that zig-
zag down the hill from the house to the dock. Old Boy, my
dad's dog, knows where we're headed; he rushes down the
slope beside us, looks back, snorts and tears up a bit of grass
as he twirls in a circle. "What is it, Old Boy, what is it," my
father says, smiling faintly, delighted to be providing excitement for the dog, whom he always called his best friend.

I was bundled up, a sweater and a windbreaker over
today's sunburn. My father stopped to examine the bottom
two steps just above the foot path that traveled from cottage
to cottage on our side of the lake. This afternoon he had put
in the new steps: fresh boards placed vertically to retain the
sand and dirt, each braced by four wooden stakes pounded
into the ground. Soon the steps would sag and sprawl and
need to be redone. Whenever I came back from a swim or a
trip in the outboard down to the village grocery store, I
passed him crouched over his eternal steps or saw him up on a
ladder painting the house, or heard his power saw arguing

with itself in the garage, still higher up the hill on the road.

My father regarded guests as nuisances who had to be entertained over and over again. Tonight's expedition was just such a duty. But the boys, our guests' sons, didn't register the cheerlessness of the occasion and thought it was exciting still to be up at such an hour. They had run on down to the water as I lingered obediently beside my father, who ran the flashlight over his steps. The boys were racing to the end of the dock, feet pounding the boards. Old Boy started out after them, but then came back to round us up. Now Kevin was threatening to push his little brother in. Squeals, breathing, a tussle, then release, followed by the sound of two boys just being—that tunnel, sometimes narrow, sometimes wide, that burrows its way under time.

As Dad and I went on down, his flashlight veered off into the water, scaring a school of minnows and illuminating bands of sand. The Chris-Craft, moored to the short end of the L formed by the dock, was big, heavy, imposing. Two tarpaulins covered it: one was a square, corners rounded, that fitted over the two seats in front; the other was a smaller, perfect rectangle that protected the bucket seat aft of the engine, which itself lay concealed, redolent of gasoline, under the double wood doors trimmed in chrome. The canvas, as I undid the grommets and gathered in its folds, had the familiar sad smell of a sour washcloth. Neither my father nor I moved very gracefully over that boat. We were both afraid of the water, he because he couldn't swim, I because I was afraid of everything.

Dad's most constant attribute was the cigar clenched between his small, stained teeth. Since he could usually be found in an air-conditioned house or office or car, the system under his control, he saw to it that the smoke and smell filtered evenly and thickly into every corner of his world, subduing those around him; perhaps like a skunk parent, he was steeping us in his protective stink.

Although it was chilly and I had on a sweater and jacket, I was wearing Bermuda shorts; the wind raised goose bumps on my legs as I installed the wood flagpole at the stern, an accoutrement patriotism would have forbidden at night had we not needed the white light that glowed from its top. How the electricity could run through this pole as soon as it was plugged into its socket mystified me, but I dared not ask Dad for an explanation lest he give me one. The leather seats were cold, though they warmed under flesh soon enough, skin to skin.

Pulling away from the dock generated high anxiety (pulling in was worse). My father, who'd been a Texas cowboy as a young man, could laugh at twisters and rattlers, but everything about this alien medium—cold, bottomless, sliding—alarmed him. He was wearing his absurd "captain's" hat (all his leisure clothes were absurd, jokes, really, as though leisure itself had to be ridiculed). He was half standing behind the wheel. The motors were churning, the spotlight on the bow was gyrating, the red tip of his cigar was pulsing. I'd ventured out on the deck, untied the ropes, tossed them in, jumped in the boat myself; now I was crouched just behind my father. I was wielding a long pole with a hook on one end, the sort used to open upper windows in stuffy grade schools. My job was to push us safely out of the berth before my father threw the toiling motors into gear. It was all an embarrassment. Other men moored their power boats with a single line, backed away from docks in a simple, graceful arc, talking all the while, and other men's sons scrambled like agile monkeys across lacquered decks, joking and smiling. Comparison, of course, is not only the root of embarrassment but also its flower.

We were under way. The speedboat lunged forward with so much force that we were pressed back against our seats. Peter, Kevin's seven-year-old brother, was in the rumble seat, his hair streaming under the rippling flag, his mouth open to scream with delighted fear, though the sound was lost behind gales of wind. He waved a skinny arm and with his other hand clutched a chromium grip beside him; even so, he was posting high in the saddle as we spanked over someone else's wake. Our own was thrown back from the prow. The night, intent seamstresss, fed the fabric of water under the needle of our hull, steadily, firmly, except the boat wasn't stitching the water together but ripping it apart into long white threads. Along the shore a few house lights here and there peered through the pines, as fleeting as stars glimpsed through the moving clouds above. We shot past an anchored boat of fishermen and their single kerosene lamp; one of them shook his fist at us.

The lake narrowed. Over to the right (I knew it was there, though I couldn't see it) lay the nine-hole golf course with its ramshackle clubhouse and wicker armchairs painted green, its porch swing on creaking chains. Once a month we showed up late there for Sunday supper, our clothes not right, our talk too distinct and forthright, the cigar a foul smudge pot set out to ward off the incoming social frost.

Now Dad's cigar had gone out and he stopped the boat to relight it. From our high windy perch we drifted down, engine cut to a mild churning. When the exhaust pipe dipped above water level, it blatted rudely. "Boy, I'm soaked!" Peter was screaming in his soprano. "I'm freezing. Gee, you sure let me have it!"

"Too much for you, young fellow?" my father asked, chuckling. He winked at me. They children of visitors (and sometimes their fathers) were usually called "young fellow" since Dad could never remember their names. Old Boy, who had been squinting into the wind, his head stuck out beyond and around the windshield, was now prancing happily across the cushions to receive a pat from his master. Kevin, sitting just behind my father, said, "Those fisherman were mad as hell. I'd of been, too, if some guy in a big fat-ass power boat scared off my fish."

My father winced, then grumbled something about how they had no business to. . . . He was hurt. I was appalled by Kevin's frankness. At such moments, tears would come to my eyes in impotent compassion for Daddy: this invalid despot, this man who bullied everyone but suffered the consequences with such a tender, uneducated heart! Tears would also well up when I had to correct my father on a matter of fact. Usually I'd avoid the bother and smugly watch him compound his mistakes. But if he asked my opinion point blank, a euphoria of sadness would overtake me, panicky wings would beat at the corners of the shrinking room and, as quietly and as levelly as possible, I'd supply the correct name or date. For I was a lot more knowledgeable than he about the things that could come up in conversation even in those days and in that place (the Midwest in the 1950s). But knowledge wasn't power. He was the one with the power, the money, the right to read the paper through dinner as my stepmother and I watched him in silence; he was the one with the thirty tailormade suits, the twenty gleaming pairs of shoes and the starched white dress shirts, the ties from Countess Mara and the two Cadillacs that waited for him in the garage, dripping oil on the concrete in the shape of a black Saturn and its gray blur of moons. It was his power that stupefied me and made me regard my knowledge as nothing more than a jester's cleverness he might choose to show off at a dinner party ("Ask this young fellow, he reads, he'll know"). Then why did his occasional faltering bring tears to my eyes? Was I grieving because he didn't possess everything, absolutely everything, or because I owned nothing?

Within a moment Kevin had made things right by asking Daddy how he thought the Red Sox would do next season. My father was soon expatiating on names and averages and strategies that meant nothing to me, the good spring training and the bad trade-off. When Kevin challenged him over one point, Dad laughed good-naturedly over the boy's spunk (and error) and set him straight. I rested my arm on the rubber tread of the gunwale beside me and my chin on my arm and stared into the shiny water which was busy analyzing a distant yellow porch light, shattering the simple glow into a hundred shifting possibilities.

The baseball talk went on for some time as we rocked in our own wake, which had overtaken us. We were drifting toward an island and its abandoned summer hotel, moth-white behind slender, silver-white birches. The motor wallowed, the sound of an old car with a bad muffler. My father usually felt uncomfortable with other men, but he and Kevin had now found a way to talk to each other and I half listened to the low murmurs of their voices—or rather of Daddy's monologue and Kevin's sounds of assent or disagreement. This was Dad's late night voice: ruminative, confiding, unending. Old Boy recognized it from their dawn walks together and circumspectly placed his nose between his paws on the cushion beside Dad. Little Peter crawled up over the hatch and listened to the sports talk; even he knew names and averages and had an opinion or two. After he'd been silent for a while I looked around and saw he'd fallen asleep, his head thrown back over the edge of the cushion and his mouth open, his right hand twitching.

By now we'd entered the narrows that led into a smaller,

colder branch of the lake. The lights of a car, after excavating a tunnel out of the pines halfway up the shore, dipped from view and then suddenly shot out across the water, which looked all the blacker and choppier in the brief glare. I had rowed laboriously over every mile of the lake; it was a mild sort of pleasure to see those sweaty distances beautifully elided by the Chris-Craft. For Dad had gunned the motors again and we were sitting once more on our high, thundering throne. We passed a point where the clipped lawns of an estate flowed down from a white mansion and its lit, curtained windows. Late last Sunday afternoon, as I was rowing home, pulling hard through the turbulent water at the point, I'd seen a young man in a seersucker suit and a girl in a party dress. They had sauntered up the hill away from me, he slightly in the lead, she swinging her arms high in an exaggerated way, as though she were a marionette. The sunlight found a feeble rainbow in the mist above a distant sprinkler and made the grass as green and uniform as baize. The light gave the couple long, important shadows.

All around me—at the post office where we had a box, in the general store, on docks, sailboats and water-skis—young people with iodine-and-baby-oil tans, trim bodies and the faultless teeth only money can buy were having fun. A boat would glide across the setting sun, the shadow of a broad-shouldered teen inhabiting the white sail. At the village dock I'd look up from my outboard to see two young men walking past, just a sliver of untanned skin visible under the hems of their shorts. As I sat high above the lake on our swing, reading, I'd hear them joking as they sunned on the white diving raft below. I'd see them up close at the country club suppers—the boy with the strong chin and honey-brown hands in blazer and white cotton pants seating his mother, her nose like his but pointier, her hair as blond but fogged with gray. These were the women who wore navy blue and a single piece of woven yellow and pink gold, whose narrow feet were shod in blue-and-white spectators, who drove jaunty station wagons, drank martinis on porches with rattan furniture and straw rugs and whose voices were lower than most men's. Up close they smelled of gin, cocoa butter and lake water; we sometimes sat next to such a woman and her family at a communal table. Or I'd see the women at the little branch of Saks Fifth Avenue in a town not far away. They pretended they were bored or exasperated by their children's comings and goings: "Don't even bother to tell me when you'll be home, Scott, you know you've never kept your word yet." I saw it all and envied those sons their parents and those parents their sons.

My father was never tan. He had a huge belly; his glasses weren't horn rim or translucent pink plastic (the two acceptable styles) but black with bronze metallic wings; he seldom drank cocktails; he didn't act as if he were on stage—he had no attractive affectations. Although my stepmother had risen socially as high as one could rise in that world, she'd done so on her own. My father never took her anywhere; she was as free as a spinster and as respectable as a matron. When she was with us in Michigan during the summer, she forgot about society and helped my father with his steps or his painting, she read as much as I did, arranged for good meals and rusticated. Once in a while, one of her elegant friends would drop by for lunch, and suddenly the house was electrified by the energy of those women—their excitement, their approval, their laughter, their thrillingly professional small talk, an art as refined (and now as rare) as marquetry. My father would beam at these guests and pat their hands and pour them thimblefuls of brandy after their doll-size luncheons. Then they'd limp away in a broken-down car, millionairesses in old cardigans covered with cat hairs, their wonderful vibrant voices their only badge of breeding. Silence would fall back over our house in the way snow fills up a forest.

My father was courtly but dim. I was even dimmer. I read so much in the house (on the bed in my room, on the couch in the living room, on the shaded bench at the foot of the dock) that I hadn't gotten a tan. I, too, wore awful glasses, black and gray tortoise shells my father had selected. I didn't have chinos with a brass-buckled garrison belt or droopy jeans but rather green work pants and a shiny alligator belt my Dad had bought. I didn't have plain white sneakers but rather tall black and white gym shoes from gym class. I did have the requisite red and yellow checked short-sleeved shirt, but I didn't know how to roll up the sleeves and, besides, the shirt was a size too big and hung on me. I had a horrible crew-cut two years after crew-cuts had gone out of style.

Unlike my idols I couldn't play tennis or baseball or swim freestyle. My sports were volleyball and Ping-Pong, my only stroke the side-stroke. I couldn't make small talk; I wasn't charming or at ease with other teenagers except intellectual girls, professors' daughters whom I would tax with endless recitations of my poetry, all formal and inhuman, rime royal about the changing seasons, that sort of thing. I fell in love with three of these girls; we'd sit in movies and after forty minutes of inner debate, I'd make a move. Our glasses would click and lock horns. We'd laugh with the polite, rueful laugh that our parents had invented to subvert passion, a laugh that turned every strong impulse into a small embarrassment.

Most of the time I daydreamed of escape. I concocted a plan of running away from home to New York, but I never implemented it. I wrote a novel I was going to sell for millions, which would have enabled me to ascend from my father's porch on a cloud of glory, but I never mailed the manuscript off. I was an orphan, I was a prince, I would be a general, another Napoleon. I wrote an opera, I painted dozens of paintings, I studied every musical instrument including the harp and harpsichord, I wrote plays that I put on at school with myself in the starring role (usually a king in disguise)—and all of these ventures were ways of leaving home, but I never once made a move.

I was a sissy. My hands were always in the air. In eighth grade I had portrayed Literature in the class pageant, a word I'd always pronounced as two mumbled syllables ("lit-chur") but that the Creative Dramatics teacher now taught me to say as four tripping ones ("lit-tah-rah-tour"). We all wore togas and marched solemnly in to a record of Schubert's *Unfinished*. My sister couldn't wait to tell me I had been the only boy who'd sat not cross-legged on the gym floor but resting on one hand and hip like the White Rock girl. A popular quiz for masculinity in those days had three questions, all of which I flunked: 1. Look at your nails (a girl extends her fingers, a boy cups his in his upturned palm); 2. Look up (a girl lifts just her eyes, a boy throws back his whole head); 3. Light a match (a girl strikes away from her body, a boy toward—or perhaps the reverse, I can't recall). But there were less esoteric signs as well. A man crosses his leg by resting an ankle on his knee; a sissy drapes one leg over the other. A man never enthuses; men are either silent or loud. I didn't know how to swear; I always said the final *g* in *fucking* and I didn't know where in the sentence to place the *damn* or *hell*.

My father was just a bit of a sissy. He crossed his legs the wrong way. He was too fussy about his nails (he had an elaborate manicuring kit). He liked classical music. He was not an easygoing guy, the sort Auden says likes "hard liquor, horseplay and noise." But otherwise he passed muster: he was courageous in a fight, he was a strong, skilled athlete, not many things frightened him, he had towering rages, he knew how to swear, he was tirelessly assertive, and he had a gambler's good grace about losing money. He could lose lots of it in business and walk away, smiling and shrugging.

Kevin was the sort of son who would have pleased my father more than I did. He was captain of his Little League baseball team. On the surface he had good manners, but they were born of training, not timidity. No irony, no superior smirks, no fits of longing or flights of fancy removed him from the present. He hadn't invented another life; this one seemed good enough. Although he was only twelve, he already throbbed with the pressure to contend, to be noticed, to be right, to win, to make others bend to his will. I found him rather frightening, certainly sexy (the two aspects seemed linked). Because I was three years older, I guessed he expected me to be ahead of him in most ways, and that first night in the boat I was silent in order not to disillusion him. I wanted him to like me. Since I didn't look like a sissy or a brain (I'd taken my glasses off), I thought maybe I could fool him.

Kevin may have been cocky, but he wasn't one of those suave country club boys. He wasn't well groomed and I don't think he thought about such things; he didn't date girls yet and he wore clothes unironed out of the drier until his mother threw them back into the washer. He still watched cartoons on television before an early supper and when he was sleepy he leaned sulkily against his father, eyes blinking and registering nothing. His seven-year-old brother Peter was a nervous boy, morbidly eager to be just like Kevin; he made me uncomfortable, since I could be tempted to behave in the same way. Except I didn't want to *be* Kevin, not anymore, if ever.

As my father barked commands, Kevin and Peter and I secured the Chris-Craft to the dock and covered it with canvas. We climbed the many steps up to the house, Old Boy blazing the trail, then darting back to urge my father on. The house was brilliant with lights. Kevin's parents had bumped me from my upstairs room, the place where last week I had read *Death in Venice* and luxuriated in the tale of a dignified grownup who died for the love of an indifferent boy my age. The plot, however, quickly evaporated in my memory; what lingered was the feeling that somewhere a great world existed in which things happened and people changed, took risks— more, took notice: a world so sensitive, like a grand piano, that even a step or a word could awaken vibrations in its taut strings.

Since the house was built on a very steep hill, the basement wasn't underground, though its cinderblock walls did smell of damp soil. There were only two rooms in the basement. One was a "rumpus room" with a semi-circular glass brick bar that could be lit from within by a pink, a green and an orange bulb (the blue had burnt out).

The other room was long and skinny, the wall facing the lake broken by two large windows. Ordinarily a Ping-Pong table was set up in here, its green net never quite taut. Under the overhead lamp my father would lunge and swear and shout and slam or stretch to the very edge of the net to tap the ball delicately into the enemy's court (for his opponent was inevitably "the enemy," challenging his wind, strength, skill, intelligence). Whenever my sister, a champion athlete, was at the cottage, she enjoyed this interesting power over Dad, while my stepmother and I sat upstairs and read, curled up in front of the fire with Herr Pogner the Persian cat (named after my harpsichord teacher). The cat dozed, feet tucked under her chest, though her raised ears, thin enough to let the lamplight through, twitched and cocked independently of one another with each "Damn!" or "Son of a bitch!" or "Gotcha, young lady, *got* you there" floating up through the hot air vents in the floor. My sister's fainter but delighted reproaches ("Oh, *Daddy*" or "Really, Daddy") didn't merit even the tiniest adjustment of those feline ears. My stepmother, deep in her Taylor Caldwell or Jane Austen (she was a compulsive, venturesome reader), was never too mesmerized by the page not to know when to hurry to the kitchen to present the inevitable victor—drawn, grinning—with his pint of peach ice cream and box of chocolate grahams, which my father would eat in his preferred way, a pat of cold butter on each cracker.

Tonight there was no game. The grownups were sitting around the fire sipping highballs. Downstairs the table had been replaced by three cots for us boys. Kevin's parents sent their sons to bed but I was allowed to stay up for another half hour. I was even given a weak highball of my own, though my stepmother murmured, "I'm sure he would rather have orange juice."

"For Chrissake," my father said, smiling, "give the fella a break." I was grateful for this unusual display of chumminess and, to please him, I said nothing and grinned a lot at what the others said.

Kevin's parents, especially his mother, were unlike any other grownups I'd met. They were both Irish, she by origin, he by derivation. He drank till he became drunk, his eyes moist, his laugh general. He had a handsome face projected onto too much flesh, black hair that geysered up at the end of the formal walkway of his part, large red hands that went white at the knuckles when he picked something up (a glass of whiskey, say) and a tender, satirical manner towards his wife, as though he were a lazy dreamer who'd been stirred into action by this spitfire.

She said *damn* and *hell* and drank whiskey and had two moods—rage (she was always shouting at Kevin) and mock rage, an appealingly ardent sort of simmering, Virtue Stymied: "All right then, be gone with you," she'd say, feisty and submissive, or "Of course you'll be having another drink."

It was all play acting and intended to be viewed as such. She had "temperament" because she was Irish and had been trained as an opera singer. If she wandered into a room and found Kevin's T-shirt balled and hurled in a chair, she'd start bellowing, "Kevin O'Malley Cork, get in here and get in here *now*. Look alive!" Nothing could restrain these outbursts, not even the knowledge Kevin was out of earshot. Her arms would stiffen, her clenched fists would dig into her slim flanks and bunch up her dress, her nose would pale and her thin hair, the color of weathered bricks, would seem to go into shock and rise to reveal still more of her scalp. Because of her operatic training, her voice penetrated every corner of the house and had an alto after-hum that buzzed on in the round metal tabletop from Morocco. During the mornings she chain smoked, drank coffee and sat around in a silk robe that revealed and highlighed her bony body. With her freckled face, devoid of makeup, rising above this slippery red sheen, she looked like an angry young man trapped in travesty as a practical joke.

This couple, with their liquor and cigarettes and roguish, periodic spats, struck my stepmother as "cheap." Or rather, the woman was cheap (men can't be cheap). The husband, my father later decided, wasn't "stable" (their money was by no means secure). Though they lived in a mansion with a swimming pool and antique furniture, they rented it, probably the furniture as well.

The Corks were both "climbers," he in business, she in society; they seemed to me fascinating shams. I especially admired the way Kevin's mother, so obviously a bohemian, hard drinker and hell raiser, had toned down her exuberance long enough to win invitations to a few polite "functions," those given by the Women's Club if not by the Keyboard Club (the Keyboard pretended to be nothing but a little gathering of ladies who liked to play four-hand versions of "Mister Haydn's" symphonies, though it was in fact the highest social pinnacle). As though in pursuit of such heights, Mrs. Cork had reduced her *damns* and *hells* by the end of the week with us to *darns* and *hecks*. And I, as someone who was already at fifteen widely experienced in low life though ever vigilant against revealing these sordid connections—I had to admire the way Mrs. Cork was pretending to be shocked by the innocent improprieties that so excited my stepmother. I could tell Mrs. Cork had palled around with screwballs, even unwed couples—it was just a sense I had. When I took her out one day in a motor boat alone, she and I happily discussed opera. We cut the motor and drifted. I relaxed and became animated to the point of effeminacy; she relaxed and became coarser. "Oh, my boy," she promised me in her brogue, "you want to hear fine singing, I'll play you my John McCormack records, make you weep your damn eyes out of their bloody sockets. That *Lucevan le stelle*, it'll freeze your balls." I shrieked with delight—we were conspirators who'd somehow found ourselves stranded together here in a world of unthrillable souls. I dreamed of running off and becoming a great singer; I walked through the woods and vocalized.

Tonight we had not yet made our rapport explicit, but I

was already wise to her. She had through circumstances ended up not on the La Scala stage but in this Michigan cottage, married to an affable, overweight businessman. Now her job was to ingratiate herself with people who would help her husband in his career (lawyer for industry); she was retaining just enough brogue and temperament to be a "character." Characters—conventional women with minor eccentricities—flourished in our world, as Mrs. Cork had no doubt observed. But she'd failed to notice that the characters were all old, rich and pedigreed. Newcomers, especially those of moderate means, were expected to form an attractive but featureless chorus behind our few madcap divas.

"Time for bed, young fella," my father said at last.

Downstairs I undressed by the colored light of the glass-brick bar and, wearing just a T-shirt and jockey shorts, hurried into the dark dormitory and slipped into my cot. Northern Michigan nights are cold even in July; the bed had two thick blankets on it that had been aired outside today and smelled of pine needles. I listened to the grownups; the metal vents conducted sound better than heat. Their conversation, which had seemed so lively and sincere when I had witnessed it, now sounded stilted and halting. Lots of fake laughter. Silences became longer and longer. At last everyone said goodnight and headed upstairs. Another five minutes of moaning pipes, flushing toilets and padding feet. Then long murmured consultations in bed by each couple. Then silence.

"You still awake?" Kevin called from his bed.

"Yes," I said. I couldn't see him in the dark but I could tell his cot was at the other end of the room; Peter was audibly asleep on the cot between.

"How old are you?" Kevin asked.

"Fifteen. And you?"

"Twelve. You ever done it with girls?"

"Sure," I lied. "You?"

"Naw. Not yet." Pause. "I hear you gotta warm 'em up."

"That's correct."

"How do you do it?"

I had read a marriage manual. "Well, you turn the lights down and kiss a long time first."

"With your clothes on?"

"Of course. Then you take off her top and play with her breasts. But very gently. Don't get too rough—they don't like that."

"Does she play with your boner?"

"Not usually. An older, experienced woman might."

"You been with an older woman?"

"Once."

"They get kinda saggy, don't they?"

"My friend was beautiful," I said, offended on behalf of the imaginary lady.

"Is it real wet and slippery in there? Some guy told me it was like wet liver in a milk bottle."

"Only if the romantic foreplay has gone on long enough."

"How long's enough?"

"An hour."

The silence was thoughtful, as though it were an eyelash beating against a pillowcase.

"The guys back home? Guys in my neighborhood?"

"Yes?" I said.

"We all cornhole each other. You ever do that?"

"Sure."

"What?"

"I said sure."

"Guess you've outgrown that by now."

"Well, yeah, but since there aren't any girls around . . ." I felt as a scientist must when he knows he's about to bring off the experiment of his career: outwardly calm, inwardly jubilant, already braced for disappointment. "We could do it now." Pause. "If you want to." As soon as the words were out of my mouth I felt he wouldn't care to come to my bed; he had found something wrong with me, he thought I was a sissy, I should have said "Right" instead of "That's correct."

"Got any stuff?" he asked.

"What?"

"You know. Like Vaseline?"

"No, but we don't need it. Spit will—" I started to say "do," but men say "work"—"work." My penis was hard but still bent painfully down in the jockey shorts; I released it and placed the head under the taut elastic waist band.

"Naw, you gotta have Vaseline." I might be knowledgeable about real sex, but apparently Kevin was to be the expert when it came to cornholing.

"Well, let's try spit."

"I don't know. Okay." His voice was small and his mouth sounded dry.

I watched him come toward me. He, too, had jockey shorts on, which appeared to glow. Though barechested now, he'd worn a T-shirt all through Little League season that had left his torso and upper arms pale; this ghost shirt excited me, because it reminded me he was captain of his team.

I had already made love to quite a few adult men by this time. Most of them, alarmed by my age, had been rough or at least rushed in satisfying their needs. But four or five had called me affectionate names and kissed me on the mouth. That was what I wanted: romance. We pulled off our shorts. I opened my arms to Kevin and closed my eyes. He said, "It's colder than a witch's tit." I lay on my side facing him and he slipped in beside me. His breath smelled of milk. His hands and feet were cold. I kept my lower arm scrunched under me, but with the upper one I nervously patted his back. His back and chest and legs were silky and hairless, though I could see a tuft of eiderdown under his arm, which he'd lifted to pat my back in reciprocation. A thin layer of baby fat still formed a pad just under his skin. Beneath the fat I could feel the hard, rounded muscles. He reached down under the sheet to touch my penis, and I touched his.

"Ever put them together in your hand?" he asked.

"No," I lied. "Show me."

"You spit on your hand first, get it real wet. See? Then you—scoot closer, up a bit—you put them together like this. It feels neat."

"Yes," I said. "Neat."

Since I couldn't kiss him, I put my head beside his and pressed my lips silently to his neck. His neck was smooth and long and thin, too thin for the size of his head; in this way, too, he still resembled a child. In the rising heat of our bodies I caught a slight whiff of his odor, not pungent like a grownup's but faintly acrid, the smell of scallions in the rain.

"Who's first?" he asked.

"Cornholing?"

"I think we need some stuff. It won't work without stuff."

"I'll go first," I said. I didn't like taking it up the rear; it hurt going in; it sometimes felt as though I had to go to the bathroom. After I came I really couldn't stand it; I'd lie there staring into my pillow and hating the guy above me. If he took too long I'd make him pull out and whack off while I dashed, white with scorn, for the toilet and the shower. I assumed Kevin hated getting screwed as much as I did— that's why I wanted to give him a break, have him come last. I knew I'd want to repeat this experiment, but I wasn't sure he would unless he enjoyed it this time.

Although I put lots of spit on him and me, he still said it

hurt. I'd get about half an inch in and he'd say, "Take it out! Quick!" He was lying on his side with his back to me, but I could still look over and see him wince in profile. "Jesus," he said. "It's like a knife all through me." The pain subsided and with the bravery of an Eagle Scout he said, "Okay. Try it again. But take it easy and promise you'll pull out when I say so."

This time I went in a millimeter at a time, waiting between each advance. I could feel his muscles relaxing.

"Is it in?" he asked.

"Yep."

"All the way in?"

"Almost. There. It's all in."

"Really?" He reached back for my crotch to make sure. "Yeah, it is," he said. "Feel good?"

"Terrific."

"Okay," he instructed, "go in and out, but slow, okay?"

"Sure."

I tried a few short thrusts and asked if I was hurting him. He shook his head.

He bent his knees up toward his chest and I flowed around him. Whereas face to face I had felt timid and unable to get enough of his body against enough of mine, now I was glued to him and he didn't object—it was understood that this was my turn and I could do what I liked. I tunneled my lower arm under him and folded it across his chest; his ribs were unexpectedly small and countable, and now that he'd completely relaxed I could get deeper and deeper into him. That such a tough, muscled little guy, whose words were so flat and eyes so without depth or humor, could be so richly taken—oh, he was as glamorous as a gardenia in that cot. But the sensation he was giving didn't seem like something afforded by his body, or if so, then it was a secret gift,

shameful and pungent, one he didn't dare acknowledge. In
the Chris-Craft I'd been afraid of him. He had been the usual
intimidating winner, beyond enticement—but here he was,
pushing this tendoned, shifting pleasure back into me, the
fine hair on his neck curling with his sweat just above
the hollows the sculptor had pressed with his thumbs into the
clay. His tan hand was resting on his white hip. The ends of
his lashes were pulsing just beyond the line of his full cheek.

"Does it feel good?" he asked. "Want it tighter?" he asked,
as a shoe salesman might.

"No, it's fine."

"See, I can make it tighter," and indeed he could. His
eagerness to please me reminded me that I needn't have
worried, that in his own eyes he was just a kid and I a high
school guy who'd done it with girls and one older lady and
everything. Most of the time I had dreamed of an English
lord who'd kidnap and take me away forever, but now it
seemed that Kevin and I didn't need anyone older, we could
run away together, I would be our protector. We were
already sleeping in a field under a sheet of breezes and taking
turns feeding on each other's bodies, wet from the dew.

"I'm getting close," I said. "Want me to pull out?"

"Go ahead," he said. "Fill 'er up."

"Okay. Here goes. Oh, God. Jesus!" I couldn't help kissing
his cheek.

"Your beard hurts," he said. "You shave every day?"

"Yeah. You?"

"Not yet. But the fuzz is gettin' dark. Some guy told me
the sooner you start shavin', the faster it comes in. Jew
Legree?"

It took me a second to realize he'd said, "Do you agree?" "I
think so. Well," I said, "I'm pullin' out. Your turn."

I turned my back to Kevin and I could hear him spitting on

his hand. I didn't like getting cornholed this time any more than before, but I was peaceful and happy because we loved each other. People say young love or love of the moment isn't real, but I think the only love is the first and its fleeting recapitulations throughout our lives, brief echoes of the original, aching theme in a work that increasingly becomes all development, the mechanical elaboration of a crab canon with too many parts. I was aware of the treacherous air vents above us, conducting the sounds we were making upstairs. Maybe my dad was listening. Or maybe, just like Kevin, he was unaware of anything but the pleasure spurting up out of his body and into mine.

My father had started his own business fifteen years earlier in order to make money, be his own boss and keep his own hours. These were imperatives, not simple wishes, and whenever they were set aside he suffered, even physically. Money was for him the air certain superior people needed to breathe; wealth and superiority coincided, though when he said someone was from a "good" family, he meant rich first and only secondarily respectable or virtuous. But his real reason for wanting money, I imagine, was that it was a distinction as absolute as genius and as solitary; any other thing people think is worth getting would have struck him as too arbitrary and congenial.

His need for independence was less explicit, more shaded but just as strong. Independence conferred upon him feudal rights of the purse and gavel and allowed him to dictate his fate and ours. The fate he chose for himself was misanthropic and poetic. He slept all day, rose at three at the earliest or five at the latest and at six, the winter sky already dark, sat down to a breakfast of a pound of bacon, six scrambled eggs and eight slices of toast freighted with preserves. He took no lunch but at three or four in the morning ate a supper of a plate-size steak, three vegetables, a salad, more bread, and a dessert, preferably sugared strawberries over vanilla ice cream. His only drink was spring water delivered to the house in twenty-gallon glass jugs, tinted a faint blue, inverted above an office-style electric water cooler. Before bedtime he had his snack of buttered chocolate grahams. Then he'd brush Old Boy in the basement and take him out for a long dawn walk; he talked to the dog in a man-to-man but deeply solicitous way, somewhat as though the animal were a great man gone senile. His hours gave Dad the cool and silence of the night and took away the populated disorder of the day. Had he liked poetry, he might have cited Vaughan:

> Dear night! this world's defeat;
> The stop to busy fools; care's check and curb;
> The day of Spirits; my soul's calm retreat
> Which none disturb!

He worked all night at his desk, wielding a calculating machine and slide rule and printing out page after page of specifications and instructions. At home he sat in his office at the top of his house, which had been built to resemble a Norman castle, and from his windows he could survey the floodlit lawn. On the wall behind him hung a big bad painting of waves crashing in the moonlight. He smoked his cigars until the last hour before bedtime, when he switched to a pipe. Its sweet smoke filtered through the central heating or air conditioning into ever corner of the sealed house. The pipe hour was the time to approach him for a favor or just a few pleasant words; I'd sit on the loveseat beside his blond mahogany desk and watch him work. Hour after hour he wrote with an onyx fountain pen in lower case block letters that had the angle and lean elegance of art deco design; his smoke drifted up through the rosy light cast by the matching red shades on floor stands that flanked the desk.

Even in Michigan he would set up an office and work till dawn when he wasn't outdoors doing manual labor under artificial light, his "hobby." But now a houseful of guests had forced him to modify his hours and habits. Had Mrs. Cork been a beauty he might have suffered the presence of her family more gladly; he was a great fancier of women and they brought out in him a courtliness as sweet and clear as the best sherry. His irritable misanthropy vanished in the presence of a beautiful woman. She could even be a child, a lovely little girl; she would still excite gallantry in him. Once a ten-year-old charmer who was staying with us announced at midnight that she wanted chocolate and my father drove fifty miles to Charlevoix, dragged the owner of a candy store out of bed and paid a hundred dollars for twenty opera creams. He once gave the same amount as a tip to a full-bodied, glossy-lipped singer in an Italian restaurant who had serenaded him with a wobbling but surprisingly intimate rendition of *Vissi d'arte* to an accordion accompaniment executed by a hunchback with Bell's Palsy freezing half his face while the other half modestly winked and smiled.

The only part of his customary life my father could maintain during the Corks' visit was filling every waking moment with what used to be called "classical" music, though most of it was romantic, Brahms and Mahler in particular. He had always had hundreds of records, which he played on a Meissen phonograph that stood as a separate, massive piece of furniture in one corner of his office. In the past before long-playing records he had constantly been leaping up to change the 78's.

I mention the constant music because, to my mind at least, it served as an invisible link between my father and me. He never discussed music beyond saying that the *German Requiem* was "damn nice" or that the violin and cello concerto was "one hell of a piece," and even these judgments he made with a trace of embarrassment; for him, music was emotion, and he did not believe in discussing feelings.

His real love was the late Brahms, the piano *Intermezzi* and especially the two clarinet sonatas. These pieces, as unpredictable as thought and as human as conversation, filled the house night after night. He could not have liked them as background music to work to, since their abrupt changes of volume and dynamics must have made them too arresting to dismiss. I never showered with my dad, I never saw him naked, not once, but we did immerse ourselves, side by side, in those passionate streams every night. As he worked at his desk and I sat on his couch, reading or daydreaming, we bathed in music. Did he feel the same things I felt? Perhaps I ask this only because now that he's dead I fear we shared nothing and my long captivity in his house represented to him only a slight inconvenience, a major expense, a fair to middling disappointment, but I like to think that music spoke to us in similar ways and acted as the source and transcript of a shared rapture. I feel sorry for a man who never wanted to go to bed with his father; when the father dies, how can his ghost get warm except in such an intimate embrace? For that matter, how does the survivor get warm?

Kevin hated the music. When he was horsing around with his little brother, he'd fall back into the silliness of boyhood. Like all boys, they loved cracking stupid jokes which became funnier and funnier to them the more they were repeated. The opera singers specially tickled them (strangely enough, consisdering their mother was a singer) and they'd jounce

2 5

along with warbling falsettos, holding the right hand on the stomach and rolling their eyes. I was chagrined by this clowning because I'd already imagined Kevin as a sort of husband. No matter that he was younger; his cockiness had turned him into the Older One. But this poignantly young groom I couldn't reconcile with the brat he had become today. Perhaps he wanted to push me away. It occurred to me that last night he may have ventured farther than he had with the other guys; they were neighbor kids, all Catholic, all twelve, and mostly on his team. They had a sort of sex club, he told me; they exchanged dirty playing cards, cigarettes, information about the female anatomy, jokes about the nuns, a purloined beer. No romantic sentiment and no specific lust drew them together; the emotion was camaraderie and the desire general, a scientific curiosity about what went where and to what result. Had they been living in what calls itself a progressive society, they might have skipped the cornholing altogether and moved right along to heterosexual beach parties or heavy petting sessions in someone's unlit basement. Nor would the sex club have gotten off the ground, I suspected, if it had not been led by someone as self-assured and popular as Kevin. Sex among boys differed from clique to clique. It would flourish if a gang included two or three daredevils—those kids made arrogant through fistfights on back lots and triumphs on the field, boys who alternately tormented and cajoled their teachers and challenged their followers to perform ever more outrageous deeds (stealing Mom's money, breaking curfew, hopping a commuter train). The other needed ingredient was for the idea to be handed down to them by a slightly older guy, someone who had passed on to his brat brothers the tradition of this temporary pleasure before he himself was absorbed into the teen world of cars and dating. The irony, of course, is that such gangs almost always excluded anyone destined to be an adult homosexual; they had, at least, excluded me. I was fully aware that only circumstance had brought together someone as neat as Kevin and someone as out of it as I; I also knew that I mustn't let on how much I adored him. As I looked at him, I thought *I adore you*, and silently I murmured *darling* to him: expressions that dignified and excited my feelings by turning them into tags from literature or at least my highly literary notion of a sophisticated milieu.

In the afternoon everyone except Kevin and me left on a boat ride. We went swimming off the dock. Clouds had covered the sun, gray clouds with black bellies and veins of fiery silver. After a while they blew away and released the late sun's warmth. We were standing side by side. I was at least half a foot taller than Kevin. We both had erections and we pulled our suits open under the cold water and looked down at them. Kevin pointed out that there were two openings at the head of his penis, separated by just the thinnest isthmus of flesh. I touched his penis and he touched mine. "Somebody might see us," I said, backing away. "So what," he said.

For quite a while we lolled on the dock. One opulent drop of water rolled down his high, compact chest into the hollow between his nipples, the right one still small and white from the cold, the left fuller and just beginning to color. The other drops were not so heavy; studding his body impressionistically with light, they didn't move; they slowly evaporated. His sides and childishly rounded stomach dried faster than the glossy epaulets on his shoulders. For a second a diamond depended from his nose. Three or four houses away little kids were screaming in the water. One was impersonating a motor boat, another had comically lowered her voice. An older boy was trying to scare the younger ones; he was a bomber, they helpless civilians, and his way of imitating a plane was really very good. The kids were thrilled and squealed. Some of them were laughing, though their laughter contained no warmth, no irony and no humor.

Kevin was restless; he belly-flopped into the water, spraying me, stood, turned and scudded more water on me with the heel of his hand. I knew I should shout "Geronimo!" and leap in after him, clamber up on his back and push him under. The horseplay would dissolve the tension and sexual melancholy; my body would become not a snare but a friendly sort of weapon. But I couldn't go against the decorum of my own fantasies, which were all romantic.

Kevin swam freestyle away from me, way out to the white diving raft. I watched, then rested my head on the board beside my arm. A tiny ant shaped like a dumbbell crawled through the flaring, glittering hairs on my forearm. The water flowing through the pylons under me gurgled urbanely. I propped myself up on my elbow and watched Kevin diving. After a bit he found what looked like the pink plastic lid of a bucket. He tossed it again and again into the air and swam to retrieve it, The late sun, masked once more by clouds, did not send its path across the water toward us but hollowed out beneath it a golden amphitheater. The light was behind Kevin; when he held up the pink disk it went pale and seductive like a hibiscus. His head was about the same size as the lid. When he turned his face my way it was dark and illegible, but his back and shoulders were carving up strips of light, carving them this way and that as he twisted and bobbed. The water was dark, opaque, but it caught the sun's gold light, dragon scales writhing under a saint's halo. At last Kevin swam up beside me; although his head was life-size, his

submerged body had become a small, boneless fetus. He said
we should go down to the store to buy some Vaseline.

"But we don't really need it," I said.

"Let's get it."

In the distance two gray-mauve clouds, like the huge
rectangular sails of caravels, hung darkly, becalmed, imma-
nent, behind mist. Kevin's lips were blue and he was covered
with goose bumps as he vaulted up onto the dock. His legs
were smooth except for the first signs of hair above his ankles
(the first place an old man's legs go bald). He dried himself
and put on a shirt. We took the outboard to the village. I went
into the store with him, though I made him ask for the
Vaseline; I was blushing and couldn't raise my eyes. He
pulled it off without a trace of guilt, even asked to see the
medium size jar before settling for the small one. Outside, a
film of oil opalesced on the water under a great axle of red
light rolling across the sky from azimuth to zenith. That little
round jar of grease would be a clue for my father or his to
find. Worse, it was the application of method to sex, the
outward betrayal of what I wanted to consider love, the
inward state. At last the sun went down and the lake seemed
colder and bigger and the two of us seemed much older.

That night the two families, all of us, went out to dinner at
a restaurant thirty miles away, a place where the overweight
ate iceberg lettuce under a dressing of ketchup and mayon-
naise, steaks under A-1 Sauce, feed corn under butter, ice
cream under chocolate, where a man wearing a black toupee
and a madras sports jacket bounced merrily up and down an
electric organ while a frisky couple lunged and dipped before
him in cloudy recollections of ancient dance steps. The
waitress was at once buddy ("How we doing here?") and

temptress ("C'mon, go on"). She had meticulously carded bronze hair, an exuberant hankie exploding above a name tag ("Susie"), a patient smile and, hanging on a chain, lunettes that she wore only when writing an order or totaling the check. In one corner a colorful canopy hung over a round bar, just so the whole place could be called "The Big Top." No one was sitting at the bar. On its tiered glass shelves, lit from below, stood rank after rank of liquor bottles, soldiers at attention and glowing from within. Everything smelled of the kerosene heater and the pine-scented Air Wick wafting out of the toilets. Except for the circus theme, the dominant motif seemed to be hunting, demonstrated by the rifles and glassy-eyed, dusty-antlered deer heads on the wall.

The place was smelly and oppressive, but the grownups, their fires banked by martinis, settled in for a long stay. The two women, seated next to each other, talked Paris fashions and assured each other *no one* would wear the Parachute. Mr. Cork, more Republican than the republic, was discerning a communist conspiracy in every national mishap; like all conspiracy theories, his assumed perfect intelligence and canniness on the part of the enemy. I could see my father wasn't convinced, least of all by Mr. Cork's ardor; Dad took off his glasses, rubbed his eyes and nodded rhythmically through the harangue, his polite way of shielding himself from a loudmouth, of immigrating inwards. Little Peter had turned a celery stalk from the relish tray into an Indian canoe and Kevin was sniping at it from the chalky promontory of a flour-dusted dinner roll; the massacre was carried out in whispered sound effects. "Kevin O'Malley Cork, how many times must I tell you not to play with your food!" "Aw, Maw."

On and on the meal devolved. The organist's pale forehead

glittering under his black wig, his teeth bared, he moved from a pathetic "Now Is the Hour" with copious vibrato into a "Zippity-Doo-Dah" with a Latin beat. The waitress tempted everyone with pie—stewed apples and cinnamon enclosed in envelopes of pastry that looked like pressed leatherette, each wedge, of course, à la mode. Coffee for the grownups, more milk for the kids. The bill. The argument over it. The change. The second cigar. The mints. The toothpicks. The crème de menthe frappés and the B and B's. More coffee. The tip. "Goodnight, folks. Hurry back!" Another tip for the organist, who nods grateful acknowledgment while staying right in there with "Kitten on the Keys."

All seven of us squeezed into my father's Cadillac and rolled off into a chilly night gray-blue and streaked with the smell of burning wood. My stepmother, Mrs. Cork and Kevin and I were in the back seat; Peter was soon sleeping on his father's shoulder up front, as my father drove. The dinner had left me bleak with rage. Something (books, perhaps) had given me a quite different idea of how people should talk and feed. I entertained fancy ideas about elegant behavior and cuisine and friendship. When I grew up I would always be frank and loving and generous. We'd feast on iced grapes and wine and talk till dawn about the heart and listen to music. *I don't belong here*, I shouted at them silently. I wanted to run through surf or speed off with a brilliant blond in a convertible or rhapsodize on a grand piano somewhere above Europe. Or I wanted the white and gold doors to open as my loving, true, but not-yet-found friends came toward me, their gently smiling faces lit from below by candles on the cake. This longing for lovers and friends was so full within me that it could spill over at any provocation—from listening to my own piano rendition of a waltz, from looking at a reproduction of two lovers in kimonos and tall clogs under an umbrella shielding them from slanted lines of snow, or from sensing a change of seasons (the first smell of spring in winter, say).

Once, when I was Kevin's age, I'd wanted my father to love me and take me away. I had sat night after night outside his bedroom door in the dark, crazy with fantasies of seducing him, eloping with him, covering him with kisses as we shot through space against a night field flowered with stars. But now I hated him and felt he was what I must run away from. To be sure, had he pulled the car off the highway right now and turned to say he loved me, I would have taken his hand and walked with him away from the stunned vehicle that creaked as it cooled, our only spoor the sparks flying from Dad's cigar.

Kevin took my hand. He was sitting next to me in the dark. I had scooted forward on the cushion to give the others more room. Now our linked hands, were concealed by his left leg, which he'd crossed over the other. Just as I'd almost given up on him with his Vaseline, he placed that hot hand in mine. I could feel the calloused pads on his palm where he'd gripped the bat. Outside, the half moon sped through the tall pines, spilled out across a glimpse of water, hid behind a billboard, twinkled faintly in the windows of a train rolling slowly along beside us, only a few windows still lit, one framing the face of a woman crowned by white hair. Dogs barked, then stopped as the trees came quicker and quicker and pushed closer to the winding road. Only here and there could a light be seen. Now none. We were in the deep forest. The change from scattered farms to dense trees felt like an entry into something chilled and holy, a packed congregation of robed and mitered men whose form of worship was to wait in a tense, century-long silence. Kevin had made me very happy—a gleeful, spiteful happiness. Here we were, right under the noses of these bores, and we were two guys holding hands. Maybe I wouldn't have to run away. Maybe I could live here among them, act normal, go through the paces—all the while holding the hand of this wonderful kid.

Back in the basement, we three undressed under the glaring Ping-Pong light. Peter had blue rings under his drooping eyes; he stumbled out of his clothes, which he left in a puddle on the floor. His shoulders were bony, his waist tiny, his genitals a pale blue snail peeping up out of its rounded shell. He mumbled something about the cold sheets and turned his back on us. Kevin and I, at either end of the long, narrow room, undressed more deliberately, said nothing and scarcely looked at each other. Lights out. Then the long wait for Peter's breathing to slow and thicken. The silence was thoughtful, like a pulse heard in an ear pressed to the mattress. Peter said, "Because I don't *want* to . . . squirrel . . . yeah, but you . . ." and was gone. Still Kevin waited, and I feared he too had gone to sleep. But no, here he was, floating toward me, the ghost T-shirt on his torso browner from today's sun. With the Vaseline jar in hand. Its light medicinal odor. The cold jelly that warms quickly to body temperature. As I went in him, he said straight out, as clear as a bell, "That feels really great." It was the first time it had ever occurred to me that sex between two men could please both simultaneously.

The next afternoon my father, painfully patient but haggard from these unusual daytime hours, took us kids water-skiing. Again I walked on the lacquered deck, pushing us away from the dock with the long pole, my movements stiff, almost arthritic with fright. Again my father shouted orders that betrayed his own anxiety: "Kids, I smell something burning. The engine's on fire! Goddam it, quick, young fellow, open those doors." "Nothing, sir, everything's fine." "You sure?" "Yessir. Positive." "Sure?" "Yes." I was clinging to the windshield with claws of fear—and I caught a glimpse of Kevin and Peter smirking at each other. They thought my father and I were both fools.

Skiing off his boat wasn't simple. The velocity of such a massive, powerful vessel almost pulled your arms out of your sockets. The wake fanning out on either side of you once aloft seemed intimidating and to jump over it foolhardy, if not suicidal. Kevin, of course, handled it all beautifully, though he'd never skied before. Soon he was clowning around and lifting first one ski and then the other, and he raced from side to side with great speed. I was in the bucket seat watching him. If we lost him I was supposed to signal Peter up ahead, who was to relay the message on to the captain—but Kevin fell only twice. We went past the diving raft and its company of teenage swimmers; I was pleased that our boat was pulling someone as athletic as Kevin. In our family the virtues were all invisible to a stranger's eye. My stepmother's social eminence, my brains, my dad's dough—they couldn't be seen. But Kevin's body as he crouched and jumped over the wake, *that* could be seen. When at last he became tired he waited till we went past our house and then released the rope and slowly sank ten paces from our dock.

That night he came to my bed again, but I irritated him by trying to kiss him. "I don't go for that," he said brusquely, though later, when we stood together in the maid's half-bathroom washing up, he looked at me with an expression that could have been either weariness or tenderness, I couldn't tell. In the morning he went swimming with his father. I watched the two of them talking away with each other. Kevin gave his father a hand and pulled him up on the dock. They were obviously friends, and I felt all the more rebuffed.

That afternoon Peter, Kevin and I went fishing in the little outboard. The weather was hot, muggy, clouded over, and we waited in vain for a bite. We'd dropped anchor in a marsh where hollow reeds surrounded us and scratched the metal sides of the boat. I was sweating freely. Sweat stung my right eye. A mosquito spoke in my ear. The smell of gasoline from the engine (tilted up out of the shallow water) refused to lift and float away. The boys were threatening each other with dead worms out of the bait jar and Peter's calls and pounding feet had scared off every fish in the lake. When I asked them to sit still, they gave each other that same smirk and started mocking me, repeating my words, their voices sliding up and down the scale, "You *could* be more considerate." After a while the joke wore thin and they moved on to something else. Somehow—but at what precise moment?—I had shown I was a sissy; I replayed a moment here, a moment there of the past days, in an attempt to locate the exact instant when I'd betrayed myself. We motored back over the glassy, steaming lake; everything was colorless and hot and drained of immediacy. This place could be any place, these people any people. This day was interchangeable with any other. In such a listless, enfeebled world the whine of the motor seemed particularly cruel, like a scar on the void. I went off on a walk by myself.

I plodded up and down the hills on the narrow road that passed the backs of cottages, which turned their faces to the lake. An old car full of black maids sputtered past. It was Wednesday evening; tomorrow was their day off. Tonight they'd stay at a Negro resort twenty miles away and dance and laugh far into the night, eat ribs, wear gowns, talk louder and laugh harder than they could the rest of the week in the staid houses where they served. Most of the time they were exiled, dispersed, one by one, into the alien population; only once a week did the authorities allow the tribe to reconvene. They were exuberant people forced to douse their merry flames and maintain just the palest pilot light. At that moment I really believed I, too, was exuberant and merry by nature, had I the chance to show it.

In the silence that ebbed in after the last sound of the departing car, the air was filled with the one-note, polyvocal chant of crickets. Their song seemed like the heartbeat of loneliness, a beat that sang up and down the wires of my veins. I was desolate. I toyed again with the idea of switching back to military school and becoming a general. I wanted power so badly that I had convinced myself I already had too much of it, that I was an evil schemer who might destroy everyone around me through the poison seeping out of my pores. I was appalled by my own majesty.

Kevin and his family stayed on three more days. Mr. Cork became incoherent with drink one night and cracked the banister as he reeled up to bed. Mrs. Cork exploded the next morning and told my stepmother she *loathed* eggs "swimming in grease." Katy, the Hungarian cook, locked herself in her room and emerged red-eyed and sniffling two hours later. Kevin and Mrs. Cork argued with each other, or rather she nagged him and he ridiculed her; when they made up, their embrace was shockingly intimate—prolonged, wordless nuzzling. On a rainy afternoon the boys rough-housed until Peter overturned a coffee table and smashed one of the hand-painted tiles set into the top; his parents seemed almost indifferent to the damage and allowed the pushing and shoving to continue. Mrs. Cork's way of conspicuously ignoring the pandemonium was to vocalize, full voice. Each night Kevin came to my bed, though now I no longer elaborated daydreams of running away with him. I was a little bit afraid of him; now that he knew I was a sissy, he could make fun of me whenever he chose to. Who knew what he'd do? After witnessing his vituperation against his mother, followed by the weird nuzzling, I could not continue to think of him as the boy next door. The last night I tried kissing him again, but he turned his head away.

On the afternoon they left, Mrs. Cork flushed a deep, indignant red and chased Kevin halfway up the stairs. He crouched and shouted, his face contorted, "You scumbag, you old scumbag" and pushed her down the stairs. My father was furious. He lifted the woman from the floor and said to Kevin, "I think you've done enough for one day, young man." Mr. Cork, not completely sober, kept counting the pieces of luggage and pretended he hadn't noticed the outbreak. His wife took on an injured silence as though in heavy mourning. She barely went through the motions of bidding us farewell, but once they were out the door and on the steps toward the garage, I saw her flash a sad little crooked smile at her son. He rushed into her open arms and they stroked each other.

At last they were gone. My father and stepmother were lighthearted with relief, as was I. My stepmother, ever fastidious, had found them almost savagely dirty and cited lots of evidence, beginning with the pint bottles under the bed and ending with the used ear swabs smoldering in the bathroom ashtray. My father said they were all "screwballs" and their boys more fit for a reformitory than a house. And that Cork fellow talked and drank too much and knew too little and seemed unstable; Dad thought Cork would not do well in business—nor did he, as it turned out. I said the sons struck me as "babyish." My stepmother apologized to Katy for the rude guests and reported back to us that they had not left Katy a tip; my father rewarded her for the extra bother she'd been put to.

Then we all rushed into solitude, my stepmother and I to our books and Dad to his puttering. My father now seemed to like me better. I might not be the son he thought he wanted, but I was what he deserved—someone patient, appreciative, as addicted to books as he was to work, as isolated by my loneliness as he was by his misanthropy, someone he could speak to only in the best if least direct way through the recorded concert that filled the house deep into the night, even until dawn.

I was moved back into my room. We ate very late and gave ourselves to the sonorous, spacious night. My father did desk work. We were three dreamers, each musing happily in a different cubicle. The sound of the calculating machine, jumping with sums on its metal wheels. The aroma of burning pine logs. The remarkable fairness and good humor with which the piano and clarinet took turns singing the melody. At last, the sweet smell of the pipe. My father was in the basement, which had been restored to his dog. Through the air filter I could hear him: "What is it, Old Boy? Tell me. You can tell me."

Then, unexpectedly, he invited me to join them for their walk. It was strangely chilly, the first reminder of autumn, and my father had put on a ridiculous blue cap with a bill and earflaps and a baggy tan car coat that zipped up the front. Wherever we stopped we were enveloped in a cloak of sweet smoke, like the disguised king and his favorite who'd slipped out of the palace to visit the peasants' fair. Nothing could hurry my father or Old Boy along. We stopped at every bush and every overflowing garbage can behind every silent, darkened cottage. We went all the way down to the deserted village: the store, the post office, the boat works. A speedboat, its bottom leprous and in need of sanding and painting, was turned upside down on trestles. A chain rattled against the flagpole in front of the post office. A woman wearing a nurse's uniform drove past, the only car we'd seen.

We retraced our steps. As daybreak came closer, the birds began to twitter and the leaves on birches fluttered in the rising breeze. Down the sloped shore the lake slowly took shape, then color. Behind a door an unseen dog yapped at us, and Old Boy became frantic with curiosity. "What is it? Tell me. You can tell me. What is it, Old Boy?"

As the sun, like life returning to a body, stole over the world, the beam from my father's flashlight grew less and less distinct until it had been absorbed in the clarity of something that was new yet again.

The Killer Chicken and the Closet Queen

At thirty-seven Stephen Ashe
was the youngest member of the Wall Street law firm of
Webster, Eggleston, Larrabee and Smythe. He was quite as
important a member as any of the four whose surnames
comprised the firm's title and the name Ashe was not
included only because it was felt that five names to the title
would overload it. The oldest member, fifty-nine-year-old
Nathaniel Webster the Fifth, was on his way out, having
suffered a stroke the day of President Nixon's resignation and
another on the night of his wedding to his nephew's adolescent widow from the Arkansas Ozarks. The day that he
mistook Larrabee for Smythe in the elevator ascending to the
firm's thirty-second floor offices in the Providential Building,
Jerry Smythe had slipped a business card of the firm into
Stephen Ashe's pocket as they went down the elevator for
lunch, giving Stephen a smiling wink and a slight pat on the
butt. When Stephen looked at the card he saw that the name
Webster had been scratched and the name Ashe appended to
the three remaining, printed on it with a ball-point pen.

In the next few days the same conniving winks and little

butt-pats had been delivered to Stephen by Jack Larrabee and Ralph Eggleston, and it was now fully apparent to Stephen that there was no dissident voice in the matter, that is, none excepting that of the senior gentleman who was on his way out. Of course it was a bit unnerving the way that Nat Webster hung in. A work day never passed at the law firm without Nat, secretly known as the old hound dog, shouting out exuberantly, his door having banged open, "Pressure down five more points, I'm in the clear!"

Stephen and Jerry Smythe went directly from work every evening to the Ivy League Club, for a splash in the pool, a massage and a sauna. They each had an interest in keeping physically fit: both were under forty and on good days or evenings didn't look as if they'd been out of law school for more than a couple of years. They undressed in the same cubicle at the club. Smythe would wait until Stephen had found a cubicle that was vacant and gone in it and then Smythe would enter it, too, and as they undressed together, Stephen could hardly ignore how frequently Smythe's hands would brush against his thighs and, once or twice, even his crotch.

They had their massages on adjoining tables and Stephen's was administered by a good-looking young Italian, and whenever this masseur's fingers worked up Stephen's thighs, Stephen would get an erection. He tried to resist it but he couldn't. The Italian would chuckle a little under his breath but Smythe would make a loud, jocular comment, such as, "Hey, Steve, who're you thinking of?"

One Friday evening Stephen replied, "I was thinking of Nat Webster's little teenage wife."

"Oh, did I tell you, she's got her kid brother up here, he was staying with Nat and her but Nat threw him out on his ass last weekend."

"Why'd Nat throw him out?"

"Found out he was delinquent."

"Delinquent *how?*"

"Jailed for lewd vagrancy, peddling his goodies, you know," said Smythe, his voice lowered to a theatrical whisper.

Stephen wanted, for some reason, to extract more information on the boy's delinquencies but he refrained from pursuing the subject with Smythe because he found himself wondering, as he had sometimes wondered before, if Smythe's freedom of speech and behavior with him were not a kind of espionage. It was altogether possible that Eggleston and Larrabee were using Smythe's closer familiarity with Stephen to delve a bit more into his, Stephen's, private life. It was more than altogether possible that this was the case. Stephen remembered a little closed council among the partners a few months ago when they had discussed the advisability of discharging a junior accountant on suspicion of homosexual inclinations, a suspicion based on nothing more than the facts that he was still unmarried at thirty-one and sharing an apartment with a younger man whose photograph had appeared in a magazine advertisement for Marlboro cigarettes.

Stephen had felt himself flushing but said nothing at this council; Smythe had spoken up loudly, saying, "I don't see how it can affect the prestige of the firm one way or another."

Stephen's head had lifted involuntarily, it sort of jerked up, and he had seen Smythe's eyes fastened on his flushed face.

"What do *you* say, Steve?" Smythe had asked him, challengingly.

Despising himself a bit, Stephen had cleared his throat and said, "Well, I don't think it's to our advantage to be associated in any way with this sort of deviation from the norm. I mean we don't want to be associated with it even by—" For a moment he dried up, then he had completed the sentence too loudly with the word "association!"

"Exactly," Larrabee had said.

The junior accountant had been given two weeks notice that day.

Now the Italian masseur had turned Stephen on his belly and was kneading his buttocks.

Smythe was continuing his discussion of Nat Webster's wife's kid brother's precociously colorful past.

"In Arkansas he was involved in the beating up of an old homo who is still in traction in a Hot Springs hospital. Well, the old hound dog told this kid to hit the streets and I understand he is now living at the Y. You know what that means, don't you?"

"Does it mean something besides living at the Y?" Stephen enquired with affected indifference.

At this moment the masseur's fingers entered Stephen's natal cleave, and Stephen said, "Is there any truth in the report that there is going to be a merger between Fuller, Cohen, Stern and the Morris Brothers?"

"Steve, are you in dreamland? Why, the Morris Brothers declared bankruptcy last week, and have flown to Hong Kong!"

"A massage makes me sleepy," said Stephen, affecting a great yawn.

***

One evening in early spring Stephen was viewing an old Johnny Weismuller film on his bedroom TV set when the persistent ringing of the phone brought him out of a state that verged on entrancement.

"Aw, let it go," was his first impulse, but the phone would

not shut up. At length he got up from his vibra-chair, turning the TV set so that he could still admire it while at the phone.

"Yes, yes, what is it?" he shouted with irrepressible annoyance.

"Oh, I'm sorry! Did I interrupt something?"

The precocious little girl voice, reminiscent of Marilyn Monroe's, was recognizable to Stephen instantly. It was Nat Webster's adolescent wife's.

"No, no, not a bit, Maude, not a bit in this world or the next one. In fact I was just about to phone you and Nat and invite you over for Sunday brunch to meet my mother who is flying up from Palm Beach for my birthday."

"You are havin' a *birth*-day?" Maude exclaimed as if amazed that he had ever been born.

"How is Nat doing, Maude?"

"Let's not discuss the condition of Nat," Maude said with abrupt firmness.

"Bad as *that?*"

"It's his lack of concern for the—sorry, I shouldn't be botherin' you about this, but, you know, Steve, you're the only one in the bunch, I mean his Wall Street buddies, that I feel I can open up with. Now, Steve, maybe you've heard about my little brother payin' us a visit from Arkansas."

"It seems to me that Jerry mentioned you had him with you right now."

"Look, Steve, I'm callin' from a coin-box because I didn't want Nat to hear this conversation. You see, a problem has come up."

"Oh?"

"Yes, you see, I think that Nat resents my attachment to this sweet kid brother of mine."

"Oh?"

"Well, I'm not going to drag out the conversation, another

party is waitin' outside the booth. But the problem is this. Nat suddenly told me an' Clove, that's my kid brother's name, sweetest, cutest little sixteen-year-old thing, that there wasn't room enough for him in our eight room penthouse on Park."

"Oh. A spatial problem."

"Space is not the problem, the problem is that Nat is resentful of youth and natural gay spirits, and that's the reason he handed Clove ten dollars—imagine, one measly ole sawbuck—over the breakfast table this week and told him to go and check in at the Y."

Stephen felt a premonitory tightening in his throat. In a guarded tone he remarked that there were a lot of physical advantages to be had at the Y, the swimming pool and the workout rooms and association with other young Christian kids.

"Steve, you're playin' dumb!" Maude almost shrieked, "Why, everyone knows that Y's are overrun with wolves out for chickens!"

"Wolves? Chickens?" Stephen gave a totally false little chuckle of incomprehension.

"Quit that, Steve, you can't play dumb with *me!* Now I am comin' straight to the point. I've got to remove little Clove from that kind of temptation that's so unattractive and it occurred to me that you might be able to give Clove a bed at your place, you being the only young bachelor in Nat's crowd, I thought that maybe—well, how *about* it, Steve?"

Stephen took a break on that one, a pause for breath.

"I've got an extra bedroom for Mother's visits, but—"

"Oh, that I didn't know, but if I remember correctly, you've also got a sofa in the livin' room, haven't you, Steve?"

Stephen again was unable to come up with an immediate, natural reply, but that was not necessary.

"Goddam, hold your hawses!" Maude shouted, presumably to the party waiting outside the coin-box. She then lowered her voice a little and said in her reminiscent-of-Marilyn tone, "We'll see you Sunday at brunch to meet your mother, she will just love Clove and so will you!"

The phone had been hung up. In a dazed fashion Stephen noted that the nearly nude backside of Johnny Sheffield, son of Tarzan and Jane whom they called Boy, was as close to perfection as, well, his *own*, when he looked at himself in the triplicate mirror in his dressing room, in the right sort of light.

"My God, why is it that—! I do get myself in for—!"

He was still awake when the midnight news came on. There was a photo of Anita Bryant with a banana cream pie on her face.

". . . thrown by a militant gay with a shout about bigots deserving no less—"

"But what will Mom *think?*" Stephen murmured aloud as he switched off the TV and the bed-lamp and cradled his crotch with a hand. . . .

***

Mom's plane was due to be delayed five hours owing to a visibility problem over Kennedy Airport. Having received this report at Kennedy, Stephen thought about Mom and what her reaction to the situation might be.

Mom is an old trouper, he thought, but definitely not one that's about to wait five hours in West Palm Beach for weather to change over Kennedy. I bet if I got on the phone and called her suite at the Royal Shores I'd find she is already back there; yes, I ought to do that.

But he didn't do that right away. Without a conscious thought of doing so, he took out the latest report on Mom's stockholdings on Wall Street.

This will put her in a bad humor, he thought. She claims she doesn't keep up with things like stock fluctuations although I know she watches them like a hawk. She won't admit that she knows the Dow Jones has slipped almost forty points in the last two months. But it's just on paper. I'll tell her again, "Just trust me, Mom, you know it is just on paper, your net worth is still a million over what it was when Dad left us."

He would give her this pitch on the ride back from J.F.K. and she would maintain a reproachful silence for the next several minutes. Then she would make some politely withering remark, something like: "Son, you must know that nobody's net worth is what it is on paper, not since they forced Richard Nixon to resign and put that peanut vendor in the White House."

"All right, I couldn't agree with you more, but you must remember, Mom, that even with an economic situation unfavorable as it is, you have not only a portfolio of stock holdings worth more than three million but nearly as much in the Manhattan Chemical Bank, I mean in your savings account alone, and as for your holdings in Switzerland, Mom—"

"Stephen, I can't imagine what you are talking about!"

Mom always pretended she hadn't the least idea that the bulk of her fortune was in diamonds and gold bricks in the vault of a bank in Zurich.

Stephen found himself standing, although he didn't remember getting up. He also found that he had sweated through his shirt, and he heard himself saying in a strident whisper, "Christ Almighty, does she think she can take it all with her?"

He was now in a phone booth, calling Mom's suite at the Royal Shores of Palm Beach.

"Thank God, Precious, you didn't wait, you went home."

"Naturally, Stephen, I knew you wouldn't expect me to wait in West Palm Beach for five hours or even one."

"No, no, Mom, I just wanted to be sure. So what *are* your travel plans now?"

"I may be a little late for your Sunday brunch. Why don't you change it to a buffet supper? Would that put you out too much?"

"I'd just have to call up about a dozen people."

"You mean it *would* be too much, then?"

"Precious, has anything for *you* ever been too much for *me*, Mom?"

"Stephen, as we both know, you have always been a paragon of filial devotion. Then it is understood. If you're tied up with preparations for the buffet supper, just have a limousine waiting at Idlewild to meet me."

"Mom, it's not Idlewild anymore, it is Kennedy Airport."

"To *me* it remains Idlewild. Understood?"

"Oh, yes, Precious, I understand completely, I was just afraid that—"

"And Stephen, one thing more."

Her voice had dropped to a level that was still firm but slightly less militant.

"What thing, Mother?"

"I trust not a thing but a person. This Miss Sue Coffin whom you mention to me as a young woman, well, she couldn't be still too young, that you are perennially 'going out' with, as you put it, as if you thought I could not see through euphemisms, however transparent. Are you still going out with this *Miss* Sue Coffin whom, for fifteen years now, Stephen, since we buried your dear father, you have described to me as a successful young career woman in some sort of promotional field?"

"Oh, yes, *her!* I am still seeing Sue Coffin, oh, yes, I see her regularly, Mom."

"I presume that you mean upon a nightly basis. Now, son, I have become increasingly disturbed by the fact that you have been 'going out' for fifteen years, slightly more than fifteen, I believe, with this young woman whom I have yet to enjoy the possible pleasure of meeting. Stephen? When I fly up to Manhattan for the buffet I shall expect to be granted that pleasure and an opportunity to discuss this situation with her in private, and before I hang up I wish to know if she is connected with the Nantucket Island Coffins with whom all the socially acceptable Coffins are connected?"

"Oh, now, Mom, I wouldn't be going out all this time with a Miss Coffin who wasn't a socially acceptable one, you know that, I wouldn't dream of it, ever!"

"Son, this extramarital alliance with a woman, socially acceptable as the Nantucket Coffins, must be legalized, Stephen, and I insist that she be produced, that she be presented to me at the buffet on Sunday. Now I'm exhausted, there's nothing more to discuss. I love you, Stephen. Good night."

Produce her, produce her, produce her, out of a hat or a sleeve, why, my God, Sue Coffin is—

Yes, there had indeed been a fleeting association of a slightly intimate nature between a Miss Sue Coffin and Stephen but that association had been terminated long since when she had married an advertising executive for whom she'd worked, and they'd moved to San Francisco. Why, even Christmas cards from her no longer came in; the last card he'd received from her was an engraved one bearing her married name and announcing the birth of twins, giving the date of their nativity and their weight at that occasion and a scribbled statement from Sue Coffin Merriwether saying *Proud mother is happy as a lark! Fond greetings, Sue.*

Not happily as a lark did Stephen emerge from the phone booth, in fact he staggered from its stifling enclosure as though about to collapse. A discreet hand clasped his elbow, steering him toward a door marked EXIT beyond which possibly there existed some reviving fresh air. . . .

***

On the long ride home Stephen's usually well-ordered mind seemed to be getting the wrong sort of feedback for the input. It was not continuing along a chosen groove but was abruptly skipping onto a series of little tangents. It was as if somebody had monkeyed with a perfectly but too delicately tooled computer. No matter how finely a machine of this sort is tooled, even if it is hand-tooled by artist-craftsmen—

"Wow!" said Stephen aloud. He said it loudly enough for the chauffeur from the rental limousine service to glance back and enquire, "Something wrong, sir?"

"No, no, no, just—"

Just what, and why three "no"s? Must be really upset, have a feverish feeling. He knew how to take his own pulse and the hands of his watch were luminous so he could time it. He was alarmed at how it was racing. One hundred and twenty a minute!

The new rental limousines were equipped with liquor cabinets. Why did Stephen open it so stealthily, since he had already pressed the button that shut him off, sound-wise, from the chauffeur?

I guess I must be afraid of getting a liquor problem like Dad's.

He was trying to remember what he had been thinking about when he had silently uttered "Wow" a short while ago as he had followed the chauffeur out of Kennedy. Was it because the chauffeur's elegantly tapered back was—?

Wow!

In the liquor cabinet was a half-full bottle of bourbon, a good brand of it, Old Nick. Stephen helped himself to half a tumbler and by the time they were passing serenely into the outskirts of Queens, the other side of La Guardia, Stephen had, with no conscious plan to, lowered the soundproof panel between himself and the chauffeur.

He knew that he was in a dreamlike, an almost trancelike condition.

"What's your name?" he asked the chauffeur in a slurred voice.

"Tony," said the chauffeur.

"Aw, Italian, are you?"

"That's right."

"Love Italy," said Stephen, "beautiful, beautiful country, beautiful people. You know—"

"Know what, sir?"

"I've got a mother."

"Me, too. I got a helluva Mama."

There was something soothing, almost caressing, about the voice of the young Italian chauffeur, and in response to those qualities, Stephen sloshed some more Old Nick into the tumbler which he had just drained.

"You've got a helluva Mama and I've got one hell of a Mom. Do you notice the difference?"

"Not sure what you mean, sir."

"How much time have you got for me to explain?"

"My time is yours, at your expense, but it's yours."

The voice of the young Italian chauffeur had undergone an indefinable change.

"Well, taking you at your word's value," said Stephen, "drive off the highway at the next turn and le's have a little talk. About Moms and Mamas."

Stephen felt a slight lurch as the limousine turned off the highway but felt nothing more until the car had stopped.

Through eyes with lids that drooped, Stephen looked about.

The personable young chauffeur had parked the limousine in a place from which the nearest lighted building was at least half a block away.

Without invitation from Stephen, the chauffeur now entered the back seat of the limo and sat rather close to Stephen. He was not only young and good looking but there was a redolence about him, a musky fragrance.

After a few moments' silence, he said to Stephen, "The next move's up to you."

"Strange remark," Stephen said in his slurred voice, now very deeply slurred.

Another few moments of silence but not altogether inactive. The Italian's left knee had swung open to encounter Stephen's right knee.

There was a wild clicking on and off of multi-colored buttons inside Stephen's head, along with electronic noises. This disturbance suddenly descended to his stomach and he began to make retching sounds.

"If you're gonna puke, stick your head out the window. Not so far, okay, I'm holding your ass."

When Stephen had vomited, he sprawled back into the lap of the chauffeur. After swabbing his mouth and chin with his monogrammed handkerchief of fine Irish linen, a customary sort of adjustment to his position in the world took precedence over all other circumstances, and to the chauffeur, still holding him on his lap, he said in a tone inherited from his mother, "Young man, I believe you are taking liberties with my person!"

"Me? Liberties? Person?"

"Yes, I am a *person*. In fact, I am a member of the Wall Street law firm of Webster, Eggleston, Larrabee and Smythe. I am in Register, Social, and headed for Dunn and Bradstreet's."

"*Marrone!*" said the chauffeur. "Didn't you tell me to drive off the highway at the next turn-off?"

"If I did, I assure you it was to have a discussion of our respective mothers, not to be subjected to liberties with my . . . person—"

"Blow that out your ass!" said the now outraged Italian, as he dumped Stephen off his lap and opened the back door of the rental limousine.

"The person you are is a goddam closet queen."

"And what is a 'closet queen,' that curious expression?"

The chauffeur grinned. "A queen in a closet with a broomstick up his butt," replied the chauffeur, slamming the back door shut and returning to the wheel.

***

Of course this bizarre experience was somewhat blurred in his recollection when Stephen woke late the next morning with a violent headache. He recalled only that a rental limousine chauffeur had made suggestions to him of a presumptuous nature on the drive back from the airport.

It was, when he woke, much too late to call off the Sunday brunch; in fact, there was barely time to prepare the Bloody Marys. He had all the ingredients for Eggs Benedict and since old Nat's young bride was on the guest list, Stephen was confident he could engage her as an assistant chef.

He was just out of the needle-sharp shower, drying off vigorously and reaching for his paisley silk robe, when the doorbell rang.

"Just a mo!" he shouted in the hall as he got himself into the robe and secured about his throat a snowy new scarf, arranging it as an ascot.

The bell rang again and again he called out "Just a mo," as he inspected himself in the full-length mirror on the door's interior surface.

He inspected himself two ways, head on and in profile, and was far from displeased, particularly by the way that the paisley silk so gracefully delineated, in profile, the masculine but prominent buttocks that Dame Nature had gifted him with.

"It's me, it's Maude. I came a little early because I thought you might need a woman's hand in the kitchen."

But Stephen was not looking at her, he was looking at her companion, a boy in blue jeans, no taller than Maude but with a—

Again the word "Wow!" exploded in Stephen's head.

"Oh, this is my kid brother, Clove," Maude was saying, "I stopped off at the Y to pick him up 'cause it's important you and him get to know each other before the others get here, especially Nat."

Wow!

"Now you two just leave the kitchen to me an' go get to know each other. Oh. Is your Mom up from Palm Beach?"

"Plane . . . delayed . . . she—"

"What a bitch," Maude said with great cheer in her voice. "I mean the plane delay."

Stephen found that he had not gone into the living room, as he had naturally intended, but had returned to the bedroom. He heard the door being closed, not by himself.

"Sis is right, we should get to know each other if you're gonna put me up here."

Stephen found himself rattling a bit, uttering words without due process of thought.

"I think I must be sort of unnerved this morning."

"Over your Mom coming up to check on you, huh?"

"There's nothing for her to check on, nothing at all, but her visits disturb the routine. Hey, now, what are you doing?"

"Feelin' the material," said the boy, Clove, breathing on Stephen's neck and running his hot little hand down the gracefully, just-enough swaybacked curvature of Stephen's spine and right onto that ellipsis of his posterior which Stephen had only a few minutes past admired with such satisfaction in the mirrored back of the front door.

"Good stuff, whacha call it?"

"I just had time to put on my silk robe, and this white cravat, before your sister and you arrived at the door."

Maude's kid brother's hot little hand was still feeling the material, as he had put it, but with increased pressure.

"Would you mind going into the kitchen to bring me a Bloody Mary, a . . . double?"

"Now you're talkin', baby. I'll bring both of us doubles, and when I come back, you are gonna forget all about your Mom's check on yuh."

A cunning idea abruptly occurred to Stephen. "Clove?"

The boy glanced back at Stephen from the door.

In a husky whisper, Stephen said to him, "Clove, don't ask

me why right now, but when Mom arrives, I want you to get her aside and tell her that you are a secret."

"What kinda secret you mean?"

"Clove, I can make it worth your while if you go through with this little conspiracy right. I want you to convince Mom that you are a secret child of mine, born fifteen years ago, and your Mom was a Miss Sue Coffin from Nantucket Island."

Clove's eyes narrowed to a look of shrewd contemplation. He had a definite attraction to deception as a practice in life. Of course he did not comprehend at all the purpose of this particular deceit but that it involved a trick about to be played on someone was immediately appealing.

"Just lemme git all this straight. You are my secret daddy? And my mom, she's also a secret named—"

"A young lady named Sue Coffin who died at your birth, Clove."

"Jeez, this is heavy, but when you say you'll make it worth my while, I reckon that I can handle it for you okay. Now you stay in here, rest on that bed there, and I'll fetch a couple of doubles, I'll be right out and then we can git it together in more detail, daddy."

As the door opened briefly for Clove's kitchen errand, Stephen heard from near, but as if from afar, the doorbell ringing again.

"Never had such a hangover, wow—" he murmured to himself, falsely, as he removed the paisley silk robe and toppled onto the bed.

* * *

Easily an hour had passed by the time Stephen emerged gradually and uncertainly from his bedroom in which he had ingested easily three and probably more Bloody Marys, fetched him by the Ganymede younger sibling of Nat Webster's adolescent bride from the Arkansas Ozarks.

He did not begin to know what faced him in the living room; he knew only that the entire complement of his colleagues in the Wall Street law firm of Webster, Eggleston, Larrabee and Smythe were there assembled, each with his respective spouse.

"Well, I want you to know—" he heard himself saying, in a slow and slurred voice as he joined the abruptly hushed assemblage.

Nat Webster, the old hound dog, was first to speak up. "I don't much think you want us to know a goddam thing which we don't know already."

"I want you to know I passed out in the bedroom and I don't know how it happened."

Nat Webster was on his feet. "If you'll drop by the office tomorrow about noon, I think your official paper of resignation from the firm will be ready for signature. Is that understood, Ashe?"

Then he marched to the door, calling back "Come on, Maude!"

Maude bestowed a sisterly kiss on Stephen's blanched cheek as she responded languidly to this summons. Then she lisped loudly and sweetly, "Thanks for putting up Clove, so much better for him than life at the Y."

"*Maude!*" shouted Nat Webster from the door.

She blew a kiss at the lingering guests and undulated into the hallway.

Eggleston, Larrabee and Smythe were all on their feet now, and their wives, conferring together in whispers, were getting into their furs.

Clove had now entered. He closed the fly of his jeans with a loud zip.

Smythe was last to leave the Sunday brunch. He came up close to Stephen, still standing stunned in the living room center, and delivered these comforting words. "Too bad, boy, you had to blow it like this."

His butt-pat, which followed, was of a fondly valedictory nature.

Vertigo took sudden hold of Stephen, he tottered in several directions, but finally fell backwards into the arms of Clove.

"Bed, bed, before Mom," he heard himself imploring before it all went black.

**

It could not be said that Stephen emerged altogether from black when he recovered consciousness in his elegantly-appointed-bachelor-bedroom. However, the black was not total, unrelieved black, although the room was not lighted by the least lingering vestige of daylight through his dormer windows. Day had withdrawn as completely and, to Stephen, as precipitately, as had his future association with the law firm of Webster, Eggleston, Larrabee and Smythe. Still, as the pupils of his eyes expanded, he could detect those sometimes comforting little irregular glimmerings of light on the river East, which the windows of the bedroom overlooked, as well as the more assertive challenges to dark that were offered by citybound Sunday night traffic on the Triboro Bridge.

"Jesus K. Morris BROTHERS!"

This extraordinary exclamation was not provoked by a reassessment of his future with Wall Street and its legal aspects but by a very precisely located physical sensation, one bitch of a pain where he had never experienced one before.

5 8

Hard upon this outcry of distress, Stephen heard from the hallway (thank God the door was closed!) the voice of his nearest and dearest still living relative, none other than his mother, her voice, yes, but not at all under its usual cool restraint.

To whom was she talking? Herself or someone other?

Although pitched rather loudly, the voice of mother was saying something incomprehensible to him.

"Oh, Precious gran'chile, I believe your daddy's awake, now, I heard him in his bedroom, le's go in and—"

"Oh, no, Mother, hello, Mother, no, no, not quite yet, dear!"

"Shun, shun, Shtephen, what a sad but beautiful shtory! Mother's naturally very upshet by the tragedy of poor Sue Coffin but undershtands why you preferred not to shpeak of it. The thing to conshider now ish the proper background and shchooling of thish adorable deshendant of an Ashe and a Coffin of the Nantucket Coffins. Thish beautiful shecret of yours, thish darlin' Clove Ashe Coffin ish comin' in there to fetch you shoon as—Oh, Clove, Preshus, I'm shtill sho unshtrung, thrilled to pieces, of course, but shtill a bit overcome by the shuddenness of it all. Sweetheart, do you think I could have another one of those marvelous ashpirin shubstitutes you gave me when I arrived, and maybe alsho another one of thoshe delishous Merry Marys to wash it down with?"

Then through the hall door, that frontier of a world in which all that remained of his particular reality was confined with Stephen Ashe, came the voice of Clove, its hillbilly coarseness and outright abrasiveness of intonation hardly recognizably muted and transfigured, as if adapted from a score for a brass instrument to one for a delicate woodwind. "Mommy, I reckoned you might want seconds and here they are, just stick your tongue out and I'll pop in this new type aspirin and . . . there! Leave mouth open for Mary! There now, slowly, drink all, don't let none spill! Good, huh, Mommy? If the drugstore man was God and the barman was Jesus, they couldn't make 'em none better, you can bet your sweet—"

"Shunny, I am afraid that shun Stephen has neglected your social training. You mustn't pat a lady on her behind, not on such short acquaintansh, regardless of . . . relashuns!"

But if there was any genuine reproof in Mom's tone, it was immediately cancelled out by her subsequent giggles, coy as a skittish schoolgirl's . . .

***

Some minutes later, fewer than might be surmised, Stephen had opened the bedroom door just a crack and had called softly, "Son?"

"Yes, Daddy?"

"Shun Shtephen!" cried out Mom in her curiously altered voice.

"Mom, I'm sorry you had to discover my little, uh, *secret* like this, but if Son will give me some help in here, I'm not feeling well, Mom. You remember that thing I had called labyrinthitis? Well, it has come back on me, there's been a little recurrence, it, it . . . affects my equilibrium, and if Sonny will help me in here, I'll, I'll make myself decent so we can talk this all out together."

Stephen heard the sound of a prolonged and moist osculation in the hall. He swayed backwards a little as Clove entered the door of the dark bedroom. Having swayed in that direction, Stephen went all the way backwards to the little bench beneath the dormer windows, where he soon found Clove beside him.

"You know, at sixteen I'm one helluva lot smarter than you are, Daddy. Your Mom likes Quaaludes, Daddy, and she got one in her first Mary."

"Quaa what?"

"Lude."

"Yes, it's all very lewd, it's almost disgustingly lewd."

"You got the wrong spellin', Daddy, but never mind about that. I think that your Mom is already hooked on Quaaludes washed down with a toddy or two. Now, here. You take this other Quaalude and then you go out to your Mom."

"And do what?"

"Shit, you'll know what to do when this big one hits you, washed down with a Merry Mary as your sweet ole Mom calls it!"

Clove thrust the Quaalude into Stephen's slack mouth, then pressed the Mary to his lips.

"Now swallow slowly, Daddy, don't slobber. Which one of the drawers in that bureau is the drawer full of drawers?"

"Bottom drawer."

"Right. Drawers for your bottom in bottom drawer."

Clove got Stephen dressed for his heart-to-heart with Mom in less time than an experienced short-order cook would need to serve up two over lightly with a side of French fries.

"How you feel, how'd it hit you, Daddy?" whispered Clove.

"No problem, no problem at all," Stephen replied with an uncertain air of assurance.

"Must run in the family but it took me to bring it out. Now git with Mom."

He headed Stephen forcibly toward the door.

Mom attempted to rise to her feet to embrace Stephen as he

entered the hall but she nearly hit the carpet. Clove caught her buttocks to his groin, and then Stephen witnessed a scene the shock of which even his Quaalude washed down with a double Mary did not insulate him against completely. Mom was now seated in the lap of Clove. Both of them were sobbing, the difference being that Clove was winking and grinning over Mom's shoulder.

Mom made a sound that was "Shun, shun, shun," but doubtless was her best effort, under the circumstances, to articulate three times the word "Son."

"Mom, can you hear me?" Stephen shouted.

"Oh, shun, oh, shun!"

"Daddy," said Clove, "your Mom is the treasure at the end of the rainbow I've waited for all my life. She understands! You understand, Daddy? Your Mom understands and is so goddam happy she's speechless!"

Mom did, indeed, appear to be overcome with felicity but she was not only in the arms of the Arkansas chicken but those of narcotized slumber. After a little colloquy between Clove and Stephen, it was agreed that she should be transferred to her suite in the Ritz Tower where she customarily stayed when in Manhattan, Stephen's room for her in his apartment being a matter of fiction.

Endlessly resourceful, Clove prepared Mom for this transference. He put over her blind but half-open eyes his own pair of shades, got her sables about her and hung her crocodile shoulder bag over her slumped shoulder.

"Now, Daddy, git with it. You got to show downstairs when I put her in the limo and you got to tell the driver to git her delivered all the way up to her room at this fat cat hotel where she sacks."

As he was conveying this command to Stephen, his hand

was busy inside Mom's shoulder bag, extricating from it some nice bits of green, well engraved.

"Mom is sharp about money."

"That's why she's loaded with it but, Daddy, it's got a price, all of it's got a price, that's one piece of education that I took with me out of the Arkansas Ozarks."

***

Late the next day, after another all-afternoon heart-to-heart among son Stephen and Mom and this treasure of an offspring Clove Coffin Ashe, Mom was carefully deposited on a jet to Palm Beach, blowing kisses to "Shun" and his "Lamb" long after the jet was airborne. In her crocodile shoulder bag was a bottle of 49 Quaaludes, the fiftieth having been ingested at the start of the highly emotional afternoon and washed down with a Merry Mary and high oh-ho. . . .

***

Stephen and Clove and a tiny French pug puppy (surprise gift for Mom who associated that breed of canine fondly with dear old Wally Windsor) were sharing a compartment on the Amtrak to Miami which would let them off at Palm Beach. They had chosen rail travel instead of plane because Stephen's infinitely precocious (and improbable) offspring felt that the extra time was needed to prepare his daddy-by-adoption for certain ideas, in the nature of projects on the agenda, which had to involve them jointly during their visit with Mom at the Golden Shores.

6 3

"I think the porter heard that goddam dog under the fruit in the basket when he was making up the beds."

"If he heard the dog in the basket, the memory of it was completely erased by that twenty bucks I got you to give him on his way out."

"Clove, you don't seem to recognize the fact that I'm an unemployed man, I can't be that loose with money."

"With all the money you got comin' in to you?"

"Money from where, Clove?"

"Man, you know and I know that your Mom is sittin' on one helluva bundle and I don't mean her fat ass."

"Clove, you don't know how close Mom is with her money, why, she—"

"Daddy, don't give me that jive, what I don't know is yet to be known by sweet Jesus. Now you jus' stick out your tongue for this lewd pill. Tha's right. Now drink this shot of Wild Turkey. Tha's right. Feel better? Feel good? Like when I'm teaching you the Arkansas Ozark way?"

Attempting to nod, Stephen moved his head in an elliptical way.

"Now, then, Daddy, jus' lissen, don't bother to speak. Your Mom is down there sittin' on this helluva bundle and high as the moon on her lewds, and what is more important to me and to you, Mom is afflicted with *tragic sickness!*"

"Sickness, tragic? I don't follow you, Clove. All that's ever been wrong with Mom is an occasional little asthmatic condition which allergy specialists say is just a touch of rose fever, so she had to insist that the gardener at Golden Shores dispose of all rosebushes on the five acre grounds."

"Shay-*it!*" Clove said with a slightly savage chuckle. "This Golden Shore boy in the garden musta stuck five acres of rosebushes up Mom's butt to bring her out of that little asthma condition, Daddy, because it so't of runs in the

family, don't it? Mom loves a little spankin' like she does her
lewds and her Merries. Well, I'll give her a spank now and
then to comfort her through this tragic sickness she's got,
because after all, I—"

At this point Clove had somehow diverted Stephen from
his effort to assimilate Clove's Dogpatch drawl by Clove's
even slower business of removing his fine-textured flesh-
colored briefs. Dear God, thought Stephen, You must've said
Let there be Clove before You said *Let there be Light,* because this
Arkansas Ozark kid, what he is now unveiling takes precedence over all other works of Yours in those six days of
creation!

Unconsciously Stephen Ashe crossed a few paces to secure
the lock on the compartment door of the Amtrak southbound
to Mom. And he thought it best not to comprehend fully
what Clove was speaking now, his words timed with the
gradual removal of his briefs.

"Daddy, I've told you but I'll tell you once more," Clove
was saying, "you got to come out of the closet, I mean all the
way out and for good, and you got to lock the door of it
behind you and forget that the goddam closet ever existed,
because—now you hear *this!*—you are alone on this Amtrak
with a *killer chicken!* An' when this chicken infawms you that
Mom is afflicted with a tragic sickness, you better rate this
chicken's word higher than words out of any medical mouth
in the world."

Clackety-clack went the wheels of the Amtrak, rhythmically unchanging over its roadbed, quite definitely not
subsonic, but Stephen heard nothing but a hum in his ears as
faint as the late night music of the river named East in the
passive view of which the ravishment of his often-patted
backside had occurred between a Sunday brunch and Mom's
oddly catered buffet.

"Clove, I didn't quite catch what you've been talking about and maybe it's better that way."

Clove's response was only an ineffably innocent smile, but from the wicker basket of Hammacher Schlemmer's "Garden of Eden" department, from under the apples, bananas, peaches and seedless grapes, the French pug puppy uttered a sound, a little "woof-woof" which had to pass for a note of moral protest in the absence of any other more consequential to events proceeding in this world whose one and only crisis is not the depletion of its energy resources.

Nipples

*O*ne has always had nipples but one became aware of them only last summer, on Fire Island, on a quiet midweek night devoid of the suppressed hysteria which defines the dinner table on Saturday night, when everyone is going out at two to dance at the Ice Palace and wondering which drug to take. No, on a Wednesday evening it is not at all imperative that you go out; the prospect is something to be considered between yawns, over coffee, around midnight, when the dog at your feet looks up as the conversation pauses and everyone stares at him. On a Wednesday evening in midsummer with the fog drifting over the dunes and a profound silence emanating from the houses on either side of ours, which until this day have played *Evita* so loudly the fact that our own tape deck is broken is irrelevant, shirtless in the light of the candles on the table and amid the intimacy that five-for-dinner allows, the conversation becomes almost grave. We talk of lovers, and if people really want them or only think they do; we talk of books we've read; someone even reads our palms and then, rather than retire, for it is still early, we talk of nipples.

It has been a strange mélange of the concrete and the purely abstract all evening, in fact. In our room downstairs on this quiet night, while we wait for our chicken to bake, a housemate says to me, "I've had a wonderful breakthrough in therapy this week."

"Oh? What?" I ask, leaning forward with the sense that something profoundly human—something elicited by the silence, the fog, the wash of the surf—is about to be revealed.

"I can suck cock now without being nauseated," he says.

"Oh," I say, sitting back in slight confusion. "I didn't know it used to nauseate you."

"Couldn't stand it," he says. "But now I'm getting better. I did it last night, for example. No problem."

"Well—" I say. The word "congratulations" hovers in the air, but it hardly seems appropriate; I allow "That's wonderful" to sink to the floor while the dog looks up at us.

The sense of communion after dinner is even stronger: the candlelit faces, the wash of the surf, the dog indifferently dozing, the burning cigarettes in hands suspended in midair before a magic circle of bronzed chests. The words which emerge are these: "Have you been noticing nipples?"

"Yes!" someone says instantly, as if he has been wondering about the same thing himself. "Nipples are in vogue this summer," he says emphatically.

"Really!"

We sit forward at the announcement of a trend.

"Absolutely. I've been noticing them for some time now. They're getting much larger, more cultivated, more distended, more prominent. I've noticed nipples becoming more . . . *distinct*, on several of my friends." Everyone is suddenly abashed, their nipples quite clearly the objects of some attention. "Have you seen————?" and here he names several people whose nipples, we have all noticed, protrude from their chests like heads of yarn. "Do you enjoy your nipples?" someone asks.

"I haven't particularly, till recently," he replies. "But I think it's something one learns; it's an erogenous zone one develops."

"Yes," agrees another.

"I love nipples on other people," he adds.

"Oh, *quite,*" the man who introduced the topic says. "I could dangle from them for hours. I wanted to go into the dunes yesterday and just munch on nipples."

"Women's nipples change color after they've had a child," I offer. "They become dark." But this is irrelevant; it elicits nothing more than a few glazed nods. "I find," I begin again, hoping to be more on point, "that in the baths nowadays, when people meet in a hallway and stop and negotiate erotic matters, they often play with one another's nipples first. Before, they simply grabbed the crotch. Now they stand there dialing each other's nipples like men trying to tune in a radio."

"I had a boyfriend once who went *crazy,*" a friend says in a slightly awed voice. "One touch and he was yours."

"Some people feel nothing at all," I add.

"Then they should go to San Francisco," he says, "where you can take a course on getting in touch with your anus. I'm sure they have something for the nipples, unless it's taken for granted, as it probably *is there,* that you're in touch with your nipples."

"In San Francisco, they paint their nipples," someone else says. "In concentric circles. On Castro Street. Which is not surprising, I guess," he finishes.

"What do you think of *pierced* nipples?" someone asks.

"Ghastly," comes the answer. We are a traditional group.

"Are nipples an index of penis size?" someone asks.

"Not at all," cries his roommate, and everyone, seated shirtless at the table, begins wondering what his nipples tell of himself. "There is no connection. A friend of mine who used to search for that El Dorado, the test for penis size, tried and had to give up using noses, feet, hands, earlobes—"

"Earlobes!" someone says.

"Earlobes," he replies. "My friend thought thick earlobes a foolproof sign. Well, it isn't so," he says indignantly.

"Thank God," someone sighs. "Imagine going to the Meat Rack tonight to feel earlobes."

"There *is* no correlation," the man continues. "It's as hopeless as looking for the Northwest Passage!"

"So nipples do not indicate penis size," says another, who, due to his experiences with hospital budget meetings, is accustomed to summing things up.

"No, they do not," says the man.

"Well, what good *are* they, then?" asks someone brightly.

"Nipples?" says my housemate, in an elevated tone. "Nipples are the windows of the soul."

At the end of July, one of my housemates hears of an opening for a houseboy in a place on the beach which has always been considered one of the most beautiful houses in the Pines, a house whose simple and elegant architecture exemplifies what is best here, an emblem of that unspoken pride gay men have in their taste and ability to produce beautiful designs. The Pines has its share of architectural junk, to be sure, flung up in the building boom which has filled nearly every empty lot in the community these past few winters, a time when, if you came to the Island, the air was contrapuntal with the sound of hammers. But the house in which my friend becomes houseboy is one of the very finest, and one evening we all decide to go over and sit with him on the deck to enjoy its beauty. It is a house purchased by men from a southern city, but to us it will always be a house which belongs to the previous owner, a New Yorker whose end was a scene from *Looking for Mr. Goodbar*. His ashes are purportedly near the deck.

Solitary runners float past the dunes, their heads bobbing up and down. The sun begins to set. We can see no other houses, only the pristine seascape, only the sloping lines of dunes, the wild roses, the wild grass and the milky blue sky which has suddenly become precisely the same shade as the ocean. We were never invited to this house by the deceased owner; he had his own circle of friends, now middle-aged, who, in the days when we first came to Fire Island, could be seen playing volleyball at a net near the house. The net still stands. The players have disappeared, although not as luridly as their former patron; they have simply vanished from the scene.

We sit sipping our wine and watching the play of light on the weathered cedar curves of the house, the pots of geraniums and petunias on the steps, and feel no remorse. Fire Island is a curiously public community, and one may find oneself in its homes through circumstances far less coincidental than these. It does not bother my friend that he has suddenly become a houseboy at thirty-three; we all have our summers at different stages in our lives. This, we declare with an odd absence of those considerations that define our lives on the mainland, is *la vie en rose*.

"You're not afraid you'll be bored?" I ask him. "I tried to live out here one summer and it drove me crazy. I thought I wanted a summer on the Island more than anything else in the world, and I was so glad the day I went back to Manhattan."

"I'll go back from time to time," he says, "if I get crazy. But darling," he says, putting down his drink and looking at me to share an ideal almost every one of us has had at some point in his youth, "I've always wanted to spend the summer out here, and who knows when I'll have the chance again?"

It is the dream of everyone who has ever hated his job, or city, or the very limitations of life itself. As the dusk deepens before us, with its ascending moon, the opalescent waves, the runner floating past the dunes, it is hard not to conclude that if an earthly paradise exists, this is it.

"One has to be rich and beautiful to go to Fire Island," a friend writes me from Oregon. "Nonsense," I reply. One has to be rich *or* beautiful, I am tempted to add; but this, if witty, would be untrue. The Pines is composed largely of people who are neither rich nor beautiful, although occasionally, as in the house next to ours, that alliance is achieved. The place belongs to an older man who simply likes to fill it with attractive youths, who spend their days naked around the pool and are endowed with the buttocks ordinarily given to dancers and to statues supporting lanterns on a bridge in Paris. The house is bursting with inflated beach toys, a pair of Afghans and countless plastic pendants. The youths turn Donna Summer up very loud, or *Evita* or KTU, and go out by the pool. It is like watching life on Fire Island as dreamed by a gay boy in Arkansas: Fire Island is lying by your pool listening to Donna Summer and drinking Piña Coladas. As opposed to the neighbors' Fire Island, which consists of Mozart and walks at dusk. But the boys are all twenty-one, and what can the neighbors, who are ten years older, say? Nothing.

The neighbors marvel as they watch them come and go

with their inflated rafts and their two Afghans, Marissa and Snowflake. The neighbors belong to the ordinary class composed of bankers, copy editors, ribbon clerks, attorneys, temporary typists, physicians, designers (apprentice and famous), novelists (aspiring and jaded), carpenters—people who return on Sundays to offices in New York and Washington; people to whom the summer is fraught with guilt (over spending what is easily enough for a month in Europe), worry (over whether or not you left the house unlocked, flirted unconsciously with a roommate's lover, or ignored a friend in the city who should have been invited out), routine (whose turn is it to cook?), and a certain absence of privacy. It is even difficult to have sex on a weekend in the Pines, for the same reason that families living together in one room in Moscow find their personal lives limited. Then, too, the social fastidiousness of the Pines—the good taste, competition, and consuming gossip—produce a certain climate in which sex is the least possible of all things here. This is why Sunday nights at the baths are crowded with people just off the bus from Sayville who have endured a weekend of sexual stimulation so powerful it amounts to torture. This is not to say there aren't houses to be found on Saturday afternoon where twelve naked men lounge around a swimming pool, and the bedrooms upstairs are filled with copulating couples. There are people who spend their entire weekends having nothing *but* sex. No, the Pines, like the Army—like life— cannot be the subject of a single descriptive sentence; it is what happens to you, just you, when you go out there.

On one of those hot, sticky, white evenings in New York, when one would *kill* just to be in the Pines, just for the breeze, I overhear a conversation at my gymnasium between two people I first saw on the Island six years ago. They discuss the exorbitant rents, the increased crowds, the absence of their friends, and conclude that it would be nice to go out once this summer, but that next year they are definitely going to Europe. I wonder which has changed, the Island or they?

Is it an illusion that the Pines is more crowded, more frenetic, more watered-down? Is the Sandpiper really filled with heterosexual teenagers from the mainland on Saturday nights? Or have we simply become more finicky? One friend of mine cannot get over the fact that pizza is sold at the harbor. It's true that the Pines is a long way from its rustic beginnings.

A friend calls up one Sunday from the Pines and says in a voice tinged with panic, "It's mobbed out here, there are Puerto Ricans on the beach, they're barbecuing a pig!"

A friend from San Francisco calls to ask, "How are the drugs out there this summer? I hear it's very heavy." I tell him I do not know. He then inquires, for a friend who is deciding when to return east, "Do you know if there are going to be any big parties before Labor Day?" I cannot answer that, either. He seems disappointed when I confess that lately I have been going to bed around midnight and have not been to a single fête; I feel guilty for not contributing to the Fire Island legend.

A housemate calls from the city one day midweek to say he is not coming out this weekend. "I have to be honest," he says. "The weekends depress me."

"Ah," I say, with the coolness of a nurse who has seen all the symptoms before, "it always gets that way at the end of

July. Take a break." The summer, like a fever, has its doldrums. "Is anyone coming back to town?" he asks. "It's not really all that important, but if someone is, I'd appreciate—"

"What?" I say. "I'll be glad to bring it in, whatever you need."

"My suntan pills," he says sheepishly.

A white tent appears on the beach the last Friday in July, and we watch from a nearby blanket as a group of men around the tent applaud individual speakers whose words are inaudible to us. It is a meeting for people interested in the Advocate Experience.

"Do you think it's just that people are tired of the baths, the bars, the discos, the Pines?" someone on our blanket asks. "Do you think it's just another way to meet people?"

Our friends are going to therapists, chanting, studying Gurdjieff, Zen, taking est, the Advocate Experience; one wonders if this is a movement of gay men in general or just of gay men my age, who turn quite naturally, in their mid-thirties, to matters which never concerned us during our more frivolous twenties. Even on the beach, which, alas, has come to stand for little more than the partying mob, this white tent reminds me of the tents in Saratoga a century ago, filled with people listening to speakers on the chatauqua circuit.

Someone on the blanket says, "So first they get their bodies together, then they get their personalities together. Then what? What is the point of a room filled with handsome, lean, muscular men with open, friendly, communicative personalities? Oh, give me a room filled with sullen beauties!" Then everyone sits up to watch the latest blond model from California, a perfect physical specimen of Man, walk by with X, after which we discuss who has the better ass.

We end with this paradox: my house is filled with men who love the Island, but none is sure he will return next year. These men are perfect housemates. Veterans of summers past, they know how important it is to be considerate, to make and abide by certain fundamental rules—say, no guests without sponsor present. They have all spent horrendous summers in houses where no one was considerate and they vowed, Never again! Those were the summers that produced the hilarious stories. This summer we kept the place neat; each asked the others if anyone needed anything from the store or if anyone had any colors because we were doing a wash. We did not interrupt when people were reading. We wrote down telephone messages, we virtually *competed* with one another to do the dishes after dinner and (in keeping with the new mood of fiscal caution which seems to have swept over even the most spendthrift of New Yorkers) whoever was cooking on Saturday night went to the trouble of buying some of the food in the city, to keep the price of dinner down.

But if the outrages, the horror shows are gone, so are the glamour, the excitement, the thrill. We have learned how to shape the Island to our tastes; it can no longer pick us up and take us on a ride we never rode before. By the time you are mature enough to be considerate, you are too mature to be susceptible to social and sexual glamour. Tea Dance repels us; the Ice Palace seems too obligatory. What *is* the Island then? We recall the answer the afternoon a friend who has not been here in two years arrives from the city and falls on his knees before the ocean, then does cartwheels up and down the beach. For this narrow line of dunes breasting the Atlantic is simply one of the most beautiful places on earth. He stands up to gush about the boy he saw on the boat coming over and we, who have allowed our experience of the place to sink beneath the weight of routine, have to smile and remember, *Yes.*

The weekend our house closes, we are irrepressibly happy. The summer is over at last, Labor Day is behind us, the weather is indescribably gorgeous. "There are no *words,*" says a housemate, coming in from the moonlit, starry night.

At the Sandpiper that night, a friend turns to me and says, "This is *Heaven!*" And it's a very good facsimile: the most handsome men we've ever seen are dancing around us.

We awaken the next day, eat blueberry pancakes and go down for our last swim. The ocean is the green of a tropical sea. We say hello to the people we pass on the boardwalk, as we did in the spring, and the summer seems like an enormous tumor which has been removed. The sheer number of people has been reduced to a civilized scale, and the Pines becomes the place that makes you wonder, against your better judgment, if you shouldn't take a share again next summer.

For that is the illogical lure of it: as with perfect sex, an experience which may be rare in proportion to the time spent searching for it, we go back, nevertheless, for a few incomparable moments. One forgets being depressed by the crowds, the routine, the regimentation; the disco from the house next door and having to share one's house with eight men and two dogs. Where else on earth is there anything like it? The gorgeous dusks, the constellations toward the end of summer, when you walked home slowly from the bar with X, stopped to kiss, lay down in the sand to seek out Orion, and kissed again in the perfect, windy silence. Love and nipples, and stars, and deer in the darkening dusk: around March we will be starved for the very things we are relieved to see coming to an end on Labor Day.

It is perfectly understandable that a man who has come to the Pines for seven summers should awaken one sunny Sunday in August and say to himself, "There's nothing to *do* out here!" He may take an early train back to the city, go to his local delicatessen and find himself sitting happily at home with the paper, his rice pudding and his cat, while Tea Dance, which, seven years ago, so dazzled him when he came out of his room at the Botel that he decided on the spot to leave Washington and move to New York, is beginning in all its splendor.

But this is not to say that there is anything on earth quite like Fire Island, because there simply isn't. It is simply to say that after many a summer dies the swan. Or at least that particular swan, whom you will now find bicycling in SoHo or sunning himself on the pier on weekends, while on the beach near that famous house, a new team is playing volleyball, a team of newcomers whose nipples one hardly notices.

JANE RULE

◇◇◇◇◇◇◇◇◇◇◇◇◇◇◇◇◇◇◇◇◇◇◇◇◇◇◇◇◇◇◇◇

In the Attic of the House

Alice hadn't joined women's liberation; she had only rented it the main floor of her house. It might turn out to be the alternative to burning the house down, which she had threatened to do sober and had nearly accomplished when she was drunk. Since the four young women who moved in neither drank nor smoked, they might be able to save Alice from inadvertence. That was all. And the money helped. Alice had not imagined she would ever be sixty-five to have to worry about it. Now the years left were the fingers of one hand. She was going to turn out to be one of the ones too mean to die.

"I'm a lifer," she said at the beer parlor and laughed until her lungs came to a boil.

"Don't sound like it, Al. If the weed don't get you, the traffic will."

"Naw," Alice said. "Only danger on the road is the amateur drunks who can't drive when they're sober either. I always get home."

The rules were simple: stay in your own lane, and don't honk your horn. Alice was so small she peered through rather than over her steering wheel and might more easily have been arrested as a runaway kid than a drunk. But she'd never caught hell from anyone but Harriet, rest her goddamned soul. Until these females moved in.

"Come have a cup of tea," one of them would say just as Alice was making a sedate attempt at the stairs.

There she'd have to sit in what had been her own kitchen for thirty years, a guest drinking Red Zinger or some other Kool-Aid-colored wash they called tea, squinting at them through the steam: Bett, the giant postie; Trudie and Jill, who worked at the women's garage without a grease mark under their finger nails; and Angel, who was unemployed— young, all of them, incredibly young, killing her with kindness. Sober, she could refuse them with "I never learned to eat a whole beet with chop sticks" or "Brown rice sticks to my dentures," but, once she was drunk and dignified, she was caught having to prove that point and failing as she'd always failed, except that now there was the new test of the stairs.

"Do you mind having to live in the attic of your own house?" Bett asked as she offered Alice a steadying hand.

"Mind? Living on top of it is a lot better than living in the middle of it ever was. I don't think I was meant for the ground floor," Alice confessed, her spinning head pressed against Bett's enormous bosom until they reached the top stair.

"You all right now? Can you manage?"

"Sleep like a baby. Always have."

Alice began to have infantile dreams about those breasts, though awake and sober she found them comically alarming rather than erotic, eye level as she was with them. Alice liked Bett and was glad, though she didn't hold with women taking over everything, that Bett delivered the mail. Bett had not only yellow hair but yellow eyebrows, a sunny sort of face for carrying the burden of bills as well as the promise of love letters and surprise legacies. And everyone was able to see at a glance that this postie was a woman.

Angel was probably Bett's girl, though Alice couldn't tell for sure. Sometimes Alice imagined four-way orgies going on downstairs, but it could as easily be a karate lesson. It was obvious none of them was interested in men.

"We don't hate men because we don't need them," Trudy said, the one who memorized slogans, who, once she could fix a car, couldn't imagine what other use men were ever put to.

For this crew, hating men would be like hating astronauts, too remote an exercise to be meaningful. Alice knew lots of men, was more comfortable with them than with women at the beer parlor or in the employees' lounge at Safeway, where she worked. She needed them as a group far more than she needed women. Working among them and drinking among them had always been her self-esteem.

"Aren't you ashamed to sit home on a Saturday night?" Alice asked.

"We don't drink; the bars aren't our scene."

Alice certainly couldn't imagine them at her beer parlor, looking young enough to be jail bait and dressed so badly men who had taken the time to shave and change into good clothes couldn't help taking offense. Even Alice with her close-cropped hair put on a nice blouse over good slacks, sometimes even a skirt, and she didn't forget her lipstick.

"Do you buy all your clothes at the Sally Ann?" Alice asked, studying one remarkably holey and faded tank top Jill was wearing.

"Somebody gave me this one," Jill admitted irritably. "Why should you mind? You're the only one of any sex who has a haircut like that."

"Don't you like it?" Alice asked.

"It's sort of male chauvinist," Trudie put in, "as if you wanted to come on very heavy."

"I don't come on," Alice said. "I broke the switch."

At the beer parlor someone might have said, "Then I'll screw you in," or something else amiable, but this Trudie was full of sudden sympathy and instruction about coming to terms with your own body, as if she were about to invent sex, not for Alice, just for instance.

"Do you know how old I am?"

"We're not agists here," Jill said.

"I'm old enough to be your grandmother."

"Not if you're still working at Safeway, you're not. My grandma's got the old age pension."

"When I was young, we had some respect for old people."

"Everybody should respect everybody," Angel said.

"I have every respect for you," Alice said with dignity. "Even about sex."

"You know what you should do, Alice?" Angel asked. "It's not too late . . . come out."

"Come out?" Alice demanded. "Of where? This is my house, after all. You're just renting the main floor. Come out? To whom? Everyone I know is dead!"

Harriet, rest her goddamned soul. Alice mostly pretended that she never spoke Harriet's name. In fact, she almost always waited to do it until she had drunk that amount which would let her forget what she had said, so that she could say it over and over again. "Killed herself in my bathtub. Is that any way to win an argument? Is it?"

"What argument?" Trudie would ask.

IN THE ATTIC OF THE HOUSE

"This bathtub?" Jill tried to confirm.

"How?" Angel wanted to know.

Later, on her unsteady way upstairs, Alice would most resent Bett's asking, "Were you in love with Harriet?"

"In love?" Alice demanded. "Christ! I lived with her for thirty years."

Never in those thirty years had Alice spoken as openly to Harriet as she was expected to speak with these females. Never in the last twenty years had Alice and Harriet so much as touched, though they slept in the same bed. At first Alice had come home drunk and pleading. Then she came home drunk and mean, sometimes threatening rape, sometimes in a jeering moral rage.

"What have you got to be guilty about? You never so much as soil your hand. I'm the one that should be crawling off to church, for Christ's sake!"

Sometimes that kind of abuse would weaken Harriet's resolve and she would submit, whimpering like a child anticipating a beating, weeping like a lost soul when it was over.

Finally Alice simply came home drunk and slept in a drunken stupor. She learned at the beer parlor how many men did the same thing.

"Scruples," one man explained. "They've got scruples."

"Scruples, shit! On Friday night I go home with the dollars and say, 'You want this? You put out for it.'"

"So what are you doing down here? It's Friday, isn't it?"

"Yeh, well, we split—"

Harriet had her own money; she was a legal secretary. Alice remembered the first time she ever saw Harriet: in the beer parlor, wearing a prim gray suit, looking obviously out of place. Some cousin had brought her and left her for unrelated pleasures. After they'd talked a while, Alice suggested a walk along the beach. It was summer; there was still light in the sky.

Years later, Harriet would say, "You took advantage. I'd been jilted."

Sometimes, when Alice was very drunk, she could remember how appealing the young Harriet had been, how willingly she had been coaxed from kisses to petting of her shapely little breasts, protesting with no more than, "You're as bad as a boy, Al, you really are." "Do you like it?" "Well, I'm not supposed to say so, am I?" Alice also remembered that indrawn breath of surprise when she first laid her finger on that wet pulse, the moment of wonder and triumph before the first crying, "Oh, it must be terrible what we're doing! We're going to burn in hell!"

Harriet could frighten Alice then with her guilt and terror. Once Alice promised that they'd never again as Harriet called it "go all the way," if they could still kiss, touch. Guiltily, oh so guiltily, weeks later, when Alice thought Harriet had gone to sleep, very gently she pressed open Harriet's thighs and touched that forbidden center. Harriet sighed in sleeping pleasure. Three or four times a week for several years Alice waited for the breathing signal that meant Harriet was no longer officially aware of what was happening. Alice could mount her, suck at her breasts, stroke and enter her, bring her to wet coming, and hold her until she breathed in natural sleep. Then Alice would go to the bathroom and masturbate to the simple fantasy of Harriet making love to her.

It wasn't Harriet who finally quit on it. It was Alice, shaking her and shouting, "You goddamned hypocrite! You think as long as you take pleasure and never give it, you'll escape. But you won't. You'll be in hell long before I will, you goddamned *woman!*"

* * *

"We're looking for role models," Angel said. "Anybody who lived with anybody for thirty years—"

"I don't know what you're talking about," Alice said soberly on her way to work, but late that night she was willing enough. "Thirty years is longer than reality, you know that? A lifetime guarantee on a watch is only twenty. Nothing should last longer than that. Harriet should have killed herself ten years earlier, rest her goddamned soul. I always told her she'd get to hell long before I did."

"What was Harriet like?" Bett asked on the way upstairs.

"Like? I don't know. I thought she was pretty. She never thought so."

"It must be lonely for you now."

"I've never had so much company in all my damned life."

To be alone in the attic was a luxury Alice could hardly believe. It had been her resigned expectation that Harriet, whose soul had obviously not been at rest, would move up the stairs with her. She had not. If she haunted the tenants as she had haunted Alice, they didn't say so. The first time Trudie and Jill took a bath together probably exorcised the ghost from that room, and Harriet obviously would have no more taste for the vegetarian fare in the dining room than Alice did. As for what probably went on in the various beds, one night of that could finally have sent Harriet to hell where she belonged.

Alice understood, as she never had before, why suicide was an unforgivable sin. Harriet was simply out of the range of forgiveness, as she hadn't been for all her other sins from hoarding garbage to having what she called a platonic relationship with that little tart of a switchboard operator in her office.

"If you knew anything about Plato—" Alice had bellowed, knowing only that.

Killing herself was the ultimate conversation stopper, the final saying, "No backs."

"The trouble with ghosts," Alice confided to Bett, "is that they're only good for replays. You can't break any new ground."

Bett leaned down and kissed Alice good night.

"Better watch out for me," Alice said, but only after Bett had gone downstairs. "I'm a holy terror."

That night Harriet came to her in a dream, not blood-filled as all the others had been, but full of light. "I can still forgive you," she said.

"For what?" Alice cried, waking. "What did I ever do but love you, tell me that!"

That was the kind of talk she heard at the beer parlor from her male companions, all of whom had wives and girlfriends who spent their time inventing sins and then forgiving them.

"My wife is so good at forgiving, she's even forgiven me for not being the Shah of Iran, how do you like that?"

"I like it. It has dignity. My old lady forgives my beard for growing in the middle of the night."

They had also lived for years with threats of suicide.

"She's going to kill herself if I don't eat her apricot sponge, if I don't cut the lawn, if I don't kiss her mother's ass. I tell her it's OK with me as long she figures out a cheap way of doing it."

Alice was never drunk enough or off her guard enough until she got home to say, "Harriet did. She killed herself in my bathtub." Nobody at the beer parlor or at work knew that Harriet was dead.

"I didn't ever tell them she was alive," she said to Bett. "So what's the point of saying she's dead?"

"Why do you drink with those people?" Bett asked. "They can't be your real friends."

"How can you say a thing like that?"

"They don't know who you are."

"Do you?" Alice demanded. "What has a woman bleeding to death in my bathtub got to do with who I am?"

Bett was pressing Alice's drunken head against her breast.

That night Alice fell asleep with a cigarette in her hand. When she awoke, the rug was on fire. She let out a bellow of terror and began to try to stamp out the flames with her bare feet.

Jill was the first one to reach her, half drag, half carry her out of the room. Trudie and Bett went in with buckets of water while Angel phoned the fire department.

"Don't let the firemen in," Alice moaned, sitting on Harriet's old chair in their old living room. "They'll wreck the place."

The fire was out by the time the truck arrived. After the men had checked the room and praised presence of mind and quick action for saving the house, the fire chief said, "Just the same, one of these nights she's going to do it. This is the third time we know of."

Jill, with the intention of confronting Alice with that fact, was distracted by the discovery that Alice's feet were badly burned.

The painkillers gave Alice hallucinations: the floor of her hospital room on fire, her nurse's hair on fire, the tent of blankets at the foot of her bed burning, and Harriet was shouting at her, "We're going to burn in hell."

"Please," Alice begged. "I'd rather have the pain."

In pain, she made too much noise, swore, demanded whiskey, threatened to set herself on fire again and be done with it, until she was held down and given another shot.

Her co-workers from Safeway sent her flowers, but no one she worked with came to see her. No one she drank with knew what had happened. From the house, only Bett came at the end of work, still dressed in her uniform.

"Get me out of here," Alice begged. "Can't you get me out of here?"

In the night, with fire crackling all around her, Alice knew she was in hell and there was no escape, Bett with her sunny face and great breasts the cruelest hallucination of all.

Even on the day when Bett came to take her home, Alice was half convinced Bett was only a devilish trick to deliver her to greater torment; but Alice also knew she was still half crazy with drugs or pain.

There the house still stood, and Bett carried her up the stairs into an attic so clean and fresh she hardly recognized it. Alice began to believe in delivery.

"This bell by your bed," Bett explained, "all you need to do is ring it, and Angel will come."

Alice laughed until her coughing stopped her.

"It's a sort of miracle you're alive," Trudie said when she and Jill came home from work and up to see her.

"I'm indestructible," Alice said, a great world weariness in her voice.

"This place was a rat's nest," Jill complained. "You can't have thrown out a paper since we moved in—or an empty yogurt carton. Is that all you eat?"

"I eat out," Alice said, "for whatever business of yours it is. And nobody asked you to clean up after me."

"It scared us pretty badly," Trudie said. "We all came close to being killed."

"Sometimes you remind me a little of Harriet," Alice said with slow malice. "That's a friend of mine who killed herself."

"We know who Harriet is," Jill said. "Al, if we can't talk about this, we're all going to have to move out."

"Move out? What for?"

"Because we don't want to be burned to death in our sleep."

"You've got to promise us that you won't drink when you're smoking or smoke when you're drinking," Trudie said.

"This is my house. I'm the landlady. You're the tenants," Alice announced.

"We realize that. There's nothing we can do unless you'll be reasonable."

Bett came into the room with a dinner tray.

"Get out, all of you!" Alice shouted. "And take that muck with you!"

Jill and Trudie were twins in obedience. Bett didn't budge.

"I got you out because I promised we'd feed you."

"What you eat is swill!"

"Look, Angel even cooked you some hamburger."

"You can't make conditions for me in my own house."

"I know that; so do the others. Al, I don't want to leave. I don't want to leave you. I love you. I want you to do it for yourself."

"Don't say that to me unless I'm drunk. I can't handle it."

"Yes, you can. You don't have to drink."

"What in hell else am I supposed to do to pass the time?" Alice demanded.

"Read, watch TV, make friends, make love."

"Don't taunt me!" Alice cried into the tray of food on her lap.

"I'm not taunting," Bett said. "I want to help."

Until Alice could walk well enough to get out of the house on her own, there was no question of drinking. She kept nothing in the house, having always used drink as an excuse to escape from Harriet. There was nothing to steal from her tenants. She was too proud to ask even Bett to bring her a bottle. The few cigarettes she'd brought home from the hospital would have to be her comfort. She found herself opening a window every time she had one and emptying and washing the ashtray when she was through.

"You're turning me into a sneak!" she shouted at Bett.

"It all looks nice and tidy to me," Bett said. "Trudie says you're so male-identified that you can't take care of yourself. I'm going to tell her she's wrong."

Alice threw a clean ashtray at her, and she ducked and laughed.

"You're getting better, you really are."

Alice returned to the beer parlor before she returned to work. She wasn't walking well, but she was walking. She had been missed. When she told about stamping out the fire with her own bare feet, she was assured more free beer than she could drink in an evening, even when she was in practice. How good it tasted and how companionable were these friends who never asked questions and therefore didn't analyze the answers, who made connection with yarns and jokes. Alice had hung onto a couple of the best hospital stories and told them before she was drunk enough to lose her way or the punch line. She only laughed enough to cough at other people's jokes which, as the evening wore on, were less well told and not as funny. Drink did not anesthetize the pain in Alice's healing feet, and that made her critical. Getting a tit caught in a wringer wasn't funny; it hurt.

"And here's one for those tenants of yours, Al, hey? How can you stem the tide of women's liberation? Put your finger in the dyke!"

It was an ugly face shoved into her own. Alice suddenly realized why a man must be forgiven his beard growing in the night, forgiven over and over again, too, for not being the prince of a fellow you wished he were. Alice didn't forgive. She laughed until she was near to spitting blood, finished her beer and her cigarette and went out to find her car. As on so many other nights, even a few minutes after she got home, she couldn't remember the drive, but she knew she'd done it quietly and well.

"Come on," Bett said. "Those feet hurt. I'm going to carry you up."

Drunk in the arms of this sunny amazon, Alice said, "Do you know how to stem the tide of women's liberation? Do you?"

"Does anyone want to?" Bett asked, making her careful, slow way up the stairs.

"Sure. Lots of people. You put your finger—"

"In the dyke, yeah, I know."

"Don't you think that's funny?"

"No."

"I don't either," Alice agreed.

Bett carried Alice over to her bed, which had been turned down, probably by Angel.

"Now, I want you to hand over the rest of cigarettes," Bett said. "I'll leave them for you in the hall."

"Take them," Alice said.

"All right," Bett agreed and reached into Alice's blouse,

where she kept a pack tucked into her bra when she didn't have a pocket.

Alice half bit, half kissed the hand, then pressed herself up against those marvelous breasts, a hand on each, and felt the nipples, under the thin cloth of Bett's shirt, harden. Bett had the cigarettes, but she did not move away. Instead, with her free hand, she unbuttoned her shirt and gave Alice her dream.

As in a dream, Alice's vision floated above the scene, and she saw her own close-cropped head, hardly bigger than a baby's, her aging, liver-spotted face, her denture-deformed mouth, sucking like an obscene incubus at a young magnificence of breast which belonged to Angel. Then she saw Bett's face, serene with pity.

Alice pulled herself away and spat. "You pity me! What do you know about it? What could you know? Harriet, rest her goddamned soul, lived in *mortal sin* with me. She *killed herself* for me. It's not to *pity!* Get out! Get out, all of you, right now because I'm going to burn this house down when I damned well please."

"All right," Bett said.

"It's my hell. I earned it."

"All right," Bett said, her face as bright as a never-to-come morning.

Alice didn't begin to cry until Bett had left the room, tears, as hot with pain and loss as fire, that burned and burned and burned.

The Black Widow

High summer. We were lying on the beach at sundown, about seven o'clock. Everything was pink and gray. "The exact colors," commented Charlie, "of my sister's 1959 Ford convertible. Remember those Fords?" Pink shaded into gray in the waves; gray shaded into pink up out of the ocean and overarching the sky towards the hot-pink sun at our backs. We were lying on Charlie's beach blanket (you've seen it; it has the Brazilian flag in the center) facing the waves, on our bellies. Paul, Charlie, me—otherwise known as Patti Labelle and the Bluebells. Paul (Patti) was the ringleader.

Not everyone on the Island had a name other than his given name. It was by then a rather passé concept, all in all; only Island fixtures had names. Paul had a name, and the two of us, by virtue of hanging out with him all the time.

We hadn't known each other all that long, but we went everywhere together: We went to Tea Dance at six P.M. (though not that night; we'd agreed Tea on Saturday nights was overpopulated) and we went down to the Sandpiper at two A.M. (though not on Saturday nights; even we were not sufficiently iconoclastic to ignore the Ice Palace Saturday nights). We danced together and took the same drugs to be in sync with each other. Sometimes we even entered the meat rack together at 5 A.M. (and sometimes at 4 P.M., fresh from the beach) although we soon, of course, split up.

We ate together after our evening naps—long, leisurely dinners accompanied by chilled wine and (if Charlie was cooking) candlelight. We must have made a pretty picture (of course we did; we knew we did) sitting around the table in front of that big plate glass window high above Ocean Walk. We were all impeccably tan, in good shape, young (31), and rich. Our house looked like a packing crate turned upside down and we made fun of it to others, but it *was* a very big house and it *was* very impressive. We prided ourselves on our lack of ostentation while continually inventing new ways to exhibit ourselves and our superior taste. We were just plain folks—that was the image we sought to project. Any one of us might have been elected Miss Congeniality, had such contests still been held on the Island. For we were very, very friendly—"free with our charms," as Paul once put it—and through the simple expedient of pretending we did indeed know every soul on the Island, Charlie and I had almost caught up with Paul—who *did* know every single soul on the Island, or soon made his acquaintance.

You might recall that there was a fourth *Supreme* who died ignominiously in a motel in downtown Newark, or some such thing, ill and on welfare. Well, in a sense, Barry—now departed to L.A. and living anything but ignominiously in the Hollywood Hills (you saw him in the *Rolling Stone* spread)—was the fourth Bluebell. I had never met him; I was his replacement. In a larger sense, I guess *I* was the fourth Bluebell.

There was much that year I was still ignorant of, but my

natural diffidence usually masked it and I became good at tossing around names of people I'd never met but had just seen or heard about. If you refrain from actually saying something downright malicious about strangers, an easy familiarity can be assumed:

"Oh, yeah Jack Rodriguez. He had that—" (roll of the eyes) "house on Tina Walk."

Or,

"Oh, yeah. Henry Cahill. He had that—" (roll of the eyes) "house on Sky."

Or,

"Oh, yeah. Bill Murphy. He had that—" (conspiratorial glance from side to side) "house down by the co-ops."

Which would elicit from those more in the know:

"Drugged boys constantly diving off the roof into the pool."

Or,

"Do you know he paid $25,000 for the summer! For that pile of shit!"

Or,

"Oh, *you* were there that Memorial Day weekend . . ."

Fortunately, these conversations were seldom open-ended and the other would move on, perhaps having provided a bit more information for the old memory bank, perhaps not. The nightmare, of course, was:

Meeting up unknowingly with Jack Rodriguez's housemate for the past ten years, a nice older man who has never allowed drugged boys into his pool,

Or,

Discovering from Henry Cahill, after subtly applying the screws to him about his house on Sky Walk, that he paid $4,000 for the summer and thus was able to live there in blissful solitude, *and* that the landlord made prompt repairs,

Or,

That Memorial Day weekend in question, Bill Murphy had his mother out and they dined genteely on squab with three of his closest friends. "And some poor schmuck is going around saying my house had the hottest orgy weekend of the summer . . ."

WHY WAS IT SO IMPORTANT?

All that gossip, all that memorization, learning to distinguish between those hundreds of undistinguished faces?

Well, I guess I took my cue from Charlie, the junior of the Bluebells now that Barry was gone; and Charlie in turn must have taken his cue from Paul. But Charlie and I were the real fanatics. What made us care *so much* about attaching little tags to all those people? Paul cared very little. Or gave the impression of caring very little. I don't know how much he actually cared any longer, though he still continued to play the game, of course. By this point it had become habitual. It looked very easy. I'm sure it was almost effortless for Paul— to remember, for instance, who shared with Ira Lentz three summers ago in that A-frame on the bay. What was difficult, by the time we'd consolidated the Bluebells anew, was for Paul to remember who he'd tricked with last Wednesday.

A second reason just occurred to me. If we spent so much time memorizing undistinguished faces and acquiring information on them, wasn't there a higher purpose (beyond getting invited to *every* party over the course of a summer) to the exercise? Of course there was. It was all in preparation for the truly *distinguished* face, the face attached to the truly distinguished body attached to the truly distinguished mind attached to the truly distinguished career attached to the truly distinguished income—this was roughly the (naive) order of our priorities at that time.

"Who is *he*?"

"Don't know. Paul?"

"Last house on Shore. Name's Terry."

"Oh, yeah. Terry . . . Terry . . . *Brewer.*"

"Brewer, yeah. Jaguars."

"Cats? Literal cats?"

"Beautiful ass."

"Yeah. No, cars."

"He has more than—?"

"Sells them."

"Cisco."

"Terry Cisco?"

"No, that's his lover's name. Ralph Cisco. Bergdorfs. . . ."

And on and on it went, as the number in question crossed the deck of the Botel and slipped into Tea.

We'd been doing this all afternoon: pooling our resources, so to speak, lying on Charlie's beach blanket and dishing and kvetching and congratulating ourselves on our excellent grasp of the mechanics of Island social life, our impeccable tans, our discernment. *Everyone* was out on the beach that day. Few, however, were secure enough to stay in one place all afternoon and let it all flow past. We were secure; we missed *nothing.*

"It had whitewall tires."

"What?"

"My sister's pink and gray Ford convertible."

"Oh."

I flopped over on my back. It was getting chilly but the sand was still warm.

"I had a '52 Plymouth," Paul was saying. "Candy Apple Red."

"Oh, yeah? I had a—"

Whatever Charlie said in reply was lost on me . . .

As I lay on my back, my legs framed a house ("that house

on Ocean with the hanging plants flanking that nubby sort of hanging in orange and puce"), which in turn framed the ocean-side deck, which in turn framed a set of broad steps leading down to the beach from the deck, which in turn framed two golden retrievers running down the steps towards me, which in turn flanked—

"That must be the most beautiful man I've ever seen."

"Oh," said Paul, "one's always and forever seeing the most beautiful man one's ever—"

"Yes, always but always—" said Charlie.

Nevertheless, the two of them turned over like flapjacks on a griddle.

"Oh."

"Oh."

They were not gasps of delight; they were gasps of recognition.

He continued to run, almost directly towards us. He was tall and lanky. His was not a "built" body out of the catalogue; it was a golden color, fair skin nicely tanned. His hair was exactly the color of the dogs, who were bounding ahead of him over the dunes and onto the nearly deserted beach. Two black leather leashes were wound about his neck and shoulders. He wore a green bathing suit exactly (I later discovered) the color of his eyes: the green of blown glass.

The dogs heaved past us, panting and yapping. I could hear them splash into the breakers at our backs. But I was intent on another sound, the sound of *his* breathing: not labored, but audible, as he ran towards us, then veered down the beach looking neither left nor right. I soon realized it was not so much the sound of his breathing that mesmerized me, but the happy gurgle he was making, the kind infants and children are supposed to make and never do. He was glad to be alive.

I was glad to be alive. I made a mental note to thank God the next time we were at all on speaking terms: for putting this man here on the beach before me, for gilding his red-gold hair with those little tongues of fire via that spectacular hot-pink sunset.

He ran off down the beach. My eyes had followed him unmoving in their sockets, leading my head, neck, shoulders, torso—a smooth craning around on the blanket that left me supine and boneless. Gradually the steady "tamp-tamp-tamp" of his bare feet on the sand died away. I went limp.

Silence from my companions. Were they, too, as thunderstruck as I?

I was breathing through my mouth.

"Must he always pull that boy-and-his-dogs routine?" said Paul.

"Dreary and tired," said Charlie.

"Heaven on a raft," said I, like the Papal short order cook.

Silence from my friends, but for twin, sharp intakes of breath.

I turned over on my side to face them.

"Who is he?" I asked casually. (Prose can't possibly convey the urgency behind that question. Roughly translated, it was, "I MUST HAVE HIM!")

"*The Black Widow,*" they intoned with one voice.

"Huh? But that's ridiculous," I said, turning away and looking back at the tiny figure, now far down the beach, skirting the edge of the surf. "He's a redhead."

What's usually described in books as "a silvery cascade of laughter" came from my companions' throats. A dangerous sound.

"So literal," said Paul.

"Charming," said Charlie.

"Gerald Manheim," said Paul.

"Grosse Point Manheims," Charlie added.
"Stocks and bonds," Paul said.
"Chocolate," said Charlie.
"East 63rd Street," said Paul.
"Arthur Eberly."
"Hans Werther."
"Larry Holt."
"George Papadopolis."
"*Who?*" I cried.
"Dead."
"Yes, darling. All of them. They all died."
"All four. All four of his lovers," said Paul.
"Poison," said Charlie.
"Poison?" I gasped.
"Pretty poison," qualified Charlie.
"He's a no-no," said Paul.
"*The Black Widow*," they chorused.

Now let me get this straight, I said to them. This man, this beautiful, vital Gerald Manheim from Grosse Point, Michigan, whose major income is derived from stocks and bonds in his family's wildly profitable chocolate business, and who lives on East 63rd Street in a penthouse apartment (what else was I to assume from the twisted inflection Paul gave *that* one?) had four lovers, Arthur-Hans-Larry-George, and they *all died.* . . .

"But he can't be more than thirty years old," I protested.
"Out at eighteen," Paul said.
"Choate," Charlie said.

Well, we went in and took our naps. But I tossed and turned on my bed. Not even putting on the earphones and listening to the Mozart horn concerti calmed me. Every time I closed my eyes, I saw Gerald Manheim running down those steps and onto the dunes, feet sending little shockwaves of sand out in all directions about him, his dogs leaping up before him like fabulous beasts bracketing a perfect heraldic image. . . .

And I was supposed to believe, just because two jaded queens had passed on what was doubtless distorted and certainly suspect information on the beach, that this same golden Gerald Manheim was the infamous (but why hadn't *I* ever heard of him?) Black Widow. Gerald and his golden retrievers—yes, danced before my eyes at the edge of the pink-rilled waves, to the accompaniment of the Mozart horn concerti. By September, that same tape, once my favorite, would fly from the topmost flagpole of our Ocean Walk house. It would twitch in the sun, shiny side/dull side, as my nerves finally twitched in fitful sleep the day I first saw Gerald Manheim.

He never went out, he slipped unseen onto the ferry and off, his paper was delivered by the houseboy next door, he saw no one, he never dined, he was not to be found in the meat rack at any hour. As far as anyone knew, the only piece of clothing he owned was the green swim suit he wore on that daily romp in the surf when no one was expected to be awake or watching. On odd occasions, the top of his auburn head might be glimpsed above the walled deck at the top of his house where he sunned.

"Oh, yeah. The Black Widow," people would say. And I might hear the story again, hear it so many times I wondered at my previous ignorance. People weren't so very anxious to tell it—it *had* all happened so long ago, at least two years since George, two long summers, three long winters.

I listened with half an ear, attentive only for nuances or unique bits of information. The rest of me was concentrated on the image of Gerald Manheim as I'd first seen him, and on my unshakeable belief that they had to be talking about someone else when they talked about the Black Widow.

"Well George jumped, of course."

"Yes. Jumped."

"Out the window."

"Yes."

"Isn't it interesting how no one, but no one, ever does it out here?"

"Suicide? Yes. I've noticed that."

"Murders—"

"Yes, your occasional murder."

"But not suicide."

"Your occasional overdose."

"Yes, but not suicide.

"George jumped."

"I heard about it on the bus the next day."

"Well, Larry. That was the antithesis."

"Oh, yeah. Very much so."

"Long, lingering illness."

"Something to do with the blood?"

"He was very attentive."

"Gerald. Yes."

"Two, three years of it."

"Horrible."

"Sloan-Kettering."

"Leukemia?"

"What else?"

"But Hans . . . "

"Much more typical."

"Strayed out into the ocean."

"Night of the Feather Fantasy party."

"White cockatoo feathers."

"Spectacular."

"He was lifted, you know."

"*No.*"

"Yeah."

"Well, not Arthur."

"Oh, Arthur, too."

"*No.* Well, they do say it's a good idea, at forty or so, as a preventive measure, to have the first one . . . "

"What a waste of money."

"Yeah. Closed coffin."

"Grisly."

"My *dear.*"

But not one of them was able to implicate Gerald Manheim in any of those deaths. As far as I could tell, Gerald was strictly an innocent bystander to four extraordinarily coincidental deaths: one suicide, one Big C, one overdose, one freak encounter with a garbage truck.

But you see, they were his lovers, each of them. They lived with him. They all left him their estates.

That was the salient point. Or so it seemed to the myth-makers.

The Black Widow. Gerald was an Island legend in his own time, so much so that he was no longer discussed. He was not gossiped about, as were the mini-legends that flamed out over the Island for a season and then were gone; he was not regarded with the same attitude as that reserved for the ordinary legends—those who were visible, accessible, fuckable. Gerald's flacks believed as gospel truth the PR they'd created for him. But there had to be a real person behind such a legend. Didn't there?

I, a lowly Bluebell, the sophomore member, aspired to contact (OF ANY KIND!) with Gerald Manheim. It was beyond infatuation; it had deepened into sheer idolatry.

But how to meet him? Our only guides in these things are hoary old tales like *Rapunzel;* or *Pyramus and Thisbe* and their wall (the first glory hole); or the apocryphal first person accounts of lucky meetings with stars, the kind you find in fan magazines. I couldn't "accidentally" bump into Gerald Manheim at the Monster, nor was there any hope of wrestling him to the ground under cover of night in the meat rack. I couldn't fling him my cheery *Hi!* on Fire Island Boulevard, nor could I pique his curiosity with any bogus mystery of my own. I couldn't even do an Eve Harrington and wait for the maid to let herself in to do the beds, creep into Gerald's boudoir, finger his threads and try them on, and "accidentally" be discovered dozing by his pool with a terry robe pulled up to my chin.

There was no maid. There was no pool. There was just Gerald, behind that forbidding, blank façade on Ocean.

I lost interest in everybody and everything else. The focus of my entire summer became Gerald Manheim. And so, many frustrating weeks passed.

August 1. I was in town to see Daddy's lawyers and have dinner with my accountant. Wertheimer, Wertheimer, Shapiro & Pettigrew being what it is, I didn't get out onto Wall Street until well after six. There were no cabs in sight, so I decided to take the subway uptown, something I hadn't done since Daddy passed on.

After several transfers and a perplexing side trip into Canarsie, I found myself at last on the uptown IRT. It was sweltering in the subway, but I remembered that the subway is *always* sweltering. I'd bungled and was on the local train. At 42nd Street I endured the tidal onslaught of the steaming masses and was crushed against the door at the far side of the car. At 50th Street, it was full to bursting; I was pressed back against the door by a dozen bodies packed in so tight that their torsos and limbs were melted together, like clay figures that have been crushed together into a ball by a petulant child.

At 59th Street, more of the same. At 66th Street I stepped out of the car briefly, keeping a leg in, and . . .

He passed by me to step into the car.

I scuttled in behind him. The door slid closed (I pulled in my butt) and I found myself in a posture immediately up against him that, under any other circumstances whatsoever, would have gotten me arrested.

He was quite a bit taller than I, so my chin came up just to the middle of his shoulder blades. My nose was pressed into his pale green raw silk jacket. I didn't know what to do with my hands, which were crossed over my chest in the attitude you see saints and peasant girls assume in lithos when they've had the Virgin revealed to them. My knees knocked against his calves. My crotch . . . was well positioned.

Gradually, I eased my hands down. The doors opened at 72nd Street, but on the other side of the car. I let my hands fall onto his hips. No reaction. The train started up again. I worked my hands around his hips (one of them in its blind passage badly confused a woman next to him) until they were resting on his upper thighs. I let them gently caress his thighs, in a circular motion. I was just about to close in on his basket . . . when the doors opened at 79th Street and I fell out onto the platform.

He stepped out of the car. His face, yes, Gerald Manheim's face, was crimson, redder than his hair. He was horribly embarrassed, just as embarrassed as if *he* had humiliated us before the entire mass transit population of New York. Because he was so obviously worked up, I was terrified he was going to hit me.

"You'll miss the train," I said, the first thing I could think of. But the doors were already closing behind him.

He took my arm. The exit gates were before us. He pushed me through them and, still holding my arm in a vice-like grip, hustled me up to the street.

It was sweltering on the street, too. Somehow, I managed to remember that the season was summer and that I was in the U.S.A. My white summer suit was ruined. The subway doors had probably rubbed a brown smudge across my back, and Gerald Manheim's claws were now irreparably crushing the fibers on my sleeve.

He walked me down 79th Street, oblivious to the stares of passersby, and half dragged me across West End Avenue, not saying a word. He was like Spencer Tracy as God taking the Unwashed to the River.

Which was in fact his destination.

"Where are we going?"

He didn't answer, but his face, though grim, had softened up a bit, and his color had returned to normal, which is to say the exact color of the Peace roses Mummy used to raise in her garden when we lived in Locust Valley.

Children were skipping rope and molesting each other in Riverside Park. The setting sun cast its light through the trees, dappling the walks and broken benches. A jogger running in front of us twisted his ankle and fell. But Gerald did not stop.

We went through a tunnel and under an overpass, down another flight of broad steps, through an archway and into a colonnade letting out onto a plaza with a derelict fountain. In a fieldstone wall just before the landing that led down to the boat basin, a metal door stood ajar. It was through this door that Gerald thrust me.

Inside was a galvanized steel platform with steps dropping off and a vast indoor parking lot below. Homebound traffic roared overhead on the West Side Highway. Water from some obscure source ran down the walls and dripped from the I-beamed ceiling.

I wasn't afraid. Although I'd lost some feeling in the hand attached to the arm in Gerald's grasp, I wasn't otherwise injured. My shock at seeing Gerald on the subway was wearing off. As a matter of fact, I thought I was very lucky.

But I thought to myself: Is this where the Black Widow takes his victims? I couldn't help but think that.

I wasn't afraid. I would have gone down into the Black Hole of Calcutta with Gerald. I would have gone into The Mineshaft. I would even have gone to the *Hamptons*, with Gerald at my side.

"Careful . . ." he said as he steered me down the steps. His first words! His voice was melodious, lightly accented in contrast with his obvious agitation. "They're slippery."

At the bottom of the stairs, he let go of my arm and put his hands on my shoulders. From behind, he guided me into a corner, removed my jacket and let it—Hey! That's my Steve SoHo unconstructed linen blazer!—drop onto the cement floor. His hands caressed my throat, my collar, my shoulders, my arms, slipped over my hands, grasped them.

"Lean up against the wall," he whispered.

I was hard as a poker.

I followed his orders. His body covered mine in an instant. My cheek was pressed into the gritty brick wall and I was sure my silk Ronald Kolodzie slipover shirt was ruined, but his breath in my hair, and his hands (following the same route mine had taken on the subway) were transporting me back to the beach and I was lying in the sand. . . .

I pulled up what was left of my Élance briefs, pulled up my trousers.

"Gee whiz," Gerald sighed in my ear.

Several yards off in the vaulted parking garage a car engine started up. He grabbed my elbow and pulled me down next to him. "My God, do you think they saw us?"

"Who cares?" I said, losing my balance and swooning into him. We sprawled on the filthy floor.

We stayed there, in a heap, while the invisible car edged its way out of the garage.

"Well," Gerald finally said when it was so still we could hear the steady drip-drip of water off the beams again. He disengaged himself (not so reluctantly, I thought) and sat up on his haunches. He looked dazed.

"Thanks," I said, simply.

"What you did to me in the subway," he breathed. "That was the most exciting thing that's ever happened to me."

"You must be kidding," I said. I laughed an ironic little laugh. Even with Gerald Manheim, it was impossible to keep the irony out of my voice. "*Most* exciting?"

"Yes."

He meant it. And I could tell, as he stood up and made a few cursory swipes at the dirt on his slacks, not looking me in the eye, and zipped up his fly, that Gerald Manheim was very, very shy. He was coloring, very prettily.

"And what *you* did to *me*," I said, *trying* to sound sincere. But it had been so long since I'd had to sound sincere. What he'd done to me had certainly ranked high. Certainly above what Clark Vecchio and I had done in the signal house at summer camp—wow!—and barely below that night I spent with Sam Brelow and Howell Petersen in the Piper Cub over Big Sur.

He didn't respond. He just stood looking down at me and panting, eyes bright in the gloom, looking stunned.

I never made it to dinner with my accountant.

"What a *great* color! I didn't know he did them in that color! It looks *great* with your tan!"

Paul turned me this way and that, admiring my new shirt. Exactly the color of red wine grapes.

"It's my old Kolodzie," I said. "I had it dyed." Colors *were* getting stronger, but there had been only one way to save the shirt anyway.

"Where've you been?" Charlie asked, coming in and sitting on my bed. His tan had deepened even further during my week-long absence. Exactly the color of gingerbread.

"Oh," I said, packing socks into a drawer. "Business."

"What a bore."

"Yas, yas," said Paul, fanning himself with his hand in imitation of the society girls we sometimes affected being.

"Don't you ever feel, well, maybe just a pang of guilt over our . . . I don't know." I was suddenly very serious. Too suddenly for my friends to know how to respond.

"Over our what?"

"I don't know," I said, although I'd been thinking about it constantly since I'd left Gerald, all the way back on the seaplane. About the poverty of our inner cities, the growing reactionaryism of our country, even the movement for homosexual liberation. . . . I took a stack of T-shirts out of my bag. "Our lives are really so useless, aren't they? Ger—

This friend I have says that the only possible justification for wealth in our society is an energetic pursuit of spiritual values by the monied classes, values that the rest of society can't afford to cultivate any longer. That we—you and you and I— are solely responsible in a technological age for keeping, well, I guess the religious sense alive in the twentieth century. Of course one wants to do more than *that*, but—"

"Like monks," said Paul.

"Or nuns," said Charlie.

"No, really," I insisted. "And we don't cultivate the spiritual out *here* at *all*. We have no energy left. We party it all away."

"But I always set aside time for my macramé," said Paul.

"And I my bargello," said Charlie.

"Fuck you both," I said, slamming shut a drawer.

"Well, what do you mean, puss?" Paul asked. "A hobby? Take up something then. Something portable. Like hang gliding."

"Or sky diving," Charlie said.

"You could bird-watch."

"Or botanize."

"If you must know," I said, stripping off the wine-red Kolodzie and pulling on a Fruit of the Loom pocket T, "I'm thinking of taking up the clarinet again."

Their reaction was such that they had to leave the room.

Well, damn them for the style queens they are, I thought. And I thought, How unaffected, how direct Gerald is.

Gerald hadn't laughed about the clarinet. "How interesting, after all this time," he'd said when I'd confessed that I hadn't played since Trinity School except for an occasional crack at *The Great Gate of Kiev* in my old room at home when I visited Mummy. Gerald was very encouraging.

"I was once considered *very* musical," I confessed. "I sang in the St. Paul's boys' choir."

"But that's wonderful," enthused Gerald.

I felt like a fool. The conversation had come about, after all, because Gerald had confessed to me, with much stammering and blushing, that he . . . what *did* Gerald Manheim do those long nights alone in his house on Ocean Walk?

He composed music.

"Little exercises," he had put it. "Just to keep my hand in."

But when Gerald played some of his compositions for me on the Steinway in his penthouse on East 63rd Street, that third night of our honeymoon, when Gerald played his compositions—God, but they were beautiful! Contemporary but classical, impressionistic but crystalline, intellectual, subtly nuanced. His music was, like his voice, his manner, himself, completely natural.

That clinched it, of course. The music. I was already beyond infatuation with Gerald. And well beyond idolatry as well. I was *interested* in Gerald. Interest, as you know, is far more fatal than mere infatuation or hero worship. I was almost (but who would have the courage even to *breathe* the word nowadays?) in *love* with Gerald Manheim, this decent, sensitive, considerate, shy man who lived a poignantly solitary existence, not out of choice (though I could see he had great strength and deep inner resources), but because he'd been ostracized from a superficial and superstitious milieu not at all worthy of him.

I didn't, of course, mention *the lovers* to Gerald. Nor did I reveal in any way that I knew who he was, or worse, that I knew how he'd been characterized. As for me, I didn't exactly *lie* about myself (as he would later accuse me), but the fact that he regarded me as a slightly mysterious and certainly unlooked-for treasure made it easy to keep my present life and lifestyle obscure.

I didn't, of course, tell Gerald about Patti Labelle and the Bluebells. If I'd tried to, it would have taken precious minutes of our time together: defending the practice of pet names, explaining who the real Bluebells were before their transformation and eventual dissolution, what a "girl group" was, the distinctions between the Philadelphia and Motown sounds. . . . We had all sorts of educational conversations. I have to confess for Gerald (since he isn't around anymore to speak for himself) that his frame of reference vis-à-vis popular culture had developed only as far as his eighteenth year, the year Arthur Eberly discovered him at Choate. Gerald had traveled extensively, met the great and the near-great and their anonymous lovers, had been tutored in all the fine points of taste. He had a foundation in his name to dispose of unwanted funds. But he'd really seen society only from the interiors of great houses, condominium apartments and art museums. Was it a wonder he was such an ardent democrat? He adored what he called "the common man." (When he first said this, I thought he meant hard hats and other hunky stereotypes, but he didn't.) He subscribed to leftist publications, which were littered all over a pink marble coffee table in his study. He had even learned to ride the subway.

Of course even I, by the time Daddy died, had learned the salient features of what Mummy called "the real world," a world into which she herself had never ventured. Perhaps I hadn't ridden the subway for some years until the day I met Gerald on the IRT. But at least I knew the East Side of Manhattan from the West once outside my apartment or the confines of a taxicab. The day we met, Gerald had thought he was riding from Lincoln Center to the Whitney Museum. Although I never asked him outright, I'm sure he had no idea whatsoever where he was taking me, that the boat basin (which he'd probably never seen before except from the river, from George Papadopolis's yacht) was a happy accident—its discovery by him an instance of something like racial memory.

Yet however naive he was, it's for sure that when I left Gerald at the end of that week, in spite of his tears and protestations, he'd left his mark on me.

It was agony to tear myself away, but it had to be done. I understood fully why Gerald, who had a Christmas-morning outlook on sex, had had only lovers and always lovers—until, that is, his estrangement from the subculture that had for a decade nurtured sufficient replacements for the departed.

He was intoxicating. Not merely his body and the heat it threw off, or his odor, his green eyes, his skin, his white teeth. Not merely his beautiful voice, his artistic talent. All these things. But also a quality of attention. What was nothing but shoddy sleight-of-hand in others—the trick of fastening one's attention, as if completely, on another—was in Gerald utterly without sham, utterly complete. He rang true as a bell, and he tolled only for me.

But wasn't there something—well, *spooky* about Gerald? He was, of course, delightful company, so entertaining, so, well, attentive. But every once in a while, a cloud would pass over Gerald's handsome face and he would turn stock still, staring at me with an almost dumb expression that would finally turn into one of—why hold back?—adoration. But before the sun broke through . . .

The first time it happened, I'd been lying out on the terrace enjoying the sun and the relatively "good" air quality. It was two in the afternoon. Gerald was in the kitchen. He had been in there since one, except for a brief trip to my side to place a tall, iced glass of fresh-squeezed lemonade on the table, kiss me on the forehead and massage my temples with his cool fingertips.

"Darling?" he now called from the kitchen. "Would you like to eat out there or inside?"

"Oh, I don't know," I said, snapping out of my lethargy somewhat. "Whatever suits you . . ."

But I knew he had something special planned. I turned over on the chaise and peered into the dark dining room. He'd laid out linen mats and luncheon plates. A crystal vase with a single calla lily adorned the center of the table. "Shall we lunch inside?" I asked facetiously. "I fear I've already had too much sun."

"Marvelous idea, darling," he chimed from the kitchen.

I could hear sounds of metal against metal. Delicious smells—was that a nice *omelette aux fines herbes?*—wafted out onto the terrace. I sauntered into the dining room.

Gerald stood in the kitchen doorway, a bottle of wine in one hand and a Limoges platter bearing two perfect omelettes on a bed of watercress in the other.

"Oh, Gerald. I really *should* put something on," I said, glancing down at my trunks.

"Stay just the way you are," he said from the doorway. "You're gorgeous, all brown and sweaty like that."

We sat down and dug into the eggs. "Delicious," I said, mouth full. "Gerald, everything is *so* exquisitely mounted." I twirled my pistol-grip George III sterling knife. "It does a girl's heart good to see standards being maintained by *someone*. Such style."

A tiny wrinkle appeared between his eyes. He put down his fork.

"Why, Gerald," I said. He'd blanched under his peachy tan. "Are you quite well? Did I say something?"

His face softened and he looked at me with . . . that look I'd begun to expect from him.

"Please forgive me, darling," he said, placing a hand over mine. "It's just that . . . that kind of talk is . . . unworthy of you."

"Unworthy?"

"Please do forgive me." Self-consciously, he picked up his fork and prodded at his eggs.

"What is it, Gerald?"

"It's just that I'm . . . so familiar with . . . that talk."

"What talk?"

The rest came out in a torrent.

"The empty banter of the style queen. I don't want you ever to get that way. Please, please promise me," he said, his face convulsing to the extent that his regular, fine features would allow, "please promise you won't go that route. *Promise you won't change.*"

I laughed a guilty little laugh, wondering if I was, indeed, the style queen Gerald feared I was, and said that of course I wouldn't change. (*Everyone* makes one promise *that.*)

"That you'll remain as unspoiled as you are," Gerald stipulated. Then he used a little pet name, one which even *my* tattered conscience won't allow me to consign to paper. "You see," he said, "I've known so many of those typically disengaged and selfish types. I used to hear that kind of talk all the time. It was like an opiate, to dull the senses and to level social congress to the lowest, most common denominator. Island faggots . . ."

"Oh, you mean *Fire* Island," I said lightly, not daring to look up from my plate.

"God," he moaned. "Yes. *I* used to be one of those people myself, you see. A few years ago after . . . some emotional

1 1 5

difficulties . . . I realized that I'd become what I'd always feared more than anything in creation. My entire world was bounded by Water Island on the east and Les Mouches on the west; my only concerns were drugs, dildos and discos; my only amusements were fine wines, pretty boys and *L'Uomo Vogue*. Flamingo was a shrine upon which I immolated myself weekly, only to stagger home alone and then struggle out of the ashes again every Sunday afternoon, blackened, weakened. I was desolate. I was *lonely*—"

The blood had risen to his face. There was an unholy fire in Gerald's eyes.

"I longed for a savior," he sighed. Then he said, smiling ruefully, "Until I realized, darling, I finally had to save *myself*. I'm not asking you somehow to rescue me from the vacuousness and hopelessness of modern life. If only you'll *trust* me. I've been down those sorry paths you seem to find so glamorous. Oh, don't try to deny it," he said, holding up a hand. "I've watched you, seen your reactions when Regine's or Studio are mentioned on TV. But I've *been* there. I've been there and back. I finally realized, thank God, that . . . I am me. Gerald Manheim. I am *not* a style queen."

"That's inspirational, Gerald," I said, feeling wretched and unworthy.

"Oh, *so* serious," he said, attempting to brighten up a bit. "You haven't said a word about the wine."

"Delicious," I said. For some reason I'd lost my appetite completely. Nevertheless, I attempted to finish the eggs. Gerald sat with his chin propped on his hands, watching me, urging me on, and didn't take his eyes off me until I'd finished every last leaf of watercress on my plate, each tiny stuffed cherry tomato. No one had watched me like that since Nanny.

In fact, Gerald was *always* watching me. And there were more diatribes against what he called *The Life*. And there were inexplicable blank moments between us when Gerald, sitting on the couch or on the rug at my feet or crosslegged on the bed, stared at me with that queer expression. Rapt. Spooky.

I tried to ignore it. Cheap payment, those moments, for the coinage of Gerald's smooth skin, his skillful hands, his greedy mouth, his fantastic apartment . . .

I didn't, of course, reveal to my friends the Bluebells the actual reason for my week-long vacation from the Pines. I wonder now if my choice (choice?) not to was altogether a matter of wanting to avoid the derision the revelation would have brought on me, the concern news of my affair with the Black Widow (conveyed to me in mocking tones, of course) would have elicited. No, I wanted Gerald Manheim all to myself. And didn't I also, perhaps subconsciously (even after a crash course in sincerity with Gerald) still feel enough of an attachment to the values (*values?*) of Island society not to want to dispel the legend of the Black Widow?

"Oh, no. He's a very ordinary guy, really. Very childlike and trusting. Very sweet. You'd like him."

Not a word. I wanted to keep Gerald to myself. But it was confusing, keeping a lie alive and inventing new ones to cover up the incongruities of the old. I was either testy and remote all that next week, or else I was wildly affectionate and madcap. I wasn't myself, and Paul and Charlie noticed. But there is a decorum, even among fast friends, that can't easily be breached. So they didn't intrude.

"But *why* can't you see me?"

"I told you, Gerald. I have to see my mother. Family business."

"But you saw your mother *last* week."

"I have to go out again. Really, Gerald. I'll be back in a few days."

"I *never* see you anymore,"

"Gerald, we just saw each other last night."

"But you left right after breakfast."

"Gerald, we've talked about this until we're both blue in the—"

A long sigh, then silence at the other end of the line. I fiddled with the phone cord. I was confused, feeling as if I were taking a corkscrew slide down an enormous funnel.

Finally, he said in the low, childish voice he sometimes assumed, "Talked about *what?*"

"Gerald, I *have* to have a life of my own."

"You don't love me," he bawled disingenuously.

"I *do* love you," I said patiently. "But I can't be joined at the hip to you."

"Why not?"

"That's nonsense, Gerald. Because I'm not. *That's* why not."

"Well, *I* can't help it if you're not. *I* can't help the way I feel." This had been a refrain recently. "If you'd just stop being silly and move in with me—"

"But I *can't* just move in with you."

"Why not?"

"Because I have a co-op apartment and a maintenance charge so sky high that—"

"I'll *pay* it for you. I *told* you."

"Because I've never lived with anyone before and—"

"There's a first time for everything."

"Because I'm not ready!"

Silence again. I covered the mouthpiece with my hand and

allowed myself a good scream. Then I uncovered the phone. "Gerald, I do adore you . . ."

"And I you."

"You're really the most extraordinary thing that's ever happened to me." (In more ways than one, I'd begun to think.)

"And you me."

(Was this true? Arthur-Hans-Larry-George all rolled into one?)

"I need a mate," he said. "I'm weary to death of the single life."

"But Gerald, your life is charmed, so perfectly ordered, so productive. I'd only gum it up. Can't we just—"

"I need a mate," he repeated. "All of it seems hollow and purposeless without a mate."

I knew he was telling the truth. "Gerald, I swear I'm not avoiding a commitment. I *am* committed. But I can't just move in with you . . ."

"Why not?"

And around we went again.

Although Gerald was as exciting as ever, his conversation, *this* conversation was becoming . . . a trial. It was confined to one topic and one alone: marriage.

When I was a boy at Trinity School, we used to play hooky now and then, three or four of us, and we'd roam the forbidden precincts of upper Broadway. We were outrageously, obviously truants. We wore blazers and rep ties. But we were never, amidst the jumble of nationalities, classes and disabilities on that street, apprehended or otherwise interfered with.

We always used to gravitate toward one particular shop in the nineties. It was a novelty store, with plastic buttocks, rubber spiders and rubber noses in the windows, where we'd buy all sorts of repulsive, marvelous things. I remember one item in particular—a packet of lozenges exactly the color of cockroaches. When one of these lozenges was set on the sidewalk and touched with a match, it began to fume and erupt into ash. Miraculously, it gave birth to a long black snake. We were so crazy about these Dr. Howard's Asp Kits that the sidewalks of the Upper West Side bore the mark of their birthings for blocks, all around Trinity School.

Well, Gerald was rather like the Asp Kit lozenges of my childhood, although I was ashamed to admit it to myself as the weeks went on—two, then three, then four. He'd been slumbering, innocent, but I'd ignited him again. And love is almost always a tragically solitary state for *anyone* to be in. His love was consuming him as it extended him, and the spectacle was rather frightening to watch.

It was not at all easy being loved by Gerald, as I was discovering. For instance, he had a habit of lying on my back (perhaps an allusion to that first exciting encounter in the parking garage) and pressing me into the mattress with his big hands on the back of my head until I gasped for air and begged him to let me go. He only smothered me in the throes of passion and I have to acknowledge I found this quirk very stimulating. But his love had begun to smother me more figuratively as well.

"What *are* you doing?" Paul asked me.

I was lying in bed with the earphones on, listening to the Mozart horn concerti.

"What?" I removed the headset.

"Don't you know it's one in the afternoon?"

"What about it?"

He was wearing his blue Speedo, exactly the color of the summer sea.

"You've already missed two hours of the best sun we've had all season. The beach is packed. *Everyone* is out. It's August 31st and you're in here alone in the dark" (I'd merely drawn the shades) "listening to music. You haven't changed those gym shorts in three days." He leaned down and put his hand on my forehead. I shook it off.

"I'm fine," I said.

He sat down on the bed.

"You know, of course, that you haven't cooked or paid your share of the house in two weeks."

"I know," I said.

"And you haven't been to Tea for three."

"I know."

"And you missed *Royal Scandal* at the movies last night."

"Yes, yes, I know."

"But those are relatively minor points, aren't they? *Everyone* has to find occasionally *some* means to rebel against the mainstream. For some, it's staying no longer than half an hour at any one party; for others, it's forgetting to bring the party invitation along; for still others, it's not going to the party at all and staying home to read *Mansfield Park;* for others yet, it's not even R.S.V.P.ing. But *you* . . ."

"I don't feel very well."

"You're ruining our reputation."

I sat up in bed.

"Yes," he said.

"What *are* you talking about?"

"You've cut *everyone* left and right. When you *do* go out to the store, for cigarettes or cough drops or whatever it is you're living on, you look *terrible*. Even if you *would* go anywhere, we wouldn't be able to *take* you."

"Well, ex*cuse me*," I said, flouncing over onto my side so I was facing the wall.

"Go ahead," he said, steel. "Pout."

"I'm not pouting. I'm in the midst of a terrible dilemma and you're *some* kind of friend."

"Is that what all this has been? A cry for help?"

"I have problems the nature of which none of you could possibly guess."

"I'm sure you do. But you don't sulk with much style. You should see your hair."

I turned around to face him.

"You *style queens* just can't bear to take *any*thing seriously, can you? Everything's a joke. Everything about you is so fucking superior and surface. You make me sick."

He stood up and left the room.

I was shocked at my behavior, yet at the same time felt somewhat satisfied that I'd finally spoken my mind. I put on the earphones again and rewound the tape. I listened to the horn concerti from the beginning. But I found myself searching, through their fields and forests, vales and dells, for what had so enamored me of them in the first place. Charlie and Paul went riding through the landscape on beautiful bay horses exactly the color of roasted chestnuts, sprinkling confetti in their wake. But search as I might, I couldn't find Gerald. His image, my image of him as he was the evening of the hot-pink sunset, had grown dim, opalescent—exactly the color of a pearl set out on peach satin. It faded and was dispelled for good when Terry Brewer came riding over the hill with a phalanx of red-coated huntsmen behind him, red red against the green green of the countryside, hounds baying at their flanks. Terry bore aloft the insignia of the Pines

Volunteer Fire Department. Gaily colored ribbons streamed off it and tumbled about Terry's curls . . .

When I woke up, it was pitch black outside. I stumbled out of bed, inadvertently yanking the earphones out of the amplifier. I looked in the mirror above my bureau. There were deep red marks in my temples where I'd slept on the headset.

Paul was right. I *did* look terrible. I went to the bathroom, rinsed the hairs out of the sink, filled it with hot water, draped a towel over my head and steamed for a while. Feeling much better then, I took a pair of scissors and trimmed my mustache and the thatch that had sprung out over my ears. Then I showered, shampooed, conditioned, braced, deodorized, creamed and moisturized. It was a slapdash job, but I didn't look half bad when I had finished. A few swipes with the bronzer helped.

I went out.

Labor Day. Well, you know what Labor Day weekends are like out here. Daytrippers, teenyboppers, groupers—*everyone* is out for Labor Day weekend. From our table on the deck at the Botel, we watched boatload after boatload come over from the mainland. The three of us were reunited and looking forward to the rest of September, when the Island would again be ours in that last glorious gasp of summer. I'd sent Gerald Manheim a letter. In essence, I'd agreed that I *was* a silly queen incapable of a real commitment; too much of my life lay ahead of me and there were just too many pleasures yet to taste before I was ready to settle down; the pull of the very lifestyle he'd deplored and attempted to warn me of was too seductive for me to resist.

Not a word from Gerald in reply. No letter, no message. I'd begun to relax for the first time in weeks.

My own theory about the fatal charm of the Black Widow was that Gerald was not *just* perfect husband material; husband material was *all* Gerald could be. I'd suffered the cutting edge of his laser-like love and felt fortunate to have escaped it in time.

It was six o'clock and we'd been sitting on the Botel deck drinking piña coladas since four. Lots of piña coladas. *Everyone* was there and we were just saying how Tea really was out of the question that day. . . . It was clear that since we had such good seats we weren't about to budge for some time.

Another ferry chugged into the harbor.

"Look at that, will you?" Charlie said, pointing to a rusty old scow we'd never seen before. The traffic was so heavy that weekend, they were hauling out anything that would float. The ferry shuddered into the habor, careened into the pier and began unloading passengers.

On the top deck, standing a little apart from the motley collection of urban refugees, was a lone figure in a white trench coat, male, a slouch hat pulled down over his eyes, outsized avaitor glasses covering much of his face, collar up, two golden retrievers leashed at his side.

"The Black Widow," breathed Paul excitedly.

"Get *her*," said Charlie.

But I'd turned around 180 degrees in my chair, back to the water. I knew he was staring directly at me, burning holes in my shirt—which was, after all, hard to miss, being exactly the color of the Candy Apple Red Plymouth of Paul's youth.

I was totally freaked out. My one glimpse of the Black Widow standing on the top deck of the ferry with his dogs, incognito and supernaturally sentient of my presence in the crush of that harbor—one glimpse did me in. My stomach shifted uncomfortably, as if seeking a way out of my torso. In the red shirt, I was a moving target. Gerald's passion was that acute, his pain that palpable. And I was the source of it all. I was both the sun and the tuft of kindling; Gerald was the necessary lens. And I prayed he would simply step off the ferry and disappear into his Ocean Walk hermitage. For if we came face to face, we would start a nice little blaze the likes of which the Island might never recover from.

Don't be so hyperbolic, I said to myself.

"Dear me," said Charlie at my side.

"Goodness," said Paul.

"What?" I croaked.

"She's coming up *here*."

"Out*rage*ous."

"Up here?" I gasped.

There was a slight stirring amidst the crowd on the Botel deck. As I said, *everyone* was at Tea that day. A slight sensation rippled through the crowd, as a breeze runs over aspen leaves. Heads turned ever so slightly. Stances were reordered.

"Up *here?*"

"Look, puss!" Paul said. "You're missing *everything*."

"I underestimated him," Charlie offered. "He's truly a great lady after all."

Curiosity got the best of me. Before I realized what I was doing, I turned around to see . . .

The trench-coated figure approached the Botel down an avenue of bodies mysteriously parted to allow his swift progress. His golden retrievers strained at their leashes, prancing before him. His face was obscured by his disguise, but of course *everyone* knew who he was.

"He *is* coming up here!" Charlie squealed.

"At last," Paul said, attempting to affect the proper tone of disinterest, "something to write home about."

No, I thought to myself, he can't have spotted poor little me in all this multitude, not *me*, whom he would have no reason to suspect of being within a hundred miles of the Island.

People were *pretending* not to notice—hard and conclusive evidence that *everyone* at Tea was intensely engaged in the spectacle of the Black Widow's imminent arrival on the deck of the Botel. Labor Day Tea had been, in the space of a few minutes, elevated from an obligatory ritual to a full-blown Event. Ever after, it would be "The day that—" What? The Black Widow *throttled?* Spat on? Shot dead? Gave high attitude to?

"I, uh, think I'd better be going," I said, struggling to my feet. Don't let anyone ever tell you that a sudden shock sobers you up. It doesn't.

"You *can't* leave *now!*" Paul said, clasping my hand.

"What *are* you thinking of?" Charlie said, pulling me back into my chair.

All six of our eyes, throughout this struggle, were fixed on . . .

The Black Widow. He mounted the three broad steps to the Botel deck. People fell back in his wake. Spines stiffened as he approached.

Now, you know what those three steps up to the Botel deck constitute. They are to the Island what the *eccyclema* was to classical Greek drama: that great shadow box revolving on its pivot to reveal a god or an animus or the gory remains of the tragedy's machine. Those three steps are the *eccyclema* upon which those who would enter Tea must ride, the portal through which each of us must pass on our way to Judgment, the gates to Heaven or Hell—or worse, the limbo of social indifference.

It was an entrance every bit worthy of the legend, partly because Gerald was clad *all* in white but for his mirrored shades. The dogs were a veiled complement to his hair, hidden under the white straw slouch hat. He was re-entering the society which he'd spurned (but had not entirely forsaken, oh no) with no trace of diffidence and no apologies. He took center stage. Even incognito, he was quite obviously the most beautiful man any of us had seen that day, or would see tomorrow, or the next day. Oh, and he was seen—from behind dark glasses and over shoulders and from beneath lowered lashes and out of the corners of eyes and in the reflections on the plate glass windows—seen by *everyone*. Only a few, however, stared outright.

He strode across the deck, his dogs not daring to stop to piss or snoop, but seemingly bent on the mission of sniffing out . . .

Who but me?

I sat in my canvas chair, rigid with fright, half turned away from him (as were, of course, Charlie and Paul by now) with a stale piña colada in my hand, feigning mute interest in the waves gently lapping against the *Barbara*, tied up dockside.

The Black Widow's progress to our table was unimpeded. The crowd parted before him as if by telepathy, like rushes before a royal barge. Twosomes and threesomes sauntered around him like well-choreographed supers in a grand opera piazza. But something in the scene was out of tune.

All conversation had completely halted on the Botel deck.

A heavy hand fell on my shoulder. It wasn't, of course, necessary to turn, to confront him and make sure it was Gerald. I'd felt that heat before.

"Have you come for a drink?" I asked, trying to brazen it out. "Have we quite fallen out of our tower?"

My friends' mouths were hanging open.

I turned to face Gerald. I'm sure it was my imagination, but the whole Island was absolutely silent as he took off his dark glasses. His eyes were swollen and red-rimmed.

"You lied to me," he hissed.

"I didn't lie to you," I hissed back, shrugging away his hand and looking down at the deck, as if the boards might have opened up and afforded me some escape. "I just didn't tell you the whole truth, Gerald, and I'm sorry." And indeed I *was* sorry, on account of his eyes.

"That you're a *style queen?*" he asked, looking about him with disgust.

There was a low murmur from the crowd. Paul opened his mouth (which he'd managed to close in the interim) to say something, but I cut him with a look and said to Gerald, "I *am* a style queen. I admit it. I'm not good enough for you, Gerald."

"*But I love you!*" he wailed.

Conversation on the Botel deck resumed.

"Oh, is *that* all," I heard someone say.

"That's what I tried to tell you in my letter—" I began.

"Lies!" Gerald cried, grasping my shoulder again. It hurt.

"Ouch," I said, and tried to wriggle away. But my canvas chair began to fold up. Charlie, sitting next to me, was half in, half out of his. Paul was watching the scene still as death, bug-eyed with rapture.

Gerald struggled to pull me into his arms, but my chair collapsed and I fell onto the deck, taking Charlie down with me. The dogs, happy to see me again, jumped on top of me, evidently thinking this was the cue for a romp. In the process, they pulled Gerald into the tangle of arms and legs on the deck. His hat rolled over the edge, bounced, and dropped into the water.

Conversation on the deck became extremely animated.

"Get away from me!" I screamed, at the dogs, at Gerald. "Go back to Manhattan! Go back to your two-bit penthouse! Get your slimy hands off me!"

"I only want to talk to you," Gerald panted, wound up in the leashes.

"Do you *mind?*" Charlie said, trying to ease out from under me and the dogs. "These are *satin* painter's pants, you know." He scrambled to his feet.

"I just want to *talk* to you," Gerald said, arms around my legs.

I kicked at him with one Adidas-ed foot. He fell back onto the deck. A wide circle had formed around us. A few people were even gawking. I saw Richard Sacks making signs at Paul, trying to get the scoop before *everyone* knew what was behind this. Paul was shaking his head back and forth, fixed on us, on the deck, and I think actually oblivious to everything but the fact that there was something of major social import going on that he hadn't predicted.

"Why'd you lie to me?" Gerald said, crouched on his knees, trenchcoat awry, close to tears. One auburn curl had fallen onto his forehead in the melée.

"Because you didn't want a style queen, Gerald. Because I was infatuated. Because I didn't want to lose you."

"What on *earth?*" said Paul, in a deep, husky voice. "What on earth has been going *on* between you two? You *must* tell me."

"Keep out of this," I snapped.

"Gerald," Paul said, pushing me aside, "whatever has been going *on* between you two?"

"But I LOVE you!" Gerald cried again.

My reaction to this second, more shrill protestation couldn't have been more electric if he'd put a cold revolver to my temple. I began to scurry away backwards under the table. Gerald grabbed my ankle. An animal cry escaped his throat.

"Oh, give her a *down*," someone drawled.

"What is this all *about?*" Paul asked, crawling under the table with me.

Gerald froze. He looked perplexed. He shook his head. Like a person awakened from a long dream, he glanced furtively around him. Then he smiled. He got up off me and backed out from under the table. Still on his hands and knees, he said in a normal voice, as if to coax me out, as if I'd gone under the table from sheer perversity:

"This is *so* silly, isn't it?" He shrugged, fell back on his haunches, lifted his hands. "I mean, this whole thing. . . ."

I felt my lips curving into a smile to match Gerald's. Perhaps something could be salvaged from this fiasco after all (Paul was muttering, "I won't tell a *soul*") if we just— But my mouth was forming something closer to a grimace than a smile. My veins were running cold. I pulled my face back together and said:

"Isn't it?"

I gave Gerald my hand and he helped me up. The dogs lay down on the deck. Charlie was back in his chair. Only Paul looked disheveled and a little mad. I put a hand on Gerald's back and steered him over to the railing. The crowd, still insanely curious but already, I was sure, discussing the encounter in the past tense, turned away.

"But Gerald," I said, gently patting his trembling back. "I *knew* something like this would happen if we actually *saw* each other. It's just impossible. I suppose I *did* lie. A bit. In that I allowed you to continue to think—"

"You hurt me very, very much," he said, like a scolding parent.

"In that I allowed you to continue to think I was something I wasn't."

Now he was looking at me with that megawatt intensity, frying my circuits. What was it? What *was* it that was so frightening about Gerald Manheim? This: that his face displayed *hope* in all its awful facets.

"But that's all over now," he said hoarsely.

"How? Over?" I asked.

"Yes," said Paul eagerly. "How over?"

"Butt out," I barked at Paul.

"You keep out of this," Gerald warned him.

"Don't pay any attention to *him*," I said, glaring at Paul. Charlie was sitting with his chin on Paul's shoulder.

"Darling," Gerald said, lowering his voice. "I can bend. Do you know I have a marvelous house right here in the Pines? Yes! Right on Ocean Walk! If you'd just please"—his voice was down to an urgent whisper again—"spend a couple of days with me there. And then perhaps we can work it out, shake me out of that dreadful misanthropy I've fallen into. I *promise* I won't press you for a full commitment."

I can't say I wasn't tempted. I thought of what wonderful parties could be thrown in that house; of how adorable Gerald would look in lime trunks, against the gray-beige of the weathered siding; of what a spectacle we'd make, the two of us, running down the beach with his golden retrievers ahead of us . . .

"I'm sorry, Gerald," I said. "No."

"BUT NO ONE'S EVER DONE ANYTHING LIKE THIS TO ME BEFORE!" he bawled. He grabbed my throat.

"Gerald, *please* understand." I grunted as we wrestled

against the rail. "I'm involved with *someone else.* I *have* been for some time now."

Charlie and Paul backed away, neither anxious to be singled out as my paramour. I wrenched myself free from Gerald's grip. I scuttled down the rail. He was fast on my heels. "That's just an excuse," he panted, trying to get me into the corner. "Like all the excuses you style queens use. You're—oh, God!" he cried, as we turned over another table, "You're trying to let me down easy!"

"But Gerald," I said, twisting free again and sidestepping some frightened muscle queens. "It's *true!* I have a *lover!*" We stumbled out into the open. Gerald crashed headfirst into the bar. Three perfect oranges, exactly the color of croquet balls, rolled across the deck. Women shrieked. Men stifled giggles behind their hands.

"It was a *horrible* thing to do to you, I know, Gerald," I grunted. He got hold of the waistband of my parachute-silk trousers. "It was a *terrible* thing to do. Capricious. Irresponsible. A summer romance."

"*I am not a summer romance!*" he cried, as we fell into Tea Dance, knocking down several dancers. We'd managed by this time to create an authentic commotion. Some actually stopped boogying; but that was only because we were directly in their way.

"*Lies!*" Gerald reiterated. "Why don't you tell me the truth?" He had me in a modified half-nelson. We cartwheeled out the other door, colliding with a waiter and a clutch of old aunties. I struggled free and leapt onto a table. Gerald hit the table with an "Oomph!" and went crashing to the deck.

He struggled to his feet, using the table for support. I stood on the balls of my feet, ready to jump one way or the other.

"Why don't you tell me the *truth?*" he moaned.

"The truth? You want the truth?"

I've read accounts of demonic possession, the real kind, not the double feature variety. I can authenticate my own case with some confidence. I was possessed. By the Devil? By the World? By the Truth Gerald was begging to hear?

"The truth is . . . *Gerald Manheim.*"

He shuddered.

Everyone was watching.

"*Of the Grosse Point Manheims! Chocolate! Stocks and bonds!*"

We now had the utter, direct and undivided attention of the entire population of Fire Island. Even the D.J. in his booth.

"THE TRUTH IS, GERALD," I screamed, beside myself as he struggled to reach my feet, "YOU'RE *BORING!*"

He gasped and groaned, threw himself across the table.

"Dear Gerald," I said, in a regular voice that nevertheless carried in the utter silence all the way across the bay to Sayville. "Poor Gerald. You *bored* them all. To *death!* You killed them with kindness. Whatever tragic—and we're all truly sorry, Gerald—twists fate supplied to help you along, you bored them all *to death.* You killed them with your perfect love!"

(Scattered applause.)

Well, I don't suppose *I* can say much more about Gerald Manheim that hasn't all been said before. You know how people are prone to talk, how they blow things up all out of proportion. He did *not* stray into the ocean à *la* Hans Werther. He did *not* overdose in his East 63rd Street penthouse. Nor was he strangled there by a hustler with a silk bathrobe cord as *some people* have said. No, Gerald Manheim simply sold his house and disappeared.

And for the rest of the season, the tape of the Mozart horn

concerti that I broke open and cast into the winds the next day fluttered from the topmost flagpole on our house.

When we returned in the spring to open up, the tape was gone. But then, so was the oceanside deck and most of the pool, the plate glass doors letting out onto them and the furniture from the livingroom. It had been the winter of the Great Storm, the winter of the—but who can remember from year to year? It was the winter I got a Christmas card (Neiman-Marcus, exactly the color of café au lait) from Gerald Manheim, from Key West, Florida:

> Having a great time, weather's divine.
> In my element *completely*. Great humpy
> numbers *everywhere*, almost as *boring*
> as I am (ha-ha). Met a man
>
> > Love,
> > Gerald Manheim

There was not one trace left after the Great Storm of the former lair of the Black Widow on Ocean Walk.

Love Lifted Me

When nothing else would help
Love lifted me.
                        —Songs of Praise

Come down and redeem us from
virtue, Our Lady . . .
                        —Swinburne

*T*retona and Belinda certainly
had a very jolly junior year in high school. They sat together
every night on the school bus (unless Belinda had decided to
subject Tretona to temporary torture for some minor mis-
deed). One of them generally managed to get the car for ball
games and they always took each other home last. Tretona
talked her dad into getting a "necker's knob" for the steering
wheel so she could turn corners with one hand. If Belinda
was driving, Tretona caressed her thighs and tickled her
underpants so much that generally she gave up and let
Tretona drive so they wouldn't have an accident.

There were lots of lovers' lanes leading back into woods or cornfields. One time down in the bottoms they interrupted their love-making to watch a raccoon clean his food by the creek bridge.

Tretona and Belinda spent a lot of time practicing kissing. They worked on each other's eyelashes and ears and what Tretona later learned in linguistics class are called alveolar ridges. Tretona gave Belinda tiny hickies on the inside of her elbows. (She never dared to bite her neck.) She learned how to mold and tease Belinda's nipples until they were stiff and quivering like tuning forks. Then she would smelt them down into little limp rose buds with her tongue. She chewed the hair on Belinda's arms and threatened to braid the hair between her legs.

Tretona never let Belinda make love to her, except on very special occasions. Once when Belinda stayed all night they shared a double bed in the loft. What a luxury after cold nights in the back seat of a Plymouth! They even both took off their pajamas and let their breasts play with each other. Tretona really liked the way Belinda made love to her that night, but it also scared her. When boys rubbed her down there, it was real exciting but she always felt in control. When Belinda did it, she felt like she was going to burn out something in her brain—maybe go crazy or insane. Besides, it just didn't seem right for Belinda to be doing that sort of thing. She was somehow too good and pure to be initiating sex. Somehow getting swept off your feet wasn't so bad. The next morning they had to hide the pillowcase because it had bloody handprints on it. It seemed that one of them was always getting her period.

Somehow, miraculously, they were never discovered, even though they took more and more chances: bribing Belinda's sister to go out to play, jumping into their clothes just before her folks came home, passing thinly disguised notes in assembly hall, stealing kisses on the bus. One Sunday afternoon in early spring they drove down in the bottoms and started necking. It was so muddy they couldn't pull off the narrow road. Tretona had her head buried in Belinda's stomach kissing her navel and Belinda had her head tipped back, her legs spread, and her eyes closed. Suddenly they realized that a man in a pick-up had stopped in front of them and was staring in amazement. Tretona had to back the car up for about a quarter of a mile before there was room for him to pass by. She and Belinda were relieved that he was a stranger, but mortified that they had been so careless.

And yet they wanted to talk to someone about what they were feeling. For hours they discussed the pros and cons of telling Sister Naomi. Some survival instinct always stopped them in the end. The events of the following summer proved the wisdom of keeping things secret.

The tent meeting during the summer before their senior year was the biggest ever. Brother Jode preached for the second time and Brother Don helped out on the long altar calls—he was more soothing and coaxing than Jode and provided a nice counterpoint to Jode's frightening, punitive tone. Sister Naomi was the pianist, of course, but Tretona was the assistant musical director. That meant she got to play for the morning prayer meetings and arrange some special numbers. One evening she and Jackie played "Pass Me Not Oh Gentle Savior" as a trombone duet. Tretona played the alto part on a real trombone and Jackie carried the melody on a tromboneshaped kazoo. Everyone laughed when they walked out carrying their music racks because Tretona's was so tall and his was so short. But everyone shut up when they began. Jackie got started on the right note and stuck right on tune even though he was only five. And he moved the slide of his toy trombone just like Tretona moved hers. She almost couldn't play for smiling because she was so proud of him.

The biggest attraction of the tent meeting was the new song leading team, James and Lenore Clayton. They were song evangelists from the Nazarene Church, and boy, did *they* get everybody singing and clapping. They would divide the congregation into sections and teach them rounds and question-answer songs. Then they would have contests to see which group could sing loudest. "Praise ye the Lord," one side would sing. "Hallelujah," would come the answer. Sister Clayton's group always sang loudest. She was dark-skinned and wore navy blue dresses and black stockings. Her thick, straight hair was pulled back in French braids and a bun, but wisps would work loose and frame her sweaty face. She had strong cheekbones (Tretona later found out she was part Oklahoma Indian) and prominent, full lips of a blue-purple color.

The most remarkable thing about Sister Clayton was the way she moved her body. Her breasts were big and obviously crammed into her crepe dresses. It often seemed to Tretona that the dress might split open any minute. She imagined it happening with a slow cracking noise, like when you open up a ripe watermelon and loose pieces of juicy heart fall out. After the tightness over the bosom, the dress fell in soft, lazy folds down across her belly and hips.

Sister Clayton would sway her lower body back and forth as she directed. Sometimes when she was trying to get everyone to sing louder she would spread her legs slightly and make her thighs tight. You could sort of see them under the dress and her stomach when she breathed. The louder people sang, the tenser her legs would get. Finally, on the last chorus, they would start to quiver just enough so you could notice it. Tretona and Belinda watched pretty carefully and they decided that she probably wasn't wearing a girdle. Tretona's mom didn't like Sister Clayton one bit, but her dad said that Nazarenes just felt the music more than Methodists did.

Tretona also got to observe Sister Clayton in the morning prayer meetings. She was always whispering to people and touching their arms. And she would kneel by folks and comfort them if they had any sins or weaknesses to confess. One morning when Tretona turned around from the piano she saw that her dad was crying at the altar. It turned out that he had gone into the pool room behind Wilcox's filling station intending to invite some of the crowd there to come to the tent meeting. He was just working the conversation around to the subject when someone started telling dirty jokes. Then he not only lost his nerve, he also laughed at the jokes. Tretona thought it was real nice how Sister Clayton consoled her father, saying that she knew Brother Getroek would be braver next time and that he would surely become a mighty soldier in God's war against evil and filth.

Tretona didn't tell her mom about it though.

One evening during the altar call Belinda and Tretona were side by side in the same pew as usual. They liked to share a hymnal and feel their fingertips touch across the spine of the book. It was also safe to rub their shoulders and ankles together, and when they stood up sometimes their hips would touch momentarily. Suddenly, their cocoon of blended voices, electric skin and honeyed underpants was invaded by Sister Clayton. She had come up from the back of the tent and stood behind them in the pew without being noticed.

Now she thrust her body between them and whispered harshly, "OK, cut it out, you two." She grabbed each of them by the shoulder. Her hips felt firmer than Tretona had imagined. "What do you mean?" Tretona weakly asked. "You know very well what I'm talking about," said Sister Clayton. "And to do it in church, too."

During the rest of the service Tretona and Belinda sat nice and far apart. Afterwards they talked a lot about what to do.

The next evening during the prayer circle at six o'clock Belinda told Sister Clayton that she was just trying to lead Tretona to Christ, but Sister Clayton said, "Sure, kid" and walked away. Then they were really scared about what Sister Clayton might do.

It got more frightening when Tretona found out that the Claytons were coming out for Sunday dinner.

Saturday she had to babysit Jackie, and she tried to calm down and think what to do. She couldn't concentrate, though, because Jackie and Troy were in a wild mood. They had decided to play revival meeting and had rolled up all the throw rugs to make an altar and put the davenport cushions on the floor for church seats. Teddy Bear was the preacher and all the Jumbo family were the sinners. "Come to the altar," said Jackie for Teddy. Troy and the stuffed elephants refused. "Bless you," said Teddy, "if you don't get up to the altar right now, I'll come back and kick you up!" A big scuffle ensued. Tretona tried to get them to start over again so she could use Slinky, the loose-jointed green snake, as Sister Clayton, but Troy and Jackie soon got bored and went back to fighting.

When Brother Don came to pick up Jackie, Tretona managed to bring up the topic of Sister Clayton and remarked that she sure seemed to have a powerful imagination. Don looked sort of confused, so then Tretona had to mumble something about her big stories about Oklahoma. Don said that probably things really were quite a bit different down there.

When Sunday came, Tretona decided all she could do was to stick around the house and make sure Sister Clayton didn't get a chance to talk to her mom alone. Dinner went OK. Brother Clayton did most of the talking, punctuating his stories about faith healing and stingy congregations that didn't pay their evangelists enough with an occasional "Isn't that right, Lenore?" Sister Clayton seemed smaller when she wasn't walking around in front of the tent. She sat across from Tretona. Whenever Tretona looked up to pass the noodles or to see if her mom needed something brought in from the kitchen, Sister Clayton was looking at her. Tretona felt flustered, but her experience playing Stare helped her not to look away. Sister Clayton would give her a funny little smile and then slowly drop her gaze to Tretona's neck and breasts and hands. It happened several times and Tretona was sure she wasn't imagining it.

Tretona managed not to have to talk to Sister Clayton even after the meal when, as usual, Tretona's mom started bragging about her and Tretona had to answer questions about stuff like the essay contest and her classical record collection. Her mother was so dumb she even wanted her to play some Stravinsky for the group.

But unexpectedly things got out of hand. Troy had gone down in the basement after the noon meal to play. When James Clayton started coughing Tretona immediately figured out what had happened. Troy had her old chemistry set downstairs, and they had supplemented it with muriatic acid from the drugstore, baking soda, lye, cut-up zinc-can lids, fertilizer, and sulfur disinfecting candles left over from when her mom had had scarlet fever.

Tretona always tried to get Troy to be careful, but he liked to make what he called "Mud Pie Mountains"—big, seething, colored mixtures. The best concoctions occurred in the half-gallon glass jar he used as a slop bucket. Today Troy had tried to melt sulfur in a spoon and it had caught on fire. The brimstone fumes got worse and all of a sudden Troy appeared in the gas mask her dad used when he mauled back hay.

Tretona went down to help Troy air out the basement. When she got back upstairs the men and kids were all out in the yard and her mom and Sister Clayton were in the front bedroom with the door shut. Tretona nearly went wild with worry, and it didn't help her any when she saw how puzzled her mother looked when the two of them came out. No one said anything, but Sister Clayton shot Tretona a triumphant glance. Tretona didn't like the looks of the half smile on Sister Clayton's face either.

As soon as the company left, Tretona's mom called her dad into the bedroom to talk. Tretona went crazy. What was she going to do? Try to lie? But they wouldn't believe her. Run away from home? But probably Belinda wouldn't go along. Ask Naomi for help? But she wouldn't buy the leading-Tretona-to-Jesus argument either. The only person in the whole world that Tretona could think of who might be willing to take her in was her Grandmother Getroek, who was really gentle and loving. But then she imagined trying to explain things to her grandmother and knew immediately it'd never work.

Suddenly her mind stopped churning over possibilities and got cold, clear and factual.

1. She and Belinda loved each other.
2. Their love had nothing to do with Jesus.

3. No one would tolerate their love—everyone would try to destroy it.

4. Tretona would never give up that love no matter what, but she wasn't sure about Belinda being able to stick it through.

Tretona pulled her cheeks in tight and made her eyes very hard and dry. She pointed her toes in a little, like Indians did, stuck her hands in her back pockets, and looked straight at her folks' bedroom door.

"Oh, there you are, Tretona," said her mother, suddenly coming out. "We were just discussing what Sister Clayton told us." Tretona was surprised at how calm, even warm, her mother's voice was. "Your father and I have decided we can afford it if you want to go." Only slowly and with much amazement did Tretona finally understand that Sister Clayton had invited her to go along to a Nazarene music camp for teenagers. And Belinda was probably going too. Sister Clayton wanted them to learn duets and practice leading songs in a team the way she and James did. The camp was clear over by St. Louis, but they could get a ride one way with Jim and Lenore (her mother seemed to have become quite chummy with the Claytons all of a sudden). "Lenore thinks you have lots of talent and a great future in church music," her mother said proudly.

A question flashed through Tretona's mind about why Sister Clayton was doing this. But she immediately moved on to the problems of making sure Belinda got to go, convincing her folks she had to have new tennis shoes, working up the piano accompaniment to some of the new choruses Jim and Lenore were teaching them, and figuring out what to use as a suitcase. She also noticed that Sister Naomi and Brother Don didn't seem too thrilled about the camp idea, but she reckoned that might be because it was run by the Nazarenes.

* * *

A few days later they set off in the Claytons' old Buick. The trip was pretty boring. Jim was a cautious, jerky driver and told lots of long, pointless stories. Lenore was sort of broody and didn't say much. Tretona would have liked to sit close to Belinda, but Sister Clayton had piled some junk in the middle of the back seat, saying firmly, "You'll both want to sit by a window." She and Belinda held hands behind the stuff part of the time, but it wasn't very comfortable, and besides, Lenore kept looking back every once in a while and frowning.

They arrived at the camp late on Friday night and the three women were assigned cots in an overflow tent all by themselves. As soon as Jim left, Lenore moved the cots close together and chose the middle one. Everyone turned her back to undress. When they finished Tretona was surprised to see that Sister Clayton was wearing a nice flowered nightgown. Everyone in her own family wore pajamas. Sister Clayton looked younger when she wasn't wearing navy blue and her face seemed a lot softer and prettier when she undid her hair and started brushing it. Tretona really wanted to kiss Belinda goodnight but she didn't have a chance.

As soon as the lights went out Tretona felt Sister Clayton's arm under her. Instinctively she rolled her head up on Sister Clayton's shoulder. Sister Clayton was talking aloud about how much she cared for both of them and how Christ wanted his daughters to love each other. Her voice was soft but Tretona could feel the intensity of her breathing. She put her hand very casually on Sister Clayton's upper chest. Immediately Sister Clayton slipped her hand under Tretona's arm and around her breast.

All of a sudden alarm bells went off in Tretona's mind. What if Sister Clayton was doing the same thing to Belinda?

She vaulted over the middle cot and crawled on top of Belinda.

"What are you doing?" Sister Clayton hissed.

"Just leave us alone," said Tretona. Belinda didn't know what was happening but she responded to the urgency of Tretona's kisses. Sister Clayton watched for a while, saying things like "Better come up for air," and then left. Tretona made love to Belinda more fiercely than she ever had before. When they had finished, Tretona covered Belinda for a long time with her entire weight. Then she put their cots side by side and moved Sister Clayton's several feet away.

When Sister Clayton came back she turned the lights on. She was carrying two wet wash rags and a towel. "Wash yourselves. It smells like pussy in here." Meekly, like two kids with chocolate on their faces, Tretona and Belinda complied. Nothing more was said and Sister Clayton didn't rearrange the cots. Tretona was surprised at how quickly she fell asleep.

The next morning they all attended the big farewell session for the old campers; Saturday was the day when the old batch left and the new people came in. Tretona and Belinda were very impressed with the way the Nazarenes ran their meetings. There was a band with lots of brass as well as a piano and an organ. The chorus was really peppy and sang lots of fast numbers that had four parts going off in different directions. Tretona's favorite was "Oh the Glory Did Roll," and she resolved to learn it and teach it to her brothers and sisters. The most unusual part was the Popcorn Testimony Meeting. The idea was that people should pop up and just explode with praise for what God had done for them, preferably several at one time. In no case should one person finish testifying before someone else started. Some people made long speeches about prayers that had been answered. Others just stood up and gave a canned testimony, such as "I'm glad I'm saved, sanctified, and a Nazarene." Tretona felt like getting up and testifying that she was glad to be a Methodist, but of course she didn't.

That night the women were moved into a cabin. Not all of the new campers had arrived, so they had one corner pretty much to themselves. Sister Clayton and Belinda chose lower beds and Tretona picked the bunk over Belinda's so that she could reach down and hold hands with Belinda after the lights went out. Besides, she was good at climbing up on things. Tretona woke up early the next morning just as the night was turning from black to gray. For some reason she glanced down at Sister Clayton. To her surprise Sister Clayton was awake and staring at her. She was about to turn over and go back to sleep when Sister Clayton slowly pulled her long hair out from behind her head, brought it over her shoulder, and arranged it on top of her breast. Then she laid a finger very gently on her lips to signal Tretona to be quiet. Almost as if she were sleepwalking, Tretona slipped down off the upper bunk and lay beside Sister Clayton.

Tretona closed her eyes as they began to kiss. Belinda had a cozy moist little mouth and her tongue was always shy and gentle. But Sister Clayton's mouth was large and wet and her tongue was like a wild animal's. Tretona felt like she was going to be swallowed alive or turned wrong side out. She almost got scared when Sister Clayton started pulling Tretona's lower lip in between her teeth and sort of bit and chewed it. In defense Tretona kissed back real hard and didn't bother to shield her own teeth, and she boldly put her hand right up under Sister Clayton's nightgown and into her crotch.

Belinda had a soft little cunt that reminded Tretona of a little moleskin purse with a rabbit-fur border. Sister Clayton had wiry hair and her vagina was somewhat like the bubbling mud pots in Yellowstone. Tretona thrust in two fingers and then four as Sister Clayton began to buck like a horse. Tretona was afraid someone—especially Belinda—might wake up from the noise, so she tried to hold Sister Clayton down flat. She hooked one foot onto the side of the bunk and tried to pin Sister Clayton's legs. She got her left arm around Sister Clayton's neck in a wrestler's grip. But then somehow Tretona stopped trying to hold her back and really got into the ride. She found that if she moved her thumb around just right, Sister Clayton really went wild, and then she started biting Sister Clayton on the neck and holding her breasts really hard and doing all sorts of rough stuff that she never would have dreamed of doing with Belinda.

And then Sister Clayton went stiff and shook like she was having little spastic fits and then her body turned all soft and she kissed Tretona's face all over and kept saying, "You devil, you."

After a while Tretona went off to the john and washed her face and hands and combed her hair. She was surprised at how normal her face looked.

Inside she felt very different. She now realized that Belinda might not be the only woman in the world that she could love.

Aphrodisiac

*T*he revolving drum of the multilith printer spun with a rhythmic chatter. Sheet after sheet of clean white paper shot beneath the drum, then jumped into a cradle, each page stamped with Carpenter's face and politics.

It was unnerving. Imagine being in love, and suddenly the object of your affections begins to divide, multiply in a sort of amoebic frenzy, until the world holds a hundred duplicates of the unique person who'd earned your total devotion. What then?

The original Carpenter stood beside the machine, adjusting the feed of paper, correcting the ink flow, talking to me over the gentle noise of the machine. His smooth, boyish face was tilted forward and a sheaf of blond hair was caught behind one lens of his old-fashioned steel-rimmed glasses. Carpenter was twenty-eight, three years older than I, but the only thing about him that looked adult were his hands. They were oversized and tough, ridged along the edges. I have always had great respect for his hands.

"No. I've been meaning to come by and see you people,"

Carp was saying. "Or at least let you know what was up. But I've been occupied with this." He gestured at the stack of handbills rising in the cradle.

It was lunch hour, and Carp was using his free time to run off material for his city-council campaign. Every few years Carp ran for city council, affiliating himself with one or another of the left-wing groups that seemed to come and go in Richmond with the life expectancy of a fruit fly. He had vanished from view a month before; and although I knew about the campaign, I couldn't quite believe that it was the only reason he was staying away. He had to know what was going on, and if he did, he would want no part of it. Carpenter had always been a terrible moralist. I had driven all the way across town during my lunch hour to learn how much Carp knew, and I stood there now in the empty print shop, watching Carp, feeling out of place in my three-piece suit.

"That's the only reason you haven't been around?" I asked. "There's nothing wrong?"

He looked at me, surprised. "Not at all. What could be wrong?"

"Nothing," I mumbled. I invented a reason. "Cathy thought you might be bored with us."

"*Bored?* Lord, no. I'm sorry I haven't been able to see y'all. But this nonsense—"

"Good. Cathy'll be glad to hear that. She was afraid you'd gotten tired of hobnobbing with the bourgeoisie."

He prodded the last sheets of paper through the machine and cut off the power. "On the contrary."

So he didn't know after all. The news pleased me and I could enjoy watching the rubbery way he moved when he stooped to stack his bills and posters. "You like some help with that?" I asked.

"Nope. Friendship doesn't require it."

"For crying out loud, Carp. Carrying your propaganda's not going to subvert me. Besides, that's what you're *supposed* to do," I said, picking up a bundle and trying to hold it so that the ink didn't rub off on my vest. "Subvert, pervert, and seduce. You're not a very good socialist, you know."

"I'm a *r-r-rotten* socialist," he said with a grin and led the way out back to his car.

It took several trips to fill the trunk and I was able to brush clumsily against him each time we passed; for the moment, that was all the contact I needed. Carpenter and I shook hands, promised to visit each other as soon as the election was over, shook hands again and parted. My afternoon at the insurance office was spent reviewing claims, but the work soothed me; I knew I had another life hidden beneath my button-down respectability.

During the next few weeks we saw Carp only in the form of his campaign leaflets and posters. The bills I had seen being run off by the hundreds were suddenly all over town. There were other candidates, and a flood of other people's posters, but it was only Carp's that I noticed. The photograph was old, something saved from a previous campaign; he was dressed in a Robert Hall jacket and the kind of narrow necktie worn by working-class grandfathers. He looked exactly like a kid dressed up for church back home in Nansemond County. Printed beneath the picture were the words *Socialist People's Party*. The incongruity of picture and caption made me think of the bland high school photos you see in the newspaper under such headlines as HONOR STUDENT SLAYS OWN FAMILY.

The picture was suddenly everywhere; the whole world

seemed to have been papered over with Carpenter's face. Wherever I went, surfaces mocked me with his beaming-boy image, the boy in the Sunday school suit, the Socialist People's candidate. He was on telephone poles, on alley walls, on the soaped-over windows of shops that had gone out of business. He even peered winsomely from a wastebasket in the downstairs lobby of the insurance office. Cathy thought it might be funny to peel a poster off and tack it up in the apartment; she called me a stuffy prig when I wouldn't let her.

Cathy and I weren't very happy in Richmond. We had never been very good at meeting strangers, but when we lived in Maryland we had Cathy's family and a few of her friends from college. The only person we knew in Richmond was Andrew Carpenter. Carp and I had come from the same county in southside Virginia. When I met him, he was already halfway through college; I was still in high school. I trailed after him like a puppy, thinking I was only attracted to him because he was what I, foolishly, wanted to be: an intellectual. It was only now, after the insurance company had transferred me to Richmond, that I understood the real reason for the attraction; I understood only because I had tripped over backwards and fallen into it again. Here I was, happily married, and not only had I fallen in love with somebody else, I had fallen in love with a guy.

It bothered me, but not in the way I might have expected. There was no guilt, perhaps only because I was too busy wondering what I could do with this new feeling. I liked the feeling very much and did not want to throw it away. The obvious thing would have been to go to bed with Carp, but I wasn't sure what you could *do* in bed with him. Even if I were capable of it, I thought there should be something beyond that, perhaps something like marriage. I wondered about adoption.

Several weeks without Carpenter passed. Cathy was as bored with Richmond as I was, so bored she finally overcame her snobbery and insisted we buy a television. We hunted for things to keep each other entertained. A week before the election we drove out to the University of Richmond to see *Children of Paradise.* I'd found out that a film society was going to show it and reported the news to Cathy as though it were a gift just for her. But I wanted to see it as much as she did. Our isolation in Richmond had made us very dependent on each other; all our pleasures and desires seemed to blur together. The blurring was nice, in a way, but I found myself missing the sharp edges things had had when we were first discovering each other. Now, we were too easy with each other, even at night when we went to bed.

Cathy was all shivery and excited after the movie. It was a clear, cold October night and we delayed our return home by walking around the campus. I tried to put my arm around her, but she kept breaking away to wave her hands and repeat a favorite line or remember some lush scene. I was very happy, too. Under a streetlight I stopped her and asked to hear the line Arletty uses to invite the actor into her room.

"Hmmmm? Which one?"

"You know. Right after he asks if her door is locked."

She displayed her big teeth in an enormous grin. I often tease her for having a mouth like a cupboard full of china. "Oh, I *love* it!" She clapped her hands and grabbed me by the collar to pull me down to her level. She gave her head a shake, pretending to get into character. Eyeing me from beneath her hood of disheveled hair, she mimicked Arletty's seductive purr: *"What do I have that thieves can steal?"* Then she burst out laughing and shoved me away.

I watched her parade down the walk, her head thrown back so far she couldn't see. She nearly fell over a fire hydrant. I continued my amused strut behind her and didn't catch up again until she had stopped in front of a kiosk plastered with one of Carpenter's posters. She leaned against it and hooked one arm over the picture, pretending it was real. "Be nice to see Andy again. In flesh and blood, I mean."

I clutched her hand and pulled her away. "See him soon enough," I said.

We resumed our walk, leaning against each other's shoulder for support. "You're not bored by Carp?" I asked. It was a silly question, but I wanted an excuse to talk about him. From the start, she had made it clear she enjoyed his company. The first time we had had him over to dinner, Cathy was charmed by the way he had repeatedly interrupted his defense of socialism to identify each piece of classical music played on the stereo with the Warner Brothers cartoon he had first heard it in.

She clicked her tongue. "You keep insisting I should be bored by Andy. Believe me, Scott, I'm not. I actually *like* the goof. And not just because he's your friend, either."

"But why? You've got nothing in common."

"Maybe that's it. Maybe I find him . . . *exotic*." She growled the word. "I don't know. Why does anyone like anybody else? Well for one thing, he's not an insurance person."

"Then you find *me* boring?"

"Oh, get out of here." She butted my shoulder with her head. "Your *friends*, dope. Your friends and Daddy's. Insurance people always seem the same. Cynical about everybody and everything except themselves."

"They're not really friends."

"Okay then, acquaintances. Oh, you know what I mean. But don't worry, Scottie. You're different. You're a mutant."

I gave Cathy a squeeze around the waist and softly whispered in her ear, "And you're my little mutant, too." Our shoulders began to ache; we had to straighten up.

The walkway climbed a small hill and gradually swung to the left. There were fewer lights here and as we walked we saw a full moon slowly shift into the gap between the tall, black dormitories. Close to the horizon, the moon looked enormous, as wonderfully theatrical and fake as the canvas disc used for the Pierrot mimes in the movie. I began whistling one of the tunes that had accompanied the mimes.

"Funny thing," said Cathy, wearily, "but I've gotten so used to seeing Andy's face all over town, I can't even look at the moon without seeing that goof in it."

I laughed with her over her silliness. My eyes, too, were twisting the lunar geography into a copy of Carpenter's face, but I proudly believed my reasons were more dangerous and exciting than Cathy's.

Love. Sloppy, romantic love. Love so clichéd you saw the loved one in the moon. It takes no talent to fall in love, but I was proud to be in love with Carp. I may have been disturbed that I didn't know what to do with it, but I wasn't bothered by the unnaturalness of the love. I was already familiar with natural love, the domestic kind I shared with Cathy. Love with her was love that justified, protected, soothed; it was as commonplace and necessary as a loaf of bread. No matter what tensions might develop between us, my dumb faith in the success of domestic love created the feeling that there was a safety net strung beneath us and that we were absolutely free from danger. It was my love for Carpenter—a sort of ecstatic nervousness—that now supplied me with the missing danger.

Election day. Cathy and I had not been residents of Richmond long enough to be able to vote, but after dinner I suggested we visit Carpenter and sit out the returns with him.

Cathy studied me for a moment, then screwed up her mouth and shook her head. "I don't think we should. He's probably off with some friends. Don't you think?"

"If I know Carp, I'll make a bet he's alone reading. He could probably use some company."

"You really think so?" She was skeptical. Cathy has always been leery of spending evenings with strangers. I promised and teased her into giving in.

Carpenter lived on the edge of the Fan district in a small upstairs apartment behind a shoe repair shop. I had seen the place only once before: walls painted a clinical shade of white, a few straight-back chairs and an unvarnished desk, a wooden floor with no carpet. Tacked above the desk was a solitary picture: an overripe figure of Death towed a frightened monk by his cowl toward places unknown. It was a morbid picture, but oddly it seemed a humanizing touch in the stark setting of the room. An exposed flight of stairs descended from his doorway to the alley.

"So this is where Andy lives?" said Cathy as she followed me up the rattling stairs. The flaking frame shook under our combined weight.

"I've pointed it out to you," I said, rapping on the door.

"Have you?" Holding her embroidered purse against her throat, she looked over the rail at the pile of cans and flattened boxes below. "I don't think so. Are there any rats down there?"

"Big black socialist rats," I said, irritated by her sudden delicacy. She seemed to be in one of her prim and stuffy moods tonight.

The knob turned with a sharp snap and the door opened. A stocky woman with rust-red hair faced us. "Yeah?" she said, arrogantly cocking her head as though she expected us to sell her something. Pop music played in the room behind her.

A female. I was stunned to find a female in Carpenter's doorway. It was a possibility I had never considered.

"Something we can do for you?" the woman asked impatiently, her eyes as black and tiny as the heads of carpet tacks.

"We've come to see Andrew Carpenter," I stammered.

She bellowed into the apartment, "Hey! Turkey! You got visitors!"

"Don't be rude. Ask them in," Carp quietly commanded.

The woman shrugged her big shoulders, motioned us inside, and closed the door.

I advanced nervously, my head bent forward. All over the floor were empty beer cans and jar lids filled with cigarette butts. Next to Carpenter's stocking feet was half a bottle of red wine. He sat rigid in a chair in the center of the room. I was afraid we had stumbled in on something that shouldn't be stumbled in on, but when my eyes finally reached Carpenter's face, I found his smooth cheeks pocked with two enormous dimples and a grim that lifted his eyeglasses halfway up his forehead. "Why, *hello* there," he said warmly. "What brings you people down here tonight?"

"Cordial visit," I said, working up a smile. Cathy stared at the red-haired woman. "We thought you might like company on your big election night. If we're disturbing any—"

"Marsha's my co-worker." Carpenter waved his cup at Marsha, who was studying Cathy. "We had Marsha's gang of undergrads over earlier, but they wanted to get drunk and we'd run out of beer. Political campaigns are supposed to be kept well oiled with alcohol. I keep forgetting that fact." Carp himself did not seem at all well oiled; he spoke with his usual sober cheerfulness. "Marsh. These are the friends I was telling you about. That's Cathy there. And her husband is Scott."

"Pleased to meet you," Marsha said with a smirk. She looked somewhere in her late twenties and wore jeans and a floppy, untucked shirt. Whenever she moved, her breasts bounced inside the shirt like a pair of cats squirming in a bag. She spoke with a deep, bearish voice. "You're the insurance salesman."

"Oh, nothing that adventurous," I said with a nervous laugh. "I don't do any actual selling. I just march figures up and down sheets of paper and make sure they all arrive at the same place. Like the exercises they gave you over and over again in third grade, only now I get paid for it."

"If you don't like your work, get out of it," she said and turned to Carpenter. "You need more chairs. I'll get the one in the bedroom."

"You sit here," said Carpenter, setting his own chair beside Cathy. She smoothed her coat behind her and cautiously lowered her bottom to the chair. She looked down at the radio that sat on the floor, tuned to an AM station. "Marsha's," Carp explained.

No, I didn't like Marsha. And it worried me that she was familiar with Carpenter's bedroom.

"Well, what do you think your chances are with the election?" I asked, trying to forget about Marsha.

"He doesn't want to get elected," Marsha snarled, bringing in the chair. She pushed the chair at me and added, "He's chicken. If he thought he might win, he'd never run."

Carpenter only smiled at the attack and drank his wine.

More cups were brought out; Carpenter sat cross-legged on the floor and poured the rest of the bottle. "Marsha's an interesting person," he said, watching the liquid rise to the same level in each cup. "The token southpaw in the V.C.U. sociology department. According to her, I'm much too conservative, Tory radical. Oh well. I've been called worse." Marsha snorted in agreement. "But it's thanks to her that my name's splashed all over town. She's got the kind of dedication rarely found outside a meeting of Young Republicans."

"Screw you," said Marsha.

More insults followed, and the exchange turned into an argument on politics. Marsha insisted on the need for strong, decisive action. Carpenter advocated a quieter approach. They spoke as though Cathy and I weren't even there. I was able just to sit and watch for clues to their relationship. It was Marsha's strident tone that worried me most; she seemed positively marital, as if she already had him. In Carp's voice, I found nothing. He spoke just as he always did, spinning his ideas with his slow, rural drawl. The southside Virginia accent didn't match the ideology under discussion. It made me think of Gary Cooper cast as Trotsky. Cathy was looking lost and bored and I felt guilty for having misled her. Every now and then I tried to give her a special glance and a nod to let her know she had my sympathy. Her cup of wine sat on her knee untouched. She answered my concern with a brittle smile.

"I know you've heard me say it a hundred times," Carp said. "But if you're going to be a southpaw in this country, you've got to keep your goals limited."

"Must be pitiful to be a defeatist at such an early age," said Marsha.

"Perhaps. But when you have big plans, it's easier to become disillusioned. You get disappointed, maybe over-react, and end up on the other side."

"I hear you," said Marsha. She greeted the possibility with a lip fart, then shifted her nail eyes towards me. "Is that what happened to you?"

"Me? What?" The need to answer took me by surprise. "No, I was never . . . I've been friends with Carp but I . . . at no time. No. I've not been a socialist. Never." I looked around the room for help.

"No," said Carp, smiling kindly. "Scottie's always been a capitalist lackey."

"I see," said Marsha, leaning back. "Very good. I was afraid you were a sellout. But you're the real thing, huh?"

I assured her I was, and attempted a few jokes about the sins I'd committed in the name of the oppressor class. None of the jokes took, and Marsha began to hammer at me about the half-heartedness of my beliefs. Why this? What did I really think about the world I lived in? Carpenter had never violated me in this way, never poked and forced me to twist my feelings into ideas I knew nothing about. I waited for him to come to my aid again, but he simply sat there, amused by what was going on. He had a misplaced faith in my ability to defend myself. Cathy was too lost or bored to help me. I was left to myself, and trotted out the only argument I have ever used on the subject of revolution. "Suppose . . . suppose you're a fish living in a dirty bowl. You got the choice of either putting up with the filth and mess of the dirty water or you can jump out, flop around on the carpet. Maybe get eaten by the cat. So I've decided to stay in the bowl and accept all the imperfections as part of life." I have always been a little proud of that argument without completely believing it. I folded my arms together, assuming that would be the final word and that we could move on to more interesting questions. Such as was Marsha sleeping with Carpenter?

Marsha slammed her heel against the floor. "You can *change* the bowl you live in, you smug little jerk."

CHRISTOPHER BRAM

Cathy suddenly woke up. "What're you two getting so nasty for?" she muttered to her shoes. "You're only talking about *ideas*. Nothing to get nasty about."

"That's only what *they* want us to believe," said Marsha, leaning closer to Cathy and speaking to her as if to an equal. "That these things are *only* ideas. They want us to believe that there's real life over here, and ideas over there, and no connection between the two." Marsha glared at me. "And they want us to think that real life is only a dirty fishbowl you can never change but only talk about. Like the weather."

"In Marsha's mind, *they* are men," Carpenter explained, shaking his head and not making it clear whether or not he agreed with her.

Marsha began to twist a strand of her hair around one finger. "That's a vulgarization of what I believe," she muttered, then picked up the wine bottle and examined it. "Empty," she said. "Pitiful the party has to end so soon. We ought to get some more wine."

I jumped out of my chair and rubbed my hands together. "No, it's getting late, I'm afraid. Cathy and I should be moving on."

Cathy looked up at me over her shoulder. "We don't have to go, do we, Scott? It won't hurt us to stay a little longer."

"You want to stay?" She surprised me. I looked her up and down, wondering about her motives. It seemed masochistic for her to want to stay any longer. "Well. Whatever you say," I said reluctantly. I was afraid of making a scene by insisting we leave. "Uh, since I'm up," I said to Carpenter, "why don't I go get the wine?"

Marsha rose, clomped over to the desk and picked up an Army jacket. "I'll go too."

"That's not necessary."

"Hey, Marsh. Why don't you stay here?" said Carp.

160

"Nope." She turned to me. "I can show you the best place," she insisted, and before I could object again, Marsha and I were outside, headed for the car. With her sneakers planted on my dashboard, Marsha gave directions.

As soon as we were moving down the street she turned to me and said, "Tell me. I'm curious. How come you're foisting your wife on poor old Carp?"

I couldn't understand what she was talking about and spent a good twenty seconds trying to understand before I finally said, "Come again?"

"She's in love with him, isn't she? I always thought your kind kept their wives locked up whenever something like that happens. Never imagined a husband would offer personal delivery. I guess I should find it admirable." She tittered through her nose. "Unless it's just bourgeois kinkiness."

This was hilarious. I couldn't believe it. I nearly choked trying to hold back my laughter. She was so damn right in her general picture of what was going on. And so damn wrong in the particulars. "You know, you're nuts," I said. "What gives you a crazy idea like that?"

"Come off it. You don't have to pretend with me. Sweet little things like that can never hide their feelings. Soon as she walked in, the place smelled like love and kisses."

"My wife is no 'sweet little thing,'" I said, dutifully going to Cathy's defense.

"But she *is*. Sweet, frail, *Cosmopolitan* girl. Not her fault, though."

I didn't like to hear Cathy mocked like this. "I can't . . . I can't *imagine* how you'd see what you see. You wouldn't talk like that unless you were in love with Carpenter yourself."

"Me?" There was a laugh like pebbles dropping onto a snare drum. "If I ever fall in love—and I won't—it'll never be for the likes of good old Carp."

"Then why are you being such a bitch about it?"

"I merely report the obvious."

We pulled up in front of a delicatessen. Marsha ran inside with long, leaping strides. *Cathy in love with Carpenter. Husband delivering wife. Sweet little thing.* Very droll. I kept turning it around and around in my head until Marsha returned with the wine.

Marsha kept her mouth shut for several minutes. I was hoping for complete silence, when she suddenly shifted sideways in her seat and confessed, "I'm needling you. Scott. Can't you see that? I have no obections to what you're doing. It goes along with everything I believe. Sexual democracy." She came closer to me. "But I'm curious why you're doing it. It's not the norm for people of your ilk. Something like this runs against the grain, doesn't it? Or are you and your wife so bored you'll jump at anything?"

"My *ilk?* You think you have me pegged, don't you?"

"I know you a lot better than you think. You're one of those types who thinks to himself, 'I'm complicated. I'm so wonderfully complicated.'" She mimicked my thoughts with a squeaky whimper. "And you take great pride in it. Cozy sensitivity. But, you know? You're not really so complicated. A few contradictions, a few hypocrisies. Things you could reconcile if you put your mind to it. Only you don't want to bother. It would put an end to the cozy notion you're a deep person."

Marsha settled back into her seat. I was relieved to have some distance between us again. I took refuge in silence.

"Of course, you realize your wife doesn't have a black man's chance with Carp."

I refused to rise to the bait.

"Perfect nickname. Carp. He's a cold fish, all right." She

waited for a reply, then snidely added, "Your wife might as well be flirting with a fag."

"Carp's gay?" I asked, trying to hide my sudden interest.

She shifted her big shoulders. "I don't know. You know him better than I do. Is he?"

One of the many idiotic things about the whole idiotic mess was the fact that I did not know Carpenter's sexual affiliation. Through all the years of our friendship, all the letters and visits, there had never been mention of a girlfriend and never any mention of the alternatives. Whenever the subject of love or lust came up, Carpenter only smiled and wiggled his head until the subject went away.

"Don't know," I said to Marsha.

"Might as well be for all the luck she's going to have. Couldn't get him to do *anything* with me," she said, and sighed, "much less fall in love. Not that I'd want that. The love part, I mean."

"You asked Carpenter to go to bed?"

"Why not?" she said, wistfully indifferent.

"And what did he say?"

"I think he laughed. Carpenter can be a jerk."

When we arrived at the apartment, Marsha made a big show of stomping noisily up the stairs, as if to warn them of our return. There was a clownish grin on her face.

We entered and found Cathy and Carpenter exactly as we had left them, seated six feet apart. Cathy's look of discomfort was gone; she appeared relaxed and easy, and not even Marsha's return disturbed her. The radio had been changed to an FM station: a baroque fanfare of trumpets added to the happiness.

"Mountain chablis," Marsha announced proudly, stripping the bag from the bottle. She broke the seal and the wine was passed around while we returned to our positions in the circle. I tried to be sociable by asking for news of the election.

"Andy's writing a book," Cathy declared. She was quite excited that Carpenter had confided this to her; the outcome of the election seemed to interest her as little as it did the candidate.

"He's always writing some book," I said. "What's this one about?"

"It's, uh, fictional institutions."

Carpenter politely corrected her. "Institutional fictions. Assumptions about reality that make up the basis of different social institutions." He gave himself an embarrassed sigh.

Marsha smiled at me, apparently reading my thoughts and highly amused by them. But she could not have been reading them correctly. I gave no consideration at all to her goofy ideas about Cathy's affections. Marsha was a joker, I decided. I felt a fondness for her now that I knew she had failed and that I wouldn't have to compete against her. And I felt a great fondness for Cathy because she seemed happy now and I no longer had to feel responsible for her discomfort. I was set free to sit back and enjoy the fact that I was in love with Carpenter.

Marsha left shortly after midnight, and things became very peaceful. There were times when there was nothing to say, but there was no embarrassment over the stretches of silence.

As Cathy and I got ready to leave, Carpenter said he was pleased the nonsense was over and that he'd be free to see us more often. There was a prolonged exchange of smiles and handshakes, then Carp watched from his open door as Cathy and I made our way down his stairs.

The interior of the car was cold as a refrigerator; the heater

I had heard Cathy express similar sympathy for her father, for my older brother, and before she had met him, for Andrew Carpenter. When I stopped at the next traffic light, I was able to bend over, kiss the top of her head, slip my hand beneath her long hair, touch the down on her neck.

There was eerie energy in our lovemaking that night. Sex again became the invention of two teenagers petting under the bushes, only with adult privacy now, and no restraints. Each intimate move was smoothly answered and there was a slippery, licensed roving of hands and mouths. I did not fake any of it. I could not pretend it was Carpenter who shared me. No, it was definitely Cathy whose knees and shoulders, breasts and hair were the targets of all my energy and it was irrelevant that the energy had been created by my feelings for Carpenter.

In that extended instant after sex, before you remember you are not alone, I felt pleased with myself and the life I lived. Gradually, I reawakened to Cathy, and found her looking at me with one open eye.

"You—" she began lovingly, and never finished. Suddenly, she rose up on her knees and stretched her body like a cat. She sank down again and rested her chin on my chest.

We lay like that for a very long time. I could look past the loops of her hair and see our legs, stacked together like hand-dipped candles.

"Know what?" she finally said. There was a bit of flirtation in her voice, and the warm breath with the words tickled my chest.

"What?"

"Kind of funny but—"

"Yes?" I closed my eyes and brushed my hand up and

did not begin to ease the cold until we were halfway to the suburbs. Cathy stretched over the console and huddled close to my side.

My head ticked with possibilities. In the narrow space of a couple of hours, I had found my path blocked and then had found the obstacle totally imaginary. Carpenter was available after all; my love had come through the ordeal stronger than before and I knew I would have to act on it. I would take my chances; I would actually do something with this incredible feeling I carried. There would be love, out in the open, dangerous love, love so strong it would be indistinguishable from fear. The only question was how to move Carpenter to join me in it.

"You've certainly been spacy tonight," said Cathy, her face buried in my coat.

"Yeah? Just toward the end. I got to thinking about things. You were pretty spacy yourself. At the beginning."

"Was I?" she asked sleepily. "Yeah, I guess so. We're not the world's greatest guests. Wonder if we could get tutored somewhere on social charm. Take night classes in party behavior, maybe."

"Don't know."

"Oh, doesn't matter. I think we could've acted any old way and Andy wouldn't have minded. Scott? Did you think that girl and Andy were lovers? I mean when we first walked in, did you think that?"

"Hard to imagine her being anyone's lover. Too dogmatic. Too much the—you know." I wanted to say "bitch" but the word angers Cathy. "Why? Did you think that?"

"At first. But I talked to Andy while you were out and I got the impression they were barely friends. She really was too dogmatic. I feel sorry for people like that. They must be very lonely before they can go and get like that."

down the solid muscles on either side of her back. I was waiting to be teased or complimented.

"I think I have a slight crush on your Andrew Carpenter."

She spoke too soon to disguise it. And all along I had thought her excitement had been in response to mine, that it had been something I created in her. "Do you mean . . . you're in love with him?"

"*Noooo*. Nothing stupid like that. Do you think I'd tell you if it was something like that?" She hugged me around the waist and giggled, then looked up at me with her lower lip sucked behind her front teeth, grinning while she watched and waited for me to share her amusement.

My hand drew tiny circles on the cooled mounds of her bottom.

"No," she said. She had to shift her eyes away from my face. "No. It's just a silly crush. All in my head. Nobody could *really* fall in love with Andy." There was a tremor in the pupils of her eyes as they looked straight into mine again. "You dope!" she suddenly laughed. "You have nothing to fear," and she reached up to sweep some hair back from my forehead.

Slashed to Ribbons in Defense of Love

"*I*t's about time you decided to wake up! We have a brunch at one o'clock, as you very well know."

Gary was up, dressed, sitting across the room sipping coffee and smoking a cigarillo. He'd been out; the Sunday *Times* sat unopened on a chair nearby.

"It's almost twelve now. A cab will take at least fifteen minutes. If we can *find* one. Go shower. You know you take forever in there."

Behind Gary's head, sunlight came in through the sky-lighted dressing room and the flecked fibers of the shoji screen. Spence could see the gold flecking on the rice paper very clearly today. The undulating fields of lacquered flowers were backlighted, bright as persimmons. Gary's face was in shadow.

"I want you to know beforehand that this brunch is extremely important to me. Arnie has invited Seitelman, the Oriental art expert. I've been trying to get near him for months. I want him to come look at those *Monoyama* scrolls I picked up last month."

Gary exhaled blue smoke. It floated into the sunlight, turned gray, then yellow, then gray again. He exhaled again and a second cloud rose to meet the first in a billow. It spread thinly, forming a tiny tornado around the head of the smiling Shinto statue precariously perched on a wall shelf. The Shinto idol kept smiling; it never seemed to notice the smoke descending to form a flat halo directly over Gary's head. Spence noticed, though. He laughed.

"I'm not kidding, Spence. Arnie's gone to a lot of trouble to get Seitelman. And it will take a lot of tact to keep him there. So I don't want any interference from you. Is that clear?"

Gary exhaled forcefully and broke the halo. He began picking at the edge of the cup he was drinking from, as though it were crusted with something. It was his favorite china, from the Northern Sung, and invaluable. Spence never touched it. He only used china that could be dropped— or thrown. Gary frowned. Spence turned over in bed.

"As soon as you've met him, go to the other end of the room or table or wherever we are. And stay there. And Spence, do try to keep your pin-sized knowledge of art to yourself. No one is interested, I assure you."

If Gary weren't dressed, if he were still in bed, he would have been vulnerable. Spence was bigger, stronger. He'd roll Gary over, pin him down, wrestle with him: anything to make him shut up. Sometimes fucking helped. But Gary wouldn't fuck now. He was already dressed. He'd been up for hours. Up smoking one cigarillo after another. Up drinking one cup of coffee after another. Up scheming about the art and Seitelman. Up, thinking, thinking, thinking.

"I don't even know why Arnie and Rise invited you. I suppose as a compliment to me. Either that, or they think it's the enlightened thing to do."

Enlightened, my ass! Spence thought. Ah, enlightenment.

Spence could see it all. He and Gary were on the Johnny Carson Show. Johnny was asking Gary about his career as New York's most successful male model in decades. Gary was saying how boring it all was—boring and superficial. The only real benefits, he would admit, were the money he made, the investments—the hotel in the Colorado Rockies, the model agency he owned on the Coast—and the freedom it gave him. He was such a prig he wouldn't realize Johnny was looking for a sensational exposé, hinting at it with all those sly innuendos and lousy one-liners. Gary would begin talking about Oriental art, detailing the difference between *Kano* and *Genre*, and those with *Ukiyo-E*. Johnny and his audience would be bored stiff. In desperation, the talk show host would turn to Spence and ask if he shared Gary's interests. "Only fucking," Spence would answer. Tumult, Delight. The camera would remain on Spence as he went on, describing the last orgy he attended, holding Johnny and the audience rapt. Enlightenment ruled all!

"Don't think I'm going to ask you to *behave* at this brunch. I know that will only incite you to turn it into a three-ring circus."

Spence turned over again. The sunlight was above the shoji screen now, creeping towards him along the arabesques of the Shiraz carpet. More sun came in through the side windows, lightening the dark corner where Gary sat in his Regency wing chair, next to the little Hepplewhite table. Everything Gary had was either antique or invaluable. Everything but Spence.

"Seitelman doesn't socialize much. Arnie says he's very sensitive. So even you can fathom that this brunch ought to be as pleasant as possible."

Gary's head was in the light now. He shaded his eyes. His arms, neck and face were a perfect tan from Long Island summers and Caribbean winters, so evenly tan he could be a Coppertone advertisement. Spence was tan too. Spence also passed his summers at Amagansett, his winters in Dominique or Palm Springs or St. Thomas; they were all interchangeable by now.

"The other guests either know you already or have been warned. Try not to lecture Kate Halliday about Jung today. *She's* the psychoanalyst. Not you."

Spence leaned over the bed, opened one of the drawers built into the bedboard, and lifted out a flowered cloissoné box. A gift from Gary. Everything was a gift from Gary. A tiny silver spoon was attached to the side of the box by a silver turnaway hasp. Spence removed the spoon, opened the box, dipped the spoon and lifted a tiny mountain of snow-white powder. Gary always kept cocaine in the house. He said it was the only civilized drug: it costs an arm and a leg and you need a bushel basket of it to get hooked. Spence propped himself up against the pillows, held a finger to one nostril, inhaled through the other one, then reversed the process.

"Christ! Spence! You're not even awake and you're already into that!"

Spence had closed the box. Reconsidering, he reopened it and snorted twice more. Carefully—he was already feeling the rush—he closed the box and replaced it in the drawer. Then he slumped back.

"Didn't you have enough last night? You were like a maniac. Chasing that dark little number around with your spoon all night. He was covered with it when he left."

Wasn't it Beckett who said that a light isn't necessary, that a taper would do to live in strangeness if it burned faithfully? Yes. Beckett. A taper, Spence thought, and a spoon of coke.

The sun was playing hide and go seek in the infrequent

gray hairs among the chestnut brown of Gary's head: They would glint for an instant, then die away, glint somewhere else, and die away. Little signals. Maybe a glint was all you needed. And a spoon of coke, of course.

"I hope you're not going to wear these filthy denims again?"

Gary threw the pants at Spence. They hit the side of the bed and fell. Motes of dust shook off them, rose in the air and performed an intricate ballet to a silent score.

"When was the last time you washed them? People know you're coming a hundred yards away. You have so many new, clean slacks in the closet, Spence. Why do you insist on wearing these?"

Spence wondered if dust motes had senses of perception.

"I don't care if you make a good impression today. I would rather you made no impression at all. But there are certain rules of hygiene. I'm surprised you don't have lice. And those people you call your friends are no better. God, what a bunch! The Allies' liberation of Bergen-Belsen couldn't have been more unsavory than that party you took me to last week."

Could dust motes be sentient? Even intelligent? Look how they danced! Spence shook the denims once more. More dust motes flew up into the sunlight. God, they were lovely when they danced. Stately.

"While Seitelman and I are discussing our business, why not talk to Rise? She always asks about you. She wants to help you. She really does know a lot of useful people."

Could man communicate with dust motes? They had to be intelligent to dance like that. So organized!

"Rise thinks I'm holding you back from doing something wonderful. *Me!* If they only knew how shiftless you are. Someone who needs an hour just to get out of bed."

Spence would ask the dust motes to dance for Gary.

"You have to begin to do something with your life. You can't just hang around here and party all the time."

No. Gary wouldn't recognize a million dust motes dancing for him.

"I'm not saying you have to be a great success. You don't even have to earn a lot of money. But just do something!"

If communicable, and friendly, the dust motes might be persuaded to dance around Gary's head. Then, one by one, without his noticing it, they could enter his ears, his nose, his mouth. One by one. Little by little. So subtly Gary wouldn't notice a thing, until it was too late. At first he would cough a little. Then he'd begin to gag. His multicolored eyes would begin to fill up with tears. Then he'd really begin choking. His handsome, craggy features would be distorted in agony. It would be a sad struggle.

"If you weren't bright, it would be different. But you are. Imaginative too. Why, I've never met anyone with as many crazy ideas as you have. Write them down. Draw them up. Make them work for you."

No fingerprints on the throat. No murder weapon at all. Spence wouldn't even have to get out of bed. The perfect murder. He could see the headlines already:

WEALTHY MALE MODEL DIES

MYSTERIOUSLY IN UPTOWN TRIPLEX.

NO CLUES.

Spence would confess, naturally. He'd call the press and explain how he'd entered into a conspiracy with the dust motes, how they'd waited patiently for his signal to attack. He'd explain that dust motes are not only sentient, but intelligent, too. He'd reveal their highly organized cultural heritage—based on their major pastime, the art of the sunlight dance.

"We could turn the greenhouse into a studio for you. We hardly ever use it. And that big closet, that could be used as a darkroom. Arnie would help find you a distributor. He knows *everyone.*"

At first his confession would be ignored. Spence might be asked to take a lie detector test, a mental examination even. He'd pass it with flying colors, return to the triplex—his, now that Gary was gone; he'd have almost unlimited resources. Once home, he'd contact the dust motes again. He'd study their dance patterns, draw diagrams—he could see them as variations of the double helix already. It would take years of study to get to understand their habits, their customs. But it would be worth it.

"You know I'll pay for whatever lessons or extra equipment you need. It's just that you have to do something, Spence. Man cannot live by partying alone."

He'd compile his findings, edit them carefully and send an article to *Scientific American*. They'd be impressed. They'd print it with four-color diagrams and half-page photographs he'd taken of the dances. In an editorial, he'd be hailed as a pioneer. He'd call his new science Motology.

"Jack and I talked about you last week at Ron's. He thinks this crazy life you're leading is simply compensation for having no real motivation. Everyone needs a goal."

Spence would go beyond science. He'd wait until his work was fully accepted. Then he'd reveal the true meaning of the dust motes' dance, how it embodied their philosophy of life, endless flowing, total dance. He'd try to show how this could be of supreme advantage to people, too. He'd be the first and foremost Theomotologist in history.

"Without a goal, you're working against yourself all the time. Kate said so, too. And she ought to know."

Naturally, Theomotology would attract many others. To

stay ahead, Spence would specialize. He was certain the dust motes held the secret of levitation: He'd learn it from their elders and apply it. NASA would approach him. Imagine floating immense spacecraft on molecular motology. MAN FLIES TO PLUTO ON DUST the headline would read in the *New York Times.*

"You don't have to be self-defeating, you know. You and I aren't in competition. I'm done now. Retired. It's your turn, Spence."

On Pluto, Spence would make his greatest discoveries: he'd find out how dust motes propagate. Beginning as nonessential carbon crystals from pollution, they develop externally—like all crystalline forms—by simple geometric accretion. On Pluto, of course, there would be no pollution. The motes would have to evolve along other lines to survive.

"What kind of life is this for you, Spence? I have my friends, my businesses, my collections. What do you have?"

At first the adjustment would be difficult; all selective evolution was. Millions, perhaps trillions of them would fail to develop, and perish. But one day it would just happen. One mote would make the changeover, and discover how simple it was. The others would follow. Spence would be hailed as a new Darwin.

"Spence, are you *listening* to me? I asked you a question."

Spence would remain on Pluto. He'd crystallize himself.

"Spence? You haven't fallen asleep again?"

He already suspected the minuscule viruses found in every living body were crystal compounds. He would use them as a point of focus for the process.

"I see you moving. You're awake. Are you getting up today?"

It would take years, possibly decades, for the process of autocrystallization to work. Meanwhile he would derive nourishment from airtight gardens in which only nitrogen-high greens were grown. He suspected the crystallization would require absolute stillness.

"It's ten minutes to one, Spence. I'm going. If you aren't getting up, I'm going alone."

Spence might be four hundred years old when his last remaining living tissues, the stomach lining, crystallized.

"And when I get home, you and I are going to fill out that registration application on the back of the Film School catalogue. If you insist on acting like a child, you'll be treated like one."

On Earth Spence would be a legend.

"Since classes won't begin for another month or two, you'll have time to get a job. I know plenty of people who need work done in their gardens or in their apartments. That'll keep you busy."

On Pluto Spence would metamorphose into pure crystal. He'd be immortal.

"I've put up with your nonsense long enough. I will not have you lying around the house stoned all day. And if you don't care for my plans, you know where the door is."

Spence would disperse into many smaller crystals, all of them immortal.

"That's *it*. Either go to work or get out!"

Millions of crystals levitating around the universe.

"Spence! Are you listening? Are you?"

"Fuck you," Spence said.

"I see it's clear then. I'll be back by four. You have three hours to make up your mind. And make up that bed when you decide to get out of it."

Gary left the room. A few minutes later, Spence heard closet doors crack open and shut downstairs. Then the front door slammed.

Gary had never talked like that before, never about going to work or leaving. He must be nervous as hell about meeting this Seitelman. Perhaps if their meeting worked out all right at brunch, Gary would forget what he said, forget this morning's hysteria. Fat chance. That would probably only convince him he was right. Gary was so terrified of being thought inconsistent he always did precisely what he said he would do, even if it went against his best interest. Ah well, Spence thought. He'd at least have three more hours of peace. He'd make breakfast, listen to some music, enjoy himself while he still could—until the ax fell.

The sun had already reached halfway up the sheets. Spence threw them onto the floor. It was warm, hot, really. Hot as Mexico. The way the sun advanced along the room, it would take another hour for him to be completely bathed in sunlight. He wouldn't even have to go out onto Gary's terrace to sun today.

Those Who Are Dreaming

> *Where is he? He is everywhere, he*
> *is not a character, he is a person,*
> *and therefore general.*
> —Frank O'Hara,
> *Those Who Are Dreaming:*
> *A Play About St. Paul*

1

*T*he room is small, high in a white house with many gables and a view toward the bay. Beyond the bay a thin arm of land circles the harbor affectionately; beyond the land is the sea. The harbor is safe, calm, its entrance protected from the perils of night and fog by a small lighthouse steadily blinking blue-green, like a cat's eye. Today, the fogburns off late, the sunlight lies palely on the water; in the distance a dog takes his time nosing along the surf line. Over all, the two foghorns call to each other at intervals, sometimes sounding together, a slightly dissonant chord in some minor key.

In her room is a couch, and a table with a lamp whose gentle light at night softens the contours of the room. The room holds no surprises; a sea breeze billows the curtains, filling it with a briny, sunny smell, enlarging it like the drawing in of a breath. Outside from a near distance is a hammering of some sort, then a pause; then low male voices, then a pause. The hammering begins again.

Over all the two foghorns call to each other at intervals, sometimes sounding together a slightly dissonant chord, in some minor key.

A woman is at the high window, watching the people on morning porches drinking coffee and reading papers. She rests her chin on the back of the couch and watches the light on the water, the flags flapping. She is alone. There is no plan of how her story will continue and no real history of what it has been. It is as if she were playing solitaire, each turned card signifying some action that might be taken, some thought she might consider. She is a passive, yet longing observer of these cards, these signs. She dwells on them and takes no action on what they say to her.

Another breeze tosses the ash from her cigarette onto the mauve carpet. She watches it for a moment, then rubs it with the toe of her bare foot. She mustn't go too fast. Overhead a small plane drones by.

She is holding herself in preparation for two others who will arrive today on the boat from Boston; both are her lovers. She has not planned what she will say to them, has not speculated about what might happen. She watches the water and smokes, waiting for the ferry horn. The words she thinks of make no sense to her, are unimportant. What she does during the next several days will be entirely in response to what these two will say to her, to what they will do. She feels as if her strength were flowing out in a slow turning. She feels no tension, no caring; just a longing passiveness. Only the waiting is real now.

Idly, she begins to touch her body. She feels her breasts, soft but small through her thin Indian shirt. Her hands relax and go downwards, her belly arching slightly beneath their movement, and she lowers herself beneath the breeze onto the couch. She moves her fingers, long and brown from the sun, along the inside of her thighs until she encounters that part of her that produces a different sensation, more poignant, more urgent. She moves rhythmically against herself and finally as she closes her eyes tightly she hears the sound of the ferry horn, echoing as if from her own throat.

For a few moments, she lies calmly; then she rises, straightening herself, and reaches for her sunglasses.

***

"Take off your sunglasses, I can't see your eyes." The older woman speaks above the murmur and clinking of glasses in the sidewalk café. She still has a firm body although it is no longer youthful, and she is dressed stylishly. Her hair, not naturally auburn, is tastefully done and blends subtly with the sunlight. The younger woman removes her dark glasses and places them on the white metal table top. "Can we have another, Will?"

Will, startled, focuses his gaze through his thin, wire-framed glasses, and a waiter appears. "I forget what you're drinking, Mrs. Medina."

"Vermouth Cassis."

"Very well." The waiter departs.

"Very well indeed."

Will's sandy hair curls lightly on his neck. He is a boy, really; he paints with words. Huge canvases covered with words, phrases, the sounds of animals. He carries them constantly in his head. Although his shoulders are broad, he reacts with confusion when asked to play the male. Mrs. Medina is amused by this and has startled him several times.

The younger woman stares at her glass, which she has been turning in a small pool of water, then raises her eyes to look beyond her two companions to the street, which has filled with a jostling noon crowd: tourists, summer people, people in from the beaches. Their various exotic scents mingle with the smells of pizza and frying clams.

"I once knew a woman," Mrs. Medina begins, "this was before I married—"

Will pushes his glasses up on his nose; the town hall clock strikes one. "Were we here together once, in the winter, during a snowstorm?" he asks the younger woman.

"You know we were."

Mrs. Medina rises. "Shall we get some lunch?"

On the beach, Will is lovely; he attracts the attention of several men who pass by, giving him dark glances. He misses the glances, since he has a towel over his eyes.

The young woman raises herself on her elbows. "Mrs. Medina is asleep."

"Where?"

"In my room."

Will removes his towel and puts on his glasses. "What does that mean?"

She shrugs. "Nothing." She lies back down.

"Well, what is it then?" She is silent. He turns over and puts his arm about her belly. "You're nice and brown." She smiles.

After a while she says, "Let's walk up there into the dunes for a minute." He looks at her solemnly.

Behind the dunes she kneels in the hot sand and lowers his nylon briefs.

He comes quickly, his cheeks wet, and pulls her head convulsively against his body, his hands tight in her hair. He falls back softly into the sand. She sighs and rubs the curly golden hair on his abdomen, letting the sun dry him. She leans over him and peers intently into his closed, peaceful face. Nearby, someone cries out; there are others in these dunes. She imagines she is the only woman.

The sun is brilliant. Will rests lightly in the sharp dune grass; she studies him for a long while. She wakes him when he begins to turn red. "You can stay if you want, I need to wake Mrs. Medina," she says.

"What else is there to do?" he asks. The tide is coming in.

***

"You smell like semen," says Mrs. Medina. Mrs. Medina smells of Madame Rochas. The younger woman draws away from her and begins slowly to undress. "Is he nice to make love to?"

She nods yes.

"Can you work out what is happening to you then?"

The younger woman steps into the shower. Mrs. Medina nods to herself, then moves gracefully to the window in her emerald and cream flowered gown. She draws aside the curtain. The hot glare of the day is cooling into a slowly bluing sky over the sea.

"I think we were *all* here during that snowstorm," she says, after a while.

At night, Mrs. Medina holds the girl (that is how she thinks of her) loosely in her arms, hearing the cry of the foghorns, sensing the fog, feeling it dampen the sheets. The girl is restless, dreaming; her body moves against the older woman's as if to awaken a passion. Mrs. Medina thinks this is all she has now, all she has to give. She wakes the girl softly, touching her breasts. She tastes the saltiness of her neck but is afraid to kiss her, afraid of that youthful intimacy. Her hands move over the girl as if they were not part of her; the girl responds in half sleep, without a sound.

Mrs. Medina pulls herself up beside the girl and listens as her breathing calms and returns to a sleeping rhythm. Car lights reflect briefly on the ceiling. She wonders for a moment where the cynicism is that was supposed to come with age. Although she does not consider herself old, and in fact is not, she wonders where the experience is that she can follow from beginning to end, with no turns, no surprises. Should she expect this experience? Yes, certainly, after years of waiting patiently for a sign that some circle was near completion; years of pushing against a presence that gave, deceptively, again and again; of finding always that she passed through the presence entirely, as easily as through a phantom, and that the circle had twisted and begun again. Yes, she should have been cynical, or at least indifferent, but going on was a type of cynicism, perhaps?

With this thought she falls asleep, the girl's head like a child's against her breast.

***

"I do remember that snowstorm, and we were all here. You came later, Will, because the airfield was closed." Will nods, remembering. "It was only last year, last winter. After the storm that day—don't you remember?—we almost froze on the beach, watching the dark red sun set fiercely into a sea of black clouds. And an old car was on fire in the dunes, burning quietly, nobody around." Will nods again and turns nervously in his chair. "She's coming, Will. We can get coffee at least, can't we?" Her doctor had advised against coffee. "Where did you sleep?"

He sighs. "With a friend. Someone I got to know."

"Well, tonight I will sleep at the Inn; you can stay with her."

He grimaces. "I don't like—" He rests his palm on the side of his face and turns his head. "How is she to sleep with?"

Mrs. Medina raises her eyebrows. "There are differences involved here. You must find your own intimacies." She pauses. "Sometimes I don't like it either; it confuses my sense of beginnings and endings."

Will says, "I'm starting to get an idea of something."

"Well, work it out then." She rises. "I'm flying up to Boston for the day. Enjoy the beach. I'll see you at dinner."

They are on the beach. The tiny cries of gulls sound high above the surf. He studies her back, the soft blond hairs along her spine. She wears no top but has kept on her briefs. She is breathing softly and he is filled with a sudden urgency for her.

"I'm staying with you tonight. Mrs. Medina has agreed."

She rolls on her back and shades her eyes with her hand. "No," she says. "No, it won't do."

"Why am I here then?" he says, suddenly very young in his anger.

She reaches for her top and sits up; his eyes follow her breasts, the movement of her arms. "Why do you ask now? You've never asked, not for a long time." He is silent. "It's how I want it." She lights a cigarette. He grasps his chest with his arms and watches her brush the sand idly from her thighs. Sensing his look, she begins to move her hands more purposefully along the inner parts of her legs. Although he is sitting, he feels his legs weaken, but he says nothing for a while, until he feels her watching him. Then, when he speaks, his words catch against the dryness of his throat.

These are days of bright, brilliant heat. The beaches are strewn with bodies: burning, hypnotized by the sun. At midday, the sea is white. Couplings in the dunes and in the shaded rooms of old white guest houses occur spontaneously, compulsively, in response to the heat. At night, when the sand cools, and darker, private areas regain their density, meetings are more intense, sometimes violent.

In a darkened bar two women are involved in an explicitly erotic dance, oblivious to the groups at tables and at the bar who pretend not to watch. They are dancing to music with a heavy beat but are not moving harshly; they move almost against the rhythm, circling about each other, touching a waist, a hand. One of the women draws her partner's hips forward and holds them tightly against her own, against the movement of their bodies; their eyes never leave each other's eyes; they are swallowed into one another entirely. As the music dissolves into a harder, quicker beat they kiss, briefly but intensely, and leave the floor. The others stir in their chairs. There is an expulsion of breath. The sexual tension can almost be inhaled. Arms touch at the bar, breasts brush in the line waiting for the john.

The music is louder now, building toward closing time. The dance floor is filled with female bodies dancing a ritual from some unpronounced part of their pasts. There are no partners; there are only bodies moving, bodies touching, the smell of female sweat. They are the hunters tonight, theirs is the celebration. There is no story; only the movement, the locking of eyes, the rhythm of a sexuality they have been conditioned to forget.

The bartender calls *time*, and formal pairings begin again. The two women who were dancing by themselves are dreamlike in anticipation. Release from this room into the night will provide them with the energy they need to carry them the three blocks to their welcoming bed. Autumn seems very far away.

Mrs. Medina and the girl, with their own urgency, pass two women embracing passionately in a doorway. "You should be with one of them," Mrs. Medina says.

"I am," the girl replies.

They turn down an unlit, sandy side street, toward the beach; the street is lined with old frame buildings. They move beyond them and approach the sand and the quiet lapping surf. To the east, the moon is rising, three-quarters full over the bay; the shore lights swing southward along the curve of the Cape, to Truro and Wellfleet. On the beach are other pairs of bodies at discreet distances and one or two people alone; the darkness obscures their actions. The girl sits on the sand, which is still slightly warm from the day, and makes a movement with her hand that Mrs. Medina thinks she understands. "Here?" Mrs. Medina asks, watching her intently. "Let me at least put my jacket down."

She kneels and grasps the girl's hips, then moves one hand slowly down between her breasts, across her belly, to part her thighs. The girl makes a sound in her throat and Mrs. Medina lowers herself to her side, thinking of what most other women of her age might be doing at this moment: sleeping beside a snoring husband, waiting for the first pain of that final blow to the heart. Instead. *Instead.* She wants the girl very much.

Afterward, the girl lies sprawled in the sand: Mrs. Medina's body aches as she raises herself on one elbow and sees Will sitting a few feet away. They stare at each other for a moment, then Mrs. Medina stands up. She and Will begin to walk softly along the damp sand close to the water, keeping the girl in view. Mrs Medina smokes.

"Why did you come *here?*" Will asks.

"It seemed that was what she wanted." Mrs. Medina shrugs.

"Ah." Will nods. "I was sleeping on the beach, you see." They turn and head back to where the girl is lying. "She saw me, you know. She knew I was there."

Mrs. Medina raises her eyebrows. "Is that so. Well what could she do?"

"I could have left. But I saw she didn't want me to." His glasses are misting with a fine salt spray.

They stop as they see the girl sit up some yards in front of them. Mrs. Medina turns to Will. "Did I look grotesque, Will? Is this a thing for me to be doing?" The girl has risen and is staring out across the bay towards the tiny lighthouse on Long Point.

Will touches Mrs. Medina lightly on the shoulder. "Sleeping here is grotesque," he says.

Someone down the beach begins to play a flute of some sort; Will turns and follows the sound, disappearing quickly into the darkness.

My bones ache from all this dampness, Mrs. Medina thinks. She hopes Will has a warm blanket.

The girl sleeps in Mrs. Medina's arms, smelling of a musky, salty, female odor, her skin damp. Mrs. Medina sleeps lightly and does not dream.

It is difficult to describe the lack of direction, the absence of cause and effect, the impossibility of following one action to its natural consequence that mark the days in a resort town such as Provincetown in July. If anything, there is a series of encounters, a series of series that do not begin or end but are simply part of a pattern whose design would be the same whether traced in a single room or in the entire town. Relationships are formed on more singular, fundamental impulses than in other places and other seasons; people choose not to relate them to what their lives may be back in the city or wherever they come from, to who or what may be back there waiting for their return. Those who wish to make more out of this life, to find some controlling factors to it, are almost always disillusioned. Personalities vanish. A night may be decided by an accidental tilt of the head.

During the days, the heat is a narcotic. The sun burns off the fog, which rises from the sand, lapping around the bodies, lying vulnerable, passive, as if drugged on the beaches. There are no sudden movements; even the eyes dull. An occasional racing dog, a young boy doing a graceful ballet along the surf, the constant passage and re-passage of the parade of searching eyes just below the sea of towels: all are observed through half-closed, expressionless eyes.

The ambience is sexual, but encounters are enjoyed with a certain indifference, a passion dazed by the heat. The sun indulges the body, enters and surrounds it, plays in its rhythms. At noon, the body turns in the hot white sand, in air that is white, too. The sea glances fire. The dune grass rustles dryly in the sea breeze. In town, fragrant smoke billows from wooden seaside decks where hamburgers are drowned in blue cheese and downed with heavy mugs of beer. Over all the gulls swoop and dip, and the beat of disco music thrusts incessantly.

The hours, the days move around each other as if in a great twisted waltz; the dancers move in and out of each other's terrible grasp as if there were no boundaries to the body. There are not, really; there is only the dance, the exchange of energy, the spinoff into the territory of other eyes and promises, the synthesis into a single vertiginous body that turns through feverish days cooling into nights; the body, released from its hypnosis by the sun, explodes the energy it has gathered into an androgynous mating that consumes night beaches, doorways and dampened beds and expends itself before the dawn, leaving the soft slap of the surf, the hoot of the foghorns and the creeping fog.

The evenings begin with a shift of color: the sea becomes blue again; the dimming heat releases individuals back into their ordinary colors. Those on the beaches leave for guest rooms, showers; from there, into the streets; the gentle blue-rose of the sunset lies high and calm above the darkening waters of the incoming tide. In seconds the light will change again, the rose will become scarlet, the blue indigo.

For about one hour, the town is gentle, almost exquisite, in anticipation.

2

Mrs. Medina and Will were sitting in the same streetside bar. The girl was at her guest house, showering.

Will was very serious. "I wish I could feel a little better about myself, about all of this. I don't like not knowing where it's going, *why* things happen. Why I can't say I don't like it," he shrugged, "why I go on with it. Probably I don't belong here, I'm waiting for someone to tell me I should go." He glanced up through his glasses at Mrs. Medina, who looked quite elegant this evening as she sat smoking: her hair settled softly about her face, a dark blue silk blouse billowed loosely from her arms, her legs, in well-cut white trousers, crossed casually.

After a moment, she said, "Years ago, before I married Mr. Medina, I worked in the Paris office of the *Tribune*. I was a good journalist and had some useful social connections. I covered several—more than several—important social and political events during those years, none of which you will remember. It was my business, and I took it very seriously, to track people about, to catch a train with an hour's notice to Vienna or Geneva to follow someone who was selling a Rembrandt, or selling his soul, or simply on the heels of his wife's lover." She paused.

The pianist in the bar across Commercial Street had begun quietly to play something by Legrand, the candles on his piano flickering in small orange pots.

"In those days I lived in a hotel around the corner from the Place Vendôme—do you know Paris? No.—on the Rue St. Honoré. Interesting people stopped there, those who didn't care for the ostentatiousness of the Ritz, who wanted a little more privacy but service just as attentive. The hotel was built around a large stone courtyard where in nice weather one could have a meal or a drink. I was having my coffee there one summer morning, I recall it was sunny, and a young woman came in alone. She was tall and her hair was dark and curly in an attractive disarray. When she smiled at the maître d' it almost took my breath away. Her teeth were so white, her smile was so spontaneous and lovely. She carried herself like a dancer or an actress, but it happened that she was a singer, an American, of all things, who had had a reasonable success in the European opera houses and was preparing to return to the States. I found this out later from the maître d', with whom I was quite good friends, because strangely enough I didn't know who she was. You would know her name, probably—she is well known now—but it is not important.

"I was attracted to her instantly. It didn't bother me much; I was nearly forty then and one knows by that time that not all passions require consummation to provide pleasure. I would have been perfectly content to watch her at meals or to observe her returning to the hotel late in the evenings. She was rehearsing at the Opera at the time. After rehearsal she went out, presumably for food or some entertainment. In any case, I watched for her and eventually she noticed me observing her and asked the maître d' about me. One morning she joined me for breakfast. Shortly after that, very naturally, we became lovers, and this didn't bother me much either, although I did care for her in a special way and there was a tremendous passion between us. She was of southern European descent and did much to mellow my Anglo-Saxon guilt feelings about sex."

She stopped to light a cigarette, noticing Will's frown. "Yes, I know Medina is a Spanish name, but I hadn't yet met Mr. Medina, remember." The crowds in the street were thinning, heading for dinners at Ciro's, Front Street, the Boatslip. The piano player continued; the tune was unfamiliar. The street lights came on suddenly.

"She was traveling with a friend, a certain Steva, a Czech who at various times had been her accompanist, her accountant, and probably her lover as well—I don't think I ever asked. He was now a playwright, and serious about it, even rather good, I was told. Several of his plays had middling success in eastern European cities, and one was currently playing to good houses in Munich. My singer was giving him friendly support; he was traveling with her, as I said, and demanded a good deal of her time. She seemed to like him. She was rather single-minded about her singing—we rarely saw each other more than two or three times a week. Which was all right with me; I had work to do too.

"Steva did not like the fact that she and I were involved, even to the modest and temporary extent that we were; in fact he was smoldering. After a week or so he began to come down sleepily and quite ill-temperedly to join us for breakfast. His working hours coincided with and sometimes were longer than hers at the Opera, and he was getting very little rest. My presence seemed to reignite a passion for her on his part that I think he felt he had overcome. He rarely looked happy—he was tall, dark, almost gaunt—in any case, his countenance did not encourage one to talk easily with him. I never saw him eat or drink much besides coffee and an occasional brioche. He would appear at our table and sit, looking gloomily and with sad bewilderment at her, never at me, as if he were attempting to solve a great riddle. She was always lovely to him. She spoke affectionately to him, touched him, smoothed his wild hair. I must admit that he amused me somewhat, he was so very intense.

"One night, while she was working, or out somewhere, I was in my rooms attempting to finish a piece that was hard in coming. Irritated, I lit a cigarette and went to the window. For a bit, I watched the chairs and tables being taken in from the courtyard. Then I raised my eyes and found Steva looking at me from his window across the court. After a second, he disappeared. Shortly after, he knocked at my door. He was in a shambles. His shirt was soaked in sweat, he had the chalky look of a serious illness, he reeked of wine and tobacco. I asked him in, but he shook his head and said, 'I have just destroyed my play. It was almost finished, but it was false. I have been reading. I am having great difficulty in separating the fantasy I must write from that in which I am forced to participate every day.' He was greatly agitated. 'So I will not try any more, you see. I will give up this struggle against that which is natural and true after all.'

"I couldn't make much of this and repeated my invitation to come in, but he declined again. 'It all comes from her. I cannot connect with her any more. Not in the old way. *Something new must happen.* You will help, will you please, when I ask?' I nodded yes, with a quizzical look on my face, I am sure. He left hurriedly along the carpeted hall.

"For a few days he did not appear at all; my singer tried his room on a number of occasions, but he replied that he was preparing his new drama and wished to be left alone. The fact that she heard his voice was something of a relief to me, for I had been worried about him after his visit to my room. But we moved along, sophisticated as we were, and left him to his own mysterious devices, whatever he was working out. Our affair was static but passionate; we found each other at whatever times we could. Late one morning, while still in bed with her, I thought I heard movement outside my door, but when I rushed into the hall there was no one there. My singer was amused, but her mind was already moving toward her evening performance and she wasn't altogether with me.

"That night on an impulse, she came by after she left the theater to ask if I would have supper with her. I agreed readily. My editor had called earlier in the evening to tell me I would be going to Brussels later in the week, and I didn't know when I would return; my singer was nearing the end of her engagement at the Opera and I wanted to see her as often as I could before our paths diverged. We went alone to some small restaurant, on the Cité I believe it was. There was a dampness in the air; the sky was very low and the lights of the city reflected dully against it. I was glad to be with her but uneasy for some reason, and she, too, seemed pre-occupied."

Mrs. Medina stopped for a moment, as if to re-experience the way she had felt then. Will stared at her, with his chin in his hand, fascinated, not knowing how any of this could possibly relate to him.

"We were drinking our coffee when Steva came in. He moved gracefully to our table, and I was shocked to see he was smiling. I don't think I had ever seen him smile before. He was carrying a portfolio of papers. He greeted us cordially and sat down. The waiter brought him a cognac, which he apparently had ordered on his way in. After sipping it, he looked at my singer and said, 'Well. It is finished. It will be my masterpiece. All my other works will be judged by this one. I am celebrating now. In a moment you will both assist with the première performance.'

"We looked at him blankly. He turned his darkened eyes to me and said almost triumphantly, 'You promised you would help.'

"'But,' I replied, 'it is late; we are tired; can we do it tomorrow, perhaps?'

"He shook his head. 'Let us return to the hotel. We will have a reading there. There are parts for each of you.'

"We were puzzled, but my singer shrugged; I supposed she was glad to see his mood had changed. We traveled back to the hotel in silence through a light drizzle. The night porter nodded sleepily as we made our way past his desk. We crossed the echoing stone courtyard and went up the carpeted stairs. 'Your room,' Steva said to my singer. I was very tired. I hoped it wouldn't last long.

"Once in her room, his excitement heightened. He rearranged some chairs into a pattern that seemed vaguely familiar to me and drew back the bedspread on the big bed, gently and with precision. He opened the windows and the wide shutters that gave onto the central court and turned to face us. 'Now the reading will begin.'

"My singer threw her wrap on a chair and said, with fatigue in her voice, 'All right, what is my part?'

"He smiled. 'You must read the part of the singer.'

"'How appropriate,' I remarked. 'And what is my role?'

"He handed me a sheaf of papers rather violently. 'You will recognize it,' he said. As I began to read the script I did indeed recognize it, for the words were real, almost verbatim transcriptions of conversations I had had with my lover, both in bed and out. As she glanced at the script, she too recognized the dialogue, although I must say she reacted with a bit more composure than I did.

"'You must have gone to a bit of trouble to overhear all this,' I said with hostility. 'This is not a good joke.'

"He picked up the remaining script and searched through it quickly. He found a certain page and said, 'Ah no, madame, it is no joke. This is in fact real drama, the truest there is. I am simply, simply—' he paused and glanced down at his script—'an agent only. But also involved as a player—a greater sacrifice, you see, for I know the end of this particular production.'

"'Well,' my singer said, and she was more amused than I, 'we can skip the first part, can't we, since it's been played and we know the lines?'

"'No, I don't think so.' He began to pace about; I suddenly realized he was very angry. 'We must play it *all*.'

"I said, 'I've had enough; this is silly, Steva. Goodnight, I'm going to my room.'

"He sat on the edge of a chair and lit a cigarette. 'Look at page seventeen.'

"'What?' I was gathering my things.

"'Page seventeen. Look at page seventeen of the script.'

"In exasperation, I picked up my copy and flipped to page seventeen. About halfway down the page, I read: 'WOMAN: *I've had enough; this is silly, Steva. Goodnight, I'm going to my room.*' I frowned, amazed, and turned to glance at my singer, who had also found the page. For a moment, I was silent, then said, 'Some trick—' He shook his head, smiling.

"I didn't dare lower my eyes again to the script. But my singer said suddenly and decisively, 'Let's play this out, then.' I was startled. Steva was delighted. My singer rose and began slowly to remove her outer garments. I watched, fascinated, uneasy, but my curiosity was beginning to nag at me. I knew what my role was, having formerly played it, so in a moment I joined her in bed. We both had our scripts.

Steva sat down in a chair by the window, and the play began.

"I can't explain the strangeness that began to settle over that room or, and I must admit this, the pleasure I began to derive from playing out those scenes that I already knew so well. I began to lose interest in how Steva had come upon the dialogue; he couldn't have been present, even surreptitiously, at all of the encounters he had reproduced so accurately. And yet they were not reproductions, exactly; our words, our actions became more sensual, heightened in this form. I found I meant them more, more than when I had actually lived them, said them. The whole thing was so removed from what I knew to be real or what I thought to be real. It was eerie, totally self-conscious; there were to be no consequences from what was said or done, no danger of misconstruing a remark or a look in the eye, no danger of offense. *Whatever happened meant nothing.* Strangely though, my passion for my singer, my feelings, whatever they were, began to quicken in a new way. I delivered my lines with meaning, with force, and she did, too. We did not deviate from the script or its stage directions by a word or gesture.

"Gradually, the script began to move out of the familiar into dialogues we had never had. They were intelligent, witty, loving, many of them, and I found myself believing wholeheartedly in Steva's words that were emerging from my mouth, believing they were my own. But in the same sense, not responsible for them. If an idea was aborted before its resolution it would be picked up again and reworked. If I was called upon to be angry, on the next page I would not be; it was as if the anger had never existed. Ah! How I remember the voluptuousness of that freedom! The absence of concern about what would remain when the night would finish!"

Now Will and Mrs. Medina were almost alone in the café. Will's eyes glittered behind his glasses; Mrs. Medina seemed lost, her eyes out somewhere over the darkening waters of the bay.

"I was not surprised when Steva began to enter into the dialogue, because I had seen his character written in. He had used his own name, but I didn't wonder at that. His part at the outset seemed to be a running commentary on what my singer and I were saying and doing. One of my lines was, *'How do you explain yourself in this situation?'*

"His reply was, *'I have come to resolve it.'*

"I believe I then said, with some irritation, *'Surely we don't need you to do that,'* and his retort was, *'You cannot really act upon the unreal. I have come to show you the real.'* Or something like that.

"My singer's line then was, *'But we are acting upon the real; what is present is what is real. What we are doing now is real.'*

"And Steva: *'No act is real unless it has a consequence, unless it causes some other act to occur as its result.'* I laughed for the first time; this was a departure from the script. But we continued in this serious, philosophical vein, Steva becoming more and more intense. He had written long monologues for himself concerning the vagaries of his life, his relationships with people, the sources of his plays. Finally, he pointed to the window and shouted, *'There! That is my proof!'*

"I looked, and saw nothing. My singer, however, haggard by this time with fatigue, was staring incredulously at Steva, who had leapt to his feet and was pacing the floor, shaking his script above his head (he did not need it; I saw, however, that he was following it with precision). I suppressed an impulse to look ahead and see how and when this all might end; since it had become his show it had begun to irritate me.

"The dialogue swung suddenly into an exchange between Steva and my singer. Steva's voice became louder and hers more frightened. I began to feel slightly anxious myself, as he said to her, '*You cannot see! You are afraid to commit yourself to an action, any action that would make you responsible for your own life. Your art is passive, your life is passive, you are not responsible, therefore you are* not. *We pass through you like a mirror. Your reality is here, when I tell you what to say, when she—*' (and here he pointed at me, although his gaze never left her) '—*acts for me, gives you your cues.*'

"Her script had lain on the bed for some time now, but there had not been much for her to say. She began to make a low sound in her throat, a low crying sound. Steva's eyes were glowing with pleasure. '*That is your response, as I might have expected.*' He was taunting, hostile. '*I am so tired of people who cannot* act!' He was close to hysteria. '*I have to write their lives for them, direct their motions. Who am I to do this?*'

"Suddenly, miraculously, he was on the window sill, the windows still open to the court. '*This, too,*' he said between clenched teeth to my singer, who was now trembling violently. I took hold of her shoulders from behind, but she shook me free and almost fell out of the bed.

"'*I have arranged it all,*' Steva said, his voice softer. '*It is your part.*' I had the sudden feeling that this was a continuation, a culmination, of some conversation they had begun long before. She didn't move. His eyes widened and his mouth wrung itself open in a howl: '*It is your* part!'

"Then, before my eyes, my singer walked swiftly to the window and pushed him gently on the belly. His face impassive at last, he fell without a sound until we heard him crumple on the stones below.

"She stood for a while at the window. I was aghast, not yet comprehending what had happened. She didn't look out; she made no move at all. I could not utter a word. Finally, a damp dawn breeze stirred the curtains; this seemed to prompt her to turn and look at me. There was no emotion in her gaze, no recognition of me. She knelt and began to gather together the sheets of her script that had fallen to the floor. After a moment of this, I made some kind of verbal overture that came out as a croak; she put her hand to stop me, then put her pages precisely in order.

"The artificial brightness in the room was dimming in the growing light from the courtyard, from above the upper windows of the hotel. She looked at me solemnly and said without pain, 'We must finish the script, the play.'

"I looked at her in disbelief, but then, with a beautiful flood of relief, I realized that this *was* the only way to conclude it.

"We began softly; there was not much left: questioning and answering each other as Steva had written, resolving things between ourselves. Our absolution—or perhaps only hers, I have never really decided—occurred in the final line, just as the night porter knocked excitedly at our door."

***

They were both silent for a long time: Will gazed at her, stunned; she, with her eyes averted, was finishing the story in her own mind. Night had entered the town during the time she had been talking. The girl had not yet arrived.

Finally, Will said, "I don't know what to say."

Mrs. Medina reclaimed herself and turned to face him. "That drama is over. There are no questions to ask about it. It taught me one thing, however, which I continue to forget and consequently have to relearn continually. It is always possible for you to become a character in another person's drama. With or without your consent. It is important always to be aware of this. You can play your parts, and not be concerned about them, until you know enough to construct your own roles. Or you can resist, and never learn a thing. If you are able to relax and step in, you will eventually experience everything, even the roles of others." She looked at him. "Do you understand?"

"I don't know." He paused. "That is an extreme story."

"And your story is not extreme? Or hers? One does not calculate extremes by degrees." She thought for a moment. "Although perhaps her story will not be extreme, after all. One of the few. She is a strange girl." They exchanged small smiles.

"It's hard for me not to be upset sometimes, not to wonder what will happen."

"It will *all* happen, don't worry. Probably not when you want, or in the manner you dream about. You must simply wait. And accept variations."

"But—" he took a breath. "Love . . ." He could barely say the word.

"A learned response," she said gently. "It will pass. Pass, or change. You can learn to enjoy even the passing of love."

He shook his head.

Across the street, the piano player began a slow tune. Will sat silently, seemingly in pain, long enough for Mrs. Medina to smoke one cigarette. Then he stood up and took her hand. Together they crossed the street, entered the small bar and began to dance. There was no one else on the floor, or, indeed, in the bar, and they moved slowly and gracefully among the tables. The music continued; the pianist became captivated by their dance and joined its rhythm, swaying gently at his seat.

At a certain point they broke. Will stared at Mrs. Medina. "Don't you get tired of waiting? What do you do?" She shook her head, smiling. "You *must* get tired of waiting. Or *bored.* I can't imagine you—"

"I don't wait," she said.

Then she took his hand and they entered the filling street. They found the girl waiting, under the trees by the town hall, expecting them.

That evening, the three of them were together for the last time. Will and the girl danced; Mrs. Medina sat quietly, smoking, watching them. At one bar or another they met up with some people who were having a party, so when the bars closed they all went there and did not sleep, but danced and danced, with a dull sense of going on. They found themselves at various times with one person or another, some they knew, some they didn't, embracing them with a cold and violent passion. They continued to lose and find each other again throughout the night.

At dawn, Will and the girl stumbled out with blurry eyes into the growing light. They had not seen Mrs. Medina for several hours. Neither of them, in fact, ever saw her again. Will parted from the girl at a deserted corner; she shrugged and vanished up the street.

That afternoon, Will caught the boat to Boston. He examined the boarding passengers carefully but saw no one he knew. As the ferry moved slowly away from the wharf, he suddenly realized he was exhausted and on the deck, in the sun, he fell into a deep sleep that carried him dreamless all the way back to the city.

The Savoy Taverne

One way for a piece of suede trade to get himself de-balled fast is to cruise me in front of Cocker. What happens is the little lumpy muscle on Cocker's right jaw just in front of his ear starts to jump. I can spot it twitching even if Cocker's way over the other side of the bar by the pool table. But the suede trade, being new to the Savoy, might miss the signal, especially since Cocker only shaves once a week maybe. And if the trade puts a hand, say, on my shoulder, say, he's going to get a surprise telegram from a certain Cocker.

Cocker is the one and only Steel Knite who's ever been inside a college for the regular reasons, and he pretends he's not proud of it. Cocker is also my old man, and he pretends he doesn't give one sweet one about me either, just like I pretend to be hot to trot after every piece of suede trade that tiptoes into the Savoy Taverne.

We—the Steel Knites Cycle Club—own all the tables on the left side of the Savoy Taverne as you walk in. From there we can keep a check on all the bikes parked outside and split fast if there's a need for it, which there very seldom is.

Mainly, we like the front left tables because we get a very fine close-up of the suede trade arriving at the door.

Usually they take a deep breath out on the sidewalk while pretending to examine all the Steel Knite bikes, which suede trade like to call "choppers" even if they're *not* choppers. Then they take a big step through the door to show the world inside what heavy studs they are. Or if they're in a group, they smile a lot and chat at each other like they're giving each other a sightseeing tour and they touch the pocket where their money is about every ten seconds.

It doesn't take long for this kind of trade to spot the Steel Knites, though. And that's when they start playing with their beer and rotating their heads like someone's just oiled their necks. Eight or ten Steel Knites in studs and straps and old denim drilling their eyes into one little suede pair of hundred-buck French army surplus pants makes trade nervous. Cocker says they love it, that's why they cruise the Savoy. The "fear orgasm," he calls it, and he figures it's the only kind most suede trade ever get.

I guess that's why he invented the Steel Knites' favorite number. How it works is two Steel Knites pick out one piece of suede trade and go to work on him, being very friendly and whispering dirty into his ear and patting his tight little butt end and letting him buy them a couple of beers. For some reason, suede trade love to buy beer for Steel Knites, which is fine with us, especially me since I'm trying to develop a small pillow for my old man's head. Anyway, after a while the two Steel Knites suggest going off to the suede trade's apartment for a little action. At this point, most trade gets nervous as all hell and suggests an alternate location, like the alley behind the Savoy. Cocker says all suede trade is as scared of its doorman as it is of its mom. But the two Steel Knites start groping the trade very persuasively, and finally he gets so hot he says *yes* and the two Steel Knite bikes escort the trade's Camaro like fuzz around a Mercedes limo.

Once inside his apartment, the trade laughs very loudly and tries to convince himself it's just like bringing two friends home for martinis. But that doesn't quite work in his head, so he asks the Steel Knites if he can just sort of watch *them* do it for a while. Of course, that sounds even worse, so the trade puts a very sincere hand on each of the Steel Knites' shoulders and tells them to please stop if he says stop, *OK?*

That's the signal for the Steel Knites to do their number. First, they both sit down on the nelliest-looking chairs and cross their legs like in a pantyhose ad and ask the trade very politely for beer in a glass, please. The trade tries not to worry about stains on his sofas and serves the Steel Knites their beer in his second-best crystal, hoping. The Steel Knites hold their glasses pinky finger up and say how yummy and refreshing the beer is and how elegant the glassware. Suddenly, one of the Steel Knites jumps up and swans over to the framed Michelangelo bare-ass with the fake cracked finish over the credenza and says, "Oooh, what a gorgeous hunk, is this a portrait of you, honey?" The other Steel Knite dances into the bedroom and calls out, "Sweetie, quick, come here, it's just darling and *so* masculine, too." By this time, the trade doesn't know whether to scream or mess his pants. The Steel Knites are now flitting around the apartment picking up all the little leather boxes and tiny marble ashtrays and stone eggs on gold chicken-foot stands and iridescent glass bud vases and saying how exquisite everything is and winking at the trade.

Now the trade has definitely decided something terrible is about to happen and he edges towards the front door while trying to smile very casually and says from the back of his throat something like, "Listen, take anything you like, heh

heh. It's an old Chinese custom, you know, heh heh, for a host to give his guests gifts, heh heh."

So the two Steel Knites say, "Oh, you really mean it?" and load up with all the junk that's portable and swish to the door and kissy-face the trade and leave. The door bangs so hard the two Steel Knites say, "Oooh, Loretta, my poor ears!" and fall all over the hallway laughing. Most of the crap they set out in the elevator like some nelly flea market, some of it they dump on the doorman, some of it they hand out to freaks in the street outside, and one thing they keep to show the rest of the Steel Knites back at the Savoy.

The first time Cocker let me do this number, he was amazed how good I was. He figured I was going to laugh or overact, but I didn't. And I know that's about when he started being proud to be my old man, though he never said anything like that. Later that same night, I told him the reason I was good at his number was probably from practicing a number of my own that I do. Well, it's not so much a number as maybe a habit. What I do once in a while is go downtown to one of the big office plazas and park the bike where I can get a good view of all the freaks coming and going. Lunch hour's the best time. At five o'clock there are too many freaks at once and they're all moving too fast. I sit on the bike, making sure all my tattoos and body metal are visible. Sometimes I take off my Steel Knites jacket and hang it over the bars of the bike, sometimes I don't. I try to look very heavy and never say anything to anybody except maybe for the growling noise I make to certain office pussies who speed up when they see me staring at them and pretend not to be turned on. Cocker thinks this growl is very funny and sometimes he does it at pussy too. It's a good feeling to teach your old man a trick for a change, at least I think so.

Anyhow, the office pussies are the last thing I'm hot for, of course. What I'm trying to spot is a certain kind of freak in a certain kind of drag. It has to be dark blue and pin-striped with a vest. The shirt has to be white or light blue. The tie has to be striped diagonally, preferably in blood-red, off-white, or navy blue; or else the tie can be blue with white dots. The freak has to be skinny and tall with no facial hair. Bald on top is permissible, but I prefer neat hair if possible. The age doesn't matter too much, although too young is nelly and too old is depressing. The skin should be clear and pale and the freak should never be smiling though he must always look alert. His walk should be loose but fairly fast.

Most lunch hours are busts. But every so often some freak comes very close to perfection. When I spot a possible, I drill him with a Steel Knite stare, because it's better for me if he knows I'm there. I follow him on foot until he turns into a restaurant or meets up with someone else, or until I figure I'm plenty hot enough. Sometimes the freak suddenly hails a cab or stops in front of a store window to let me pass. Which I don't. But no freak has ever spoken to me, which is fine, since if one asked I'd probably do him, and I know for sure Cocker would find out somehow and I wouldn't want that.

Anyhow, on the days I spot one of my particular freaks, I get so hot that only a buzz through some suburbs can half cool me down. So I bike out to where the streets are called Wildwillow or Shadyglade and I gun it around the block a few times sounding like God farting and watching all the kids look up at me the way their daddies wish they'd look at them. After a good buzz, I go find Cocker and work the rest off on him if he wants, which he usually doesn't. Even so, Cocker understands why I have to do what I do. He says everyone has a drug, even a dumb kid. I guess he's right, too, it must be a drug, because one time I went for months without spotting one single freak worth watching and I got twitchy as all hell. One night it was so bad Cocker told me to go find one of those nelly fashion magazines and get off on the pictures, for God's sake. All the Steel Knites in the Savoy made fun of me so bad that I said the hell with all of them, even Cocker.

I buzzed around for a while growling at pussy and trade but that was no good, so I figured maybe Cocker was right and I found a cruddy little store with lights that make everything green and a fat freak mama stuck behind the cash register eating margarine out of a plastic tub with a popsicle stick. In the cruddy magazine rack, I saw something called *Gentlemen's Quarterly* and flipped through it. Suddenly I felt bad for cursing Cocker the way I did. This magazine was full of pictures of freaks in *exactly* the drag I get off on. Even the ties were perfect, even the facial expressions. Too many neat beards, but what the hell. And even though I knew they were all trade models getting paid to wear the drag, I got hot. I was overdue. And before I knew it, I flipped myself out of my jeans and was doing it right there in the store in front of the fat freak mama. She started screaming, of course, but there was no one else around and I kept it up as long as I felt like. After I finished, I just leaned up to the counter, still hanging out, and tossed the magazine all covered with cum right over the mama's margarine tub. Then I went back to the Savoy and told the Steel Knites all about it. Cocker said he wished he'd been there and he bought me all the beer I wanted all night.

It wasn't long after that that Cocker and I went to collect my mother's stuff. After she'd been gone—disappeared for two weeks—the freaks who owned the rooming house cleared out my mother's room and rented it again. They'd put my mother's stuff in two old green garbage bags and a Carlsberg beer carton. Cocker grabbed the freak by the shirt and said he wanted new, unused garbage bags—or else. The freak's wife went and got them and rewrapped my mother's junk. Then Cocker demanded a beer, to be sociable, and the freak said he had none, so Cocker shoved into the kitchen and found two warm six-packs in a closet and he popped them all open, all twelve. We each took one, plus my mother's belongings, and went to the Savoy.

I wanted to stash the stuff out back but Cocker said there might be something important in the green garbage bags and anyway, where was my respect? So we emptied the stuff on the pool table. It was all just old drag and all kinds of make-up and stuff, but a few of the Steel Knites thought it was funny and started playing around with it. I didn't really care, but Cocker hit them and they stopped. Then Cocker picked out a gold plastic frame with a photo in it and stared at it. Then he stared at me, then at the picture again. Then he put it down and I looked at it and I remembered it always sitting on my mother's little white-painted table. I told Cocker it was supposed to be my father; my mother always told me it was him, although I never met him in my life. She always said that she knew lots of fine men when she was younger.

Cocker was still staring at me strangely and suddenly I realized what he was thinking. Just because the freak in the picture was wearing a dark pin-striped suit and vest and had a striped tie and a pale face with one eyebrow sort of raised alertly, Cocker was figuring that this was the freak I was looking for when I went downtown at lunch hours. I asked him if that was it, eh? and when he didn't answer, I knew damn well it was. I told him he was full of it and what the hell did he think I was, some weird freak kid? And I laughed in his face and chucked the old picture back with the rest of my mother's junk. Then Chiot came over to poke around like he always does and he pulled the gold plastic frame apart to get at the picture. He laughed through his nose and waved the picture around, pointing to something on the back of it.

Suddenly, Cocker blasted Chiot across the teeth. He kept on smashing like he was going to kill him. After we got Cocker cooled off with some beer over his head, I found the picture again and looked at what was on the back: a printed design that said *Paramount Studios, Hollywood, U.S.A.* and under that, written in old ink, *William Holden, 1953.*

I went back to Cocker and said, "Hey, you knew all the time, didn't you? Didn't you, Cocker?" He tried to swat me away and yelled for more beer. So even though I know he doesn't like me to do it, I put my arm around his neck and told him it was OK, not to feel bad about it because I didn't feel bad about it and I squeezed him in a friendly hammerlock. He looked at me the way he sometimes does when he thinks I'm not watching and I said, "Hell, I got all the old man I need right here and now and he's going to get me a beer, right?"

FRAN ROSS
◇◇

How She Lost It

*L*et's see now. Bubbling bath oil: apple-blossom-scented, $.96. Sexy bra: 36-C, gray, see-through, front-opening, $6.00 (matching panties already among my possessions). Digital watch: band of blocky interlocking E's tapering like a scream around my wrist, $172.80. Train ticket: round trip, $35.00. Hotel: room and morning-after breakfast, $41.34. (I am tempted to include subway and cab fare, but let's not be tacky for the sake of niggling accuracy.) *Ka-choong, ka-choong.* So: it cost me $256.10, and a two-hundred-mile trip, to lose my virginity.

There's a book called *Maiden* in which the heroine's virginity is said to have "burrowed in" by the time she was thirty. Well, move over, Fortune Dundy. I, Maggie Wallace, until recently laid unchallengeable claim to the title of oldest living walking-around uncloistered intact lady, beflowered to a fare-thee-well. I'd gone Miss Dundy a half decade better, and "burrowed in," with its overtones of cozy hibernation ("Oh, how warm and snuggly Bertha Bear was in her nice winter home!"), is the stuff of children's books. A certain obduracy and sophistication are missing.

I mean, this was hardscrabble territory, Fortunée. Oh yes, a clutch of pioneering hands, fingers, and tongues had been on it, around it, near it, and even smack up against it, but never far enough *in* to make it a homestead. I'd even managed to make do with only one gynecological examination in my thirty-five years. When I first came to the city, I chose a woman doctor, all wrinkles and dry bones, a priestess. I called her Dr. Vesta: reverent keeper of the hearth, consecrated guardian of my sacred fire, hawk-faced yet benign, something Jacques-Yves Cousteauish about the nose and protuberant eyes. Her voice seemed to begin somewhere above her head, high and keening like the wind, but after dying down to an extruded *sifflerie*, it escaped her kitish mouth chopped off, portentous, on the edge of emergency, like an ambulance siren warming up for the second chorus.

"Oh, I see. Well, Miss Wallace, you've been too good a girl. I shall try not to damage the hymen." Old-fashioned: she advised against the use of tampons. "Only one thing is supposed to go in there, Miss Wallace." So, not even a Tampax, Fortunée. If "it" ever happened, I expected moths to fly out.

You must understand: I was not sexually frustrated. I could come with the best of them, and better than most. It sounds like a movie title *(All the Brothers Were Valiant)*, but there's no help for it: all my lovers were breasted, and they knew what they were doing, although sometimes they didn't think I did. To my cries of "Higher, higher," Susan, my first lover, would reply, "One more inch and I'll be in your navel," among other, equally unamusing exaggerations. I considered the possibility of being deflowered by hand or tongue unaesthetic. I'd even been known to brag about my unbreached fortifications. "You still have it?" my friends would ask, giving me and my lover funny looks. We returned creamy, self-satisfied smiles. Why the surprise, ladies? Before transistors, it was probably hard to envision a radio no bigger than a hand that nevertheless was more sophisticated and gave better reception than the big-shouldered Silvertone console hunkering on the living-room oriental. And Russian spaceships are bigger, but we got to the moon first. Et cetera.

No matter. For two years I'd wanted to sleep with a man JUST TO SEE WHAT IT WAS LIKE. The capitals are important—I was a happy woman, living with the love of my life, someone who fulfilled all my physical and emotional needs. But that was the problem. How could I be unfaithful to my Pat? Pat had always been wary of any attentions paid me by men. I am just the opposite. I have never been sexually jealous of a man in my life. If a woman I was seeing made it with a man, I questioned her with scientific objectivity— more research into WHAT IT WAS LIKE. The woman who brought me out, in every way except laying hand or tongue on me where it counted, was married. I liked her husband. He was all chest, with overdeveloped, almost matronly pectorals that made me think he was wearing football gear under his shirt. In my naiveté, I said, "You and Skip seem so happy. Why are you interested in me?" "It's as different as chalk and cheese," she said, and continued fondling my breasts in the ladies' room of the place where we worked. The Living Bra, I called her. Chalk versus cheese made sense to me. I didn't care what men did with the women I loved. It was other *women* I was jealous of; it's easier to compare Brie with Camembert.

I couldn't untrack myself from my shuttling indecision: if sleeping with a man was merely a matter of satisfying my curiosity, I might as well do it, but if it meant so little, why bother? Why risk Pat's finding out? Why jeopardize our relationship? My faith in Pat's love went beyond security through complacency to the level of an axiom of the universe. No matter what (cheating aside), Pat would love me. Never mind my mountain-size rages over her trifling shortcomings. We'd been arguing about the same things for five years and would go on arguing so long as she (to cull three from a garden of trifles—pesky weeds, those), one, forgot to turn the stove off under empty pots and I refused to consider it charming the 1,825th time (which is what you get when you multiply the days of the year by five); two, stood in the middle of the floor with an important paper in her hand that she would manage to lose without moving from the spot (Pat could lose the wax in her ears); and, three, failed to master the intricacies of walking *with* me, she of the festinating gait, unconsciously accelerating as we made our way down the street.

The last I put down to unresolved ambition, unrecognized competitiveness. "Pat," I'd explain calmly, jumping up and down, "you have longer legs and are a faster walker. This isn't an Olympic event. Please slow down so I don't have to *trot!*" A split second's yoking, then back in tandem as she edged ahead once more. "Pat, goddammit to hell! Can't you see that our shoulders aren't *parallel!* A fucking moron could learn to walk *with* someone, for Christ's sake!"

What did these tirades matter? Hadn't she always forgiven me (if not my profanity) for calling her a bloody stupid ass every time she did one of her daily stupid-ass routines? Wouldn't she always forgive me?

No.

No? My Pat?

No.

I won't go into how much I hurt. The appropriate metaphors have been reserved for the sufferings of Christ. Let's just say that I went through all the stages that terminal patients are said to experience: disbelief, denial, anger, resignation, acceptance—along with a "fuck you" stage that the newly dead couldn't possibly hope to match. I went through them over and over again, from minute to minute and month to month. The area of the brain that should have registered my loss is idiot-smooth. Two years after the fact, I pound my hospital bed/coffin lid: What! It can't be! Why me! Why not me? All right—but fuck you, kiddo!

A few weeks after Pat left, I revived enough to remember the Why should I?/Why shouldn't I? shuttle—and to get off. First I had to choose a man, someone who would be worth my giving up a sensitive distant-early-warning signal. My little sealed box vibrated in phase with the crystal stutter of impending trauma. Whenever I heard automobiles screech toward impact outside my door, or saw someone slip on a banana peel, or followed the trajectory of a horsehide that had "beanball" written all over it, I felt a sharp spasm in my cunt. Who knew when I might need this signal for myself, when—with no one around to yell "Look out!"—it might be all I had to depend on to know when to duck? (I have since learned that the integrity of the membrane is not essential for clear reception of the signal.)

It had been so long since I'd thought of a specific man as a sex object. . . . Hank had the hots for me, but he was married to Ellen, whom I liked. I'd watched my first blue movies with Jim, who'd seemed to be trying to widen his eyes to a circumference large enough to enclose Candy Barr's breasts and sat rubbing my back (poor substitute) in ever more sweeping circles. "I could turn you into a marvelous lover," he said, babying his broken capillaries with a slow blink. Wrong approach. I was tempted to say "You first." Instead, I got up and left while he was ransacking the medicine chest, presumably for something to get the red out. No, Jim wouldn't do.

In the end it was all done with letters. I have a Herzogian appetite for letter writing, if not his illustrious addressees or subject matter (I have nothing to say to Nietzsche). But at least I mail my letters (even when I shouldn't). I often write to friends who live a few blocks away instead of calling. The phone is only for business or for when I get the feeling-good blathers after too much to drink. I write very effective letters to magazines and I never get form letters back. My comments are either published (my business letterhead helps) or someone with masthead authority becomes so enraged that he personally bypasses the underlings who are usually stuck with the task of writing to subscribers. Criticism of my comments (which are always initially civilized) brings out the Torquemada in me. I believe that the appropriate response is overkill. I want to shove a hot poker up the offender's ass. Failing that, I become Emily Dickinson's Steel, dealing my pretty words like blades, unbaring nerve, wantoning with bone. After a heated exchange between me and a D. W. Bassano, the sports editor of a TV magazine, I wrote a letter to his boss (with a carbon copy to Bassano), wherein I detailed the sports editor's discourtesies and called him, among other phrases baroque in construction and malign in intent, a "disturbed, full-flowering jock sniffer." I could almost hear the foam percolating at the corners of Bassano's mouth. The managing editor apologized for his staff man, and the enjoyable (to me) correspondence ended. With letters, sooner or later I got what I wanted: capitulation.

So I wrote to Eric Rasmussen, a blond Viking chiropractor, more than a casual acquaintance but less than a friend. He was also as gay as pink mud. But he'd always bragged about his appeal to and sexual marathons with women.

Whenever we met, it was always "Maggie darling, where have you *been?* You look so good I might go straight" (forgetting that it would take two of us). Kissy-kissy. I knew it was just a faggot game, but now was the time to separate the bluff from the balls. The man *was* good-looking. Better still, as a man of science, knowledgeable about the manipulation of the spinal column, he could bring extravagance to narrow, hand-bound chiropractic and jump on my bones, advance the state of the art.

Most of all, I didn't want it to hurt too much. Avoidance of pain was a not inconsiderable outpost of the palisade I had constructed around my maidenhead. I have the hyperope's view of pain: the further away it is, the more clearly I perceive it; at close quarters, its outline blurs—I scarcely recognize it. Two weeks before a dental appointment, fear mounts sneak attacks that turn my bowels into a gruel pot. But in the chair, with the buzzing prelude of the drill in my ear, I refuse novocaine, bear up bravely under the shuddering excavation, and tell the dentist as I leave that the session was a piece of cake. But mastery of pain is easily forgotten. I pictured my hymen as a cabochon carnelian, convex, unfaceted, pinkly glowing, a seal worthy of the cunt of Elizabeth I. I dreaded subjecting this gem to a chiseling cock's tremor of intent. For my first time, I wanted someone who knew me, who could be depended upon for both expertise and wonderment ("Marry! What maiden blush at such an ungreen age!"). True, a gay man could not be expected to bring the appropriate reverence, awe, or even unambiguous irritation to the task. But what the hell. So:

Dear Eric,
    There are many reasons why I'm still a virgin (as far as men are concerned) at the rather advanced age of

thirty-five. I was brought up during the time when "nice" girls didn't do it until they were married. Needless to say, I did have opportunities (who doesn't?), but during my teenage and college years I was more interested in school than in sex. Then I discovered women (again at an advanced age), or rather they discovered me. Pat and I have been together for five years now. I still love her, and I know she still loves me, but in the past few weeks (much to her surprise) she's become interested in someone else and wants to see where it leads. I don't know what will happen. Up to now, neither of us has even looked seriously at anyone else. However, for about two years before my milestone thirty-fifth birthday, I have wanted to sleep with a man, for many reasons (which I won't go into now.) Not just any man, of course. If I'm to lose my so-called virginity at this late stage, it should at least be with someone I find attractive.

I went to Florida alone on business recently and thought I might meet someone there—and away from Pat, presumably wouldn't feel so guilty about being "unfaithful" to her. As it turned out, I couldn't do it (I had a chance the first night I arrived). Now I don't feel so many compunctions about sleeping with someone else. But that is beside the point (this isn't "revenge"). You know, of course, that both men and women are attracted to you. You are my candidate for helping me find out what sex with a man is like. I know this is rather blunt and forward, but I mean it as a compliment. I also know that in sex, one can't be expected to "perform" on command. If my proposal shocks you or turns you off, please accept my apologies. I'll just have to look elsewhere. But if you are interested, please let me know so that we can get together. (I mean this less cold-bloodedly than is conveyed here.)

Fondly, Maggie

Pat has come in to pick up a few things she left behind. I fold the letter so that she cannot see Eric's name and let her read it.

"Are you really going to send that?"

I nod.

"I think it's a very cold letter."

I shrug. "How is Lockjaw?" That is the nicest of several nicknames I have given her new lover. You don't hand Steel spare blades and not expect to be nicked: Pat has confided that the woman doesn't know how to kiss, is not the lover I am, and—get this—cannot open her mouth more than a smidgeon because of a structural problem, which her dentist is trying (unsuccessfully, I hope) to correct. I showed uncharacteristic restraint at the time—I didn't fall down on the floor kicking and screaming with laughter—because I thought this news meant that hot-blooded Pat wouldn't stay away for long. (I was wrong.)

She doesn't answer. The expression on her face says: You are cruel. You'll never change. I am justified in leaving you. (She is wrong.) She looks at the letter again. "I know who this is. Chuck."

I smile. Let her think it is Chuck. In fact, Chuck would have been a far better choice—except that Chuck doesn't know I'm gay, and I don't feel like rewriting the letter. Chuck goes into the memory bank under "possibles."

"Sexy lady," she says. She seems wistful. At least that's the way I want to interpret the look on her face, which, I tell myself, mingles yearning for me, regret over her betrayal of what we had, and misgivings about her new liaison.

But I am in the "fuck you" stage of my terminal-patient routine. "Yes," I agree. Calm, smug, sure she'll come back.

The letter is an envelope marked PERSONAL, followed by a bristle of exclamation marks, so that Eric's see-no-evil secretary won't open it. I sit in a coffee shop around the corner from his office/apartment, not believing I am actually going to go and put it under his door.

Coward. Faggot. From that day to this, I have neither seen nor heard from Eric the Craven. I expected at least a kindly worded note suggesting I take my body elsewhere. After a reasonable amount of time, I send *him* a note. Letter ill-advised, I say. Tear it up, I say. I know he won't. He has probably shown it to every drag queen in town. "See, hot buns, women can't keep their paws off me." They share a few high-pitched Munchkin titters. Actually, Eric has a Marlboro Country voice. I'm just mean when I'm thwarted.

This is ridiculous. Here I am, a woman in the prime of life, who on her good days looks this young:

I am wearing my hooded blue sweatshirt, shooting baskets in the school yard. The ball gets stuck between the rim and the backboard, and sneaker-throwing avails not. A dog walker rescues me, lifting me up so that I can get my ball. "I thought you were a kid," he says. "A boy kid, I mean. But you are definitely a girl kid," he adds, eyeing the C cups.

I feign noncomprehension and go back to the foul line. Like most women, I get passes from the wrong people: dog walkers, my liquor store man, truck drivers, hardhats, the mailman, winos, minors. The usual.

Anyway, here I am, mink-brown feather-duster hair, gray-blue eyes, smooth skin, firm flesh, and the legs aren't half bad—all this good stuff, sex all around me, and I can't get laid.

Then I get a letter from Aaron Rubin. Aaron's letters are like lawyers' briefs: not brief. This is another two-pounder on the narrow light-blue school stationery he always uses. About a year or so before, Aaron saw one of my screeds in a national magazine. He wrote me a funny letter saying I must be the same Maggie Wallace he'd known in high school because of a reference I'd made to good old Emily Dickinson in my letter to the editor, but if I wasn't, well, I could just sit back and enjoy it anyway, because he was going to entertain me with the story of his life since he'd last seen Maggie. We'd corresponded ever since, in a hit-or-miss, whenever-the-mood-struck-us fashion. Our letters were long on candor and our mutual angst about growing old—chatty, intimate, self-revealing (although I'd never said which sex my lovers were). I'd had a mild crush on him in high school. But in those days, Jews dated Jews, and gentiles—well, at Dickinson High, the minuscule gentile population was tolerated but not encouraged. I was the only kid on the staff of the *Firesider* who wasn't numbered among the Chosen. As we cut and pasted, Aaron and I discovered that we shared an irreverent sense of humor and, unlike the other wheels who ran the school, not being rich. We weren't poor, but we were definitely among the not rich.

Aaron is now a happily married high-school English teacher who lives in Providence, Rhode Island, with his wife (also a teacher) and three sons. He would never have made my "hit" list if not for the question he posed in the letter I was now holding: "Is there a Shecky in real life?" Shecky was a character in a satiric story I'd written for self-therapy and sent to Aaron. It was either that or take out an ad in the

Alchemist's Daily Mercury: "Look No Further for the Universal Solvent." I was manufacturing something alkahestic by the gutful, and I had to get rid of it *somewhere*. All I could think about was Pat, and the story became my universal container. All Shecky and Becky do in the story is fuck. Aaron had taken the heroine to be me (right) and Shecky to be a man (wrong).

Instead of leaving Aaron's letter on my desk for weeks until I felt like being witty, I wrote back immediately. The crucial paragraph was well down on the second page: "No, Shecky is not a real person, and neither are his exploits. But I'm taking applications and would be happy to have you apply. If your wife reads this, I'm only kidding. If she doesn't, I'm not."

I expected Aaron to cover his retreat with a fanfarade of one-liners. Instead, the pace of our correspondence picked up. The letters on both sides were still long, funny, and frank but, a little buried, arrangements were being made.

The highlights: Aaron writes that my letter is the first mash note he's received in twenty years. Yes, his wife does read my letters, so why don't I write him at school sometime, marking the letter thus, to make sure the gym teacher (A. for Adele Rubin) won't get it.

I write: I am a virgin. I am gay.

Aaron: Yes, I know you're gay, because all the male characters in "Shecky and Becky" are unsympathetic, and because you've never been married.

I am so furious I almost stop the correspondence. I reread the carbon copy of my story. I write again: Typical male misreading. Take ninety-nine out of a hundred stories written by men. The females are invariably twits or twats, but nobody hollers that the writer is gay or antifemale. Nobody even notices; it's called "gritty realism." Take *any* story written by a woman. If the men are not shown to be saints, the writer is a manhater. In fact, "Shecky and Becky" has at least three sympathetic males (admittedly minor characters) and *no* sympathetic females. Furthermore, it's a *comic* story, and my kind of humor (and yours, I might add) is based on hostility. Come now, Aaron, haven't you ever heard of lesbian mothers? You hear of them because they were *married* and are fighting their ex-husbands for custody of the children.

Aaron: Call me Inspector Clouseau. I misinterpret all the clues and blunder into the right answer anyway. By the way, I took out our high-school yearbook to refresh my memory about what you look like. You are not exactly the kind of silky blondes I fantasize about, but do you ever get to Boston? I'll be there on such and such a date.

I always did admire his frankness, but things were getting out of hand here. I tried to arouse his competitive spirit by telling him how good my female lovers have been. "I hope I won't display unseemly maidenly panic because you're a man. As for the silky blondes, fantasize away. Whatever turns you on." This to warn him not to expect too much help from a novice like me.

Aaron (heatedly): I have it on good authority that I'm a damn good lover.

I think I spy a white flag, General Wallace.

I have more to offer than my yearbook picture shows, in many ways: I could stand to lose a few pounds. After all, the poor man can't be expected to get it up if he's not turned on. I can read: the cock's "rise from the root" (Mailer) is ever ready to desert some poor bastard. Sent for you yesterday, here you come today. Aaron might need his fantasy blondes for props. I need only flesh, to touch, taste, and smell skin—O warm and glidy casing! So let men have fantasy, pornography, dirty jokes, all the words with *c* and *k* that so energize them. I've always thought that the macho frou-frou—sucking noises, whistles, improper invitations—that turns a woman walking down the street into a mere collection of ambulatory sexual parts is essentially the male need for a recharging of sexual batteries, a shot from the booster cable, an input against the time of memory and fantasy when the penile motor simply won't turn over of itself. *The Erection Set* by Mickey Spillane—one of Mick's wives inspired the title. A "dog" constitutes a threat to male performance; she provides no sexual current. If suddenly every hymen were a permanent "valve" that opened or didn't open in the way that the penis erects or doesn't, women might begin to understand (and share) the pathetic piggishness of men. I don't care what the fuckers *think*; I just wish they'd keep their mouths shut on the streets.

Grief over Pat will later melt the pounds from me (the body's logic: if you disappear, there is less of you that can hurt), but right now I have a month to work on what I call "happy weight." (Pat and I were successful career women. We ate—expensively—to celebrate, fanning our credit cards like bridge hands before we trumped the check. When business was booming, we gained weight faster than a pair of woodchucks.) I know that Aaron keeps himself in shape playing squash, the one sport I know nothing about. I get out my basketball and head for the school yard.

* * *

I cross Twelfth Street and Seventh Avenue. A young man on the corner is watching my approach. He is eighteen or nineteen, neatly dressed, with a beautiful forehead, bones close to the surface. When he speaks, feathers of vapor drift from his mouth and plume into miniature cartoon balloons. His breath is full of iron. I imagine pockets of anemic air gaining strength as they rise off his fillings and flow out to me. My body is sending signals I am unaware of.

"Hello, my name is Theodore. You are very attractive. Can I be your man for tonight?"

A courteous approach. I am almost horny enough to say yes. "Go home, Theodore. I'm old enough to be your mother."

He smiles. "My *mother?*"

I am pleased to see that he does not believe me. I walk on.

At the party in Kate's new apartment, I try her water bed, the first time I've ever been on one. I roll once and almost come.

Sandy is watching me. She thinks I'm seasick. "That bed is overloaded," she says solicitously.

I roll again and smile. "No, I am."

She covers her mouth and points at me, her substitute for laughter.

Memory of another party at Kate's, Pat and I together: Kate teases me and then, her banter unaccountably sprouting prickles, tells me to go fuck myself. "I don't have to," I say without a beat. "Besides, the trouble with masturbation is I'm not my type." She plays Harvey Korman to my Tim Conway, Sammy Davis to my Richard Pryor, dependably breaking up.

In the elevator of my apartment building, a dog is sniffing me. His owner frantically jerks the leash. I am usually embarrassed by canine attentions of this sort. Tonight I want to look my fellow tenant dead in the eye and say, "It smells good, like good cunt should." The words tickle the back of my throat. With effort, I suppress the impulse.

On Channel 13, I watch a film on shire horses. It is the first time I have seen a horse's penis in full extension. It has dropped from his belly like a stuffed sleeve, dark at the top but white for most of its length, like a bad dye job. The rough British farmers watching the stallion serve the mare say, "Oh, he's really givin' it to her, by jingo." The stallion works and works; the mare looks as if she's unaware he's even in the barnyard. Oh dear, oh dear, poor peter, poor mare, poor me.

* * *

I tell my friend Teddy what I'm going to do. Our bull sessions on sex always bothered Pat, but Teddy and I talk because we are not *about* to do anything with each other. I could never sleep with a man so obviously fearful of and disgusted by the very thought of cunt: nightmares of an all-powerful milking machine, moist and muscular, that turns the cock into a glorified teat, the Great Mother's tribute and revenge.

"Do you want some pointers?" he says playfully, as later the first question out of his mouth will be "Did you go down on him?" Typical faggot attitude. Not "How was it for you, Maggie?" but did I service the man properly.

I stop down my deep anger by half. "*He's* the one who needs the pointers," I snap.

On the way to the hotel from the station, the cab driver, with a lack of deftness that is almost admirable, tries to find out where I'm from, how long I'll be in Boston, what I do for a living, whether I'm in town alone. The curiosity of hirelings annoys me. I grunt out answers, all lies. I give the impression that the state of the union (or at the very least Filene's) hinges on my presence here in Ben Franklin's birthplace, yet he still has the nerve to proposition me. I do not answer him. I arrange my face so that his rearview mirror will show how amused I am at his presumption. As I get out of the cab, he gets even by falling back on the condescension that men use, without even realizing it, in the presence of children and women they do not know. He calls me (pick one—it doesn't matter) "girlie" or "love," "honey" or "dear." As I give him half the tip he expects (which he would have earned by keeping his trap shut), I say, "It's impossible to condescend *up*." Incomprehension laminates the dullness already clouding his eyes. I hate it that one can effectively insult only one's peers.

I recall that I have been in this hotel before, at a convention. As I am registering, I see Aaron. I am not ready. My traveling clothes are a touch on the butch side: swash-buckler's cape, lumberjack jeans, desert boots. I'd planned to be all airy femininity by the time we met. Didn't want to give dykes a bad name. Great care had gone into the selection of the dress nestling in my suitcase.

The lines from nose to mouth run deeper than I'd imagined, and gray edges the dark scrollwork of the hair, but it is the same Aaron I'd aged in my mind. His face is oval but is saved from being unmanly by a knob of a chin, balanced by full, gently bowed lips and deep-brown eyes under a heavy browridge. His gray suit could come from an ad in *Gentlemen's Quarterly*. Squash must be a good game. He is obviously very fit.

"You caught me in my traveling clothes." Information, not apology or nervousness.

"You look fine." Polite, well-mannered, no trace of his correspondence cockiness.

"I'll just finish here and go up and change."

He sits in a chair in the lobby and lights a cigarette.

The hallways of the hotel are red-carpeted bowling lanes. ("Prepare the alleys. Her Majesty will bowl today.") My room invites excess: it is double double-bedded. I remove the dress from its tissue-paper nest. Picture an Indonesian tablecloth, lavender tree roots coolly spreading under soft green sod. Edge the green with saffron-kissed yellow. Fold the tablecloth in half and cut out a V for the neck. Halfway down the length of the cloth and four inches in, on each side stitch a green tendril echoing the sod seven inches long. No buttons, no zippers, no snaps. Let me not to the marriage of two bodies admit impediments. The dress is a self-conscious fusion of the sacred and the profane: the graceful folds evoke Greek statuary and divinity; the hemline undulates above the knee. I slip on Italian leather shoes—openwork and ankle strap, heels stacked just high enough to give me a hip action that borders on the sluttish with no effort on my part.

We are eating omelettes in a restaurant a few blocks away from the hotel. (A week from now, at this exact hour, while I am sitting in the audience at a Wednesday matinee, I will have a sudden urge for an omelette.) Although we haven't seen each other in twenty years, our correspondence has made it unnecessary to fill in boring details. In our letters we are Lenny Bruce and Phyllis Diller. In person, Aaron is subdued, not funny. I try to entertain him, pull out my sure-fire stories: my run-in with gangsters, my brief abduction in Guadeloupe, names-in-the-news I've met.

He says his life is dull compared with mine. "I love my

family, but I hate my life." Aaron belongs behind the wheel of a vintage sports car tooling around California freeways on his way to Tandem Productions to talk to Norman Lear about deals, packages, pilots. Instead, he must try to teach indifferent adolescents the subtleties of the semicolon.

I have had two margaritas and a glass of white wine and am slightly high. All to the good: I am warm and pliable when I drink too much.

Aaron has merely touched his wineglass to his lips once or twice. "Don't want to take the edge off," he explains when I notice, smiling briefly.

Oblique, but it is the first reference either of us has made to why we are both in Boston.

"Shall we go?" he asks, but he waits patiently while I drain my glass to the last drop's delay.

"Let me pay the check so you can feel like a gigolo," I say. I started this, after all, and I sort of like the idea of paying the expenses for the day, of renting his services.

But Aaron won't hear of it. He pays and leaves the waiter a generous tip. His punctiliousness surprises me. He opens doors, maneuvers to the street side of the pavement (*he'll* take the splash when horse-drawn carriages come along or the chambermaid's pot-emptying falls short of the gutter), apologizing as he does so in case my feminist sensibilities are offended. I am never offended by courtesy, I explain, and would be delighted to open a door for him if I should happen to get to it first.

At the hotel, I disappear into the bathroom, but I am not doing what a sensible woman would be doing in this situation. I am only peeing and performing the necessary follow-up ablutions. (One of my ex-lovers thought that having to pee enhanced her orgasms; to me it was just confusing one sensation with another.) I am "going bare," as they say in the underwriting business: I am uninsured. I decide to take off my see-through bra, panties, and shoes. I leave on my tablecloth to give Aaron something to remove. I unclasp my digital watch, which I plan to press at the exact second of entry. (It will give my friends who are "into astrology" something to play with on rainy days. When you don't know the hour-minute-second of your birth, they work out your destiny by the time of "significant events" in your life. Regressive charts, I think they call it. I call it bullshit.)

When I come out, Aaron is lying on the bed nearer the window. Hands locked behind his head, dark eyes studying the ceiling. He is wearing an undershirt and Jockey briefs, still looking like a men's magazine ad. The hair on his legs startles me; all the women I know, whatever the height of their consciousness, either shave or are hairless enough not to have to. Like a dunce-eyed student, I will be surprised by hair all afternoon: on the chest, the balls.

I sit on the bed and (here goes) bend down to kiss him. The pink snake dance of our tongues. Too much air is rushing in. I like to trap the tongue, seal it off with my lips like the rubber ring on a preserve jar, but he prefers to dart and probe and pull back.

By some sleight of hand, he has magicked away my shift and his underwear without my seeing it (how did he *do* that?). His mouth is on my mauve-pink nipples and his hand explores my cunt. I am so ready I am worried that I will slide off the bed on my own lubrication. But he adds to it: he turns and, with arms extended as though at the apex of a push-up, bends his elbows and takes to my clit like a cat to milk, lapping delicately. He is not doing it hard enough, but even so, two more licks and I'll come. But no, when he hears my soft "stay there" moan, he turns again, and before I can take the measure of his cock, he is entering me. Arms extended again, he pumps, gently but firmly. I imagine a foot bouncing up and down on a trampoline, stretching the fabric to the thinness and transparency of a balloon. I picture the head of his cock getting bruised, blueing like a pestle pounding indigo.

"Doesn't that hurt you?" I gasp, eyes squeezed shut. Because it sure as hell is hurting me, but not as much as I'd expected. I'd felt the shadowed edge of this pain when Dr. Vesta examined me. Now it is high-noon bright, sharp and blunt, knife and hammer at the same time.

"No," he pants, keeping up the rhythm.

I grit my teeth, then look down to see that he is all the way in. (I realize later that I'd forgotten all about my digital watch. I also forgot how nearsighted I am. I wouldn't have been able to see the damn thing without plucking it off the telephone table between the beds and bringing it up to my face—which, not to put too fine a point on it, would have been impolite. I'm too vain to wear glasses, and contact lenses feel like a truck in my eye.)

I don't think I can take much more and manage to whisper, "Come whenever you want to."

He pulls out. When he falls back on the bed, the significance of what I'm seeing at first escapes me. I am looking at the first fully erect penis I have ever seen in the flesh. It is pointing straight at the ceiling.

Aaron gets up and goes to the bathroom. I feel sore but good. The surgery is over. ("A brief convalescence, don't baby yourself, Miss Wallace. The worst is over. Have fun.") When he returns he is in full underwear again. I've missed the transition from limp to erect and back again and I'm disappointed. I didn't *see* enough. Is that all?

"I can't understand what happened," he says. "It was probably the Valium."

"Valium?"

"Yeah, I was worried about the business meeting I had this morning. Lawyers, a lot of red tape about a will. Shouldn't have taken it. Also, my wife was horny last night, and I couldn't put her off."

Dunce, numbskull, blockhead! How could I be so dumb? The poor man didn't come. He was probably in the bathroom . . . uh, unstiffening, as it were. "Guilt?" I offer tentatively, but he neither affirms nor denies.

"Don't you want a towel?"

Before I can even begin to understand the question, or the impatience that colors it, he flings me a small white bath mat. While his back is turned as he goes to sit on the other bed, I gingerly wipe myself. The family honor is upheld. Rejoicing in the village. I show him the carmine evidence. "See? I told you."

"My wife says she was a virgin too, but I don't know whether I believe her." He shrugs. A matter of no importance.

We talk about penis sizes. He says his is average and jokes about the sights he's seen in locker rooms and showers. "Some of the black guys in the service—frightening."

"One of Gore Vidal's characters says that's because black men are about the same size erect as they are at rest. What you see is what you get."

"I wouldn't know," he says pointedly.

I smile. I know from his letters that the subject of gay men embarrasses him.

Very deliberately, he takes off his underwear again. He is lying on "our" bed now, cock erect, rosy-red and shiny. Again I have missed the transition (perhaps he doesn't want me to see him vulnerable). The scrotal sacs are bigger and longer than I'd imagined. His eyes are closed, his face looks strained, suffering, as though he's staked to the bed by his baton of flesh.

I watch amazed. "If that's average—"

"You talk too much," he interrupts, eyes still closed.

Unfair, but let it ride. In other circumstances I would have drawn my sword, but I don't want to break his concentration as he rummages through his fantasy storehouse. Then I surprise myself: my mouth and tongue play with the head of his cock as I grasp it by the root. "Hmm, smooth," I hear myself say.

He is amused. "What did you expect?"

I shrug and suck. But I am inexpert and abandon my raspberry popsicle. Teddy would know what to do. Exceptions granted, I am convinced that in terms of mechanics alone, men make the best lovers for men, and women for women. A matter of familiarity with the plumbing.

I look at his feet and laugh. "I don't believe this. You still have your socks on. Just like dirty movies."

"The difference is, my socks are *clean.*" He takes them off. He has beautiful bony feet, like Donald Sutherland's *(Klute)*.

He is in me again, and this time I wrap my legs around his back. Once when he is about to slip too far out, I peremptorily grab his cock and guide it back in. When he pulls out, this time I hear the soft lisp and bubble of his withdrawal. I am disappointed that he makes no sound, apart from hard breathing. Decorous moans would do, a little sigh wouldn't hurt.

Back to the bathroom and into the Fruit of the Looms again. Why *won't* this man let me see him soft! He takes up his post on the opposite bed. "You sure everything's okay?" he asks, concerned. "The little buggers last a long time."

I dismiss the question with an airy wave. "No problem. Don't worry about it."

Maggie: "I can't believe I'm doing this."
Aaron: "Neither can I. Did you know your back's not sensitive?"

Yes, I know, and neither are my breasts. I am a cunt-centered woman. You don't have to wander all over the place. I'm right here, under the grassy mound. "Has anybody ever sat on you?" I inquire politely. I want to do that next, and be entered from the back. It always felt so good when Pat did it.

"We don't have time for tricks," he says on a long breath. He comes and eases off me. "I have to leave soon."

What! Just when I'm beginning to ignore the small discomforts of the shakedown cruise? His arm is crooked like a boomerang. I lie against his shoulder, my hand resting on his chest. I'd thought I might embarrass myself scrabbling around looking for breasts, but his mossy chest has the attraction of novelty. Aaron has well and truly earned the Order of the Golden Balls. To get it up three times within a few hours with someone who's not his type and whom he hasn't seen in twenty years, well . . . I thank him, and he is embarrassed. I didn't come but, the breakthrough's raw edges aside, I've enjoyed it and am relaxed, languorous. I did miss the smells, though. Woman-smell, sea-smell ("I'll have some more lobster with garlic butter, waiter"): sometimes a smell rose off Pat that was redolent of a delicate bouillabaisse. She says my skin smells like cinnamon buns. Aaron's smell has a drugstore air: soap, tobacco, aftershave, aluminum chlorohydrate. Only now is there a faint exhalation of a more personal odor, not yet enough musk for a turn-on.

When he comes out of the bathroom this time, he is in his

suit. I draw my knees up to conserve warmth and turn toward him, resting my head on my hands and the pillow. He looks at his watch and sits on the other bed. I realize that all this time we have not turned back the bedcovers. God knows what new patterns have been broadcast on the millefleur camouflage of the quilted spread I lie on.

Aaron laughs and shakes his head. "I almost brought along a jar of Vaseline."

I wonder if I was too juicy. Teddy said he'd once slept with a woman who was too wet. I'd assumed it was just another rationalization for his repugnance to the female body. Is an asshole tighter than a cunt? Must ask him. "Are you going back to Providence tonight?" I ask.

He spreads his hands. "All my time is accounted for." He looks at his watch again. "Still have a few more minutes."

We talk briefly about his wife and kids, and he shows me a picture of Beth. Blonde, clear-eyed, soap-and-water attractive. "She has a nice face," I say now, meaning only that. (Later I will tell a friend, "He made the mistake of showing me his wife's picture. Now I want to sleep with her too," playing for and getting a cheap laugh.)

"She's a teacher too." I nod. A pause. "She thinks we have a perfect sex life. Doesn't realize what a chore it is sometimes." He smiles. A memory: "On our wedding night, she went into the bathroom and shaved her pubic hair. Can you imagine that?"

I picture a poppy seed bun with a delicately curled tongue of baloney peeping out. Tongue calls to tongue from the little seeded bun. I smile. "She wanted to stay a little girl."

Soon after Aaron leaves, I am sliding into a tubful of apple-blossom-scented bubbling bath oil when I hear a knock at the outer door. The bathroom mirror shows a woman who has just been pelted by a berserk cotton-candy machine. I run to the door in my sugarplum decoration and peek around it.

Aaron has brought back a package I'd left in his rented car when we decided to find a restaurant within walking distance. It is a stack of Dickinson High *Firesiders* I'd brought along in the event we'd have to rely on reminiscence to get through the day. "I already have a full set, remember?" he says as he hands the package to me.

I thank him again, embarrass him again.

"Please stop thanking me." Stop making this a service call instead of an adventure. "Nice outfit," he says over his shoulder, pointing to my bubbles, and goes off down the hall.

I am using a towel for a bath mat, since the real bath mat has my hymenal blood on it. I have never stolen anything from a hotel, but I am going to keep this mat. A plan forms: I will cut out a good smeary swatch of the artwork and send it to Pat, with a concise annotation on its provenance. It is too evil an idea to pass up. Aaron is a sweet man, and sex with him was fun, but I know this: he could never make me cry. No man could make me cry over him the way I cry over Pat. I want her tears as recompense. I leave it to a piece of nubbly white terry cloth stained with the rubrics of my lost virginity.

The tub is narrow and deep. I lie back, images of the afternoon recurring, overlapping, dissolving. It is a while before I notice that something is happening that has never happened to me in a bathtub before. I am floating.

On the train the next morning, too late I remember that Boston is a city of accidents for me. Once, while visiting relatives during the summer when I was seven, I was run over by a car. In slow motion, the car passed over me without touching me. Lying on the couch in my grandmother's house, I remembered only the car's hot, metallic breath, an animal, brass-clawed and -fanged, about to devour me. I lay under it, not daring to move, peeing in my drawers. I got up from the couch and, in a fit of exultation at having escaped the brazen beast, danced madly in front of the antique pier glass. Then I looked down and saw that the beast had exacted its blood tribute after all. I had skinned my knee when I fell under the car. I stopped dancing and began to cry.

As the train nears New York, I know that I am about to be pregnant.

All my life, my period has been a clockwork rose, making its timely appearance every twenty-eight days. (I have kept track of it for twenty-three years with a red underline on my datebook and wall calendars.) This accutron precision lulled me into believing that I would ovulate exactly in the middle of my cycle, giving me one to three days' grace with Aaron's sperm even if they were particularly long-lived. Stupid? Cutting it close? True, of course. But Fate wouldn't be mean-spirited enough to turn a person's first fuck in thirty-five years into an instant lottery winner, would it? Come now, what are the odds on that? "Fate is a son of a bitch," answers a wise woman from the crowd.

Doctors say there is no estrous cycle in the human female. Doctors are stupid assholes. About five days after the end of my period, I sprout horns that take almost a week to molt. I realize now that this season of heat, when I would sleep with a moose if I didn't take myself firmly in hand, corresponds with my ovulation.

I read somewhere that the human female is born with all

the eggs she'll ever have, and releases only about four hundred of them during her reproductive lifetime.

I feel a twinge in my left side sharp enough to make me shift in my seat. It is like the pain inflicted by a visiting aunt who tweaks your chubby little cheek. I recognize it for what it is: *Mittelschmerz* (middle pain), so polite for twenty-three years I scarcely noticed it, now giving me a vengeful pinch to get my attention.

My eggs have lain there disconsolately, growing staler and more bitter by the month, with no hope of parole, no shot at merging with the Mark Spitz of sperm. Here is Sarah's chance at last. (For reasons obscure to me, that is the name I gave the egg.) I think of her leaping to meet the sperm cell, not the other way around. She wouldn't just sit there passively, not Sarah, not with the others—envious but encouraging (I ask no forgiveness for this)—egging her on.

"Sarah, it's you, it's you! Go, Sarah! *Now!*"

With all the energy of her remaining cellmates behind her, Sarah leaps. And she doesn't miss.

Two Weekends

1

Saturday, November 12

*V*eronique had sounded strange on the phone that morning. At first she had asked, then she demanded that Jonathan come out to New London immediately. His initial reaction was to say no and continue with the skiing plans he had made for the weekend. Veronique pleaded only malaise, but Jon sensed urgency and almost despite himself said yes.

He left work early and fought his way to a 3:20 train at Penn Station. The ride, or rather the idea of it, had appealed to Jon. It was long, and it afforded some unaccustomed time for reflection on himself and Veronique. An encroaching headache soon transformed it into time for sleep.

* * *

239

The train was late, and Veronique was nervous when Jon finally arrived. She said little as the car made its way down the dark road to the cabin.

"Bob Kibbe closed the Pindar deal today," Jon said.

"Oh, will you get the account now?"

"Yeah. Jeff told me just before I left. Why did you ask me out here?"

"Why did you come?"

When they arrived the cabin was cold.

"Why didn't you start the fire?" Jon asked.

"I was waiting for you."

"So you sat here and froze all day? You're fuckin' crazy." He put down his suitcase and went over to the fireplace. Wood had already been cut and placed in the grill.

"Do you really think I'm crazy?"

"Don't be an ass. All you had to do was light it; the wood's here."

"I know. The boy brought it in this morning."

The matches were damp, and Jon had difficulty lighting them.

"Jonathan?"

"Yes."

"Please hold me?"

"Just a minute, I've almost got it." One of the matches finally caught. Jon crumpled newspaper to feed the fire.

"Jon—" Veronique bent down to kiss him. He started to speak, but she put one hand to his mouth to stop the sound, and with the other reached behind his back. Her tongue found its way between her fingers and slowly entered his mouth.

Without undressing, they moved violently on the floor before the fire. Then Veronique stood, and silently undressed. She reached down for his fly, undid it and pulled out his already hard cock. She sat on it in a movement at once graceful and hesitant.

Jon lay still, entranced by her inexplicable aggression. For a moment, he wondered whether or not to tell her about Peter. The thought passed as Veronique placed three of her fingers into his mouth.

Afterward, she sat and stared into the center of the flames. Jon went to the kitchen and poured some vodka into two iced glasses.

When he returned, the touch of the cold beads of water on the glass broke her spell. "Jon, my father died this morning."

"I'm sorry," he said, unable to devise another response.

"That's why I asked you to come up. I needed you here."

"Why didn't you say something sooner? Shouldn't we be in Rhinebeck with your mother?"

"I don't want to go. There's no point. He always hated funeral nonsense, but mother will drag everyone through it anyway. I just want to be alone here with you, to think about him for a while."

Then they argued. Jon insisted they should leave for her mother's in the morning, but finally let the matter drop. Veronique went upstairs to bed alone.

Jon remained in the den watching the fire. He tried to think only of the heat from the fire and the cold vodka, but Peter, Veronique, and her father kept intruding. He was glad nothing had been mentioned of Peter. The weekend would be tense enough.

The vodka and the fire could not clear his mind, and soon lured Jon to sleep.

A white cot. A boy, Jon, lying, eyes closed, asleep.   No, not asleep, awakening. He is bleeding, no, he has bled. Blood is everywhere near his head. He sees a clock.

***

Jon awoke suddenly when a falling metal poker clanged against the grate of the fireplace. He hesitated for a moment, disoriented by sleep and the odd dream, then went to the fireplace to retrieve the poker.

As he reached for it, he thought of Veronique. Had the noise awakened her also? Had she been able to sleep at all? He grabbed the far end of the poker, not realizing how close it had been to the fire. The hot metal seared his left hand.

Jon didn't yell. He put the poker quietly into its stand, stood and stared at the hand. A gash of whitened skin cut diagonally across the palm. Actually, it didn't hurt; at least not immediately. Then a sharp sensation slowly overcame him and he went to the kitchen to run cold water over the hand. Vaseline and a dish towel served as a temporary bandage.

He climbed the stairs to join Veronique, and realized she had not entered his thoughts once in the last ten minutes.

Veronique lay naked under an afghan. Her chest rose and fell irregularly. Jon stood in the doorway and watched her. He wanted to reach out, wake her, make her father's death disappear.

But he could not, and for one strange moment knew he would not even if he could. He got into bed quietly and rested his arm on her shoulder. The pressure of her cool skin on his hand caused the burning pain to return. Jon reached for some Demerol he always kept on the night table, but then returned the bottle unopened. The pain was a comfort in itself.

He awoke much later, alone and unrested. Going downstairs, he was surprised to see Veronique rebuilding the fire. "Good morning," he said.

"Good afternoon."

"Why did you start the fire yourself?"

"Somebody had to. What did you do to your hand?"

"Just a small accident."

"Another one?"

"It's nothing. Would you call Dr. Mognasz for me? I'd like him to look at it before we leave for Rhinebeck."

"Call him yourself, Jon. I'm not going. Don't you listen?"

"Well, I'm going."

"Goddamn, go ahead."

"What will you do?"

"Sit here and watch the fire."

"Look, I won't go to the fucking funeral, I'll go back to New York. Please come with me?"

"No, Jon. I won't."

2

Friday, September 5

Jonathan sat, naked, in the wicker chair and finished a glass of white burgundy, poured in haste, earlier. The night air was still, so still that when a small breeze passed through the open porch and touched his nipples, it startled him slightly. He glanced down and slowly flexed the muscles in his chest. Rounded and taut, they had always seemed among his major assets.

He returned to the experiment. His large palm encircled the bowl of the wine glass, tightening its grip slowly, deliberately. The glass shattered, quietly severing the tendon that connected thumb and forefinger. He winced momentarily. The reaction upset him. It had marred an otherwise perfect attempt not to flinch. He threw the remaining glass far out, to the water's edge, where a small wave pulled it away.

Blood trickled from the open wound to the straw mat below. Jonathan pulled the cut to his mouth and nicked his tongue on a clinging shard. One of Peter's socks, which Jon had pulled off before they had fucked, served as a bandage. Pain shot from the hand to the center of his brain.

Jon thought back to the afternoon's car ride. It had been cool, unusually so for early September. The cold air streaming through the car window had been all that kept Jon awake.

The weekend with Peter lay ahead: three days with a man who three months ago had appeared to be the answer to so many problems. Now, Peter was only a vague figure on a clear Southampton beach. It would be awkward.

Peter had been cautious when planning the weekend, perhaps the last one they would spend at the summer house this season; he had avoided any indication of what Jon often saw as manipulative tendencies. Even so, Jon had almost begged off, but had ultimately given in, restless and needing an opportunity to break the news of his impending trip.

Traffic had been heavy; Peter was nervous when Jon finally arrived two hours late.

"Did you eat?" Jon asked.

"No, I was waiting for you."

"You didn't have to."

"I know."

Jon had put down his suitcase and gone to the oven. Cold moussaka sat on the top rack, waiting for the oven to be lit. A book of matches had fallen into the sink amidst what appeared to be a few days' accumulation of dishes, which seemed out of place in the otherwise immaculate kitchen.

"I'm sorry I was late. Some trouble came up at the Pindar plant in France."

"Oh."

"I'll have to leave for Aix on Monday."

"Oh. You wanted to pacify me tonight. I wondered why you came."

Jon let it drop. There was a strong breeze blowing in from the ocean. Peter went to close the windows. Jon retrieved the damp matches from the sink.

"Peter," Jon called out. "Why did you ask me to come out here?"

Peter appeared in the kitchen doorway and without expression replied, "I was bored."

"I see."

"Oh Christ, Jon, I just wanted us to be together, all right?"

The matches refused to light.

"Jon?"

"What?"

"Please hold me?"

"Just a minute. I've almost got it."

He found a half-dry match and got it to light. Peter bent down to kiss him and ran his hand lightly between Jon's thighs.

"Later. It's cold in here, I'll light a fire. You finish with dinner."

After dinner, by the fire, he grabbed Peter and undressed first Peter, then himself. Jon played roughly with Peter's nipples until he screamed, then kissed him full on the mouth to stop the sound.

After, Peter lay beside him and began to speak, but Jon had already fallen asleep.

***

Another drink? he thought now. *No.* Jon went inside to get a book, then returned to the porch. A small light outside on the house reflected on the water beyond. He approached the edge to look and, forgetting, reached for the railing with his injured hand. Pain shot through it. New blood soaked the bandage.

He thought of Peter, who lay upstairs asleep. What would he think if he knew of Jon's failed experiment? Jon wouldn't begin to guess, scarcely knowing what to make of it himself. His eyes moved from the water to the book he had brought and he began to read: *As soon as the idea of the deluge had subsided,* . . . He fell asleep.

A white cot. A boy, Jon, lying, eyes closed, asleep, no, awakening. Coming around. He bleeds, no, he has bled. Blood is everywhere near his head. He sees a clock. He speaks, no, a tube in his throat, two more in his nostrils. He cannot speak, he gags, he screams silently. A nurse approaches. She smiles, kisses him, and says, "Relax." A needle puts him to sleep.

Dawn crept upon the porch from across the water. Whether it was the light or a sudden realization of the cold and his nakedness that awakened him, he could not tell, but was glad. Peter should not find him like this.

He went upstairs and stood in the bedroom doorway, contemplating another experiment. If he couldn't eliminate feeling, perhaps he should wallow in it. He watched Peter, who lay naked under the afghan, watched Peter's chest as it rose and fell. Jon suddenly wanted to awaken him violently, hold him and scream. Instead, he lay down on the bed and watched Peter sleep and breathe. He held out the injured hand above Peter's tightly muscled chest. He wanted to grab him and tell him . . . what? *What could he tell him?* A drop of blood fell from the still tender wound and passed through the synapse between the hand and breast, falling lightly onto Peter's nipple. For a moment, he thought he saw strands of Veronique's blond hair brushing over the spot of blood.

Jon drew back his hand, with the other, he reached for the Demerol on the night table.

He awoke much later, alone, unrested, cold. The day had not warmed at all. Going downstairs, he saw Peter rebuilding the fire. "Good morning."

"Good afternoon. I'm glad you're up."

"I was exhausted. It's been—"

"I called Jim Hastry, he'll be here in half an hour."

"What do you mean? What for?"

"Your hand."

"Oh, you saw it. It's nothing."

"There's blood all over the bed."

"It must have dried by now. I'm fine."

"I've already called the hospital."

"What? And what the fuck does Jim Hastry have to do with this?"

"I called. He'll drive you."

"What about you?"

"No, Jon."

The White Knight Is Dead

The laundry room door swung open and there he stood, a vision of everything youthful, innocent and vital. At first I thought he might be some strange illusion brought on by the dense humidity of the rumbling machines.

"Hi John," he said.

Do illusions speak? I seemed to remember that they do in the Bible. Perhaps this was to be my first religious experience. My mother would have been so proud. I supposed I'd better be friendly. He knew my name, so I felt I should have known his, but names have never been my forte. "Hey, how's it going?" I asked, looking for some hint of recognition.

"Fine," he said with a smile. "I just thought I'd drop by and see you."

See me? This was more serious than I had thought. Maybe he was one of the guys I had made drunken passes at last night during the Student Association party and in two seconds the entire Phi Upsilon Kappa fraternity would burst through the door and beat the shit out of me. That had to be it. But I couldn't afford to let him know I knew. "So, how'd you find me down here?" I asked.

"I just asked around," he answered as he picked up a robin's-egg-blue Lacoste shirt from the basket and casually began to fold it. Either he was going to strangle me with it right there or he was one of the friendliest guys I'd ever met. When he put the shirt down and started to fold a second, I was fairly certain I could rule out the strangulation theory. I knew I was safe as I watched him turn back the sleeves meticulously and center every fold.

But who the hell *was* he?

"Who else do you know here?"

"Why Donny, of course," he replied, in a tone that seemed to question my sanity or intelligence.

Then it hit me: This was the guy wearing the pants Donny had been trying to get into for the last six months. Seeing him up close, I could understand why. He was a beauty, ready to take his proper place in a Greek temple. As he helped carry my laundry, like a schoolgirl's books, to my room, my mind spun with fantasies of all the possibilities. *Surely he must know*, I thought; *if not, he will soon.* My room was decorated conspicuously, if not stylishly, in a mid-seventies gay lib motif, my considerable collection of skin gazettes prominently displayed.

He never blinked.

When I finally had all of the clothes put away, I started to sit down. But where was I to sit? My cracker-box dorm room had only two chairs, one of which he occupied. If I sat in the other one I'd be looking at him straight on from about two feet away. If I sat on the bed I would feel like Cleopatra entertaining Marc Antony on the barge. The chair it was.

Our conversation was constant, if a bit strained and

insignificant. He was a freshman architecture student, eighteen years old and the son of a prosperous business executive. The deep tan was from spending the summer in Nantucket. In comparison, I felt old, poor, and hopelessly pale from working all summer in a department store.

The talk was coming around to one of those awkward, pregnant silences when he asked, "Do you have anything to drink around here?"

Damn, I thought, the Boy Scouts were right about being prepared; I'm sure Eagle Scouts never got caught without a drop in the place. "No," I replied grimly, "oh, hold on. Maybe my friend Bill has some beer in his refrigerator. I'll go check and be right back."

Racing down the hallway, I felt exuberant and shameless, a twenty-two-year-old panting at the prospect of seducing an eighteen-year-old innocent. Bill, although bursting with curiosity, handed over a cold six pack with only a few unsolicited theories about my sudden taste for alcohol. Pleading temporary insanity, I sprinted away before he could shut the refrigerator door.

I must have looked pretty stupid running back to my room, gasping for breath, flushed, trying to maintain an air of worldliness, the six pack attached to one hand. Under the circumstances, I didn't really stop to worry about it. He didn't seem to mind if I looked a little foolish.

We attacked the beer with the ferocity of people stranded in a desert. Soon the familiar mellow buzz set in; and we began to open up to each other. Our conversation became more and more uninhibited. I was dropping hints like bricks. Finally I dropped the full load: "You know I'm gay, don't you?"

"Sure," he answered, without the slightest change of expression, "Donny told me a few weeks ago."

Thank heaven for Donny's big mouth.

"As a matter of fact," he continued, "that's why I came to see you. I was hoping we could talk about it. You see"—he ducked his head in an "aw shucks" gesture that almost made me grin—"I think I'm gay, but I don't want to be."

I couldn't help but wonder why all the best looking ones were always so fucked up. But, as a homosexual in good standing, I assumed it was my duty to assuage his doubts, fears—and desires that dared not speak their names. I was a regular Florence Nightingale.

It was strange to relive, through his urgent, anguished reflections, the awkward emotions I had once thought earth-shattering. As I listened to him dig up his buried fears and guilts by the shovelful, I found myself longing for those tumultuous days when I understood so little about myself and the world seemed full of mountains to climb, when it seemed as if all you had to do was yell "Here I am world" and the world would take notice. I had long since given up my youthful, blind optimism; but this was the first time I realized that what I lost was so precious.

Of course, he had one problem I had never thought much about before: He was Catholic. I've always thought the fundamentalist religions have to be the most insidious guilt merchants in the market. It seemed that those pious old priests could lay it on pound for pound and then some. He was dead sure his soul would rot in Hell forever if he acted on any of his "unnatural" desires. I tried to assure him that, at least from my experience, if this were the case he'd have no trouble finding a few priests down there doing penance too. But it was no use. Catholicism is somewhat like hepatitis; once you get it, you never quite get rid of it. Personally, I can't imagine anything worse than going to some paradise with a bunch of goody-goodies. At least in Hell I'd know folks. They might even have a special section for gays.

None of these observations seemed to relieve him in the least. I consoled him and counseled him to the best of my abilities, feeling like Plato speaking to one of his students.

Finally, the beer, which had inspired the philosophical mood, demanded egress. So we trotted off down the hall to relieve ourselves of at least one burden. It was strangely erotic listening to him trickle into the pool of water in the next stall, his foot only inches from mine.

We walked in silence to my room and settled back into our seats. The intellectual weight of our conversation seemed to have drained off. I tried to keep up a sociable patter; finding out his favorite musical group, sport and hobby.

We suddenly hit one of those black holes. The silence was crackling like static electricity; shivers ran up and down my body. I stretched out my legs and let them rest between his, so close I could feel him quiver.

I was determined not to ask him. It couldn't happen because of my coercion or even my suggestion. He had to be the one responsible.

"Would you like to go to bed?" he asked softly, breaking the silence which had been like so many tons of ice.

My mind exploded with excitement. But wait, I thought, is he asking me if I want him to leave so I can get some sleep? I asked him bluntly, "You mean have sex?"

"Yeah. Of course," he answered, probably thinking I was extremely dense.

I didn't give it another thought. "Sure," I said, as I bounced up and began undressing. "Why not?"

At first he just watched me undress. For a moment I was afraid he might back out, but he certainly seemed to appreciate each new area of my bared flesh. He was undressed in a flash. If all the blood hadn't rushed from my head downwards, I might have been inspired to write sonnets to his perfect beauty.

I didn't have to lead him along, far from it. I was drowned in his passion. Either he was one hell of a natural or he had left his innocence behind with his last diaper.

We wrestled, kissed, and held each other so close he seemed to be part of me, working in symmetry. His broad shoulders surrounded me with protective warmth. Tender passion flushed through me, filling long-forgotten places. Sharing every softness, exposing every weakness, we trusted each other's arms.

We lay together in silence, removed from the rest of humanity, free. I kissed him again, brushing my fingers across his forehead. We made love again, this time more subdued, as if filtered through a haze. We were no one's concern, concerned with no one but each other.

Afterwards, we showered together, but no one saw us. Back in my room I watched like an adoring child as he toweldried his hair. "You know," he said, "I probably won't have sex with another guy for quite a while." I sat silently on the bed, trying to ignore the temporary nature of our relationship. Responding to my silence, he added, "It may be five or six months before I do it again." He became more and more nervous at my silence. "I just don't want you to think—"

"I know, I know," I broke in. "Don't worry, I understand. I was the same way, a few years back."

Pulling on his pants, he started again, "I just don't want you to get any ideas. I've never been in love or anything." With a quick zip of the fly, he said, "Sex is just . . . *sex* to me."

Aha. The old post-orgasm guilt complex. I had been

prepared for that, although I'd hoped it wouldn't happen. I told him not to worry, patted him on the head and sent him on his merry way. If he was gone forever, I was perfectly willing to accept it.

Precisely one week later he was at my door again with a smile broad as the horizon. We talked much less this time. The end result was the same. Luckily, I had thought ahead and stocked up on a good bourbon; he seemed to find liquor the only way to get the ball rolling.

As he dressed, he admitted, rather self-consciously, "Well, it wasn't six months, was it?"

I grinned and sent him off into his other world.

Although I didn't particularly care who knew the campus golden boy and I were doing it, I was certain he did. Much of the excitement of our relationship probably came from its veiled, mysterious nature. I did my best to preserve its secrecy.

Despite my efforts, it wasn't long before Donny discovered our affair. Our friendship crumbled like decayed leaves.

It wasn't when I started telephoning him all the time, or even when I realized he was monopolizing my fantasies, that I first understood the depth of my obsession for him. It was one particular night, after we had been to see a movie. I had been bristling with anticipation all evening, wondering if he would once again be able to keep his monstrous guilt at bay. Driving back, as we approached a decisive intersection, I asked, "Would you like to come up for a drink?" I used the most naive tone I could muster, but my facial expression (that of a starving dog) undoubtedly gave me away.

Feeling my anxiety, he looked out the window and said,

"That would be great, but I have to get up early tomorrow and study for a German test."

"Oh," I moaned, as my heart slipped through the hole in my jockey shorts down to the floorboard, "I see."

I didn't see. Did he really have to get up early, or had he decided I was no longer attractive? Or was he simply unable to fight off the beast of his guilt? After I dropped him off, I knew I was hooked. I screamed at myself all the way home, earning a dirty look from an older lady crossing the street in front of me.

I set out to forget the sexual part of our relationship, telling myself he was too young and inexperienced for me to expect anything more than a friendship from him. I fortified myself with two theories: that you had to enjoy every moment without expecting anything more, and that friendship was much more important than sex. Now I realize that the first was impossible and the second only half-true.

By the end of two weeks of friendship I felt fairly sure of having doused the flames of my obsession. I had gotten back into the habit of visiting the bars in search of love at first sight. Naturally, I ended up settling for lust at the last minute. But that was business as usual, and I had grown accustomed to the games.

It has been my experience that well enough is seldom if ever left alone; this case was no exception. Donny decided to give a birthday party for a mutual friend of ours. Although he never forgave me for messing around with the object of his desire, good manners dictated that I be invited—as well as the object himself. Rumor had it that neither of us would show up. But neither of us heeded rumor; we both appeared, together no less.

The party rambled along its uneventful course. Everyone

was tipping his glass rather frequently; one poor fellow tipped his right into the lap of the guest of honor. It was beginning to look as if that would be the highlight of the evening.

As I was making another run for chips and dips, I noticed the absence of my fair young friend. Thinking he might have gone to the bathroom, I decided to follow him.

He wasn't there. I don't really know what drove me, but before my blurry mind could give it much thought I was going to my room. The wheels inside my head were spinning with unease. Dimly perceiving the colors around me, I subconsciously increased my pace, walking, then trotting, then running through the halls.

When I opened the door to my room, I was gasping for breath. There he was, flipping through one of my more . . . vivid magazines.

"Hi," he said, looking up for a second. He returned to the page in front of him, absorbing every detail, then he put it down and looked at me the same way.

"You disappeared," I blurted between breaths.

He slowly surveyed the room, then replied, "Yeah, I was tired of the party." Realizing that I was still standing in the doorway, I shut the door, walked over and fell on the bed. "You know," he said, relaxed, "I've always liked the way you did up this room."

"Thanks," I muttered. He was in a strange mood. He rose and began to move silently and subtly around the small room. I didn't notice he had locked the door until several hours later.

"Wanna have sex?" he blurted.

I wasn't sure I'd heard him correctly. I asked, "What?"

He turned his attention away from the room and stared hard into my eyes. I was caught off guard, totally magnetized by his cobalt eyes. In one motion, he scooped me into his arms and kissed me, gulled me into his tightness.

When all the layers of tension had broken, we lay together in quiet. Then he whispered, "I'm sorry."

"Sorry?" Regret was the furthest thing from my mind.

"I shouldn't have come." He stared at the ceiling, continuing very softly, "It's just that I'm so attracted to you"—I *had* to be hallucinating—"and I lose control when I've been drinking." I was speechless. "I'm really attracted to you"—there it was again—"but I don't want to be."

Aha, the clincher. That was too much. I had to interject. "So what do you want me to do?"

"Nothing," he replied, looking me in the eyes again. "That's just it. You know you're gay and you can accept it. But I just can't."

I felt strangely complimented and yet debased at the same time, as if I had won an honor for accepting second best. "Look," I said forcefully, "I don't *care* whether you're gay or straight, or anything at all. I don't want to make any decisions for you." He looked back to the ceiling, but I continued, "I've tried to tell you what I went through, but you've got to learn to *like* yourself. It's not *healthy* to go around kicking yourself in the ass every time you feel attracted to a cute guy."

There was a long pause; my words hung stagnant in the air. Finally he sighed. "I guess we shouldn't see each other any more, should we?"

My eyes drifted away from him for the first time. It was true. I'd known it all along. I wanted to agree and be finished with it, yet I wanted to hold on to a fragment, however small, of what we had shared. "We could still be friends, couldn't we?" I asked, almost hopelessly.

"I *don't* want to be friends." He spoke more harshly, but still in a whisper. "I *never* wanted to be friends."

It was difficult to believe what I was hearing. I'd never considered myself as just a physical object before. My feelings were so confused I could only ask, "You mean, you only wanted me for sex?"

"From the first time I came here," he answered coolly.

As he dressed, I was tense. I couldn't continue in such a shallow relationship, yet I couldn't say goodbye forever. I was positive that, given the chance, we could develop something more. But I wouldn't be able to pull an unwilling partner along.

When he had finished dressing, he sat on the bed beside me. Nothing was said: We stayed there for several minutes, unable to make the final break. He let out a strong sigh, braced himself on my knee, pushed to his feet. I felt certain he would walk out the door without another word.

He didn't. Confused, he began walking around the room like an animal circling in a cage. "Hey, you've got that new record," he said loudly.

Startled, I looked up. "Huh? Oh, yeah." I lowered my head.

"Would you mind if I borrowed it?" he asked.

I stared at him for a couple of seconds.

"No, go ahead."

Sita

*T*he sound of Hare Krishna people along Telegraph Avenue. Dark of a coffeehouse. Loneliness of the afternoon. A rainy day in Berkeley. Why am I wasting myself here, far from home, pursuing what has already fled? Why, when death is so soon? Around me beards and coffee cups, madras bedspreads on the wall, other people's conversations. The impenetrable lives of strangers. On the street a young woman carrying an infant covered with a blanket against the light rain. She looks utterly lost but has more purpose in life than I do. Young men in their ponchos and hats and padded jackets, their big boots and watch caps. All the paraphernalia of youth. I become old, watching. A youngster crowing over his professor: "This guy used to teach at Harvard." Waiters on their listless feet. "So I went into his office this morning and he told me two or three things that are gonna be on the midterm. With the answers, man. Be no problem there." The busboy picks up a dirty cup. "This guy writes so smooth, you know, it just flows." Pull of the espresso machine. A girl in the corner behind dark glasses drinks coffee soulfully. The espresso machine pulls again, suction and whistle.

She will be home late again tonight. Only an hour, an hour and a half together before she sleeps. A couple come in and discuss God. Are they madder than I? "They can still be saved," the woman's voice labors on, didactic, anxious. Ineffably tedious. He rattles her with questions, objections. "No, no, when you are praying, ask the Lord to help you with the things you can't accept. Having been a Christian for twenty years, I can understand a lot more than someone who's been in the movement for just a few months." He quibbles over her age, closer to nineteen really. Idiot reactionary fanaticism and this child calls it a "movement." How self-important they all are, what a collection of phonies, of mediocre minds. Berkeley. The waiter finally brings my coffee.

I must not dig in too hard, hold on, anchor myself in her, I thought to myself last night at the Riviera, watching her arm, enjoying the rose flesh of it, my eyes touching it like fingers. Watching her during an Italian film. And Sita, her mouth half open in delight, following the play of dialogue in both languages. The look of joy on her face as she heard her own Italian spoken. And later, outside the café, coming upon an Italian professor: *"E Mario." "Come va." "Va bene."* How her voice dances over the words, rises and falls and sings them. Her English so much more restrained, restraining. But seeing her again speaking Italian, how she lights up, how she relishes each word in her mouth. Her laughter, her gaiety. I go on a few steps to wait for her apart, enjoying her from afar, happy for her happiness. She calls me back to introduce me. "You do not speak Italian?" the professor asks. I admit my ignorance, feeling irredeemably stupid before his surprise. It would take too long to explain my lust for the language last summer, my eagerness to learn it, and then the wall she lowered between me and her country. "I could have picked up a lot, just didn't seem to have the knack"—but no one hears me; they are reminiscing about friends in Sacramento. After he leaves she tells a long and naughty story about the professor's wife, the mood of the evening still with her as she drinks cappuccino, her voice still floating into laughter, into that particular lilt and vivacity it takes from contact with the Italian. As if English were a kind of prison and America too a duller place, heavy and plodding like its language, somewhere you might go to escape a war or a depression, but tepid and ugly finally, a cold exile from the Tuscan hills she loves so deeply. That summer, especially the last time she saw them, en route back to Germany and the charter flight, tears in her eyes so that she could barely drive, she hated so to leave them. And I, looking at them that last time, had actually come to hate them. And Italy. All that I had loved so in my Oxford days, the great trip to Italy alone after my examinations. Years ago, and had loved the place, the people, the profusion of art and excitement and good nature. And by the end of a summer there with her had come to hate it, the heat and the tiled roofs, even her good and always impeccably polite family. A hate that was love utterly disappointed. How easy it would have been to learn the language, how easy to love her family—how easy if she had not been there. Preventing. In some mysterious way preventing me from speaking or from becoming friends.

Her brother was invariably, even punctiliously kind. So it is hard to explain, but perhaps it was that little incident even before we got down to the villa and the shore and the countryside, the second day actually, just a few hours after we left Milan. I needed cigarettes. Paolo was not very eager to stop the car. And it was hot that day, not yet lunchtime, but the traffic was heavy already. I had to plead a little to get him to stop. Then I jumped right out and into the store, thinking to hurry. Hardly noticing his command that I wait until he was at my back in the shop, shouting at me. I had already used my new and experimental Italian on the shopkeeper, and made my request, was rather pleased with myself, when I turned to see Paolo furious. "Who do you think you are?" I'm astonished, merely stare at him. He countermands my order for cigarettes. I stand there discredited, ridiculous. He buys another package, pays, and orders me to leave. "What on earth is the matter, Paolo?" "Who do you think you are, going around like you know everyone?" He slams the door on his side of the car. I look back to Sita for guidance. She hasn't any. Like Paolo, she merely assumes that I stay in the car while a male deals with the world, keep silent in a country where I do not know the language. And be served. But paid for too? How many times has it been made clear to me that Paolo finds it hard to pay for the life he leads. I had meant only to save my host the trouble. And I had also taken it for granted that one helps oneself, is independent, and the American woman in me had no desire to be served, still less to put up with the bullying that comes out if you show any signs of independence. I found Paolo harder to like after that, though I did like him anyway. Or rather I admired his character in maintaining an exemplary courtesy to me through a whole summer in his house, when I knew he neither liked nor approved of me. I'm not certain what he imagined my relationship with his sister to be.

On several occasions he referred to Hank as Sita's lover of the moment, a fiction I did not know whether to contradict or not. During the first week of our stay he read a book I'd written, *Flying*, that was expressly lesbian in certain passages.

Bravo, I thought, he has taken this extremely well. The next day our beds were changed from a double to two singles. The reason given was that Sita had a cold. She may well have asked for the change herself, though of course she denied it. On the rare occasions when we spoke. For she was consumed now, reabsorbed into the bosom of the family, the language, the ways, the countryside, the long afternoons at the beach, the conversation of her sister-in-law, her walks with Paolo, the hours of badinage with the children. She was lost to me, lost in the crowds of friends and relations, a couple from Milan, the grandmother, the maid, the thirteen who sat at dinner. And I was a shadow reading books in our room, grinning foolishly when addressed in English, puzzled and idiotic when addressed in Italian. Inasmuch as she could arrange it, I was simply not there. I had been the means of transport, a convenience in bringing her to Italy, but now dispensable. Inasmuch as I could arrange it, I would rather neither of us were there, but she would not leave, and our two-week visit slowly and hideously became two months. I begged and was occasionally conceded a weekend in San Gimignano, a night in Siena, and finally, by myself, fleeing really, a week in Florence.

That an entire summer in Europe could be so wasted, so boring, so friendless, seems hard to believe now. All the expectations I had had, the adventure of it, being with her in Italy, her Italy, so loved, so long talked about, imagined, planned, anticipated. And of course there was much in what we had that could have been enchanting, even glamorous. The great stone-floored villa in the fields, a farmer's house from the eighteenth century, huge, full of rooms and guests and long lunches, banquets at night, the party they gave for me the night I left alone for Florence, the champagne and cakes, the table spread outside in the mists of the evening, romantic it was, magnificent. Somehow only a mockery. Even our crazy dancing that night, the one occasion of hilarity, license, the whole lot of us, children and all in a frenzy of cha-chas and twists, tarantellas and rock 'n' roll. There will always be something lonely about remembering this, I'd thought at the time, thinking it was because I was leaving them all, leaving her here with them. But it was more than that, there was a strange betrayal even in the feast. An empty ceremony.

Remembering it now in a Berkeley coffeehouse on a rainy afternoon, I find it unspeakably bitter. To remember Italy at all is unpleasant, remembering it as I am losing her is unbearable. But why didn't I see it then? Not really believing her odd little explanations for her behavior—that she was suffering depression, that she was having a little nervous breakdown in return for my bigger one, and that I, if anyone would, should understand and sympathize. On other days she would say it was her health—glandular deficiencies, hormones, nerves, her doctor would look into all of it further when she got home. Poor lady, she was simply bored to death with me and had not yet found the way to relieve herself of the affliction. Coming home in September, she could serenely tell Sherman the affair was over and rearrange her house and life and associates accordingly. She had simply neglected to tell me. Till being here becomes finding out. And letting me come was a weakness she permitted herself after the visit at Christmas. There was still a spark. She wouldn't quite give it a chance, but perhaps she could not quite bring herself to extinguish it completely. She'd wait and see. So do I. I wait and see.

And I drink bad coffee in cafés on rainy days in Berkeley,

and prowl bookstores, and have nothing to do for whole afternoons. Because I am waiting. Knowing already that if ever I were to win, I would be just as confused. I have done her the disservice of making her my need. I have used her to find purpose in my life. You can't do that to someone. My own terror lies like a mat under a rug; makes me tremble browsing through a bit of Henry Miller, his *Insomnia*, the obsession of an old man with a young and indifferent girl, but my story too. Yet whatever fool he was in the middle of the night, he was still a writer. And I have lost who I am. A follower following nothing, my hands empty along the way. Do I cling and pursue this love because I have really nothing else to do—or am I unable to write because my slavery to this infatuation makes work impossible? The former. No, the latter. The former because you have not finished a book in three years. The latter, because that is the period of time you have known her. Never blame problems with your work on other people; you have simply had no book to write for three years. Probably never again. Done for. And done for with her too. Both at the same moment. Nice timing. That curly-haired boy waiting on table knows who he is. The religious fanatic knows who she is. Even the wavering and uncertain figures passing the windows in the rain, even they understand who they are, each in his lazy California manner, "mellowed out," "laid back," whatever occult fizz passes for wisdom in their confused minds, they all know what they are doing. But ⁚ am only waiting for nightfall.

I spread her out on the couch. Laughing at me. "Kate! Why are you getting me to take off my clothes now? We're going out soon. You were going to call your sister before we left." "Later, later. This now." "But she'll be out here in ten days, we should confirm with her . . ." "I'll write her a note." "People can see us. If someone came up to the front door . . ." still laughing, unsure perhaps as I am unsure. How she would have adored this once, the madness, the risk, the spontaneity. Now I am very far from sure if she will even give in, permit me. But sitting near her on the floor as she sat on the sofa, it came to me, like a wildness, like a hope—the notion of spreading her legs and taking suck. Suddenly how I wanted that—how charming and offhand, how silly and willful and easy it seemed. I had only to coax off her trousers, spread her legs, and the warm dark loveliness would be there at my mouth. If I can persuade her, cajole, tease. Appearing to be utterly sure of myself, without qualm or question. If I can make it be then, that time and its willingness, its lust and hurry and ease. We never refused each other anything those days, could often hardly wait until we got home. When I landed from Seattle once, we took a room in Sausalito simply because it was a closer bed than Berkeley. Rented a room because we could not wait or drive any farther. Deciding the thing in the airport parking lot, amused, feeling wicked and a little silly but very pleased with ourselves, with our savoir faire and nonchalance, our imagination and ingenuity—or rather hers, for it was her idea, I was far too provincial and stingy to think of renting a hotel room to satisfy an urge. But how charming the idea was when she suggested it, how worldly and blasé. Scarcely able to wait till we got there, falling upon each other, each as if by some mute intuition taking each other in the anus as well. We laughed—can this be the reward of a Catholic girlhood? Just as I'd laughed when she came to me finally at my farm that September after the breakdown and the loony bins, the moment arrived at last when in touching her flesh again I would know all those nights in hell were over and had been worth it, had been lived through only that I might feel her in my arms again, her embrace, her skin under the fingers of my hand, and when she took me and entered me, I wept and said, the joke only a pretense for its utter earnestness—Ave Innocenza, do you realize you're my religion? But she had no idea what I meant. Maybe that was the beginning of the end, for we quarreled the whole time and she left three days later.

The anger of the bin was in me, my fury at what they had done in order to lock me up, to dope me and hold me and make me despair of freedom. I tried but I could not forgive her. And she would permit me no anger, imagined I was still mad. And I suppose I was, a little. And she drove me madder. The last awful business upriver at some college where she was to speak and was traveling as a big shot to confer with other big shots. I was supposed to perform as well, but hadn't accepted the invitation in time and had been replaced. So I traveled along as companion, baggage handler, nonentity, and then shamed her horribly by heckling from the audience. Stuffed-shirt chapel atmosphere and I put a bit of the old bomb-throwing radical into it, discomforting the little Wasp children in the audience and mortifying Sita. After that it was over. No' amount of begging or pleading could get her to stay. A long tearful delirious night and she left on the 6 A.M. plane. It was over, all over again. Then, in the late fall, her plans for a commune with the kids fell through and Hank left because the rent was too high for him. She began calling me. Answered my first tentative gift. It seemed she couldn't forget me. Or perhaps I was handy, other options failing her. And mine were failing too. Fumio announced his desertion. I began the long spiral downward into suicide. Six tries, two of them in earnest. When the depression had run its course, she was there for me, she had taken the house in Indian Rock. We would live together, it would be our home. Refuge and asylum and all settled. Until I failed her, or it seems I did, by taking a new loft in New York for a few months of the year. Having no idea it meant so much to her, having no idea it would bring about the disaffection that came out in Italy, the slow, but perhaps not slow, perhaps sudden erosion of trust or even interest that must have taken place in her while I was in New York these past months fixing the loft. And so we come to here, what I find when I return, the house on Indian Rock alienated. Sita absent, hostile. The process I stay here fighting, the death of love, its breakup, its wilting, its decay.

Hoping by an act of fantasy now to revive it, hoping by such reckless gestures as spreading her upon a couch to reach some spring of Eros never touched and still new, still fresh. I know, even as I perform the miracle of undressing her, I know the futility of what I do. And do anyway, doggedly, stubbornly, with the faith of desperation. Because it is desperate: to imagine it would matter at all if she gave into my whim, submitted to my obsession—this once. What is once? What would it possibly matter in the sure and relentless loss of yardage, the inevitable sliding down the bank grabbing at saplings and weeds, what would it matter if once, a mere once, she indulged me? But that is what I want. As if this once were all time in one moment. Without consequence. As time is for lovers.

Further laughing and persuasion, yes, darling, just a little whim, it occurred to me we had a good ten minutes, just right for something instant, how pretty you are, your long brown legs, your soft brown hair here. She protests again about the door, about her shower, about her long day at the office and no shower, it cannot be pleasant, she would prefer to shower, she would prefer to go upstairs. And out of my clutches. And the shower too is a canard, she is as fragrant as she always is, tasting her as she laughs in resignation and places her hand on my head, crooning as I wish now I could croon and speak, speak the words of my love and lust, the words that would excite her further, stoke her, fire her to cries and madness. For she is interested, she is finally intrigued and then warmed and then willing. But not as I would have her willing. The very act of getting my way, of succeeding, is my failure, the realization of how alone I am. I had wanted her to love me back, to love me as I love her, as much, as compulsively, as passionately as we once both loved each other. But this is then and then is not now. Now is merely my diseased persistence, seeing again the beloved skin of her thighs, the soft brown hairs over her cunt. Her cunt that is almost a being to me, so long have I loved it, known it, kissed it, wept for its wounds, its small twisted clitoris. After the rape in the desert, the six drunks who stopped when her car broke down—the joy that help had arrived—the nightmare that followed the surgery. Why, after such outrage, why, when penetration must be so physically as well as psychologically painful to her, why would she permit, even seek Neal's probably large and certainly painful prick? Why, when she is loath even to let me go down on her with infinite gentleness and relish? Surely he cannot know and love her as I do. The old rancor, that she would fuck a man, permit him to enter, gross and rude and large after the crime of the six drunken rapists has left her so, why of her own free will accept another one? And why in preference? There is no knowing, only the moment with the sweet salt taste of her in my mouth, trying, trying to give her joy or bliss or something to come back for, accept me again because of some particular pleasure, some satisfaction for love or skill or even adulation. Because this is surely the act of homage. Saying to her once as we walked by the sea, saying what had been so hard to say, and saying it with a bitterness that surprised me—"Why is it always I who goes down, never you? Is that some of your damn European aristocrat business?" And she of course protested. But it was true, even in the early days, when all I saw was her great and enormous desire to make love to me, to give me such pleasures as I had never known; even then, she did not often perform that act. Yet now, it is still she who is the lover, her endless and wonderful ability to make love to me, all that is left of our sensual relationship. Whereas once she assured me no one had ever really given her the pleasure before—and how easy I found it to believe that tribute, why not, there had been the rape, a succession of clumsy or inattentive husbands—now there is really nothing left but her making love to me. An exercise of power perhaps, a favor, charity, guilt. But to satisfy herself she has found men again, the one last time, others. Labor, even as I labor, listening for her cries and her hands stroking my cheeks, lighting around my head, I have no real hope. At bottom my heart already accepts defeat, expects the little sounds of her pleasure and then the sigh of her satisfaction—and knows it for fraud, if not the fraud of faked orgasm, the fraud of shallow and mere physical pleasure. I have lost my hold on her, even as I take her in my mouth, I understand how I have lost my hold. Were she to have refused me, I would not know with this same disappointed certainty. Having wanted and having gotten, now I know. Really know I have gotten nothing. Hardly even the heart to look at her as she speeds past me to her shower.

Champion

On weekends he swam in the pool his father had built in the side yard; his father clocked his speed with a stopwatch. When he performed well his father would cry, "That's my son. That's my boy."

Mr. Farrier owned an auto parts business in Hammond Falls. He drove himself hard, often working late and on Saturdays, and he was not always free to coach his son's swimming. But he had complete confidence in the school coach, Buff Chesbro, whom he had known ever since Chesbro joined the school's athletic department. Farrier sometimes stopped by the Chesbro house where he would talk about his son, sitting in the kitchen with Buff and his wife. "He's going to the *Olympics*," Farrier would insist.

"I hope so," Chesbro would say. "But it's still too soon to say, Nat. He's just finishing high school. There's a long way yet. *Anything* could happen. You shouldn't get yourself worked up like that. It isn't good for the boy."

"The *hell* it isn't," Farrier would say heatedly. "What he needs right now is *discipline*. He's got to realize that every minute counts. When he moves up into the stiffer competition, he'll thank me for pushing him now."

There was not much Farrier had overlooked. He spent entire days at the nearby university in upstate New York, which had one of the country's leading swimming teams. Farrier had checked out their standing with Chesbro, then with the American Athletic Association, before he had satisfied himself that the team was all it was supposed to be. He talked with the university's head swimming coach, then with all of his assistants, who listened patiently and then remembered something important that they had to do.

He brought Doug to the university pool and had him swim for them. His time was good, very good; the head coach was impressed. He said he would do what he could about getting an athletic scholarship for Doug. Then Farrier called on a variety of deans, who all assured him politely they would give his son every consideration but would make no commitments. Farrier brooded throughout the winter.

In the spring, a letter arrived from the university saying that Doug had been accepted with an athletic scholarship.

Farrier rushed to Chesbro's house as soon as he received the letter. Both men were jubilant and slapped each other's backs. "I tell you he's on his way to the *Olympics*," Farrier said.

For weeks thereafter, Farrier would manage to work in some reference to his son while conversing with customers at his auto parts shop.

"Oh, *say*, Nat, that's really *fine*," they would say to his Olympics line.

"I guess he takes a little after the old man," Farrier would say with a broad grin.

Farrier had two daughters, but Doug was his only son, and it was on Doug that he lavished all his attention, grooming him to be a winner.

A winner, as opposed to an also-ran, he told Doug, was someone who *felt* he was a winner, knew it in his brain and heart, in his guts, in the deepest part of himself; if he questioned for a moment if he were a winner, he would no longer be a winner; he would be worthless. He insisted Doug stand before his bedroom mirror as soon as he got up in the morning, and just before he went to bed, look at himself and say, "I am a champion." Over and over. "I am a *champion*."

On certain Saturday nights, Farrier went to the dog fights, held in a barn near Six Mile Point. They were illegal, but the police winked at their existence and many local people went, including some prominent ones. The fights were often vicious and bloody; sometimes one of the dogs would tear another to pieces. Hopefully, you put your money on one of these killers. The dogs apparently were evenly matched, but you couldn't tell by looking at them which dog had the real fight in him. A strong dog might turn out to be a poor fighter, lacking not brawn but killer instinct.

Farrier would point out the moral of the dog fights to Doug: The dog who won was the one with the unbreakable will to win, to dominate. It was the same in sports, said Farrier. When testing time came, the swimmer who came in first was the one with an absolute belief in himself, his attention totally on winning. He couldn't be distracted, couldn't have any self-doubts. His strength had to come from his belief in himself, from his certainty that he could pass every test put before him. If he failed any of these tests along the way, it would show up later: He might still be a swimmer, even come in fourth or fifth, but he couldn't be a *champion*.

Early one night, the doorbell rang unexpectedly. Farrier went to the door, and recognized the visitor through the pane of glass. "It's the outlaw," he said scornfully, and opened the door.

Jeb Nearbin came into the living room. "Hi, Mr. Farrier, Mrs. Farrier," he said, almost as if he owned the house and had come by to check on his tenants. "Nice evening, isn't it?"

Doug and Jeb Nearbin, who was two years older than Doug, and had finished his sophomore year at the university, had been inseparable that summer. Jeb admired Doug's swimming, and had talked to Doug about their rooming together later on at the university. His family was much better off than the Farriers; he had had certain advantages Doug hadn't. He had been a swimmer at high school in Hammond Falls, but had never made the team.

But it hadn't fazed him; he didn't care. He had a Honda 500 motorcycle and rocketed around town, barechested, his curly dark brown hair in the wind, wearing tight jeans and a pair of silver-lensed aviator glasses that did not reveal his eyes but shone back a reflection of the people he was looking at.

Farrier called Jeb "the outlaw" because he thought the glasses made Jeb look sinister, as if he did not want to be recognized; but also because he did not particularly like him. He had never met a boy who was so cocky. Farrier would have loved to forbid Doug to see him, but he had no real reason other than a vague distrust. And there was also the problem that Nearbin's father was a good customer of his and brought other business his way; he didn't want to lose their trade unnecessarily. Jeb was polite, but Farrier felt that Jeb did not take him seriously, did not respect him. He thought Jeb was the type of young man who would turn the head of some simple girl and then ruin her.

Farrier told his wife he suspected Jeb of taking dope and that he feared Jeb would get them both arrested, that Doug would be disqualified from sports. His wife, smiling, accused her husband of talking as if he knew everything.

"Well, I guess I *do* know everything, come to think of it," Farrier said, with a nod of his head. "Least ways, I know Doug. He's going to be a first-place winner."

But there was a lot about his son Farrier did not know. Swimming had been a natural talent for Doug and his ability as a swimmer had been recognized early; it was something he did well and was rewarded for—he pursued it for that reason, not because swimming meant more to him than anything else. Even if he had not been as good at them, there were other things he would have preferred to do if it hadn't been for Farrier's driving. Doug liked to play the guitar, but had no time to learn; he liked to draw and had done well in an art class in school, but his father had torn up his drawings when he found them hidden in Doug's room. Such stuff, he raged, would make Doug dreamy, would ruin his concentration as a swimmer. Art and music were all right for his sisters, but not for Doug, who had to train himself to focus his attention single-mindedly on *winning*.

Farrier knew nothing of Doug's emotions. He did not know that Doug found the dog fights at Six Mile Point as repellent as the greasy faces of the dirt farmers in coveralls who squatted on the barn floor while the dogs they had whipped and clubbed into a state of rage savaged each other, gouging out each other's eyes with their sharp yellow teeth. He did not know that the music Doug listened to in his bedroom before he fell asleep at night meant far more to him than almost anything, or that all summer long he listened to, and then carried in his head, a song sung by a flamboyant black chanteuse called "Every Time You Touch Me, I Get High." If Farrier had suspected Doug's addiction to that particular song he would have been enraged; he would have visualized the fine hand of Jed Nearbin drawing Doug away from the tight regimen he had prescribed for his son.

Girls were always attracted to the dark, slimly muscular Jeb Nearbin. Sometimes he would pull up into the Farriers' driveway with a buxom girl on the back of his motorcycle and they'd go over to the edge of the pool and talk to Doug as he swam. But Jeb never went steady. He was a loner and seemed to prefer open possibilities.

Farrier had once remarked that Jeb was so stuck on himself he could do almost anything he wanted. It was certainly true that Jeb could take many things for granted that Farrier, who had to work late in order to make ends meet, could not. Nearbin did not see things the way Farrier did: He took everything easily, sensually. His appearance, the way he walked across a room with a slight bounce in the buttocks, the way he sprawled in a chair were sensual. In his upstairs bedroom, by a wall of color posters of rock singers, Fleetwood Mac and Steely Dan, Jeb had an expensive stereo. When his parents were away for the weekend, which they often were, he would have some college girls up to listen to music and get stoned. Slouched in a chair, high on pot, a girl lying devotedly on the carpet by his bare feet with small tufts of dark brown hair on his long, slender toes, he made a figure that would have confirmed Farrier's distrust of him more than ever.

Farrier disliked Jeb merely from seeing him arrive in his driveway on his motorcycle, his bare chest bronzed by the sun as if he had spent the summer in the Bahamas, his wide, sensual lips parted in a smile as if he owned Farrier.

One noon, when Farrier had come home for lunch, and Doug was just finishing a workout in the pool, Nearbin zoomed up and asked Doug to join him for a ride in the country. After toweling down and changing into jeans, Doug did. Farrier shook his head, watching them ride off together, Doug seated close behind Jeb and steadying himself with his hands on Jeb's narrow hips, his straight blond hair setting him off like a topaz against the dark-skinned Nearbin.

At an easy pace, they idled through the town: past the patchwork, small frame stores, past the ugly empty paper factory that had once flourished in Hammond Falls but now stood deserted, past the long rows of box-like houses that had once been the tenant houses of millworkers.

Past the town, they came into the open spaces of the country; the sun glittered in the leaves and burned their skin, and soft warm breezes carried the odor of hay and cow dung, which was like a perfume and made them feel close to earth and animals and growing crops and each other.

Out by the county airport, on a little-traveled road, Nearbin opened the motorcycle's throttle. The speedometer needle lurched to seventy miles an hour, then ninety, then one hundred and ten. Feeling the sweet ecstasy of freedom, they zoomed halfway across the county.

***

Doug had trouble sleeping. All night, he tossed and turned, and when he woke the next morning, he felt exhausted.

At noon he competed in a swimming meet in Ontario, a neighboring town. His father and Buff Chesbro watched from the side of the pool. Sitting alone in a clear space in the bleachers, Jeb Nearbin watched behind his silver-lensed glasses.

Doug took an early lead, but midway in the heat he glanced for a moment at the spectators and lost the rhythm of his stroke. He lunged ahead to win, but only by an arm's length. He had very nearly lost; it was the worst showing he had made since his earliest swimming meets.

"God, that was close," Farrier said worriedly, looking at his stopwatch.

"It sure was, Nat," Chesbro said. "I don't *understand* it. He's been training all summer, but his swimming didn't show it today. I don't know what could have happened."

When they went to the locker room to talk to Doug, he told them he had felt tired and that he couldn't concentrate. But he said he was sure he would do better the next time.

"I hope so," Farrier intoned, "I sure as hell hope so. For your sake."

That night, Farrier came into Doug's room as he was listening to music. "It's what I've been telling you, Doug, about losing your concentration. I'll bet anything you weren't thinking right about yourself before the match started. You got to tell yourself you're the best, all the way, that nobody can stand up to you in *anything*. You got to believe that. You got to think about nothing *but* that."

"I'll try," Doug said, abstractedly.

"Trying isn't *enough*, Goddammit," Farrier blustered. "You got to think it and feel it clear through."

"OK Dad, I'll think about that and about nothing else."

"You'll be all right if you just remember what I tell you. You'll be all right. I guess I know my son."

But Farrier did not know that Doug tossed around in his sleep again that night, until perspiration broke out on his forehead. *Never fail a test . . . first-place winner* rang around in his brain until he woke up suddenly, startled, and was unable to return to sleep.

The next morning he began to practice in the pool, but after an hour he complained that he did not feel good. Mrs. Farrier took his temperature and found he was running a fever. He went to bed.

After Mrs. Farrier called her husband at work, he called a doctor immediately, then hurried home.

Doc Simpson checked Doug over for fifteen minutes. Then he came downstairs and told Farrier there was nothing organically wrong with his boy. "I expect he's just been overexcited, upset. You know, Nat, you've been driving him pretty hard. He'll be going to the university in a week and he'll be facing stiffer competition than he has here. Don't you suppose he knows how perfect you expect him to be? Don't you know it's bothering the hell out of him? Why don't you ease off for a couple of days, let him relax? That's my prescription, Nat: rest and relaxation for two or three days. And you ought to ease up a little yourself."

Farrier bit his lip with anger while hearing himself accused of causing his son's fever, of using his son for his own glory. There *was* an explanation somewhere, Farrier knew, but it had nothing to do with him. Farrier wondered if Jeb Nearbin had enslaved his son, had addicted him to drugs. He had no proof, but there *were* those telltale signs of drug use he had read about in the paper: wandering attention, jitteriness, inability to concentrate. At the meet, Doug had given Farrier a bad scare. It had *nothing* to do with him.

Jeb Nearbin came by on his motorcycle the next day and asked Doug if he would like to join him for the afternoon, for a swim at Nearbin's Island. Owned by his family, Nearbin's Island had once been a picnic ground and had been joined to the mainland by a ferry that had stopped operating years ago. Today the island could be noticed from one point on the highway, but no one ever went there any more except for Jeb, who had a rowboat tied up along the shore of the river. He said they could row over and back, and at the island they could swim and sunbathe

Doug said it sounded fine. For a moment, he hesitated, as if he were about to change his mind, then he went to get his things

It was about two in the afternoon when they rowed over to Nearbin's Island, and the midday heat was sweltering. As they worked the oars, the sun scorched their faces, its brightness multiplied by the mirror of the water's surface. When they had reached the near shore of the island, they secured the boat and went looking for the sandy spot that at one point broke the rocky shoreline. The island wasn't large and they soon found the secluded beach. It was surprising how few people knew about it. They had the whole place to themselves. Other than a bird's shrilling overhead in top of one of the trees, there was complete stillness; the highways on either side of the river seemed to recede until they were miles away. There was a soft, warm, lazy breeze off the river, and Doug felt the peace of the island steal over him.

They stripped naked. Doug found a place where he lay back to enjoy the sun. Jeb, still wearing his sunglasses, went to walk around the island for a bit.

Lying alone on the sand, which felt warm on buttocks, Doug thought back to the night before, to his father's words which still troubled him. Doug *liked* to think of himself as a champion and he thought he could be one; for a while, with deep pleasure, he thought of himself as a champion.

But then he thought of that other thing he had struggled with, the thing that made him afraid, the thing that would have filled his father with loathing. Self-doubt would defeat him, his father had preached. *His father had warned him of his ruin.* There was less than a week before he was to start at the university and become the champion. Doug felt sick, sick with self-doubt and fear.

Jeb Nearbin. It was Jeb he had thought about, all summer, when he had listened to "Every Time You Touch Me, I Get High."

Winning swimming meet after swimming meet, afterwards in the shower, he had felt some vague stirrings before for other handsome boys, but when Jeb Nearbin came back for the summer, they had focused at once on him. Doug had tried to blot out what he felt, but when Jeb was with him, physically near him, when Jeb's cat's eyes stared at his own, Doug felt drained of his will. Probably others had felt like that before, he now reasoned, and gone on to pass the test, to become winners without self-doubt. He was thinking that it might be better if he did not see Jeb Nearbin anymore. He did not feel the same way about anybody else; if he could hold out now, Doug was sure, the threat would pass. His image of himself, his aspirations were at stake. His strength lay in the power of his will and in the fact that Jeb did not suspect what his feelings were.

Seemingly out of nowhere, Jeb suddenly reappeared and came down to the sandy spot to join him, wearing the glasses that concealed his eyes.

As he sat down next to Doug, he took them off and looked directly at him. "Here's a posey for you," he said, as in an act of courtship, extending a slight, lovely blue wildflower he had found growing on the dark side of a boulder near the shore. "I picked it just for you," he said, his lips parting in an overpowering smile. It was the smile of a first-place winner.

Mothering

*A*llison Maslanka's son had run off for a couple of days this time. Ian, with yet-unshaven pale cheeks, full lower lip, cowl of uneven black hair he cut himself rather than let Allison touch, sixteen soft straight hairs on his chest, and eyebrows always lifted, was having a lesson behind the fieldhouse at the playground.

He was not learning to smoke cigarettes; he'd learned that at ten. He wasn't learning to smoke pot or trip on acid, though he may have been a little stoned. He was certainly not learning to play basketball. The idea for this lesson came neither from Ian nor from the realms behind Joey Goggins's smooth, cautious brow. The spies in the backs of both boys' heads were occupied with their cameras while each boy traced the other's fingertips. It was different from how they felt throwing Frisbee.

Joey slid his fingers over the knuckles onto Ian's hump-veined hand. Ian flinched, then relaxed. He dug in his pocket with his other hand and produced an opened Nestlé's Crunch bar. "You want some?"

Joey's broad face blushed. "Naw, man. Zit City."

***

Five blocks east, Allison spotted Lewis Goggins coming out of the Superette. Had he seen her son? He had not; he had been working at the police station until seven. He seemed tense, in a hurry. To calm him, Allison said how fond she was of Joey, how fond of Joey Ian was. Her voice traveled through the scale as she praised Lewis's boy: cello, oboe, piccolo. She thrust her stubby arms up to the elbows into the front pouch of her parka.

Officer Goggins heaved his groceries into the back of his little Healy, acting almost angry. As the car puttered away, Allison shook her head. People really have it in for themselves; they chew themselves over, she thought. No reason to bum out the rest of us. Under the dim Denver street lights her black hair hung over her shoulders.

In her mind, Ian's face replaced Lewis Goggins's.

Allison's soul was scattered with crystals, volcanoes, stream equations; she was a geologist at the Mining School. She saw several Ians: owl-eyed Ian nursing; penitent Ian with F's on his report card; howling Ian demanding a house, a yard, a father, a set of trains. The most vivid Ian resembled the one now in the playground, leaning back against the broken concrete step with his foot curled around Joey's; he was a new person for her, one whose arms she would like around her. She turned from the mountains toward Capitol Hill. I'm just taking a walk, she told herself. It will be nice if I run into him.

The fieldhouse steps cooled quickly in the long shadow of the Rockies. The spotlight over the porch gleamed on and the boys moved into the darkness. Joey's touch on Ian's belly felt different from Mandy Vallejo's uncertain stroking last week in her pick-up: It was heavier, warmer, bigger. Ian's fingers were longer than Joey's by a knuckle, but Joey's were wider. Their thighs pressed the dry July grass.

Scuffing over the broad sidewalk eight blocks north, Allison sighed. The lines around her mouth pulled her face down; her heavy glasses crushed her nose. Why didn't someone come along and lift her chin? Why didn't anybody touch her any more? Her fists clenched in her parka, then she took them out, slowly uncurled them. No good thinking that way. She had plenty of good in her life. She did interesting work. True, Allison would have preferred to work out in the field, in the mountains, instead of deciphering titrations in the lab, but work was hard to find. And Ian was proud of her.

A while ago they'd talked about the last time he'd gone off to his father's. Edgar had asked him all sorts of questions: if Allison was drinking, if she was a lesbian. "He wanted you bad off, Ma. I told him everything was ace with you. I said you were the belle of South Denver."

"Ha!" Allison had said aloud to the night that kept Edgar across the prairie. Then Ian had chuckled; then they held each other, laughing and laughing. His touch had changed completely; his stringy frame had become so strong now; he smelled wonderful, dark. And he was hers. For an instant she had forgotten all about Edgar, about bearing a son and leaving the father, forgotten how to do without a man. She longed now for Ian to touch her again.

Joey Goggins bit his salty lip; Ian caught his eye. They both half laughed, half grunted. The hand of the policeman's son on Ian's penis, his tongue soothing the thick vein up the back of it, felt different from anything Ian had felt before. His cock was like a big bird, an eagle, rising and wheeling.

But he didn't quite join it. Something held him back. He was worried. The camera in the back of his head clicked, *Faggot*. There were faggot jokes in the halls at school, wrists dangling, nasal voices saying *dearie*. He kneaded the knob of Joey's neck. Joey was big, not like Mandy; his shoulders were broader than Ian's and his chin scratched. With a girl it was all different. Ian felt a little uncomfortable. The bird soared through him but he didn't really feel it.

Pebbles stuck into his smooth ass, reminding him of the time in Michigan when he fell asleep on a riverbank and his mother Allison sang to him, *Where is the lad who tends the sheep? Under the haycock, fast asleep.* Should I tell Ma? Ian wondered, dreaming.

"What?" said Joey. Ian stirred. He opened his eyes to Joey's open face, round under a slender crust of moon. A sweet breeze licked Ian's belly, ruffled the dark feathers under his skin. He hugged Joey's head with both hands.

Allison curled her fingers around the chain-link backstop at the far end of the playground. She recalled the last time her son had kissed her—the day before yesterday, after breakfast. Had her mouth moved? Oh, God. How would she make it through this one?

The moon leered through a chink of sky; a white light flooded the playground from among the stars, guiding the machine-gun whir of propellers—the police helicopter.

The bright spot played over the field, the swings, the slide, the fieldhouse. When the helicopter circled again, Allison found herself in the middle of the light. It gave her the creeps, as if an earthquake or a glacial shift were happening, far away, where she couldn't even know. The light found two boys in the grass.

Allison had already left; the thought of the police made her anxious for home. Maybe Ian would be standing sheepishly on the stoop that very minute. Maybe she'd rest his head in her lap and stroke his long pale neck into comfort.

In a flash of light Ian saw his mouth, fishlike on Joey's curved, moon-white back. Each grass blade stood separate around them in the oval glare. Then blackness. The bird in Ian fell, fell, coasted. Rose.

He was practically there. No more spies, no cameras; he was on the bird now, he was flying. No faggot jokes. He was enormous; Joey was too, and they weren't afraid. There was nothing to worry about.

On Capitol Hill, a siren whooped. Ian got up, breathing hard. The grass was soft, the air cool. He felt happy. He looked down at Joey, who was shaking, and saying, "Sorry."

"Hey," Ian said in his voice like the reed section of his mother's voice. *"Hey."*

But Joey kept shaking. He picked up their T-shirts; his had "Goggins, Staff" over the pocket. Ian touched Joey's fingers again, pressed his lips into a kiss for Joey. *Love*, he thought; and his mouth opened up and he laughed aloud. He hugged Joey hard. Joey put the T-shirts down.

The neighborhood droned around them: motorcycles, slamming doors. Ian wondered what time it was. A car stopped at the corner. The sky said, oh, nine, nine-thirty. A pair of flashlights poked holes in the blue darkness.

"What's going on there?" a man called.

"Shit," said Joey. Shirtless, he got up and ran, hitching up his pants. Ian ran too. He caught Joey's arm as the men behind them shouted, "Halt!"

"What's up?" Ian asked. Joey's fist came down like a stone on Ian. He pushed Ian away and split into the dark.

"Who was that?"

Ian couldn't see a face, only the cocked hat and badge. The boys' two shirts hung, bright white, from the cop's hand. Another policeman, slower, was pacing through the bright circle of light by the fieldhouse.

Joey's push had made Ian dizzy; the playground swung around him. The cop with the T-shirts grabbed his arm to hold him up. Under the hat, the cop's face was fleshy; his lip curled. Would he punch Ian? Ian's fly was still undone: the zipper was down half an inch and a white strip showed.

"Faggot," the cop said. Gum snapped in his mouth; Ian smelled cloves. "Who was that?"

Blood tingled in Ian from his squeezed arm to his nose; even his eye was throbbing. The cop turned the shirts in his hand. They'd notice the name. "Joe Goggins," Ian said.

The helicopter went around the moon.

"*Goggins?*" The men looked at each other in the dark; the one holding Ian released him. "Jeez, it would kill his old man." Without support, Ian fell down. He had a slow, mounting anger. The sharp smell of turf stung his nose. Two shirts landed on his chest. "It would kill the old man," the slow cop repeated. "The shit we have to deal with," the other said, snapping his gum. "Faggot." He spat; the wet, pink gum hit the grass beside Ian.

Allison pushed her door open. The house enveloped her: one story, five dark rooms. No Ian. Well.

She crossed to a low chest under the back window that held

Ian's old blanket and his trains. Under a bunch of stuff she found a photograph of Ian at six, and Edgar. It was inscribed, "To our Mom from her two boys." Ian's tongue hung out in a goofy smile.

A bird started up outside, where saw-toothed mountains bit the stars. Allison turned the light on, took out a book on Kansas sediment. "You know, you're a good kid," she told the picture. "I wish you'd get your ass back here." Her voice filled the room with bird calls: gull, crow, nightingale, loon.

The police car followed Ian all the way back to his block. When he looped back toward the playground, the face they saw in their headlights was crusted with blood. He stumbled against a wall and pounded it. When he turned with clenched fists and went home, they left.

Allison slept on the davenport. Ian cleaned himself up in the kitchen, cracked ice cubes from a tray and wrapped them in a towel.

The living room was cool and quiet. Ian sat for a long time with Allison's head in his lap, listening to the traffic outside. He leaned sideways so the melting water from his icepack wouldn't wake her with a chill. She snored, a frog's lullaby. Their hands laced over her breast; that roused her; the world briefly rolled into her eyes and was swallowed in a monstrous yawn. He patted her, wanting to kiss her, but he hurt too mothering much.

DANIEL CURZON

◇◇◇◇◇◇◇◇◇◇◇◇◇◇◇◇◇◇◇◇◇◇◇◇◇◇◇◇◇◇◇◇

Two Bartenders, a Butcher, and Me

I'd just gotten over a bad case
of meningitis, complicated by my diabetes, and my doctor
had told me the day before that I was probably getting kidney
stones. Nobody knows what pain *is* until he has kidney
stones, believe me. So when the guy from San Francisco
stared at me in the bar and then came over and asked if I
wanted to join in an orgy, you can understand why I felt
good.

I realized I had to look a bit puny, with my thin, narrow
shoulders and thinner arms, my fat lips and dwindling hair
(though I'd cut it flat to make it look less obvious). But the
guy from San Francisco was making the overtures, saying he
and his lover Gil were arranging an orgy. I guess they liked
my face. They'd already asked the bartender if he wanted to
have a four-way, and he'd said he did. It turned out Gil was a
bartender too—up in San Francisco, not here in Fresno. For a
minute all four of us sort of eyed each other, seeing how we
felt about getting together.

To be honest, the Fresno bartender, Rory, didn't turn me

on too much. He was cute, and growing a nice beard, but somehow he seemed a little silly. I'd seen him running around the bar lots of times before, but we'd never spoken. Gil was pretty good looking, far better than me in fact, with elegant gestures and a deep voice. But the best of the lot was Bill, the guy from San Francisco, a butcher, slim and solid and lots of fun. Up close, he looked a little dissipated because of the dark marks under his eyes. That night I'd noticed he'd had about six White Russians and been smoking grass and he'd even sniffed some amyl out on the dance floor, so I wondered if I would be getting in over my head in an orgy with these guys. But Bill was really full of life, having a great time running back and forth among the three of us, finding out who liked to do what.

I began to get sleepy before the bar closed and I thought of leaving, since I had to get up and work for the Welfare Department in the morning at eight. I was going to lose my job anyway in a couple of months because the budget had been cut, but I didn't want to lose it for coming in worn out from an all-night orgy. But somehow or other I hung in there. I kept asking myself how many offers for an orgy at the Fresno Holiday Inn I got in a year, anyway.

So I waited around while the two guys from San Francisco danced and the bartender closed up. I was getting a little worried, because I don't have a very big dick and Bill talked about cock a lot, as though size was important to him; I didn't want him to be disappointed when I pulled my pants off. I know it's not supposed to matter if you have a little dick, but it *does*, it sure does. I tried looking over at Rory, but he didn't catch my eye, and I figured he wasn't attracted to me any more than I was to him. But I figured a three-and-a-half-way was better than a no-way, so I hung in there.

Somehow some Italian guy got involved. He was supposed to make up a fifth in the orgy, but when we left the bar I found out in the parking lot that Rory had lost interest in the Italian and didn't want him to follow our cars out to the Holiday Inn. I felt sorry for the Italian because he didn't catch the hint and followed us all anyway, and then, at the motel, Rory had to lie and say that all of us were acting "so weird" that he didn't plan to stay. So the Italian guy was left out in the cold; I guess he went on home. The other four of us went into the motel room and took our clothes off.

There was a big tray of dirty dishes and half-eaten food on one of the unmade double beds. Clothes were thrown everywhere. It was all a little messy, but I suppose you wouldn't want an orgy to be middle class and super-clean anyway, right?

I didn't know exactly what I was supposed to do, but the butcher gave me a sniff of amyl and asked me to fuck him while Rory was fucking him, too. It was pretty wild, I guess: the first time I'd ever seen a guy get fucked with two cocks at the same time—and I was one of the guys doing it! I kept thinking about the Italian who'd been invited and then not invited, wondering if he was still in the parking lot sitting in his car by himself. Of course, I hadn't said anything to the others about asking the Italian to join us, so I guess I made him feel not wanted, too.

So we all fucked each other in various combinations, though Rory and I didn't touch very much, just a little bit, near the end. And nobody said anything about my little dick, though I think Bill was maybe a little disappointed. But if I have to defend myself, he couldn't have been fucked by me and somebody else at the same time if we'd both had big ones, could he?

I was sitting on Gil's dick, just about to get off, and the other two were watching from the other bed encouraging me to come. I suppose if anybody had been watching from a peephole it would've all seemed nasty or depraved or something, but it didn't seem like that from my angle. We joked around a lot and hugged and told each other we were good sex. We got so loud that Bill shushed us and said we'd wake up his *mother*. I thought he was kidding, but it turned out he wasn't. His mother really was in the next room. She was traveling with them, knew about him and Gil and took it all in stride though she wouldn't talk about it.

The moment I remember most is when Rory, who was quite a good fucker, was giving it to Bill, who had his muscular legs up in the air and was grunting. Gil and I were resting on the rug and Gil said to me quietly, "I really love him. I love him so much."

He meant it, too, and I thought that was sort of nice. Here he was watching some bartender from Fresno fucking his lover up the ass, and he was glad because it gave his lover pleasure.

About four-thirty I slipped out and left the other three sleeping; didn't get a chance to say goodbye. I got to work on time. Still have a month to go in my job, and I can get unemployment for a while after that.

For some reason, that evening doesn't seem funny or depraved or anything to me. All I know is that when I was sucking dick and getting fucked and fucking all night, I didn't feel like I was a skinny thirty-eight-year-old with a little dick that nobody wanted. Of course I knew that nobody out there in the Holiday Inn "loved" me, but for a while I felt that life wasn't passing me by, and I guess I'm kind of wishing some other guy from San Francisco would come through Fresno some other night, maybe soon. It wasn't perfect, no, but it was something. Maybe it was even sort of sad if you think about it too much, but then, aren't most things in life sad?

Wild Figs

*I*n my family we were not given to dark suspicions about one another. Much of our mutual trust was based on our congenital Catholicism: faith as rich, cohesive and firm as the candied plum pudding my mother baked at Christmastime. We carried the moral dictum of Christ with us as if it were unstable proto-matter which, if sinned against, could blow us into Hell.

We were devout.

At some point in his nineteenth year, my older brother Andy discovered The Meaning of Life: The meaning of life, said Andy one evening at supper, is contained in the teachings of St. Thomas Aquinas. From that day until this, Andy has bludgeoned his way through life waving lethal moral postulates and inflicting irrefutable proofs of Divine presence onto startled libertines who, until Andy's arrival, had just been having a good party. O poor Andy, rife with metaphysics and abristle with the urgency to cure the ailing earth! Andy is exhausting to be around for any length of time and, worse, is prey to occasional drunken sprees of repellent sentimentality followed by bracing, self-righteous Irish rage against Blacks, Commies, "Pseudo-intellectuals," and, of course, the Homosexuals who, even if they did dare to speak the name of their love around Andy, could not possibly be heard above his ranting: "Queers! Perverts! Fruits!"

"More Catholic than the Pope," my father used to say of him. Once he asked Andy if he wore his longjohns in the shower to avoid temptation. "Put icecubes in your shorts, do you?"

As soon as I finished college I left St. Katherine, Montana, my mother (Papa had by then passed away), my younger brother Jack, and Andy, who lived down the valley with his glum wife Esther and their children. I left and went to New York City where I had heard that they welcomed and encouraged good young writers and where, I had also heard, but from very different sources, there were a noticeable number of homosexuals. Like me. In *my* nineteenth year I had discovered a quiet conspirator named Michael and near a lake upon whose glistening waters rested the golden reflection of an ancient coin, the moon, I breathed to Michael, "I love you."

And that was that for my sexual preference.

But Andy was never far from my mind.

I lived in New York for five years of reasonable happiness and did not find it necessary to conceal my homosexuality— except from my family, who were far away in Montana where they belonged. They excused my insistent bachelorhood by telling the neighbors I was "artistic" and too sensitive to marry so young, that my aesthetic commitment (Aquinas had much to say to buttress this fraud) shepherded its gift from uncleanliness, that many artists married late in life only after laying up a treasure in Morgan Guaranty. *Ars Longa, Vita Brevis*, I wrote home. The placebos sufficed.

Then Andy came to New York. He was teaching biology

at a small college near St. Katherine and came to New York
for a National Science Foundation conference. He was to give
a paper on "The Moral Demands of Science." My deception
was about to be rent from me.

Andy stayed uptown at the Americana where his meetings
were being held, but on Sunday afternoon he came to the
Village to take pictures of the brownstones. There was no
such graceful architecture in harsh and vertical St. Katherine
and Andy sought grace in all things. Andy was initially
alarmed, then typically fascinated by the gay life along
Greenwich Avenue. He snapped many photos of the
twitchy-bottomed dog owners being dragged about by teams
of Afghans and proud Borzois. He was splendidly aghast at
the whole Sunday extravaganza.

As if forcing some long delayed crisis into focus, I steered
him down 10th Street past Julius's. Andy peered scientifically
through the window; a smile of contempt curled like a wave
across his mouth. "Julius, uh? So that's where the queers
hang out, uh?" he said. Before I could think of an innocent,
noncommital answer (how should *I* know where the queers
hang out, brother Andy?), the side door flew open and two of
my steady cronies pranced screaming onto the sidewalk; eye
shadow, immaculate tennies, bared chests, my name wrapped in their screech, *"Teddy!* Teddy. Come inside, girl, you'll
get the vapors on a hot day like this. Well . . . and who is
this? Hi, hunky!" Andy, I admit with some despair, is indeed
a hunk, though his straightened sensibilities give a wounded
weight to his face. He recoiled as these two put their arms
around his shoulders. "Where did you find this one?" said
one; Andy took a fistful of his shirt and slammed him against
the brick wall. "I'm Eddie's brother," he snarled, "and you'd
better take a hike you fucking fairy before I knock your teeth
down your throat." "Try it," said the other friend calmly and

murderously. Panting from the rush of adrenalin, Andy shoved through us, strode down to the corner of Seventh Avenue and looked around for a cab.

One of my friends toyed with a curl near his ear. "So much for *that* cover, Teddybuns," he laughed.

I followed Andy and tried to talk to him, to explain, but we ended in a stalemate. I am what I am, I told him. It is now simply a lie for me to hide it any more and it has become necessary to tell the truth to those who require it. I am what I am and I will never change. Ever.

He said I was disgusting. Mortal sin, he said, was consciously willing serious evil and he could see now that that was what I was doing.

It is not evil, I tried to argue with him, but rather the only truly natural passion in a life lived according to the nonsense of the straight world and its categories of alienation.

You have a choice, he said hotly.

It was never choice, I said. It was more like a destiny and it was spoken in me from a hundred sources and there was a purpose in it that I could not yet understand. My sweet but hopelessly small town brother, I said, I am not unhappy. I have discovered my true brothers.

"Of all life's choices, you have chosen evil," he said, and turned and jumped into the waiting taxi and was swept away.

"I *am* happy," I called morosely after the taxi.

I did not see Andy again for two years.

Following that dark moment, my mother's weekly letters changed in tone and content. Though Jack had married his childhood sweetheart, Mama rarely mentioned them and never Andy and that fustian truce he called his marriage.

Andy, I knew, had told Mama everything and she was obviously confused by what she had heard. But characteristically, she did not snoop. Her letters, earnest and strained, became Pauline: epistolatory javelins that caught me directly in the heart. "If you are spiritually disturbed," she wrote me, "there is no Catholic priest in the world who is not willing to listen to your sins and help you to forgiveness—the forgiveness of God and a self-forgiveness which is medicinal, like good whisky." In another letter she wrote,

> I know that when a young man gets lonely he is sometimes driven to do things he would not consider if he had the proper Christian companions to guide him. Act in desperation and repent in haste. I'm not innocent myself, Eddie. You have nothing to apologize to me for because I am your mother and know your heart and I am the one who set you free to make your own choices and investigate the possibilities of whatever freedom there is on this battered planet and I know you act according to your conscience and your self respect and respect for the law and for God. Why don't you call up Fordham University and ask to visit their facilities? I'll bet there are lots of Irish priests there who would have advice and companionship for you.

Indeed there are, Mama. I slept with one.

It is not necessary to tell all of the truth all of the time. My friend at Fordham cautioned me about that. And so I said nothing to my mother regarding my love life. I mentioned only female friends by name and occasionally was able to tell her I had seen some celebrity or other in person, which I knew thrilled her for she loved the famous. I told her of my job at the newspaper, of the plays and concerts and ballets that I attended. My letters were no different from the letters of thousands of other sons and daughters of wholesome, unknown American villages who concealed from their mothers the perils of the fleshpots, of the nights in Babylon.

That silence in my mother's letters spoke insistently to me about my fall from grace. She did not, however, stop loving me. Nor I her.

Then I received a call from my brother Jack. Mama, he said, was dying: She had a rare disease of the nervous system, Lou Gehrig's disease, and there was no known cure and she would die. She had known about her malady for years. She had thought I would return home sometime for a vacation but I had not. Her nervous system is short-circuiting, he said. There is little time left.

The next day I flew home to Montana.

Jack picked me up at the tiny airport in Helena and we drove the twenty miles into the mountains where St. Katherine sat, amid aspen and birch coppices, among the angular rocky peaks in the green and ardent flourish of autumn. We drank beer and exchanged terse, tight, careful messages to one another as we bounced along the road in Jack's new Ford truck. Jack was rigid and kept his words on Mama. He had lost his boyish gentleness. He had become like Andy; he, too, feared me and what I was.

Mama was worse and worse, he said. The pain was incessant. She did not fight or mourn as her life trickled away. She teetered between sudden cheer and sudden fright and spoke frankly about being united with Papa, their souls in heaven, their mortal remains in the land itself. "She has been lonely since he died," Jack said. "Her kids were never enough to replace him."

"I felt that too," I said. On the far end of the high valley I could see the September sun glancing from the spire of St. Katherine's Church, indicating the direction of Mama's hope.

"And she drinks wine morning, noon and night," said Jack. "She's always got half a snootful on. And she chain smokes Lucky Strikes, no filter. For God's sake, don't make her feel guilty about it."

"Andy is the guilt broker, not I," I said softly.

Jack took a deep breath, as an athlete would before contesting. "Eddie, Andy will be there at the house," he said.

"It's Ted or Teddy or Edward. Not Eddie."

"Screw that. I'm telling you to watch yourself with Andy. The last thing I want to do is get Mama upset."

"Exactly what was it you thought I was going to do? Wear a dress?"

"Just don't let Andy get a handle on you, that's all."

"Fuck Andy." I said. "I owe Andy nothing. No explanation, no apology, no genuflection, nothing. And least of all a lie."

"Eddie, I'm telling you—"

"And I'm telling you, my name isn't Eddie anymore!"

"What's wrong with Eddie?"

"Eddie is bald and has freckles and a fat ass and huge teeth and every Eddie in the world always will and I'm not Eddie. That's why!"

"Weird," he muttered and shook his head, and we drove on to St. Katherine in silence.

We pulled up in front of the house, the clapboard and sandstone work of my grandfather and my father. It was stern, a house that seemed deep in contemplation there on the green slope of the high meadow where Grandpa and Grandma were buried. On Grandma's gravestone were her name, the dates of her birth and death and, beneath, the words *Wife Mother Lover Friend Helpmate*. On Grandpa's stone were his name, the dates, and this from the Book of Amos:

I am not a prophet nor am I the son of a prophet
But I am a herdsman, plucking wild figs.

The house had recently received a coat of white paint and banked up against its sides were large bushes of lilac, climbing roses, and a trellis where the last blue and yellow sweetpeas clustered. The lawn was newly cut, smooth, as if brushed. The ancient elm, twisting and pagan in its leafy fullness, swayed in green-shadowed darkness, its bark cut by many jackknives with the signatures of me and my brothers and the neighborhood children—up there in the lanky afternoon shade I had crouched hidden for much of my childhood; transformed into some Celtic legend, I worried within my blood. The tree now seemed heavy and peaceful, like an old dog.

I had known Terry, Jack's new wife, all of my life. She stood in the kitchen stirring a sweet, buttery, herbed sauce in a deep pan with a wooden spoon. She turned her head as I came in the kitchen door and smiled, saying, "Why hello, Eddie, long time no see." Her smile was clear and generous and honest. She went back to stirring. "I liked the house so much I married your brother and moved in," she laughed, a laugh whose source must have been a mountain pasture filled with wind and sunlight.

"Mama always said you'd end up with one of us," I said jokingly.

"She got that idea from me," Terry laughed again.

"I'm glad," I said.

"There's beer in the fridge, Eddie," she said, crumpling an

herb into her sauce. "Oh, excuse me. I was warned. Teddy. Ted. Have a beer, whoever you are." She smiled down into her pan. She had a blissfully predictable life. She would perish in a city. I always liked her.

"Where's Mama?" I asked as Jack came in the kitchen door carrying his beer.

"She saw you driving up and went into the bathroom for one last primp. She's been fidgeting at her hair all day."

I went down the hallway to the bathroom and rapped on the door. "Hey, you in there!" I called. "Come outta there. Someone here to see you!"

"One minute," her small, apologetic voice piped. "One minute." Water ran, the medicine cabinet door shut. A silence as she straightened her dress, lifted her chin and squinted sideways without mercy at her face. I knew every habit and gesture of her life. Then the door opened and she stood in front of me looking embarrassed but smiling hopefully as if she thought perhaps I might not remember her. Then she ran up against me and buried her head in my chest. She was fastened to me and I enfolded her (she had gotten quite stout) in my arms and my strong love and my sadness for her, holding my mother there in the hallway and feeling that a whole history of a life and purpose and understanding was there weeping happily into me "My Eddie," she cried. "My boy."

The screen door slammed in the kitchen and Terry's voice said, "Hi there, Andy. Get the wine?" She was answered by a grunt.

Mama lifted her head and sniffled. "That must be Andy," she said, her eyes wet. "I sent him to the store for provisions." She lowered her voice. "Around here that means wine and cigarettes. Don't you worry none about Andy, though." She stepped away and held my hands. "Let's go have a nice glass of wine and a big gabfest." And then she turned and took the cane she had leaned against the wall and began to limp down the hallway. Walking was deep pain for her and her plump body burdened her.

"Everyone say hello to Eddie!" she sang at the kitchen door.

"Or Teddy, or Ted, or Edward," Terry said, closing the refrigerator door.

"Any pseudonym will do," said Andy who stood bolted to the kitchen floor next to the stove. His head was drawn back and he looked at me with monumental accusation. "What we have here was never good enough for him." He sniffed. "Or should I say bad enough for him?"

"Why don't you just climb down from the cross and say hello?" I answered without congeniality.

"Now boys, now boys," Mama said, seating herself at the table. "You'll have plenty of time for that." She wheezed and smiled around the room. "Let's all just sit and get acquainted again. You bring the wine, Andy? Good. Terry? Glasses. You pour, Jack. My name's Mama," she laughed across the table at me and extended her hand. "I believe we've met before."

"Was it London or Rome I met you?" I sang to her, taking her hand.

"Paris or Nome I let you," she sang back; her laughter glittered. "Oh, I always did like funning with you, Eddie. Teddy. You gotta come home more often." Jack poured our glasses full with the wine. Andy would not sit down. He put his wine down on the sink and shakily lit a cigarette. He was very agitated.

"To us!" Mama lifted her glass and we all drank. Terry put her glass down and went back to her sauce. She dipped the wooden spoon into the pan, lifted a bit to her pursed lips, tasted, considered, opened the oven to the chicken baking within and spooned the sauce over the browning bird.

"That looks great, Terry," I said.

Andy's eyes were fixed on me with reptilian resolution; I tried to avoid his gaze but could not. He awaited some clarion.

Mama plunged her hand inside her blouse down into the cleft of her generous brassiere and brought out a packet of Lucky Strikes. She took matches from the table and began to light her cigarette and then I saw the ravages of her disease: She could not bring the match directly to the tip of the cigarette, but when I reached for the matches she frowned and drew away, lighting another and this time succeeding. She whipped the match back and forth as she exhaled a blue aureole of smoke into the air before her. "Now," she said, "Tell us something exciting from the big city."

"How's the gang down at Julius Bar?" Andy said.

"What's Julius Bar?" Mama said brightly, mistaking Andy's interest.

"It's where the fag—" Andy snarled.

"Mama said you met Walter Cronkite," Terry broke through in a loud voice. "Tell us about Walter Cronkite."

"You keep it up!" I shouted, pointing my finger at Andy. "You—"

"Now Eddie—" Jack put his hand on my shoulder.

"I'm dying to hear about Walter Cronkite," Mama said, raising her eyebrows at me.

"So am I." Jack said emphatically, giving Andy a forbidding look.

"I shook his hand at a party," I said sullenly.

"And what's he really like?" Terry went on valiantly.

"Oh, I've always thought he was such a nice man," Mama said. "I think it's wonderful you have friends like that, Eddie."

"Teddy," said Andy.

"That's correct," I answered him. "Teddy. Walter Cronkite is not my friend, Mama. I merely shook his hand at a party. He shook everyone's hand. When he is not giving the news on TV he is shaking hands. He has probably shaken more hands than any president. I said 'hello.' He said 'pleased.' I'm sure he was pleased. Famous people are always pleased. When they are not pleased they are 'morally outraged' which gives them an excellent chance to display the range of their talents but not necessarily their ability to think as most famous people and, I might add, most not-famous people, think those thoughts supplied them by their parents and their local priest, like our brother Andy here, who views everything he does not understand, which, I might add, includes just about everything, as evil. Such is life and the entropy therein. End of lecture on Walter Cronkite and selected short topics on your behalf."

Mama began to laugh and Andy said, "There's a word for people like you but I won't say it."

"I think it's 'arrogant prick,'" I said, and Mama looked away but did not stop laughing. "Two words, actually."

"You and Cronkite ought to pair up," continued Andy. "The Wally and Eddie Show. The bleeding heart liberal hour. Maybe Jane Fonda would lend you her brassiere."

"When you lapse into self-parody I almost like you, Andy," I said benevolently.

Mama pushed her chair back and struggled to her feet. She still wore her pleasant smile and said "Terry, let's go into the den and watch Merv Griffin. I've been listening to this conversation for thirty years and at least I can turn Merv off if

I don't like him." She went to the hallway entrance. "Eddie? Watch Merv Griffin?"

"In a minute, Mama." I said. "I'll be there in a minute."

Terry followed her slowly into the dusky hallway and I watched. My God, I thought. It is true. My mother is dying.

I turned back to the kitchen. "And you are a lush," I said to Andy. "You were drunk when you walked in here. I just realized."

"Oh," Andy cooed as if at an infant, "So now you have a word to call *me*. Lush, huh? I like that. It's the sort of name that keeps you in touch with your sources, our Irish origins." He began to swagger and throw his shoulders back and forth. He was very drunk, which was not an unthinkable state in our family, but I had never seen this bully-boy certitude before.

"You should have been a policeman, Andy," I said. I began to stand up. Jack, who had been watching me closely, stood up, too.

"And toady to the minorities?" His laugh indicated nothing comic. "And criminals who call themselves minorities?"

I moved around the table and Jack said simply, "Eddie, don't—"

I hit Andy and dropped him with the blow. He stumbled sideways, caught his foot in the chair and fell, hitting his head on the sink as he sank to the floor.

"Damn," Jack breathed and knelt down next to Andy. Andy's legs were crossed Indian style; he leaned forward and placed his hands flat on the floor for support. His head hung down and he shook it back and forth.

"Get up, fuckhead," I said.

Jack looked up with a plea. "Jesus, Eddie, can't you see the guy is plastered? Please let him alone. For Mama's sake."

Andy raised his head and looked around, confused. He

brought his hand to his nose as the first of the blood began to stream from his nostril and across his swelling lip. "He broke my nose," Andy cried. "Ah shit." A large drop of blood splattered across his knee.

I threw a towel on the floor next to Jack and Jack lifted Andy's head up, holding him under the chin and looking up into the damaged nose. "It's not broken." he said and began to dab at the blood flow.

Andy whispered hurriedly to Jack, "I told you. I told you he was crazy. I told you he shouldn't come back here."

Jack was shaking his head. "No, no," he said. He put his hands under Andy's armpits and began to pull him to his feet.

Andy continued to stare at Jack. "He might have a gun or something in his suitcase." Andy was upright but he clung to Jack's arm. Then he looked at me with the blank, unfocused eyes of a man who has awakened in an alien country filled with uncompanionable light. "You broke my nose," he said with sudden anger.

"Your nose isn't broken," I said.

"Let's go in the bathroom," Jack said, tugging at Andy. "I don't think it's broken."

They went into the hallway. Andy spun around, one hand on Jack's shoulder, and his eyes were banked with slag and wrath. But his focus was somewhere off to the left of me and he addressed me as merely one among many, one of his students, perhaps. "That was not a wise thing to do, Eddie. Not wise at all. Not prudent."

"Come on, dammit," Jack gave him a sharp shake.

"No," I said, emptied of revenge, "but it was wonderfully expedient."

They went into the bathroom and closed the door. The bolt slid shut and water splashed into the sink. Terry came down the hall. She went past me without looking at me or speaking; then she took the bottle of wine from the table, handed it to me and said simply, "Why don't you go keep Mama company?" She went to the oven and pouted in at the chicken.

I took the bottle of wine and my glass down the hallway and into the den. Mama sat on the couch supported by many pillows: faded, purple satin pillows with golden braided fringe. Niagara Falls was printed on one. On another, a horse. She smiled up at me, pushed the pillows away and patted the cushion next to her. "Come sit," she said.

I sat, lit a Lucky Strike and put it in her hand. She glanced at the cigarette and went back to watching Merv Griffin, who sat on a long couch with his guests and discussed the pertinence of their various lives. "Did you expand Andy's mind?" she said conspiratorially.

"Just his lip." I said.

Mama slipped her hand over and rested it on my knee. She squeezed my kneecap. She turned to me for a moment and gave me a small, trusting smile. Birds rose over the windy, furrowed fields. She turned back to the television and continued to pat my knee.

She said, "That Merv Griffin. He keeps up with everything. Never at a loss. He must read a couple books a day. Always knows what to say to folks. And Eddie, don't you think for one moment that I have any doubts about your life because I don't. I know mine and mine know me. That's what the Lord said. Yes. My, my, that Merv Griffin certainly does keep a conversation jumping along. He never hesitates and he is never rude. Gets on with everyone. And Eddie, nothing will ever change my mind about you or the other boys either. I love you all. And I know you have a perfect right to love like anyone else. Just like Papa and me. Some folks didn't want me to marry Papa. And I don't care who you love as long as you love them as honestly as you can, for you and for them. No lying or cheating or hurting, that's loving in the right way. If you can say yes to that, Eddie, you are in the right set of arms. The Lord, he loves the lovers, all right. That's what Papa would say to me at night, in bed. Oh, it's good to have you home and we can sit together and watch all your favorite shows, Merv Griffin and Carol Burnett and Mary Tyler Moore and you can watch old *Gunsmoke* shows every afternoon. Oh, sometimes I sit here watching the shows and I say God, God, don't let Eddie be lonely. Never frightened or lonely. Don't ever let that happen to him."